DEAD IN DEEP WATER

DAVE SIVERS

To Ian

Best Wishes

Dave Sivers

First published as an eBook in 2014

First published in paperback in 2015

Cover design by Jessica Bell

ISBN: 978-1511884631

For my mother, Pat Sivers
1920-2014
You taught me to love stories, mum.

ACKNOWLEDGMENTS

As usual, my thanks to the awesomely insightful Debbie Porteous and my wife, Chris Sivers, for their patience in reading the manuscript of this book, which is much better for their invaluable comments and suggestions. Grateful thanks also to my brilliant cover designer, Jessica Bell.

Thanks are also due to my very many writer friends for their support and encouragement. Writing needn't be a lonely occupation, and far more people than I can list have made sure it hasn't been. They know who they are.

Thanks also to Clare Heron and PC Kirstin Harding of Thames Valley Police for generously giving of their time when I needed to check details. Mistakes are mine and mine alone.

Many who know the beautiful part of the Chilterns I call home might think they recognise some aspects of the fictitious places I've inserted into the story. I've tried to create an Aylesbury Vale that, whilst it is a somewhat more shadowy version of the real thing, is still recognisable. I hope the liberties I have taken with the area are forgiven.

Thanks again to the real Karen Smart, and also to the real Lara Moseley, for letting me borrow their names.

Buckinghamshire, 2014

1

It was a sleepy Saturday morning in the Buckinghamshire village of Little Aston. Early July. Yesterday had been a scorcher and today promised more of the same.

Will Scott had slipped out of the house like a thief just before 7am, his parents and his brother still in their beds. The family were used to the 16-year-old going for early morning runs and so would see nothing remarkable about his absence this morning. He had no idea what cover story Emily would use, but she was waiting by her gate as he jogged along her street.

"Hi," she murmured, her eyes drowsy. She'd warned him she wasn't a mornings person, but she was still here. He wasn't sure she would be. The whole clandestine meeting thing excited him.

He moved in for a snog, but she pushed him away.

"Not here. It's bad enough that I might have been seen hanging around here waiting for you."

Will shrugged. "I said we could meet at the quarry, but you didn't want to."

"No way. I'm not going there on my own at this time of the morning."

"Well, then."

He held her hand and she let him. As they walked along, another stab of excitement hit him. He was walking hand in hand with Emily Young. He'd had the hots for her for over a year, but hadn't plucked up the courage to ask her out. Then last night, at the swimming hole, she'd actually spoken to him.

It was only the second time he'd gone there with his mates. His parents had said it was okay so long as he didn't go in the water. They said it was too dangerous, but then old people seemed to think everything was dangerous.

"Bit of a zoo here tonight, yeah?" Emily had said. "I wonder what it's like when it's quiet?"

It sounded like an invitation of sorts. When he suggested going there early this morning, it had sounded like someone else's voice. She had given him the sweetest of goodnight kisses just before she and her mates departed, her mouth open, tongues caressing. It had filled him with delicious anticipation.

They spoke quietly as they walked along the High Street to the end of the village. They crossed the road and then made their way down the lane until they came to a wide grass verge. Last night it had been thick with parked cars. Today, barely a sign that they had been there.

A gap in the hedge led them to more grass. Beyond that the quarry. Once it had been worked for its deposits of chalk for use in cement making, but it had been disused since long before either of them were born, and was now permanently filled with water, creating an artificial lake.

Here and there were bits of machinery and heaps of industrial lime, both of which were sometimes used as makeshift diving platforms by kids.

It seemed a few degrees warmer here. The morning's mist was burning off fast, sunlight sparkling on the surface of the water, an incongruous contrast to the beer cans and other litter strewn around. Birds twittered. There was the occasional drone of cars.

Will and Emily walked towards the water's edge.

"I bet it's cold in there," she said.

"Yeah, but swimming pools are always cold when you first get in. Your body soon gets used to it."

But she wasn't listening.

"Look at that." She pointed to a spot no more than a couple of yards away. At first, he wasn't sure what the splodge of colour was.

"Looks like somebody went home without their clothes," Emily remarked, going for a closer look. "And their shoes."

Will was at her elbow. They were looking at a girl's top and skirt, both neatly folded, and a pair of strappy sandals.

"No underwear, though. At least she still had her knickers on," he said, his gaze sliding from the clothes to the still surface of the water, now reflecting patches of blue sky and a couple of fluffy clouds.

"Not a skinny dipper then." She looked at him appraisingly. "So are we going in, or just standing here?"

She was unbuttoning her shirt. He could see a red bikini top with white polka dots emerging underneath. His heart caught in his throat and his fingers moved to his own buttons.

When they had stripped down to their swimming costumes, Emily cocked her head on one side and regarded him frankly.

"Not bad," she decided. "Not bad at all." She moved closer and kissed him, first a brush on his lips, then more lingering. His hardness grew, nudging against her. She stepped away, grinning. "Down boy. Save it for later."

The water was freezing, its chill not yet affected by the morning sun.

"How deep do you reckon it is?" Emily wondered.

Will was vaguely aware that it was some five metres deep, although he had no idea why he would know such a fact. He said so.

"There must be all kinds of crap on the bottom. Bet you can't get down there and bring me something up."

He looked at her, saw the dare in her eyes. This was a chance either to impress her, or to look a wuss.

"What sort of something?"

"I don't care. So long as it's not something gross, like a used condom."

He thought about challenging her to a race to the bottom, but thought he'd look bad if she beat him.

"No problemo," he said. He filled his lungs and ducked under.

He was a strong underwater swimmer, and he clove through the water, confident with each stroke that he would easily succeed. The water was a bit murky, but clearer than he had expected. As he went deeper, he began to make out outlines on the bottom. Rubbish that had either been dumped there or had been left when the quarry ceased to operate, before it had filled with water.

As he wondered what to grab for Emily, his eye was caught by a sizeable pink shape at the bottom. He idly wondered what it was. Probably too large to drag up with him, but maybe worth a closer look. He swam in its direction.

A few more strokes and he was face to face with it. Then he was clawing his way to the surface, his heart hammering in his ears, a sight he would never forget etched indelibly on his mind.

A girl, lying on her back on the bed of the water-filled quarry, her skin marble-pale, red hair streaming out like flaming seaweed.

And the eyes, glassy and staring, as if she could see right through him.

2

"Where do you want this one?" Dan Baines asked between puffs as he staggered up to the front door with yet another heavy box.

Lizzie Archer lifted a flap and peered inside, confirming what she had already guessed. More books.

"Spare bedroom," she pronounced.

Baines nodded and tottered past her, no doubt wondering why she referred to the room she was methodically filling with boxes as a bedroom, when there would never be room for a small stool, let alone a bed, if she didn't do some sorting out. She watched him lurching towards the stairs, and then headed for the van to get another box herself.

She still didn't know what was more amazing - the fact that she was moving into a Buckinghamshire village, or the fact that Baines had volunteered to help her.

It was more than a year now since she had transferred up from London to the Aylesbury Vale Division of Thames Valley Police, and she still felt like a misfit in many ways - never more so than when a case took her into one of the small villages, where everyone seemed to know each other and some families seemed to have lived for centuries. In some cases, generation upon generation had grown up in the same house or on the same farm, only to wind up cheek by jowl in the local churchyard, each headstone having its own tale to tell.

She knew that in reality many of the villages were as much a part of the commuter belt as the Vale's collection of small and larger market towns, and that those who got seriously involved in village life were usually a relatively small hard core. Yet she had come across a fair few who still regarded people who had moved into these communities more than a quarter of a century ago as incomers. Now here she was, the worst kind of townie, putting herself in that very position.

As for Baines...

They had got off on the wrong foot from the start. She was the new Detective Inspector, self-conscious about the ugly scar on her cheek and lacking in confidence. He was the ambitious Detective Sergeant who had been acting up in the higher rank and had hoped his promotion would be made substantive - until Archer came on the scene.

Neither of them had entirely shaken off their initial awkwardness around one another. It probably didn't help that both of them carried some painful baggage - Baines more so than her, in Archer's opinion.

So, when Baines had wished her a good weekend last night, and she had made a throwaway remark about moving house single-handed on the hottest day of the year so far, she had been so taken aback by his offer of help that she couldn't have found a way of refusing, even if she had wanted to.

Baines clumped back down the stairs, his tee-shirt soaked with sweat. She had to admit that he'd thrown himself into the work with astonishing enthusiasm, reporting bright and early to meet her outside the house, offering to drive the van she'd hired - a mercy, as she still loathed driving on narrow country lanes at the best of times - and helping her decant her furniture from the West London flat she was selling in double-quick time.

"I don't suppose you've managed to unearth the kettle yet?" he appealed to her. "I've lost so much moisture, I'm about to dry up and blow away."

She looked him up and down. "You think? You look pretty substantial to me, Dan, and you did have two pints in the pub at lunchtime."

Archer had decided that, if she was going to live in a place like Great Marston, the least she could do was to support local businesses, so she and Baines had made the short stroll down to The Goose for lunch, where they had found decent enough food and a cheerful atmosphere.

When she had first had her transfer confirmed, colleagues at the Met had tried to wind her up about the rustic ways of folk out in what they called 'the wilds of Buckinghamshire'. It had been mostly bollocks, including the notion that, whenever a stranger walked into a pub, the place fell silent and everyone watched you suspiciously. The patrons of The Goose hadn't given her or Baines a second glance. She could almost - but not quite - believe that no one had clocked the crescent-shaped scar on her left cheek, nor the slight droop on that side of her face, which made her smile lop-sided.

"No coffee, no more box-humping," Baines said, dragging her back to the present.

She made a show of tutting and shaking her head. "All right, already! I'll find the bloody kettle."

The truth was, she knew exactly where it was. She'd just got so caught up in the cycle of bringing things in from the van, dumping them in the appropriate room (and, yes, that did seem to be the spare bedroom most of the time), and going out to retrieve more, that refreshing her helper hadn't even crossed her mind.

She went into the kitchen, rummaged in the relevant box, drew out a limescale-encrusted electric kettle that was functional, if not aesthetic, and began to fill it. As she did so, she heard Baines's mobile phone ring and him answering it. She couldn't hear what he was saying, but she thought she caught a note of dismay.

A few moments later, he came into the kitchen looking awkward.

"Would you be okay for an hour or so? I've just had some sad news from Little Aston."

Little Aston was the village where Baines still lived, despite his wife having been murdered there some twelve years ago. Baines's young son, who had been three at the time, had been abducted by the murderer, a serial killer known as the Invisible Man, and had never been seen nor heard of again.

"What's happened?" she wanted to know.

"Have I mentioned the old quarry the kids use as a swimming hole in the summer?"

"Used to quarry chalk for cement back in the day, didn't it?"

"That's the one. On a hot night like last night, the local roadside's always awash with parked cars, and half the teenage population seems to gravitate there."

She shrugged. "So what about it?"

"It seems a young girl drowned there last night. A couple of youngsters got down there around seven this morning for an early dip. One of them dived in and spotted her on the bottom." Many people imagined a corpse would float, but the reality was that its weight would drag it under the water until gases produced by decomposition buoyed it up - a process that could take several days.

"Nothing suspicious, by the sounds of it," he said. "Joan heard about it and thought I ought to know."

Detective Constable Joanne 'Joan' Collins was a major ingredient in Archer's team - both the glue that held it together and the oil that greased its wheels. She had an eye for detail, a memory that would put an elephant to shame, and a phenomenal work ethic, often staying late or putting in appearances at the weekend. It was just like her to forewarn Baines of something nasty that had gone down in his neighbourhood.

"It seems she was reported missing late last night," he went on. "I'm surprised no one's contacted me before, living in the village and all."

"I think Lara Moseley was duty DI last night," she said. "Any search would have been mostly uniforms. No reason to involve you."

"They did what they could overnight, but the darkness obviously hampered them. They started again at first light. Apparently someone did knock on my door, but we were on our way to London by then. And then those kids found her before we did anyway."

"Bloody shame," Archer said. "Pretty stupid of the kid to go skinny-dipping on her own in a place like that." She shrugged. "Good of Joan to tell you, but presumably it's under control by now?"

"Yeah," he agreed. "I just feel I ought to show my face, to be honest. Quite a few of the locals do know I'm a copper."

"All the more reason to steer clear, then. It's not as if you know anything. And haven't you said that place was an accident waiting to happen?"

"Not quite. Kids need to take a few risks, and the quarry has always seemed benign enough to me. What I actually said was if there was ever a drowning, then no doubt the grieving parents would be blaming everyone but themselves for allowing their little darling to get within a mile of the place. "

She looked at him. "And that's what you're going there to say to them? To the locals?"

"Obviously not."

She put the kettle down on a clear square foot of work surface. "I'd better come with you. Clearing the rest of the van will seem a whole lot more appealing once we've had a little break."

* * *

Baines drove them both in his Ford Mondeo, which he'd left outside the house when they set off for London in the van. Archer's Renault was still at the van hire company's premises. It was only about five miles from Great Marston to Little Aston, and he made short work of the distance.

As he slid the car through S-bends, ignoring his boss's tension as she sat, white-knuckled, in the passenger seat, he questioned his motives for heading over there. There was apparently no crime to solve and he hadn't even heard of the dead girl, sixteen-year-old Leigh Fletcher. He had no call to start asking nosey questions, and he would have no answers for anyone who wanted to know how the police investigation into the tragedy was progressing.

The quarry itself, about half a mile outside the village, would almost certainly be being treated like a crime scene - normal procedure for an unexpected death, even where accident seemed the most probable cause - and so that was where he made for first. As they drove up, he was not surprised to see a crowd of teenagers keeping a respectful distance from the blue and white tape that cordoned the area off, nor the mountain of flowers, cards and soft toys that had clearly been piling up all day.

He squeezed the car into a space a couple of hundred yards away and they walked back, arriving just in time to witness two teenage girls adding a large teddy bear to the makeshift shrine. Their mission accomplished, the girls dissolved into tears, their arms around each other like shipwrecked sailors clinging to wreckage.

Whether they were friends of Leigh Fletcher, or simply staking a claim to a little piece of the tragedy, he couldn't tell. These days, what the media had dubbed 'grief tourism' was rife. People would travel hundreds of miles to pay their respects to people they had never met: so-called celebrities; murdered children; anyone whose death had hit the headlines. They would solemnly sign condolence books.

In this, the information age, there was also the opportunity to grieve over these total strangers on social networking sites. A particularly bizarre example had been the gunman who had gone on a rampage up North, shooting three people, one fatally, before turning the gun on himself after a six-hour stand-off with the police. A tribute site quickly appeared online, glorifying the killer's exploits and affording him cult hero status.

Baines and Archer approached the tape and showed their warrant cards to a couple of bored-looking uniformed constables.

"Do we need to suit up to go in there?" he asked.

"Probably not. Crime Scene Investigators have been there a few hours. Some stuff was taken away early on, but nothing for a while. The Crime Scene Manager's still there, with a couple of other CSIs. Might be an idea to put some overshoes on, though."

They trudged back to the car. Baines always kept a couple of plastic suits and pairs of shoe covers in the boot in case he was called urgently to a scene. DI Britton, his boss before Lizzie Archer, and also his mentor before he died of cancer last year, had given him the tip. Britton himself, in his early days as a detective, had blundered into a murder scene in his street clothes and then had to surrender every stitch. This was to eliminate any fibres or other evidence he may have inadvertently left at the scene and to check for any clues he might have picked up on his clothing. Britton had learned from the gaffe and always passed the lesson on to younger colleagues.

With their shoes suitably covered, Baines and Archer ducked under the tape and approached the former quarry. After a few warm days, the ground was perfectly dry and, with the sun shining, it was obvious why it was such a draw for youngsters.

Over the six or seven years that the swimming craze had been going on, the owners had regularly complained to the police, fearing that the site presented a hazard that would end in tears. The local MP had also got in on the act, but it wasn't that simple. No crimes were actually being committed, so all the police could do was warn of the hazards. Baines wondered if the hint of danger merely added to the attraction.

Today there was no sign of the usual litter that visitors tended to leave. Everything the CSIs found at the scene would have been removed as evidence.

Baines spotted the Crime Scene Manager, Phil Gordon, and was pleased that the whippet-thin Geordie was on duty today.

"What's the story, Phil?"

Gordon gave the two of them the once-over, taking in their crumpled tee-shirts, Baines's ripped jeans and Archer's shorts.

"You needn't have dressed up for the occasion," he told them in his thick accent, then shrugged. "Not much to tell, really. The girl was found on or near the bottom, and police divers have recovered the body. She'll be at the mortuary by now, awaiting a post mortem."

"Was she skinny dipping?"

Gordon shrugged. "In her undies. Clothes nearby, neatly folded. It seems the kids who found her spotted them and thought at first that someone had gone home without them last night."

"Really?" DI Archer looked sceptical.

"I wouldn't put anything past youngsters."

"What about her bag?"

"No, although she might not have had one with her. I gather she was just visiting a mate up the road. We found a phone in the pocket of her skirt."

"Okay," Archer said. Baines would have bet she had taken a handbag everywhere with her at 16.

"Anyhow," Gordon continued, "it looks like she got into difficulties and, with no one there to help her, she went under."

Archer frowned. "Pretty stupid to swim in a place like this on your own, don't you think? Rather strange thing to do, too."

The Crime Scene Manager spread his palms. "What can I tell you? She was a teenager. Maybe she'd been drinking, maybe she was high on drugs. Whatever. She's walking home after dark, maybe comes here just to see if anyone's about, and finds she has the place to herself. It was quite hot last night. The water's just too inviting to resist, so she strips off and takes the plunge."

He sighed. "It may be a while since I was a teenager, but I've got two of my own to remind me what stupid things we're all capable of at that age. I dare say you two have some embarrassing memories that still come back to haunt you from time to time. This poor lass paid for her stupidity with her life."

"So, nothing suspicious here?" Archer pressed.

"Not that I can see. I mean, a lot of people obviously come here and leave bits of rubbish behind. Nothing remarkable. The ground's too dry for any shoe prints. There's what looks like some scuffing at the water's edge."

Baines looked at him. "A sign of a struggle?"

"I doubt it. Could be absolutely anything." Gordon looked at them appraisingly. "What brings a DI and a DS to something routine like this on a Saturday afternoon anyway? Do you know something about this kid that I don't?"

"No," Baines said. "I live locally, and was just a bit curious, that's all."

"Aye, well, I don't see much here that needs any detecting. An open and shut case of death by misadventure, I reckon." He shook his head sadly. "A real waste. She was a pretty girl, by the looks of her, and she had her whole life in front of her."

"She's been identified as Leigh Fletcher. Sixteen."

"That's right. Your guys had been searching for her. I gather her parents got worried when she hadn't got home by midnight and started phoning her friends. They phoned the police in the early hours of the morning. You'd have to ask at the station if you want to know much more."

Baines nodded. "Thanks, Phil. We'll leave you to it."

He took a last glance round at the scene, noting the smattering of CSIs still searching the ground for clues and taking photographs, then turned away, feeling unaccountably sad.

Sixteen. One year older than his own son, Jack, would be now if he was still alive. Even though no body had ever been found, all logic told him that, like the rest of the Invisible Man's younger victims, Jack must be dead.

The Invisible Man. So dubbed because his modus operandi had been to enter and leave victims' homes without leaving any trace of himself. Always when a mother was home alone with one small child. He would murder the mother, suffocating her with plastic film, and abduct the child. Exactly one week later, the stolen child would be found at his next murder scene, killed by the same method that he used on the mothers.

At each scene, the police would find a dead woman and a dead child, and another family would have to grieve over the mother whilst enduring an agonising seven-day wait before their own abducted child turned up dead at the next victim's home.

But after the death of Baines's wife, Louise, the killings stopped. There were no more dead mothers, no new murder scene at which to discover Jack's small body. It was as if the child had disappeared into thin air.

Self-preservation had eventually forced Baines to effectively seal off his grief and the demons that had been torturing him about his son's fate. Then, just over a year ago, his dreams, and even some waking moments, had started to be haunted by visions of a teenage boy, the young man Jack might have become if he was still alive.

The sightings had gradually become rarer again, but he would still wake up in tears some mornings, or catch the occasional glimpse of teenage Jack on the edge of a crowd.

When they had arrived here earlier, his gaze had instinctively swept the crowd of youngsters assembled beyond the crime scene tape, but there had been no apparition to stir his emotions.

They walked back to the car in silence and deposited the overshoes in the boot.

"Is there any more you want to do here?" Archer asked him as he started the car.

"Not really, although I'll be interested in the post mortem report. But I'm sure it's as Phil suggested. Like you said, swimming alone in a place like that is a pretty risky thing to do if something goes wrong."

"Phil's right, though. Teenagers do daft things. I suppose what doesn't actually kill them teaches them a hard lesson. Leigh was just unlucky."

"A bloody shame," he agreed. "Oh, well. We've got a van to finish unloading."

"I wonder what sort of girl she was?" Archer mused as Baines picked up the B489. "Whether this was typical of her."

"I'd go and see the parents," he said, "but I probably don't want to get too involved with an incident on my doorstep. I just wanted to know the facts, so I don't make a complete idiot of myself if anyone asks me about it. Assuming anyone does."

"Well, they might. You said yourself, you're known for being a copper."

"True," he admitted, changing down for a sharp right-hand bend. "Although I don't know how general that is. Louise was the one who really embraced village life, knew the local mafia."

She laughed. "You make it sound like Sicily, not Aylesbury Vale."

"You know what I mean though."

Baines's late wife had fallen in love with the Little Aston community and thrown herself into it with gusto, helping with fetes, even joining the WI as one of the youngest members in its history. He'd been both touched and surprised by the genuine grief that had followed her death, as if a dark cloud had hung over the entire village for weeks.

"I do go into the village store, though - you know, for a Sunday paper, or when I run out of milk," he said. "Half the staff in there know who I am."

"It might be no bad thing if they mention it to you," she said. "I mean, I know it looks like there's no crime here, but we'll still have a role in establishing what happened. Someone might know something. You just need to listen and say as little as possible. Until there's been a post mortem, all we really have is a body and an unsubstantiated theory."

He nodded. "I'll go in there tomorrow, as usual then, but play it cagey. Best not even suggest it was simple misadventure until we know for sure."

A few minutes later he was drawing up outside Archer's new home again.

"Right," he said. "I seem to recall you were about to make coffee when a dead body intervened."

She tutted and shook her head. "Bodies, eh? No sense of timing."

3

Archer woke from the sleep of the dead, feeling stiff and achy. After the initial disorientation at being in an unfamiliar room, it dawned on her that she had spent her first night in her new home, and was now starting her first full day there. It should have been an exciting feeling, but it was tempered by all the work that she still needed to do, and how knackered she was already.

Limping to the bathroom on legs that felt as if she had just scaled Scafell Pike, she decided that the inside of her house bore a striking resemblance to council tips she had known. Getting straight was definitely a work in progress.

As she showered, she reflected again on what a godsend Baines had been yesterday, and she hoped that doing something together that was non-work related might mark a new thawing in their relationship. He had, after all, been the only person to offer her any help. Her brother, Adam, hadn't spoken to her since their mother had died last year, and her father was long dead. None of her old mates in London were really close enough friends for her to feel comfortable asking for assistance.

She supposed she could have splashed out on a removal firm, but that would have meant booking - and paying a deposit on - a moving day that the job could then have scuppered at short notice.

She had also toyed with asking her occasional lover, Ian Baker, if he could spare the time to come down from Norfolk, but he was always up to his neck in the job, and he she knew the DI was investigating the murders of two prostitutes. She saw so little of him that she sometimes wondered if they had a relationship at all.

Then, just as she'd been wondering how on earth she was going to cope single-handed, Baines had made his casual offer.

And, she had to admit, she would have been loading and unloading the van half the night without him. As it was, it had been after midnight when they'd finally called it a day. They'd finished humping boxes in from the van at around 6 pm and then dropped the vehicle back at the office and picked up her own Renault. They'd paused to pick up a takeaway on the way back, wolfed it down standing up, and then set about starting to unpack and organise. She'd asked him if he fancied lunch today, as a thank you, but it seemed he had plans. Part of her had been curious about what might be on his agenda, but she hadn't pried. It was at times like this that she realised how little she knew about the colleague she worked most closely with. Maybe after this weekend that could start to change a little.

Showered and dressed in jeans and an old tee-shirt, she sat at the kitchen table eating cereal, interspersed with swigs of coffee, with Three Counties Radio playing in the background on her battered radio/CD player combination. The BBC Channel covered Bedfordshire, Hertfordshire and Buckinghamshire, including news and travel information. A couple of colleagues had mentioned it to her soon after she arrived in the Vale, and she had found 3CR, and the local paper, The *Aylesbury Echo*, a help in finding out about her new surroundings and what was going on.

She was not really listening - too busy planning her day. But one news item caught her attention and made her turn the sound up.

"... the Little Aston schoolgirl, Leigh Fletcher, who tragically drowned in a local swimming hole on Friday night. Local MP Andrew Marling condemned local authorities, especially the police, who he said had known for years that children were using a dangerous former quarry for unsupervised swimming."

The programme cut to the MP's youthful tones:

"I get no pleasure out of saying that this tragedy has been waiting to happen for a very long time. I was a local councillor for the area before I became an MP, and even then I was repeatedly warned of the dangers the quarry posed to youngsters. You can't blame them for being lured by a nice spot to swim and enjoy the sunshine. I was a teenager not so long ago." Marling had been elected to Westminster three years ago at the 2010 General Election, becoming the youngest MP in the House. "Yet nothing has ever been done to secure it," he went on, "and no supervision arrangements were ever put in place. I just hope something will finally be done now, but it will have taken the loss of a young life to get some action."

The newsreader picked up the story again:

"A spokesman for the family said Leigh's parents and sister were devastated by what had happened. He said they were at a loss to understand why she had apparently gone late night swimming alone, and how a girl who had swum at county level and had Olympic aspirations could have got into difficulties. Other news..."

Archer took a thoughtful sip of her coffee. Coming from another MP, Marling's comments might be seen as cheap opportunism, but she knew his reputation as one of the good guys. His passion for the area had seen him elected to the local council in his teens and he had been deputy leader of Buckinghamshire County Council at a ridiculously tender age. The hugely successful music festival, The Vale Live! had been his brainchild, and had put the area on the map on the national music scene. He'd also been in a relationship with a popular fashion model, she recalled, but that hadn't lasted.

Marling had already made his mark in Parliament, and was tipped for a place in the government in a reshuffle forced upon the Prime Minister by a cabinet minister's heart attack. And he knew how to use the media. In her time in the area, Archer had not failed to notice how Marling missed no opportunity to be seen on TV, heard on the radio, or read about in the national and local press - but she had never heard him go for the banal sound bite.

Of Leigh Fletcher's death, he had said exactly what Baines had predicted people would say. Nonetheless, for all the clout Marling had locally, even he had never managed to get anything done about the quarry he insisted was a death trap.

What interested her more than the MP's sound bite, though, was Leigh Fletcher's family's statement. If she had swum at county level, presumably she had been a good, strong swimmer. So what had gone wrong on Friday night?

Phil Gordon, the Crime Scene Manager, had speculated that drink or drugs might have played a part. If so, someone was to blame for supplying a young girl with something that had impaired her normal abilities and led to her death.

She found her interest suddenly piqued, and her plans for the day were temporarily forgotten as she phoned Aylesbury police station and asked when the post mortem was expected to take place.

* * *

The village store in Little Aston was a decent size, and you could probably get everything you needed there, without ever visiting a supermarket, if you weren't too brand-conscious. Not everything was easy to find, but the staff were always ready to help.

For all that he had lived in the village for a decade and a half, he still didn't really know many people. There were five customers here, all of whom he recognised, but none of whom he could name. Behind the counter were a woman called Jan - the female half of the husband and wife team that owned the store - and a teenage girl who seemed to work weekends. Baines had a vague idea that her name might be Stacey or Tracey.

Jan nodded as he approached the counter with his paper.

"We were just talking about poor Leigh Fletcher," she told him. "I suppose you were involved in the search for her yesterday morning? Mr Baines is with the police," she informed her customers.

"Such a lovely kid," a middle aged woman said. "She was always doing sponsored swims, and she used to help out on the tombola at the village fete."

"She went to the chapel every Sunday," added another woman.

"They ought to close that bloody quarry down," opined an elderly man who seemed to wear the same uniform of brown tweed jacket and green flat cap 365 days a year. Baines privately wondered if he had a wardrobe full of them and rotated them.

"That's what the MP was saying on local radio," Jan said. "He's been saying it's dangerous for years, and no one's taken any notice of him."

Baines paid for his paper.

"Do the police know what happened?" Jan asked him. "None of us can understand it. Leigh wasn't the sort of girl to stay out late, skinny-dipping and such, and she was such a good swimmer. She wanted to swim in the Olympics one day. How could she have drowned?"

"Well, there'll have to be a post mortem," he said. "Maybe we'll know a bit more after that. But you're saying it was out of character for her to go late night swimming in the quarry?"

She seemed to consider this. "Well, I don't know the family that well, but I'd have thought so."

"They've had no luck, that family," one of the other women said. "How long is it since they were burgled?"

"Only a few months," the girl supplied. Baines vaguely recalled that there had been a break-in in the village. "And Leigh got mugged as well," she added. "Had her phone nicked."

Baines thanked Jan for the paper and left the others talking. As he made his way back up the high street, he digested what he had heard. A burglary, a mugging and now a drowning. Part of him was thinking that, when trouble comes in threes, maybe it's more than just a coincidence, and he made a mental note to find out who was dealing with Leigh Fletcher's death at the office, although a Senior Investigating Officer would most likely be appointed only if and when it was decided that there was something to investigate. Still, there was no harm in passing on this information and making sure everyone had the full picture.

Most likely, though, Leigh's drowning would turn out to be the genuine misfortune it appeared, but Baines knew that assumption could be the mother of all cockups. And, if there were cockups to be made, it was best they weren't his.

* * *

The mortuary at Stoke Mandeville Hospital was only about five or six years old, and was modern and well-equipped, putting some of those Archer had seen in London to shame. She arrived just as Barbara Carlisle, was about to start the post mortem on Leigh Fletcher. The pathologist's green eyes blinked behind her protective glasses.

"Hi, Lizzie. This is a surprise. Especially on a Sunday. What brings you here?"

"I'd like to say I just fancied keeping you company, Barbara, but the truth is I'm a bit curious about this one."

Carlisle was accompanied by her technician, Bruce Davenport. A lanky man Archer didn't recognise detached himself from the wall against which he had been leaning and held out a hand to her.

"We haven't met. Detective Inspector Rod Jarvis. I'm the duty inspector at the Child Abuse Investigation Unit. And you are...?"

Archer shook his hand and introduced herself. "Child abuse? Is that considered a possibility here?"

He shrugged. "Not from what I know of the facts, no, but protocol dictates we take an interest in the sudden and unexpected death of anyone under 18. Of course, there are all sorts of possibilities with a drowning. She may have killed herself because she was being abused, for instance. Anyway, that's our interest. What's yours? You said you were curious."

His gaze lingered on her scar for a second or so longer than necessary before sliding away from her face altogether. Little by little, she was doing her best to develop a thick skin to this sort of inspection, but still hadn't entirely succeeded.

She heaved cheerfulness into her tone. "Just being nosey, to be honest. My DS lives in the same village as Leigh, so we visited the scene yesterday afternoon. Then I heard the report on the radio this morning, and I heard some things that jarred a little."

Jarvis nodded. "Yes, I heard some of that. Of course, none of it means it's foul play. Most parents don't know their kids as well as they think they do."

"Sure. I'm probably wasting my time. Even if there is anything for CID to investigate, I might not get the case. Like I say, just being nosey."

"So I can get on, then?" Carlisle asked mildly. "Regardless of why you two are here, I'm here on a Sunday because the Coroner told me to, and I'd quite like to get back to my day of rest."

The two detectives apologised and asked her to proceed. Archer watched with as much dispassion as she could muster. She never liked seeing a body's most intimate secrets revealed, and it was rare for her to attend a post mortem she didn't have to. Muscling in when there wasn't even a criminal investigation - and probably wouldn't be - was also unlike her, and she wasn't sure why she had done it, especially with a drowning.

In her student days, she had gone with friends to see Pre-Raphaelite paintings at the Tate. One that took her eye was a depiction of Ophelia by John Everett Millais. The girl in the painting had floated amongst the flowers that she had gathered, and had looked serene and beautiful. Archer had later learned the reality that drowning was an ugly way to die.

Four or five years ago, when she had still been in the Met and had thought she had a future there, she had investigated the death of a young woman who'd been tied up and then dumped in the Thames - just one of the 80 to 100 bodies recovered from the river every year. The victim had been in the water for weeks before she was spotted and pulled out. What remained of her had given Archer horrific dreams for months afterwards, not helped by an over-enthusiastic pathologist describing in detail what he imagined death by drowning must actually be like. Archer had decided that, however she left this life behind, that was one of the last methods she would opt for, given a choice.

By comparison to that case, at least this body wasn't in too bad a condition. Leigh Fletcher had been a beautiful girl. Archer thought it was her pale skin and flame hair that might have jogged those Pre-Raphaelite recollections.

As always, Carlisle conducted her examination with compassion, respect and complete professionalism. She began with a detailed examination of the dead girl, providing a running commentary as she did so. The commentary was being recorded and would provide the basis of her report. She paused when she got to the hands.

"Nails are scrupulously clean."

That got Archer's attention. Jarvis's too.

"As in scraped clean?" Archer said carefully.

"Yes, but it's too early to read anything into that. She could have done it herself."

Archer took a closer look. "Before going into the water? How likely is it they'd be that clean if she'd done them earlier?"

"It's possible she did do them that recently," Jarvis said. "My daughter's always doing her nails. And her makeup. She can't go out for a Mars bar without being done up to the nines."

"Still. I'll ask the crime scene manager whether any manicure stuff was found at the scene. As far as I know, there were just her clothes and a phone."

Carlisle continued to work, moving on to open up the body and begin methodically to remove and weigh the internal organs. Occasionally she would ask Bruce Davenport, to take a photograph.

For Archer, the process was especially depressing when the subject was as young as this one was.

"I'll have the water in her lungs analysed," Carlisle said. "Cause of death was definitely drowning, but a comparison with the samples the CSIs collected will confirm that she drowned in the quarry and not elsewhere. The time of death I've already estimated at between 11 pm on Friday and 2 am Saturday."

She worked on. When she reached the genital examination stage, she paused and consulted a clipboard.

"I can tell you one thing," she remarked.

"What's that?" DI Jarvis asked.

"No sign of sexual assault. In fact, no sign of recent sexual activity. But she wasn't a virgin. I'd have to do some more work to see if I can determine whether she recently had intercourse."

"I think she's not long passed sixteen?" Jarvis checked.

"April 30th."

"So, maybe under age sex."

"Maybe," Archer said. "Doesn't necessarily have anything to do with her death, though. It's not like under age sex is exactly unusual these days - if it ever really was. I guess the question for you is - did she have a boyfriend, or was it abuse?"

"I'll need to look into that," Jarvis agreed, "although I agree it probably had nothing to do with her death. On the other hand, if she was being abused, that may have caused psychological problems that led to her taking her own life."

"I really think we can rule suicide out," Carlisle said briskly. "Drowning is one of the less common methods of suicide. The body has a natural tendency to come up for air, so just staying under water isn't really going to work. Throwing yourself into an icy river might do it, but we know the weather's been warm of late. No, she'd need to have weighed herself down with something heavy, which we know wasn't the case. In all probability she simply drowned by accident."

"Could her ability to survive in the water have been impeded by drink or drugs?" wondered Archer.

"Of course. I'll be sending some samples to toxicology to check that out. There are no physical signs that she was using heroin or cocaine. Ecstasy gone wrong is a possibility, or maybe some sort of date rape drug."

"Like Rohypnol or roofies? But surely there'd be signs of sexual assault?"

Carlisle shook her head. "I'll leave the detecting to you two. All I can say is if she'd, for argument's sake, had a drink spiked and somehow ended up in the water, she wouldn't have been able to do much to save herself."

"But you're not saying that's what happened?" Jarvis asked carefully.

Carlisle allowed herself a thin smile. "DI Archer will tell you she knows me better than that, Inspector. I can't possibly say at this juncture what actually happened. What I will say is that I'm not seeing anything suspicious at the moment."

Archer took in what the pathologist had said. The tox screening would be important, of course. But, assuming that came back clear, it sounded as if there was no evidence pointing to anything but accidental drowning.

So why couldn't she shake the feeling that there were still mysteries here to be solved?

* * *

The glider rode the thermals like a huge bird of prey. Baines and Karen Smart sat on the grass on Dunstable Downs, watching its progress and enjoying the relative quiet.

Part of the Chiltern Hills, the Downs were a few miles over the border in southern Bedfordshire, where they formed the highest point in that county at just over 240 metres. It was their height that attracted local gliders, kite fliers and hang gliders, and the London Gliding Club had its home nearby.

It was a very pleasant morning. Later they would have a pub lunch, then back to Baines's house to watch the Wimbledon men's final on TV, hoping to see Andy Murray become the first British winner since 1936.

Baines had just given Karen an outline of his efforts in assisting his boss's house move.

"Nice to think you two are finally playing nicely," she remarked. "And you still had time to visit a crime scene, too. Days don't come much better than that."

He searched her face for sarcasm, but she was unreadable. His late wife, Louise, had had an excellent poker face, so it was hardly surprising that her identical twin sister had the same talent.

It was that likeness that so often caused him mingled joy and sorrow. Karen was simply the closest friend he had in the world, and sometimes he wished it went further. About a year ago, they had come close to becoming much more, but the moment had somehow slipped by, and now it seemed that neither of them felt comfortable raising it again.

He thought they both knew why. There was always that fear on both their sides that there was something not quite right about a bereaved man having a relationship with someone who looked, sounded and behaved exactly like the woman he had lost. It somehow felt that he might simply be using his sister-in-law to reach out beyond the grave to Louise, rather than falling in love with her for her own sake.

Sometimes he refused to accept that. Sometimes it rang painfully true to him. It was Karen who had finally been willing to give a deeper relationship a try, and him who had got cold feet about seeing it through.

They still saw each other most Sundays and once or twice in the week, work permitting, but it was as if something between them had been damaged and could never quite be repaired.

"So what do you think about this drowned girl?" she asked. "Anything suspicious?"

A couple of kids were trying unsuccessfully to launch a kite. Baines recalled trying the same thing up here himself when he'd been a boy. He'd been crap at it too.

"I doubt it," he said. "But I'll be interested in seeing the post mortem report. There's lots of ways it could have happened, but it just sounds like we've got a girl who chose Friday night to act out of character and then drowned despite being a very good swimmer."

"But if the post mortem did show that it was foul play, would you be on the case?"

"It would depend on which DI got allocated. If it's Lizzie, I'll be working it with her. Then again, maybe they'll give it to someone else. Still, everyone's pushed, and we've just cleared up a couple of cases. The DCI's bound to think there's some slack in Lizzie's team."

She frowned. "What about that lazy bastard you're always moaning about? Ashwell?"

"Ashby," he corrected. "Please God, not that. My neighbours would be beating a path to my door demanding to know what we were doing."

DI Steven Ashby was idle and good for nothing. Lizzie Archer had confided to Baines that, when she had first arrived in the job and found herself sharing an office with Ashby, she had thought he was a pig. Later on, she had amended that, deciding that it was a little hard on pigs.

How he got away with the things he did, Baines would never know or understand. He was rarely in the office, ostensibly following leads or liaising with what he insisted was an extensive network of contacts. Baines couldn't remember the last time he'd actually cleared up a crime. He even smoked in the office, something he tried to do surreptitiously, but which everyone knew he did. Archer, whose own father had died of lung cancer, had insisted on moving out of Ashby's office, and her desk was now in the big open plan room with the DSs and DCs.

All Baines could imagine was that Ashby had compromising photos of his DCI, Paul Gillingham, perhaps involving lewd acts with farm animals. Gillingham rode all his other officers hard, yet treated Ashby like an indulgent parent treats a wayward child.

"Most probably the post mortem will show that there's nothing suspicious at all," he said. "If neither the pathologist nor the CSIs can come up with anything to point to a suspicious death, and no one who knew her can give us cause to think otherwise, then we really do have to conclude it was an accident."

"Accidents do happen, Dan."

"I know. But with the burglary and the mugging... I suppose that really could all just be bad luck."

"But you've got a feeling."

"I'm afraid so."

She squeezed his arm. "You'd better make sure there's a thorough investigation then. Now, can we stop talking shop?"

He nodded and turned his attention to the kids with the kite again. They had finally got it airborne and were trying to make it do some fancy aerobatics. He pointed them out to Karen.

"Oh, to be that age again," she sighed.

"My dad used to bring me up here," he said. "Did I mention it?"

"Only every time we come here." She smiled fondly. "In thirty-odd years' time, you're going to be one of those dozy old blokes who keep repeating themselves. And you'll keep telling people your age."

"I'm eighty-nine, you know," he said in a creaky, old-man voice.

"Really? Then you're wearing well, Mr Baines."

But he had stopped listening. Another boy had joined the group with the kite, a tall, slim lad in a blue and white hooped replica football shirt. Queen's Park Rangers' colours.

Whenever Baines thought he caught a glimpse of his son, he was always in a QPR shirt. If the Invisible Man hadn't targeted the Baines family, he and Jack would have gone to Rangers matches together, just as Baines had done with his own father, an exiled West Londoner. He thought he probably projected this unfulfilled wish onto this apparition he sometimes saw.

He wondered why he was seeing him now. The boy he thought was Jack was on the periphery of the kite-flying group. It was impossible to say whether the others were aware of his presence. Whether he was even flesh and blood. He fought against his inclination to dash over there, could imagine the other boys' blank, puzzled stares.

"Karen to Dan," Karen was saying. "Hel-*lo?*"

"Sorry," he muttered, smiling crookedly. "I just thought I saw..."

He looked back at the kite flyers. The blue and white shirt had gone.

"Jack?" she asked softly.

"Yeah," he whispered, his eyes stinging. "Jack."

4

Aylesbury had been dated back to around 650 BC through the remains of an Iron Age Fort, and had been a market town since Anglo-Saxon times. With a population of over 60,000, it had been Buckinghamshire's county town since 1529 - a status conferred by Henry VIII, probably because Anne Boleyn's father's many properties happened to include Aylesbury Manor. It was also the administrative centre of the Aylesbury Vale district.

These days it was more famous for the Aylesbury duck, bred there since the Industrial Revolution, which formed the centrepiece of the town's heraldic crest and graced the menu of several local restaurants.

The police station was based on the Wendover Road, an unprepossessing box of a building from the outside, but Archer had been in worse.

Detective Chief Inspector Paul Gillingham lounged in his leather-faced swivel chair. To Archer, it looked as if he was making an unsuccessful attempt to look like some sort of power executive. His old chair had gone to the knackers' yard recently, and he'd somehow managed, in the face of the public sector cuts that were pinching every last penny, to wheedle for this natty number.

The impression would have been enhanced by a better haircut and a suit less shiny or threadbare.

"So, let me see if I've got this straight, Lizzie," he said in a tone that she knew spelt danger. "You gate-crashed a potential crime scene on Saturday and followed that up by turning up uninvited at a post mortem yesterday. And now you think there's something to investigate?"

"I didn't quite say -"

"And you didn't think to check whether we had the bases covered?"

"I was just curious. I assumed the inquiry wouldn't really open up until the post mortem report was in." She shrugged. "In all probability it's just a tragic accident and it will just be a matter of filling in the blanks. There's a couple of things that need checking, though."

"Such as?"

"Her nails were very clean. She might just have a thing about clean nails, of course, but killers have been known to scrape them to remove DNA evidence. Plus there was no bag at the scene with her clothes. It seems her phone was in a pocket, so maybe she didn't take one out with her, but we should ask the family if that was her habit. If she did have a bag, where is it now?"

Gillingham nodded. "Most of the females I know take out voluminous sacks with them. I reckon my wife carries a Big Top around in hers, in case there's a need for an impromptu circus."

Archer laughed politely. "Right."

"Still, as you say, this kid could be the exception."

"Also, she wasn't a virgin, sir. I mean, she was sixteen - just - and it's hardly unusual. But we ought to know who she'd been seeing."

He drummed his fingers on his desk. "Just out of interest, did you manage to fit any house moving into your busy weekend?"

"Yes, sir. Well, I'm in, anyway. Lots of unpacking still to do."

"And Dan Baines gave you a hand, so the grapevine tells me. You two are good mates now, by the sound of it?"

"I wouldn't go that far," she said.

"No?" He shrugged, dismissing that line of conversation. "Well, as far as the Leigh Fletcher case is concerned, I agree we need to be able to say what happened, and to satisfy ourselves that there's nothing suspicious, but we need to see Dr Carlisle's report before we do anything else. Of course, Lara Moseley oversaw the search, but she's giving evidence in a trial this week. I was thinking about putting Steve on it."

She looked at him. "Steve Ashby?"

He visibly bridled. She knew that Gillingham and Ashby went back a long way and that the DCI instinctively defended the dodgy inspector. But every now and then she put her foot in it by letting her feelings show. Demanding a change of office, to get away from him, hadn't gone down well and had taken a long time to be forgotten. An early run in with Ashby, even before that, had knocked the shine off the reputation she had arrived with in Gillingham's eyes.

"You've got a problem with Steve taking this case?" he demanded.

She thought quickly on her feet. "No, sir, of course not. It's just that DI Ashby always seems to have such a heavy caseload." If you believed him. "We need to be seen to do this right. The local MP is already showing an interest, and if this turns into a high profile case it could seriously stretch Steve's capacity." By making him do some work.

She didn't mention that Ashby was also a PR nightmare who, on the rare occasions he had appeared on local TV, had contrived to look even shiftier than the criminals he was supposed to be catching.

Gillingham looked hard at her, probably trying to detect a hint of irony in her tone or in her eyes. Finally he held up his hands.

"Yes, well, I'm sure Steve's at full stretch, and you have already done a bit of the groundwork. And I suppose you have got Baines right on the spot."

"Yes, sir. Although I think we'd need to be careful how we use Dan," she said tentatively. "Maybe he's a bit too close. He could be vulnerable if the locals start pumping him for information, and it might be a bit strange for him to be questioning his neighbours."

"You want to sideline him?"

"God, no. His local knowledge will be useful, but perhaps keep him from the front line, at least initially."

"He might not like that, but it's for you to sort out." He drummed his fingers on his desk. "You're right about the MP, though. He's already been in touch with the Chief Constable for an update. I think his father plays golf with the Chief's husband or something, so he's got a bit of a direct line. If there's nothing in this, it's best we clear it up sooner than later."

"I'll do my best," she assured him.

"Tell you what," Gillingham said thoughtfully. "Do you want to borrow a bit of another DS's time? Jenny Ross has just finished a couple of cases."

Archer thought for a moment. It might be useful at that. It would give her a bit of flexibility about how she used Baines, although she might have to massage his ego a little.

"That would be great, sir."

"So how are you going to play it?" Gillingham asked. "I mean, as you say, I still don't see much here to interest us. There was another allotment break-in, out at Wendover on Friday night. Even that was more of a crime than this kid's death is likely to be."

"Maybe so, sir, but, I don't want to sit around waiting for Dr Carlisle's report. The MP didn't wait to go public about everyone's failure to secure or supervise the site - including ours - and he might accuse us of inertia if we're not a bit proactive."

"So...?"

"So I think I can start asking some questions without getting the village grapevine too overheated. We'll rightly stress that it's all routine at this stage, after an unexpected death. Some will have already been questioned once, but I can cover all that with the 'routine' umbrella. As you say, it's probably a clear cut case, but I want a really clear picture of Leigh Fletcher - what she was like, who her friends were, boyfriends, what she's been doing lately, and what might have changed in her life."

"I'll speak to Jenny and square it with her DI. You need to smooth it with Baines, though."

"No problem," she said confidently.

* * *

"So you're marginalising me?" Baines's eyes were wide with disbelief.

"That's not what I said," Archer placated.

"Just off the case."

"I didn't say that either, Dan." She lowered her voice, her eyes scanning the office. She knew the difference between people working and people pretending to work while they eavesdropped. She'd done it often enough herself.

"Let's go make ourselves a coffee," she said, unlocking her desk drawer and taking out her electric kettle - her little defiance of office regulations - and her jar of half-decent instant.

Still not looking happy, Baines followed her to the communal kitchen. They were in luck. There was no one else in there.

"You want some of this?" she asked. "Or will you go for vending machine muck?"

"You can buy," he said, hands in his pockets. After a few moments, he straightened his shoulders, watching her busy herself with mugs and spoons.

"Look," she said, "this case will turn out to be just what it looks like. A silly little girl does a silly little thing and pays with her life. Tragic, but life's full of tragedies. But her family deserve to know how it happened, and we need to play our part in this."

"I can't argue with that. Sorry," he added. A year ago he would have instigated a row instead of backing down. It was another sign of their improving relationship.

She smiled. "You live amongst those people, and you'll be living there when this case is closed and we've moved on. There's a thin line between trust and suspicion. We need your local knowledge, but I'd like them to see you as someone they can talk to and in front of - not the official copper coming in asking questions."

"Makes some sense," he admitted. "I dropped by the village store yesterday and they didn't press me too hard over what we might be doing to find out what happened. What was interesting, though, was how shocked people seemed to be that a girl like her would be swimming alone in the quarry late at night in the first place. Not just stupid, but quite out of character too. And she was a bloody good swimmer, too. Hoping to go to the Rio Olympics, by all accounts."

"I think people had a somewhat rose-tinted view of her character, Dan. She wasn't a virgin for starters. Athletes aren't always as squeaky clean as we'd like to imagine. Look at all those performance-enhancing drugs."

"It's hardly unusual for a teenager to have tried sex," he pointed out. "Still, they did describe her as the ultimate girl next door. Even went to the village chapel. Makes you wonder what other secrets she had."

"People will be looking for answers - including our wonder boy MP, who's already got the ear of the Chief Constable on the subject. So we're going to have to be thorough and sensitive at the same time."

He took the steaming mug she held out to him.

"Easy to say. But we're hardly thick on the ground."

"True. The boss says I can use Jenny Ross to augment the team."

He didn't say anything, but the downturn of his mouth just before he blew on his coffee and took a sip told its own story. Ross wouldn't have been Archer's first choice either, not that she knew the DS that well. But any woman who could lower herself to flirting with DI Ashby, as she had done at a recent retirement party, had to be either really desperate for male company, or just really desperate. It didn't fill Archer with enthusiasm for her new colleague, but beggars couldn't be choosers.

She sipped her own coffee thoughtfully. "So Leigh was a chapel-goer?" she said finally. "That's interesting. Are they a very religious family then?"

"Not that I know of. But then the only name I've really heard mentioned in connection with the place is the Pastor, Marc Ambrose. He's been there maybe a couple of years. Relatively young, considering the congregation seems to run on a system of elders, but quite charismatic. I know there's a youth wing, and I guess that's what Leigh must have been into."

"Find out more, if you can. We'll probably have to talk to them, and I don't want to walk into something I don't understand. Elders? It sounds a bit controlling."

Baines shrugged. "Isn't everything about religion controlling? A bunch of people who think they know God's will best, telling the rest of us how to live our lives? No wonder religion's responsible for so many wars."

She regarded him with interest. "So you're what? An atheist?"

"Nothing as committed as that. I suppose I'm C of E but, other than weddings and funerals, I don't see the inside of a church from one year to the next."

Archer seemed to remember Baines mentioning one time that, soon after his wife and son had both been taken from him, the then local vicar had taken it upon himself to knock on Baines's door and offer help and support. That had gone down well enough. Feeding him shit about how it was part of God's plan hadn't. Baines had made it clear that, if that was the best God could do for a plan, then either a new plan or a new god was needed. He hadn't gone looking to the church for comfort after that.

Archer was sure that the vicar had been well-meaning enough. It didn't make his comments any more helpful.

Before they could take the conversation any further, a round-faced woman in a suit at least a size too small for her came to join them.

"Excuse me, ma'am," said DS Jenny Ross. "Joan Collins said I'd find you here. Only DCI Gillingham has attached me to you for the preliminaries on this drowning."

Archer raised her mug in greeting. "Hi, Jenny. We were just talking about it. Grab a coffee, and we'll take them into the briefing room. I think it's free."

When she and Baines had finished bringing her up to date, Ross looked reflective.

"Taken together, it does all sound a bit odd, doesn't it? It's like there were two Leigh Fletchers. The dutiful, chapel-going daughter, helpful to everyone, county class swimmer, girl next door. And the one with a sexual past who goes late night swimming in her undies. I wonder which one got herself drowned, though?"

"Yes," Archer agreed. "I want to find out a lot more about the second one, and I don't think we're going to get to know her through her parents, or any other adult. We need to talk to her closest friends. The first thing to do is find out who's been spoken to so far, and what formal statements have been taken."

"Would you like me to check that out?" asked Ross.

"No," Archer said. "Dan, would you hunt that down, please? Jenny, perhaps you'd chase up that post mortem report. I'd like to know when we can expect the toxicology analysis."

Baines sketched a salute. "I'll get on it. Ma'am." he added, as he rose and headed for the door.

Archer stared after him. He knew full well that Archer hated being called 'ma'am'. She preferred 'guv', which all of her team used when addressing her formally. It struck her that Ross didn't know this yet, and she suppressed a smile, seeing what he was up to. Not exactly Machiavelli, but Baines was capable of some pretty evil strategies when the mood took him.

* * *

When the little meeting had broken up, Baines went over to Joan Collins and asked her to find out which officers had attended the scene where Leigh Fletcher had drowned and who had been talking to friends and family. The young black woman came back to him within ten minutes, with Tom Hall, a uniformed sergeant, in tow.

Hall was one of what Baines tended to think of as the old and bold of the uniformed division. A tad overweight, salt and pepper hair, but ramrod-straight and very by the book. In an earlier age, he would have stamped out the juvenile delinquency that plagued some of the local estates before it even got started, with a few well-aimed clips around the ear.

"I gather we're putting some effort into investigating our drowning, Dan?" he said gruffly.

"I wouldn't put it like that," Baines said. "Just dotting the Is and crossing the Ts, really. Finding out what happened for the family and making sure it's all unsuspicious."

"Fair enough," Hall said. "I didn't get any sense of anything other than misadventure myself..." He stood expectantly, clearly waiting for Baines to fill him in on any new evidence. Baines was tempted to say he agreed, but something told him to wait for Barbara Carlisle's report before saying anything.

"So who have you spoken to, Tom?" he asked, motioning for Hall to take an empty chair near his desk. "Thanks, Joan," he said, dismissing the DC.

"No problem."

As she departed, Hall fidgeted himself into a comfortable position.

"Well," he said, referring to his notebook. "I spoke to the family. Parents are Gareth and Gail Fletcher. They have an older daughter, Hayley. All absolutely destroyed by what's happened. Heartbreaking to see. I've got kids myself..." He took a handkerchief from his pocket and blew his nose. "Anyway, they all told more or less the same tale. Leigh used to spend Friday evenings at her best friend's house. Gemma Lucas. Always home by 10.30."

"But not last Friday."

"No. Even though it was unusual for her to be later than that, they left it until half eleven before first trying her phone - no reply - and then phoning Gemma's. They were told she'd left just after ten. It's no more than ten minutes walk - they live at opposite ends of the village - and the parents had never worried about her walking home alone at that time. I mean, you live in Little Aston, Dan. It's as safe as anywhere is these days."

Baines knew what he meant. Nowhere was 100% safe, but a wise parent tried not to wrap a child in too much cotton wool. His own dad still maintained that the best way to learn how to manage risk was to take a few. A view Baines supported. Life was not risk-free, and pretending you could make it so meant that when your son or daughter finally did come up against a serious problem, they would not have a clue how to deal with it.

"So what did they do when they realised she still hadn't come home an hour and a half after setting off?"

"They gave it until after midnight and then rang Stoke Mandeville Hospital in case she had been brought in. They thought maybe she'd had some sort of accident. When that yielded nothing, they called the police. The duty officer tried to reassure them that in most cases like this the child turns up safe and well. DI Moseley took charge and we tried to check out obvious places in and around the village, like the green, but it was dark, so there were limits to what we could do. We searched her own home, obviously. We considered knocking up the entire village, but the risk assessment didn't really justify it at that time of night."

"You can't win," Baines said. "We could have poured resources into a full-scale search in the dark, only to find that she'd returned home and the parents hadn't thought to let us know."

The sergeant shook his head. "They would have informed us. They're not the type to let something like that slide. But, even with the best of kids, there's a first time for everything. It was still most likely she'd met someone on the way home and been persuaded to go off with them. Peer pressure. She wouldn't have been the first kid to lose track of time and then be scared to go home and face a bollocking."

Baines sympathised. A journalist wanting a cheap headline could make quite a good police negligence story out of this, but the reality was that the police were on a hiding to nothing in cases like this. Plus, from Archer's account of the post mortem, Leigh had almost certainly been dead even before the police were contacted. Baines thought Lara Moseley had probably played it the same way he would have.

"So," Hall went on, "when there was still no sign by half seven the next morning, we started a house to house. I knocked at your door, Dan, as a matter of fact, but you weren't there."

"No, I was busy on Saturday morning." Helping Archer to move. "Early start."

"Well, we hadn't got very far when we got the call from the swimming hole to say a body had been found. Funny thing is, no one had suggested we look there."

"Not even the parents?"

"Apparently she never went there. That was what they couldn't understand. It wasn't like she was a regular swimmer there. She never did, and then suddenly she's apparently taken it into her head to go there alone, and it's ended in tragedy."

"Any possibility that she and her friend were experimenting with drugs? The kind that might have made a late-night swim seem attractive? Maybe impaired her swimming ability?"

Hall frowned. "I suppose anything's possible, but it doesn't sound like the girls I heard described."

Baines supposed another possibility was that Leigh hadn't gone to the quarry of her own accord, but they were a long way from developing those sorts of theories.

"What more did you find out about Leigh?" he asked.

"The archetypal nice girl, as far as the family were concerned. Even her sister adored her, and you know what siblings can be like. Got religion about a year ago, started going to chapel. Has helped out with village events for years. Outward going."

"Boyfriends?"

"Never, according to them. Oh, a few boys who were sort of friends, but nothing you could describe as a date." He paused. "I saw her room. Typical teenager. Place was a tip. Clothes hung up on the floor."

"Formal statements?"

"Not yet. They were in no state."

Baines nodded, concurring. Badgering a distraught family for signed statements before they'd even got used to the idea that their child wasn't coming home ever again was a bad idea, yet any piece of information fresh in their minds could prove invaluable later.

"What did you make of the family, Tom?"

"What can I say? Ordinary, fairly comfortable. Decent-sized detached house, but not ostentatious. BMW in the drive, but not an especially new one. Father works for a high street bank, mother's a part time doctor's receptionist in the village. You've probably seen her when you've been pulling a sickie."

"Right," said Baines, who hadn't taken a day's sick since falling off a garage roof chasing a suspect at least five years ago. "And how old's..." He checked his notes. "Hayley?"

"Eighteen. Got a place at Leicester University, subject to A Level results."

Baines reflected for a moment on what he'd heard. "And who formally identified the body?"

"Both parents. I was there. They were both so fucking..." He groped for the right word. "...stoic. Somehow that was worse than when they fall apart and start screaming."

"Can they account for their movements on Friday night?"

"The parents alibi each other - a night in front of the telly, apart from when dad took the dog for a walk around 10.30. Hayley was out with her boyfriend - I've got his details - and they got home around 11.30 to find her parents fretting."

"The father went out, you say?" Baines frowned. "Long enough to run into his daughter, have a row with her about coming home late?"

Hall shook his head. "What, and things get out of hand? He loses his rag, kills her, and then somehow gets her body to the quarry without the aid of a car?"

Baines nodded. "Just a thought. A pretty far-fetched one, obviously. Besides, the post mortem indicated death by drowning, so unless he walked the dog by the quarry..."

"He was only gone about ten minutes, Dan. No way there was time."

"Fair enough. And you say the sisters got on?"

"So they say. Hayley's grief seemed genuine enough."

"We'll talk to the boyfriend. Presumably someone spoke to the friend?" He checked his notes again. "Gemma Lucas?"

"Yes. Interesting. She seemed in pieces over what had happened, but... I don't know."

Baines looked at him sharply. "What don't you know, Tom?"

Hall pursed his lips. "I just got a feeling about the sort of girl Leigh was, and her best mate seemed a bit chalk and cheese to me. I could imagine Gemma being a bit flippant. Apparently they bonded on day one at senior school."

"Opposites attracting?"

"Maybe that's it. Anyhow, she said Leigh was round there, in her room, chatting and playing music, until about 10.15 and then left for home. She couldn't believe it when Leigh's mother rang to see if she was still there, Says she knew something was badly wrong there and then, but that might have been a bit more dramatisation. To be honest, if she'd been making anything up, it would have been hard to tell, but I can't see she's involved in this. As far as her parents are concerned, Leigh went home and Gemma stayed in her room doing stuff on her computer."

"What about some of the stuff you got from the family? About Leigh never going to the swimming hole, never having a boyfriend?"

"She confirmed about the swimming hole, but I thought there was something evasive about her answers when she said there were no boyfriends. I pressed her on whether there had ever been anyone, and her eyes were all over the place. She might have been hiding something."

"In that case, I think we'll do her follow-up interview at the station," Baines decided. "Make sure she gets how serious it is. Make sure there were no drugs at their get-together." He pinched the bony ridge between his eyes, tired already. Something at the back of his mind was niggling him, but what? "And are there statements from her and her parents?"

"I'll let you have copies."

"Thanks, Tom. Anything else?"

"No. Except that this was one of those times you think everything's futile, you know? You raise a kid, imagine their future, and then something like this happens." He shut up abruptly, as if suddenly realising who he was talking to. "Jesus. Sorry, Dan."

Baines waved the apology away, briefly and unkindly reflecting that the Fletchers had enjoyed 13 or 14 more years with Leigh than he'd had with Jack. He knew that was ridiculous thinking, and he immediately crushed the thought.

His heart went out to a family who were now feeling something of the agony he had experienced twelve years ago.

"If anything occurs to you," he said. "A gut feeling - anything."

"I'll let you know," Hall said.

"One other thing," Baines said. "The family were burgled not long ago, and Leigh was mugged for her phone shortly before. Did they mention that?"

"No. Probably didn't seem especially important to them in the circumstances."

"I suppose."

Just as Hall was about to depart, Baines realised what had been bothering him.

"Oh, Tom?"

"Yes, Dan."

"You saw the scene at the quarry? Before the CSIs started carting things away?"

"Yes. I was there when they got the poor kid out of the water."

"Did you notice her clothes?"

Hall frowned. "Her clothes? Well, yes, they were there. Apart from her underwear. She still had that on."

"Phil Gordon said they were neatly folded."

The uniformed sergeant looked at the ceiling, evidently trying to picture the scene. "That's right. A neat pile of folded clothes. I didn't tamper with them, obviously. Left all that to the CSIs."

"Yet you said her room was a tip. Clothes all over the place. Hung up on the floor, I think you said?"

Hall nodded, understanding dawning in his eyes. "That's right. I suppose she might have been a bit tidier in a public place."

"When she didn't expect there to be anyone around?"

"I suppose it does seem a bit odd. If there are enough other issues raising suspicions..."

Baines nodded. It was another puzzling inconsistency.

Hall left then, and Baines remained deep in thought. Some of what the sergeant had said about Leigh's best mate, Gemma, had been interesting. If Archer and Ross were going to be re-interviewing people on a more formal basis, it might do no harm to put the girl under a bit of pressure. If she had anything to hide, they needed to get to the bottom of it.

5

While Baines was talking to Hall, DS Ross managed to contact Barbara Carlisle, who had just completed her post mortem report. She said she would e-mail it through, but Archer decided to drop by the mortuary and get a verbal update.

"Quicker in the long run," she explained. "If any questions occur to us, we can just ask."

Archer took Ross with her. Carlisle didn't keep them waiting long, and soon they were studying Leigh Fletcher's corpse again and Bruce Davenport was taking some pictures of the upper part of the dead girl's torso.

"Have you found anything?" Archer asked.

The pathologist bit her lip. "I might have been premature in saying there was nothing untoward about this girl's death. Look at the shoulders. There's some pretty well defined bruising patterns there. Of course, these marks could have formed in a number of ways. What I will say is that it bears further investigation."

Archer and Ross moved closer. The bruises were quite visible. Archer would have sworn they hadn't been there yesterday, and she said as much.

"That's because they weren't," Carlisle explained. "Sometimes bruising that is incurred perimortem doesn't develop immediately, but will show up later. That striped effect suggests that fingers may have been grasping her here." She indicated the dark marks at the tops of the dead girl's arms.

"You're saying that's what happened?" Archer asked carefully. "That she was held under the water?"

Carlisle allowed herself a thin smile. "You know me better than that, Lizzie. I can't possibly say at this juncture what actually happened."

Archer took in what the pathologist had said. Clearly there was nothing conclusive yet, but Carlisle's hypothesis would certainly provide a plausible explanation for a lot of unanswered questions.

But it raised a lot more. Archer knew they were still a long way from establishing murder. But if Leigh Fletcher had been drowned deliberately, then why? Had she simply met the wrong sort of stranger, a few minutes from home? Or had she known her killer?

The stranger scenario was the real nightmare. Because it would mean a killer on the loose, someone who could strike again.

But even if Leigh had been murdered by someone she knew, what had been the catalyst for whatever chain of events that had ended in her death? Did it have anything to do with the evidence that she had probably indulged in underage sex? If so, who had her lover or lovers been?

Or was it something to do with drugs? Maybe a link to her Olympic swimming aspirations.

One thing was certain. If she'd been deliberately drowned, then surely she'd have fought for her life? Then the girl's excessively clean nails would make complete sense - someone would have scraped them to make sure any DNA picked up in a struggle had been removed.

The image of this young woman being held under water invaded Archer's mind and refused to leave. She locked eyes with Carlisle and saw her own horror reflected there.

"Any news on the analysis of that water in the lungs yet? Or the tox reports?"

"You know how long all these tests take, Lizzie. If your boss can find the budget, you can always pay for the express service."

Archer's laugh was hollow. "Funny lady. It would have to be the Prime Minister lying on that slab for our purse strings to be loosened like that at the moment."

"I'll lean on them all I can, but I dare say everyone wants their results yesterday."

She shook off the frustration. "You thought you could have a stab at how recent her last sexual activity was. Did you get anywhere?"

Carlisle made a face. "That wasn't quite what I said. I thought I might be able to tell if it was recent. It's all a bit imprecise, but I would say there's no evidence of rape, nor of any consensual recent sexual activity..."

"All the same," Ross began, then hesitated, glancing at Archer.

"Go ahead, Jenny," Archer told her. "You don't have to ask permission to speak, you know."

"Sorry, ma'am."

Archer made a mental note to ask her to stop ma'aming her.

"Can you tell whether she had intercourse more than once, doctor?" Ross asked.

"I wouldn't like to speculate on that," Carlisle said.

"A good question, though, Jenny," Archer acknowledged. "But no point in second guessing. Let's get back to base and see what Dan's turned up. Anything else before we go, Barbara?"

"No. I'll try and get those reports you need bumped up the queue, but don't hold your breath."

They thanked Carlisle and left the building. They were in a pool Ford Focus and Ross was driving.

"I hope Dan's got something for us to work with," Archer said as they headed back into Aylesbury. "I think we need to start re-interviewing Leigh's family and friends, and we need to do that knowing as much about Leigh as we possibly can."

"We don't seem to have too much at the moment," commented Ross, pointing the car towards the B4443.

"We don't," Archer agreed. "All my instincts were telling me there was some sort of story behind this drowning, even before I saw that bruising. Now that seems to confirm it. But as to what the story is? Right now it's all a bit like doing a jigsaw puzzle in the dark, wearing boxing gloves."

* * *

Back at the office, Archer hustled Baines and Ross into the briefing room earmarked for the investigation into Leigh Fletcher's death. The board that would fill up with photographs, notes, and copies of various documents, held but one item at the moment: the picture of Leigh handed to the police by her family when the search for her had got underway on Friday night.

In the photograph, she was smiling self-consciously for the camera, for all the world a bright, happy teenager with a whole future in front of her. A future that would never be.

Baines listened while Archer brought him up to date with the post mortem findings and then told her what Sergeant Hall had revealed about the dead girl's family and the events of Friday night.

"Well," she said finally, "the DCI isn't going to like it, but I think there's more than enough here for us to mark this down as at least a suspicious death."

"Not the quick apportionment of blame for a tragic accident to anyone but us he was hoping for," Baines agreed.

"And no prospect of it going away any time soon. This is obviously something Andrew Marling feels strongly about, and he's very good at campaigning. Gillingham's going to feel the heat."

"When will you tell him?"

Archer rubbed her eyes. Baines thought she looked tired.

"No time like the present. Then you're with me, Jenny. I want to pay the family a visit. Start to really get to know Leigh."

Baines felt another pang of disappointment. He was itching to get at the dead girl's family himself. But it was either accept Archer's strategy with the best grace he could muster or fall out with her. On balance, he decided to let it ride for now.

"What shall I do?" he asked.

"Yes, I was thinking on the way back from the mortuary. Can you and Joan get hold of the files on the burglary at the Fletchers and Leigh's mugging, Dan? Like you said before, that family's suffered way more than its fair share of misfortune lately."

"What am I looking for?"

"Anything that suggests a connection to Leigh's death, or anything that implies a malicious motive, rather than old-fashioned greed."

"I'll get on it. Anything else?"

Her gaze swept the almost-empty glass wall. "Actually, yes. Get Leigh's phone from evidence and see if there's anything interesting, and get Jason Bell to badger the CSIs for some photos from the scene of death. Once he's done that, he needs to get another door-to-door going in the village. See if anyone saw anything unusual on Friday night. Let's really get started on this puzzle."

* * *

Archer's surmise that Gillingham wouldn't like being told that Leigh Fletcher's death deserved serious investigation proved an understatement. His expression couldn't have been more sour if he'd bitten into an apple and found a lemon inside.

"Really?" he spluttered, eyebrows jiggling. "I mean, what we actually have here is a few bruises that she might have picked up elsewhere. Take those away, and we've got a girl dead in the quarry, probably misadventure."

"The bruising strongly suggests someone held her shoulders pretty firmly, boss, and Dr Carlisle believes it occurred perimortem. And the nails were scraped clean."

The DCI looked very sceptical. "You said yourself that there was the possibility that the girl herself was just fastidious about her grooming. And even if the bruising did occur during her drowning, isn't it possible there was some sort of horseplay that went wrong?"

"I suppose," Archer persisted, "but that would still merit a further investigation. Add the burglary at her home and the fact that she was mugged recently..."

"These things happen."

"Yes, but all to the same family? In a part of the world where they probably have to look up 'Crime Capital' on Wikipedia?"

He held up his hands in mock surrender. "All right, all right. I can see we're not going to get a quick closure on this one. We're going to have to treat it as suspicious, aren't we? So what's your next move?"

"I think I ought to take Jenny Ross and talk to the family. We should speak to Gemma Lucas, too. Apart from the killer, she appears to be the last person who saw Leigh alive."

Gillingham took a swig of machine coffee from a grimy-looking mug and grimaced. "Do that," he said, "but tread carefully. I know it's right and proper to look at the nearest and dearest, but if the Fletchers think they're being accused of something and complain to the MP, we'll really get it in the neck."

She gave him a hard look. "You're not suggesting we don't do our job properly because the local MP has connections with the Chief Constable, surely?"

"No. I'm not saying that at all. But there was that time you were interviewing a murder victim's husband and he had a heart attack."

"That was just bad luck," she protested, bristling.

"Yes, but it led to bad press. Softly, softly, Lizzie. So what other lines are you following?"

"I'm waiting on tox reports, in case Leigh had been under the influence of drink or drugs when she died. And Dan's going to go back over the burglary and mugging to see if there's anything there we need to follow up. I'm hoping we'll get more leads from these interviews."

"All right. Let's get those tox results before we go public with our suspicions." He looked gloomy. "I suppose I'd better brief the Super. Spread a little of the joy around..."

Before she and Ross set off for the Fletchers' Archer sought out Baines.

"Before I make a complete idiot of myself, is there any sort of village protocol I need to observe in Little Aston?"

"What?" he guffawed. "Like a funny handshake? A particular way of rolling up your trouser leg?"

She rolled her eyes. “That’s the Freemasons, and you know it. It’s just that I know some of these villages can have a bit of a pecking order...”

Baines looked about to add further merriment, and then simply shrugged, as if thinking better of it. “I don’t really know much more than you do, to be honest, but I do read the parish magazine, go in the store, and have even been known to have the odd pint in the pub. From what little I know, The Fletchers get involved in things, I think, but they’re probably not what you’d call community leaders. Not that I’ve witnessed much cap doffing, even to parish councillors or the vicar. I wouldn’t worry about it.”

“Okay. Anything else it would be useful to know?”

He made a great show of pondering, then said, “Just one thing.”

“Which is?”

“Left.”

“Left? What’s that supposed to mean?”

“That’s which trouser leg you roll up.”

“Piss off,” she said as she departed, but she was smiling when she said it.

6

The Fletchers' home had exactly the sense of understated comfort that Sergeant Hall had described to Baines. Gareth Fletcher opened the door to Archer and Ross and invited them in.

"We're in the sitting room," he said.

He was average height and build, but with fair, almost white hair and features that, a week ago, would probably have been described as 'boyish'. Now they were haggard and pale, his eye sockets dark pits from which cornflower-blue eyes peered dully. His clothes were rumpled and stained in places, and Archer half-suspected he'd either been sleeping in them or not had the presence of mind to change them daily.

The two detectives followed him from a good-sized hall into a spacious room with two expensive-looking sofas, one wall lined with books, and a marble-effect fireplace. The carpet was cream, and spotless.

A slightly stout, dark-haired woman in her early forties sat on one of the sofas beside a slim, attractive teenage girl, her father's white-blonde hair framing a face that combined Gareth's chiselled features with her mother's nose and mouth, although the mouth had a slightly sullen downturn.

Fletcher introduced his wife, Gail, and his older daughter, Hayley. Both nodded and attempted smiles.

A solidly built, casually attired man of indeterminate age, with a shaven head, sat in an armchair. He was introduced as Leigh's swimming coach, Graham Endean, and he looked as devastated as the family.

But Archer was more interested in the youthful, besuited figure standing by the fireplace with a more casually attired man in his early forties.

"And you probably know our local MP?"

The younger man stepped forward, hand outstretched. "I don't think I've had the pleasure, Gareth. Andrew Marling, Inspector." Archer grasped the hand. It was cool and dry, the grip firm but not bone-crunching. A perfect politician's handshake, she supposed, but there was genuine warmth in his smile.

"Andrew's been very supportive," Fletcher said.

"I wish I could do more," the MP assured Archer, looking grave.

No, not just grave. Seriously upset.

She was normally unconvinced when politicians looked emotional, but he somehow looked like the real deal. She liked that he didn't seem to be taking in her scar, either. About six foot tall, with a good haircut that looked determined not to be tamed, he looked even younger in the flesh than he did in the media. She had briefly looked him up online. He was 29, but he could easily have passed for early twenties.

She'd also read that, at the inaugural The Vale Live! festival he'd been dragged up on stage to play guitar with local chart band The Black Ducks on their number one hit 'Only You and Me'. By all accounts, he'd played a solo that had blown the crowd away. Despite the sober suit he wore today, she found that she could picture it.

"This should never have happened," Marling continued, "not to Leigh. Not to anyone. We need to know exactly what happened, so no one has to go through this again. Gareth and Gail deserve that, at least."

"And I can promise I won't rest until I can give them some answers," Archer assured him.

"Good. This family has always given me great support, you know. As a councillor and then at the general election."

His older companion nodded. "Canvassing, delivering leaflets, stuffing envelopes... we owe them a lot." He was solidly built, square jawed and starting to lose his hair at the crown. His mouth had a serious set to it.

"This is my agent, by the way," Marling said. "Chris Russell. Now, Inspector, have you any news at all on what happened to Leigh?"

"No offence, Mr Marling," Archer said, "but I'd like to talk to Mr and Mrs Fletcher alone."

"That's kind, inspector," Gail Fletcher said, in a voice that sounded like a dead woman's, "but not necessary. Anything you have to tell us, Andrew can hear."

Archer thought about objecting, but remembered her promise to Gillingham to walk on eggs, and her boss's obvious eagerness to keep Marling sweet.

"Okay," she said. "Well, first of all, I'd like to say how sorry I am about what happened to Leigh. I can't imagine what you're all going through."

"Thank you," nodded Gareth. "Thank you."

"We're trying to get to the bottom of exactly what happened to her."

"Not much mystery about that," Russell said. "Andrew's been very vocal on how dangerous that quarry is. It was only a matter of time before something went horribly wrong there."

"I'm afraid that's true," the MP confirmed. "I've had meetings with the police and with the quarry owners about finding ways of keeping people out. Leigh's accident is exactly what I was afraid of, yet everyone was pointing the finger at somebody else instead of doing something."

Gail suddenly jumped up with horribly forced gaiety. "Tea!" she warbled. "We should have some tea!"

"Oh," Marling said, "I really should leave you to it. I'm sure the Inspector has a lot to ask you all."

"Yes, come on Andrew," his agent said. "Lots to do."

"Oh, do stay," Gail pressed.

"Mum," Hayley said firmly, "Andrew's very busy. We can't expect him to stay here with us all day. Besides, he shouldn't listen to us being interviewed. Should he, inspector?"

"It's not a good idea," Archer agreed, looking at Marling. "No offence, sir."

"None taken."

The swimming coach, Graham Endean, roused himself and said he should be going too. The three men took their leave of the family then, the MP insisting that they contact him, day or night, if they needed anything, anything at all. Archer thought she knew a phoney when she heard one, but he sounded genuinely concerned for his constituents. She liked him for it and wondered if he would still be the same in twenty years' time, when two decades of dirty politics had taken their toll.

Gail insisted on making tea for all of them, which left Archer and Ross alone with Gareth and Hayley. Gareth looked like a man coming apart, but trying to hold it together on the outside for the sake of his wife and remaining daughter. Archer thought Gail was even closer to the edge.

It was Hayley who seemed the strongest at the moment. Archer sensed something simmering inside her. Probably impotent rage, which wasn't necessarily a bad emotion in the circumstances. The danger would come if she tried to internalise it and let it eat her alive from the inside.

Ross was examining family pictures on the mantelpiece. She pointed to one, looking at Gareth. "Leigh?"

The picture showed a pretty, red-haired girl, perhaps twelve years old, wearing a pink jacket and a woolly hat and poking her tongue out at the camera.

The dead girl's father nodded. "She was such a cheeky monkey at that age. Then we had the sullen phase, but she came out of that after she started going to chapel last year. We've never been a religious family, but I must admit it's worked wonders for her. She's like a different girl, isn't she, Hayley?"

"Yeah, Dad. She was."

Her father seemed to flinch at her subtle correction of the tense in which Leigh was spoken of.

"In what way was she sullen?" Archer wondered. "Just normal teenage angst, or a bit worse than that?"

"She was pretty moody and gloomy," Gareth admitted. "I suppose it was par for the course."

"No it wasn't, Dad," Hayley protested. "I wasn't like that. I mean, I had my moments, but she was like a bloody gloom cloud for about a year."

"Now's not the time to speak ill of your sister," he said, tearing up.

"No. It's not. But we can't rewrite history just because she's dead, either. You and Mum made enough of a saint of her when she was alive."

Gareth's face crumpled and he put his face in his hands. After a moment, Hayley went and sat next to him, put her arms around him and started saying she was sorry, over and over. Gail came in with a tray, laden with mugs, a plate of biscuits and, extraordinarily to Archer's mind, another plate full of slices of buttered toast. She set it down on the coffee table, glancing at her husband and daughter, her own eyes starting to moisten.

Archer gave them time to compose themselves, then apologised for running over ground that had already been covered. She needed to check that what she had been told about Leigh tallied reasonably. It seemed it did. No, she had never been to the quarry to swim before. Yes, it was completely inexplicable as to why she would have done so, alone, on Friday night, instead of going straight home. No, she had never had a boyfriend as far as the family knew.

Archer studied each of the family's faces as they responded to this last question. She thought she detected a slight alteration to the set of Hayley's mouth for an instant, like something had momentarily crawled across it, then it had gone. She decided not to press for the time being, but said she would like both Hayley and her boyfriend, Kyle, to come to the station the next day for a chat.

"What's going on?" Gareth's expression mixed anxiety with anger. "Why those two?"

"Just a formality," Archer assured him. "They were still out when Leigh should have been home, and we just need to account for their movements properly. One of you is welcome to come with Hayley and sit in, if you'd like."

"I'll come," Gareth said, still looking annoyed. "Although, why Hayley needs to account..." His eyes widened. "You think it wasn't an accident?"

"Honestly, Mr Fletcher," she soothed. "At this stage it's just an unexplained death, and we owe it to you and to Leigh to understand what happened. It's just routine, okay?"

"It's fine, Dad," Hayley said. "Whatever helps."

"I'll be coming with you."

The girl shrugged. "Whatever."

"There's one thing puzzling us," Ross put in. "Leigh had her phone in her pocket, but there was no bag at the scene. Was that normal?"

The parents exchanged glances.

"Yes, it was," Gareth said. "Since she was mugged, she hasn't liked to take out anything she doesn't need. Her phone stays in her pocket unless she's using it, and she won't take a bag or purse unless she needs them. She wouldn't take money to Gemma's, because she wouldn't need it."

Archer nodded. "Understood. There's one other thing. Could we just have another look at Leigh's room?"

"Her room?" Gareth frowned. "Fine by me, but your guys have already spent ages poking around in there. Took some things away."

"It would just help us to know her a little better."

"I'll take them up," Hayley said.

The room was pretty much what she would have expected. Lots of pink, a bit untidy, some cuddly toys, looking forlorn without their owner, boy band posters on the walls. The only thing she would not expect to see in a typical teenager's bedroom was a bible on the bedside chest.

"I think Mum made the bed," Hayley said. "And tidied up her clothes. Otherwise, it's just as she left it." She looked around, her eyes filling. "I'll leave you to it." She sounded on the verge of tears. Moments later they heard her clumping down the stairs.

* * *

As Archer had feared, there was nothing to see in Leigh's room that offered any new clues, and they left soon after. At 4 pm, Archer assembled her team for a quick update. There was a lot to do, and an atmosphere of anticipation in the room as a new enquiry started to get underway.

Photographs from the scene of Leigh's death had joined the more cheerful snapshot on the board. Archer had taken in the folded clothes, the dead girl in situ, with some leaves and other debris from the quarry still clinging to her face. It added little to what was already known, but the poignancy of the images added to her determination to get at the truth.

As agreed, she and Ross had avoided suggesting to the family that Leigh's death was suspicious. Gillingham's view - which Archer shared - was that if the toxicology lab found anything, it could point the investigations in a particular direction. Meanwhile, it would do no harm for whoever had been involved in the girl's death to think they might have got away with it; people who relaxed were more likely to make mistakes.

Archer outlined her meeting with the family.

"What do you make of Leigh's so-called moody phase?" Baines wondered.

"Could be relevant. But then, I was a right cow at around 14, which sounds like the age they're talking about."

"I found Hayley interesting," Ross offered. "I sensed that her nose was shoved out of joint by her parents making a bit of a plaster saint of Leigh. I wonder if she felt she didn't get her fair share of the love."

Archer nodded. "I got that too. She's supposed to have been really cut up when the family were told Leigh was dead, but I don't know. How much sisterly love was there really?"

"Tom Hall assured me they got on okay," Baines said, frowning.

"Maybe they did. Or maybe she was good at hiding it. Matey on the outside, but a different story on the inside."

Ross looked at her. "Different enough for Hayley to have killed Leigh?"

Archer waggled her fingers. "I don't know about that. She was home by 11.30, and the earliest Dr Carlisle reckons Leigh would have died is midnight."

"She wouldn't need to be far out in her estimation for it to work, though," Baines pointed out.

"True," Ross concurred. "Although I wonder if Hayley's physically strong enough to force a sixteen-year-old into the water and hold her under until she drowns."

"Maybe," Archer mused, "if she was angry enough. But first she'd have to get her there. It works better if she and her boyfriend intercepted her on her way home. Two of them could have handled her. Plus, we don't have that tox screen yet. She could even have been drugged. Hayley and her boyfriend are coming in for a chat tomorrow, and we'll see what buttons we can press.

"I want to talk to a few people at this chapel of hers, too," she added. "It was a big thing in Leigh's life leading up to her death. But what sort of a place is it?"

Baines raised his eyebrows. "You're not still thinking it's maybe some sort of cult? To the best of my knowledge, it's just Christian non-conformist."

"I still want to know. Who knows, maybe that's where she met whoever took her virginity. The pastor may have seen a side of her that her family never saw. It's all part of building up a picture." She thought for a moment. "That Endean character will have seen yet another side of her."

"Do you think he might have known her a bit too well?" Ross speculated.

"You think maybe he was the one sleeping with her?"

"It would be a motive for murder if she decided to tell."

"Or maybe he was giving her performance-enhancing drugs and she got an attack of conscience. But this is just speculation. Let's not get ahead of ourselves." Archer looked at Baines. "Dan, why don't you have a chat with him? The family said he was from Princes Risborough, so no local sensitivities there. Joan, can you do some research on him - see if there's been anything untoward in his past?"

"On it, guv."

"And make a nuisance of yourself with Dr Carlisle. Blame me for the hassle, but I really do want those test results."

Collins nodded and then Archer turned to DC Jason Bell. As usual, the red-haired young Scot blushed at becoming the centre of attention.

"Jason, I've got just the job for you. Take a couple of uniforms to the school tomorrow and talk to Leigh's classmates and anyone else there she spent any time with. See if she had any enemies, or whether anyone's picked up on anything that might have got her killed. You might also chat around the teachers."

"What am I looking for there?"

"You never know. Maybe there was one particular teacher she was a bit too close to. We're miles from establishing motive at the moment, but we may as well clutch at as many straws as we can." She frowned. "By the way, how did that door-to-door go?"

"I'm going through the notes, guv. Nothing jumps out at me yet, but I'll keep at it."

"One thing I don't get," Collins said. "If it really was murder, then why drowning? There are easier ways to kill someone, surely?"

"There are," Archer agreed, "but until we know what happened, we can't begin to answer that."

"One thing's for sure," Baines said. "Either she made an uncharacteristic decision to go to the quarry and met the wrong person. Or she had planned to meet someone and it all went wrong..."

"Or she was abducted and taken there against her will," Archer finished for him. Some scary scenarios there. She looked around the room. "So let's start getting organised. By the end of tomorrow I want to know everything there is to know about Leigh Fletcher and I want to know about anyone with an obvious motive for killing her."

It promised to be a long week.

* * *

A thumb pressed the power button with almost savage force, extinguishing the TV and cutting off the local newsreader in mid-sentence.

So it wasn't over, after all. It should have ended at that quarry, with the water closing over Leigh's corpse like the zip on a body bag, but now it had got a lot more complicated.

There was an Agatha Christie novel, *Murder is Easy*. Well, as it had turned out, it was, at least as far as the act itself was concerned. Afterwards there had been no attacks of conscience. But easy was not the same as simple. Instead of being nicely tied up, it was as if a seam had been picked at and now threatened to unravel.

It couldn't be allowed. Whatever needed doing would have to be done.

If that meant another death, so be it.

7

Archer had arrived home exhausted after finally calling it a day and, having taken a cursory glance at the boxes still to be unpacked, helped herself to a beer from the fridge and turned the oven on. She checked out the frozen meals in the freezer, decided a pizza was easiest and quickest, and shoved a pepperoni on the middle shelf. Food more or less taken care of, she cracked her can and took the beer into the living room.

Just as she was about to put the TV on, she heard her mobile ringing. There were a few moments of mild panic until she remembered it was in her handbag.

"How's life in the Vale?" said a familiar Norfolk accent when she answered.

"Manic," she said, grinning. "Any better in the flatlands?"

"Yes, as a matter of fact," replied DI Ian Baker. "I've just apprehended my killer. Well, when I say 'just', it was a few hours ago, but he's confessed, so it's looking like case solved."

"That's great." She took a long swig of beer, feeling the mixture of pleasure and jealousy she often felt when someone else cracked a case. Because this was Ian, pleasure won out.

"So..." he said, "I was wondering if you can get away soon? Have a bit of a celebration?"

"Sounds good, but Christ knows when. I'm up to my neck in a teenage girl's murder."

"Nasty. What happened?"

Archer outlined the case and everything that had happened so far. He listened without interruption, one of the things she really liked about him.

"Sounds a toughie," he said when she was done. "Have you had a hard look at the father? It often is, you know."

"Sure, but I've no reason to suspect him. I'd really like to know who's been sleeping with her, though. For all we know, she could have been having sex as young as thirteen. There could be at least one older man out there who needs to be stopped."

"Or maybe it will just turn out to be the old story. A boy her own age popped her cherry in a fumbling experiment when they were both just kids."

"Could be," she admitted. "Her death could be to do with something else entirely. Or to do with nothing. Joan Collins suggested it was maybe just a random thing. Wrong place, wrong time."

"Wouldn't be the first time. I do hope you haven't got a predator on the loose."

"Too soon to say, obviously."

"It must be a worry." She could hear the empathy in his voice. "The longer you go without a breakthrough, the colder the trail goes."

With that, he changed the subject, back on the subject of meeting up.

"What about Wednesday night when you finish work?" he pressed. "You might be in need of a distraction by then. I can book a room somewhere halfway again. You can be there in an hour or so. A bit of dinner, a nice night..."

"I'll be knackered at the end of the day, Ian," she told him. "I may be lucky to finish before nine. Then an hour's drive. You'd make sure I didn't get much sleep, and I'd have to make an early start to get back here for work the next day. I'd probably fall asleep at the wheel." Yet she felt some disappointment about not being able to see him. "What about the weekend? With any luck I can find a bit of time. Maybe I could come to Norfolk. Or better still, you could come here. Help me straighten the house out."

"Sorry, I can't," he said quickly. "I've, um, promised to meet some mates. Stag thing, all day Saturday, and I'll be wrecked on Sunday. I wasn't sure I could make it, what with this case, but now it's over..."

"I see," she chided. "You'd rather be pissing it up with a bunch of hairy-arsed blokes than giving me a good seeing to."

"It's not like that..."

"Oh, well. I dare say we'll get it together some time in the next hundred years. We might both be using walking frames by then, of course."

"Wednesday. Promise you'll think about it."

She felt her resolve weaken. "All right. No promises, though." But she knew she would go if she could.

They chatted for a few more minutes. Archer felt deflated as she hung up. Sometimes, life seemed to like its little joke too much. The one guy who never seemed to notice her disfigurement was a hundred miles away. Not an insurmountable distance for most people, she supposed, but quite an obstacle when both of them worked such insane hours.

It had been a year since they had fallen into bed, totally unplanned, after celebrating the solving of a case that had touched both their jurisdictions. Since then, on the rare occasions when they had got together, they really hadn't wasted time talking. With the consequence that, although he had become a big part of her life, she felt they still did not really know each other.

She didn't know his favourite meal, his taste in literature or music, nothing about his interests outside work. She knew nothing about his family, other than his parents were alive and sometimes he had to put her off to visit them. Nothing about his childhood, or even why he had joined the police.

She supposed she was similarly blurred and indistinct to him.

She downed her beer and went to get another. Whether or not it was Wednesday night, the next time she saw Ian, she would insist that when they were alone in their room they talked first, and fucked later. They should either get to know each other, like proper lovers would, or knock the whole thing on the head.

An easy enough promise to make herself now.

Harder to keep, she suspected.

* * *

The light was beginning to fade as Doug Price opened the gates that led to the Westyate allotments and headed for his plot.

Like Little Aston, Westyate sat within Andrew Marling's constituency and had also formed part of his ward in his Council days. It boasted two pubs that were still open, defying the current trend for village hostelries to go out of business, and it even had its own small railway station, with trains to and from London stopping there at least once an hour.

The village green was perhaps not as big as some in the Vale, but it was nicely central, with the church, hall, store and local junior school all adjacent. The allotments were a little outside the main drag, but still within reasonable walking distances of most homes. Price's house was no exception.

He had been up to water everything earlier on, knowing that the porous layer of chalk beneath the soil and the relentless sun would render everything bone dry within hours. What he had forgotten to do was pick peas, and he knew it was important to do so to keep the plants producing.

He liked being here at this time of day, when it was cooler and there was no one else about. The only thing you had to fear were the biting insects that started emerging at dusk, and a layer of repellent spray was essential if unsightly and itchy red blotches were to be avoided. The little buggers always found something to snack on, no matter how well you tried to cover up.

The nuisance they caused was a small price to pay for a bit of peace and quiet. That and the opportunity to have a look around and make sure everything was in order. As a parish councillor, one of his roles was that of designated allotments officer. He knew he was known as 'The Law' behind his back up here, and the nickname did not displease him. He had read the riot act on occasions when the bonfire pile had grown to formidable proportions without anyone actually striking a match.

He liked to think he treated everyone without fear or favour. To him, the allotments were one of life's great levellers. No one on the plots much cared about anyone's job, or how big their house was. What car they drove. All allotmenteers were equal, so long as they worked their plots, kept them reasonably tidy, and observed the unofficial etiquettes, like not chucking your rubbish on the communal bonfire site for someone else to burn.

His allotment was a little further from the gates than he would have liked, but it had been the first to come available after he had expressed an interest in one. He had to labour up a slight incline to get there, walking on the grassy path between the plots. He was passing Len Clough's tidy patch when a sudden movement startled him. As he spun around, he was confronted by Clough himself, brandishing his spade.

"Bloody hell, Len," he protested, "what are you doing? You frightened the life out of me."

"Then you shouldn't come up here creeping about after dark," Clough declared.

He rolled his eyes. "What are you on about? It's not dark yet. And I was hardly creeping. Not that it's any of your concern, but I've come to pick some peas. Is that all right by you?" he added with more than a pinch of sarcasm. He started to move on, then turned back to him. "Please tell me you're not doing your vigilante bit again?"

"I don't know what you mean."

There was something guilty in his tone. "You are, aren't you? Sheila Armitage said she thought you were, and I didn't believe her. But it's true, isn't it? You're lying in wait for the thieves to come back."

The last break-in had been less than three weeks ago, the third time in the past year, the modus operandi identical to all the previous occasions. Shed padlocks sheared through with bolt cutters.

The moods of the allotmenteers ranged from philosophical acceptance to seething anger. Len Clough, one of the eldest, was perhaps the angriest. Opinion varied as to who might be responsible. At first, travellers had been blamed, but none had been seen since. Clough was convinced that it was an inside job, on the basis that Outsiders probably didn't even know the allotments were here. A dense bank of trees grew between the plots and the road, so the casual passer-by would probably not spot the motley collection of wire fences, the other, equally motley arrangements to protect crops from hungry wildlife, and the sheds holding a potential treasure trove for thieves.

But Clough also suspected that the thieves bided their time between raids, waiting for people to get careless and start leaving items of value in their sheds again, and then returning for fresh plunder. According to Price's cousin in Wendover, the allotment sheds there had been targeted only last Friday.

"Well?" Price demanded. "Is that what you're up to? Some sort of one-man security patrol?"

"What if I am?" Clough drew himself up to his full height, cutting an impressive figure for his age. "Someone's got to do something about it. The police are a waste of bloody time. They'll send one of those pretend policewomen round."

Two female PCSOs - Police Community Support Officers - kept an eye on Westyate and other local villages, but they had limited powers. Clough had looked them up online, and he claimed that the most draconian thing they could do was issue a fixed penalty notice for cycling on a footpath.

After each break-in, the PCSOs had been the first uniforms on the scene. In all fairness, 'real' police officers had followed, and there had even been the odd bit of dusting for fingerprints. But no one had been apprehended and no stolen property had ever been recovered.

"There was that Inspector Ashby," Price pointed out.

"Oh, yes," Clough sneers. "Him. I remember him flirting with Sheila, even though he's probably ten years younger than her, but he didn't really give a stuff, did he?"

Price had to admit he had never actually seen the Detective Inspector take a notebook out. The reality, he suspected, was that no one thought the odd power tool or post driver that people were daft enough to leave in their shed was worthy of police time.

"I've told you," Clough growled. "It's up to us. I proposed a rota to keep guard up here, and no one was interested."

Price shook his head. They'd had this argument before. "No one's got the time for that. Besides, what if they actually turned up? It could be dangerous."

"Dangerous? I'd give the bastards bloody dangerous. I'd like them to come up here, sniffing around, when I'm lying in wait."

"And you'd do what, exactly?"

"Me?" Len Clough fixed him with a steely gaze. "I'd bloody kill 'em, that's what."

Price sighed. "Be sensible, Len. You know how Sheila talks. No wonder they're calling you the Lone Ranger in the shop. You go on like this, you'll make yourself a laughing stock at best, and get into something really bad at worst. Some poor devil will come up here and you'll brain them with that spade of yours."

"Or maybe it'll be those thieving bastards,"

"Yes, and what then?" He put his hands on his hips. "If you're lucky, you'll end up charged with assault, or even murder. If you're really unlucky, you'll be the one lying dead among your cabbages."

"That's my lookout."

"Don't be such an idiot," Price persisted. "Do yourself a favour and take yourself home." Something buzzed past his ear and he swatted at it. A horsefly. "I bet you've been bitten half to death - all your Real Men Don't Use Insect Repellent attitude."

Clough planted the spade head on the path and leaned on the handle. "I thought you had peas to pick?"

His eyes narrowed. "I wouldn't want to have to report this to the Parish Council, Len."

"What? The Head Boy, carrying tales to the teachers? Report what, Doug? That you saw me up here taking the air? Looking at my plot and thinking about watering it? I pay my rent for my patch, the same as everyone."

"I've things to do," Price snapped, giving up and walking away.

"No other bugger's doing anything," he heard Clough mutter under his breath. He sighed and decided to ignore it. If the fool had nothing better to do with his time, that was his affair.

8

Baines shuddered awake. It was still dark. The dream of Jack was still vivid, imprinted on the back of his brain like a brand.

He had been at the cemetery, laying flowers on Louise's grave. His fingers had traced the words on the cold stone:

LOUISE JANE BAINES

BELOVED WIFE AND MOTHER

CALLED TOO SOON

He had become aware of someone standing beside him and had turned his head. Jack. Fifteen year old Jack. Not in his QPR shirt this time, but in a dark suit and white shirt. The suit jacket maybe a size too big for him. No tie, a bit like the politicians these days. He held in his hand a posy of red flowers. Baines had no idea what they were. No flower that he recognised.

For some stupid reason, it seemed important to him that he could identify the flowers.

Jack bent to place his flowers alongside his father's. Straightened up and stood looking at him gravely.

"Jack," Baines whispered. "Please, son. Please. Don't disappear. Talk to me. Tell me where you are. At least tell me whether you're alive."

The boy looked at him, his eyes holding his father's gaze. He licked his lips. Glanced over his shoulder. Looked back at Baines.

"Please," Baines practically begged.

"I..."

One word. One word.

In all the dreams and visions of this almost grown up version of his son, Baines had never heard him utter a word. Now he had. Just the one.

The voice was hoarse. Tremulous. Deeper than Baines had expected. A voice full of fear.

"Come on, Jack," he urged. "You can tell me."

"I... can't," Jack said, looking over his shoulder again. "He'll... I just... can't."

Baines squeezed his eyes shut to try and stop the tears falling.

"He?" he whispered. "Who do you mean, son?"

His eyes flew open. There was no one there. Just the two sets of flowers on the grave. As he stared at them, a strong wind whipped through the graveyard. Baines's bouquet stayed put, but the flowers in Jack's posy were scattered.

Baines moved to pick some of them up, but the wind blew them away again, always just out of his reach.

* * *

Archer had also had a restless night, the case and the situation with Baker keeping her tossing and turning all night. When she could stand it no longer, she had risen, breakfasted, showered and dressed, and headed into work.

On the car radio, 3CR had a new sound bite from Andrew Marling MP. The lead in was that the reshuffle was definitely on the cards for later today, with Marling tipped for an Under Secretary role at the Home Office, but he refused to be drawn on that. Instead, he majored on crime in rural areas and the challenges the police faced. Asked about Leigh Fletcher's death, he said he was liaising with the police and that he was confident that they would "leave no stone unturned to find out how this tragedy happened, so we can ensure it never happens again."

She had to admit that, however much pressure he was applying behind the scenes, he was playing fairer publicly than some politicians she could think of.

As if they needed his urgings to make them do their jobs.

Once in the office, she was soon immersed in catching up on emails and all the other boring admin stuff that she always tried to keep on top of, even when she was buried in a case. She had learned during her time at the Met that not having read a memo could lead to some very nasty surprises.

She hadn't got far when Joan Collins appeared by her desk.

"You're looking pleased with yourself, Joan."

The DC smiled. "Am I? Maybe that's because I've got a bit of a result."

"Which is...?"

"Dr Carlisle called about ten minutes ago. She's got the toxicology results. And the analysis of the water in Leigh Fletcher's lungs."

"You must have made a real nuisance of yourself. Even so, that's quicker than I expected. Did she say how she managed it?"

"She said I didn't want to know. Anyhow, the tox screens came back clear. Nothing untoward in her system."

Archer shrugged, slightly disappointed. "Oh, well. At least we know."

"Yes, guv. Thing is, the water in the lungs is a different matter."

She shot the young woman a glance. "In what way?"

"It seems it didn't match the samples the CSIs took from the quarry at all. In fact, the most likely place it would have come from is a common or garden household tap."

"Seriously?"

"That's what she said."

Archer digested the news. "But that means she didn't drown in the quarry. She died somewhere else."

"Probably in a house. Put it together with those bruises and the scraped fingernails, guv, and..."

"... and you've got a death someone's gone to a lot of trouble to cover up."

She reached out to squeeze Collins's arm. "Great work, Joan."

"Oh, and I've got hold of those files on the Fletcher burglary and Leigh's mugging."

Archer glanced across at Baines's desk. He was a little later than usual.

"When Dan arrives, see how he wants to go through them. We're looking for any sign that the family, rather than the property, were being targeted. Probably nothing, but if there is any suggestion of a link, we need to look a bit harder at those cases than maybe we did before."

She didn't need to tell Collins that, in relative terms at least, one burglary more or less was little more than a statistic unless the police got lucky. A mugging, unless there was real violence involved, came even lower down the pecking order. It all came down to prioritising scarce resources.

"I need to bring the boss up to date," she said.

"That's the other thing, guv. I've just seen the DCI by the water cooler. He says, can he have a word?"

Archer frowned. "Did he say what about?"

"'fraid not."

"Right."

She headed for Gillingham's office, steeling herself for more pressure for results. Temperatures outside were soaring, the air conditioning wasn't coping, and her boss seemed to be at his grumpiest when he was hot and bothered. All she could do was give him the latest developments, such as they were.

Yet, when she put her head round the DCI's door, he was unnervingly genial, asking how she was and encouraging her to take the weight off her feet. She would rather he was grumpy.

Once the pleasantries were exhausted, he told her that Andrew Marling had been leaning on the Chief Constable again about the Leigh Fletcher case. Naturally, all the pressure was coming downwards and, the further up the chain it came from, the heavier it landed on Paul Gillingham.

"It's bound to happen," he said, his tone surprisingly philosophical. "Especially now. You must have heard the news about the government reshuffle?"

She nodded. “He won’t want his start to ministerial life with the unsolved murder of a teenager in his own constituency.”

Gillingham looked at her. “For Christ’s sake, Lizzie, don’t go round calling it murder. At worst it’s suspicious.”

“Sorry, Paul,” she said, “but it’s a bit more than just suspicious now.”

She told him the news from the labs. His face fell.

“Bugger! That’s all I need.” A hopeful look passed over his face. “I don’t suppose there’s a chance that this could still be an accident? Maybe someone panicked and decided to get rid of the body?”

She made a show of considering it. “I suppose it’s possible. Her and her mate, Gemma, larking around in the bathroom. The bath is conveniently full. Gemma accidentally holds her friend under water until she drowns, then she manages, single-handed, to get her up the road and dump her in the quarry, unseen. She’d have to be a very strong girl, though.”

Gillingham held up his hands in surrender. “All right, all right, I give in. I’ll tell the brass we’re now looking at a murder. Shit.”

“Good thing you gave me Jenny Ross,” she told him. “We need every pair of hands we can get now.”

His eyes became suddenly shifty. “Ah, yes,” he said. “About that...”

* * *

Baines had arrived at work feeling emotionally, as well as physically wrecked.

Whatever had been its cause, the dream had been different this time. Jack’s clothes had been different. He had been more sombre.

And he had spoken.

“He’ll...”

Who? The Invisible Man? Did it mean that Jack was alive? Still in the serial killer’s power?

In his maddest moments, he had imagined that Jack's appearances were attempts by the boy to get a message to him. Information that would somehow enable his father to save him.

Perhaps it was true.

Or maybe Jack really was dead, and whoever, or whatever, the boy feared - 'he' - was some shadowy figure from whatever afterlife he now inhabited.

Or perhaps, he reasoned, this time it truly had been nothing more than a bad dream.

Baines had arrived at his desk, noticed Archer was nowhere to be seen, and then spotted the files next to his computer, a note in Joan Collins's neat hand informing him that these were the burglary and mugging files relating to the Fletcher family. The latter was noticeably thinner than the former, and a quick scan told him there wasn't much more to see than a couple of reports.

The burglary file was a bit more substantial, and included photographs of the crime scene. He put the files aside, resolving to go through them with Collins, who had a sharp eye for small details.

His mind drifted to Karen. Their Sunday had been enjoyable but, after she'd gone home, he'd been left feeling somehow incomplete. Maybe it had to do with the latest sighting of Jack. Once, he had half-believed that the boy he kept seeing might be real. He'd since become convinced that he wasn't, at least not in the accepted sense, yet he had no idea whether this teenage Jack was some sort of ghost or something from inside his head. Nor why he kept seeing him.

What if Jack really was alive, he had wondered last night - not for the first time - before sleep took him. What if, against all the odds, he came home? How would that work? What relationship would father and son have? How would Jack react to his father having such closeness with an aunt who so perfectly resembled his mother? Would it freak him out?

Sometimes he felt that he and Karen were like a married couple, in all but the sex. There were times when he desperately wished they hadn't drawn back from the brink last year. That they'd tried to give love a chance. But there were other times when he thanked God they hadn't added to their lives' complications. Especially when, no matter how hard he tried to move on with his life, Baines would probably never entirely give up on the possibility of seeing his son in the flesh one day.

Someone had come to stand beside his desk. He looked up to see DI Steven Ashby standing there.

"Blimey, Steve. Sighted in the office? It'll be on the international news tonight."

"Fuck you, then," Ashby said, and turned on his heel.

"Sorry," Baines said with utter insincerity. "What did you want?"

Ashby returned with obvious bad grace. "I came to do you a favour, but if you're going to piss on me I'll find someone else."

"What's the favour?" Baines asked suspiciously.

"Some real work. A body's just been found in Westyate, and it looks like murder. Paul Gillingham asked me to run with the case, but I'm up to my eyes in work right now, so I can't get to the scene."

Baines stifled a belly laugh at the notion of Ashby up to his eyes in anything more challenging than cigarette butts.

"You want me to go?"

"I've cleared it with Paul. You know how short-handed we are, Dan. We're having to mix and match with our manpower, and The Bride's already pinched Ross."

Baines looked at him blankly. "The Bride?"

Ashby grinned. "Of Frankenstein."

Baines itched to smack the smirk off his face, but he bit off the retort that sprang to his lips.

"I'm already on a murder case."

"So now you're on this one. You'll be making most of the running. I remember when you were ambitious, Dan. Or has that changed since DI Archer's been here?"

Baines hesitated. If Gillingham has already sanctioned it, then Archer couldn't blame him. And he had to admit that Ashby had a point. A murder investigation that he could more or less run could do his career no harm. It was certainly a step up from his low-key role in the Fletcher case.

"So where's this body?" he asked.

* * *

"Ashby?" Archer spluttered incredulously. "You're allocating Baines to a case under DI Ashby?"

Gillingham held up a placating hand. "It's a matter of resources and priorities. You know how busy Steve is..."

"Actually, Paul, I don't," she said, "but I doubt my opinion will count for much."

"Look, I know you two don't hit it off, but we have a body, we're short of officers, and Dan Baines is a capable DS who, in my opinion, is being under-used. It was you who didn't want him in the front line on the Leigh Fletcher case, and I backed you on that. But now you've got Jenny, and I want Dan to get involved in this new case."

"But..." she massaged her temples. "He's the best DS we've got, and I have been using him fully. And Leigh Fletcher is now a murder investigation. I need him to -"

Gillingham at least had the grace to look uncomfortable, but he held up his palm again, forestalling any further objection. "The best DS is just what I need for this job, Lizzie. I've got two murders, and everyone is stretched. I'm sorry, but I've made my decision and asked Steve to brief Dan."

"So what's the case, exactly?" she wondered. In her heart, she knew she was being unreasonable, but to lose Baines to that pig?

"Someone went up to the allotments in Westyate to water their crops this morning, before the day got too hot," Gillingham said. "He found something nasty amongst the vegetable patches, and it wasn't slugs eating the lettuces."

* * *

Baines had never had cause to visit any allotments before. When Louise had been alive, she had often talked about getting one when Jack went to school, but he had never seen the appeal. Why spend hours and hours digging, tickling seedlings or whatever it was one did to them, waving a hose around during hot periods like this one, and then having to pick the stuff?

He'd never understood how all that effort could be preferable to pushing a trolley around a supermarket, grabbing the same things off the same shelves each week, chucking them in the car boot, and driving them home.

Hunter-gathering, 21st Century style.

The allotments at Westyate looked to him like some small, primitive village from another era. Sheds were dotted around, beds were nicely arranged, some neatly framed by off-cuts of wood. In some of the beds, canes had been pushed into the ground and lashed together with twine to form what resembled skeleton wigwams, with crops climbing on them.

He could imagine a sunny Sunday afternoon: all the plot holders up here, doing whatever it was they did and chatting to each other about the size of their marrows, or where to get the best manure. Quintessential English country living.

The horror that lay before him now had no place in such a setting.

"And you say this Len Clough character had been warned that something like this would happen?" he checked again with one of the uniformed constables who had already been there, containing the scene, when he had arrived.

"After the last bout of break-ins up here, he was all for setting up a rota to watch over the plots and try to catch the thief in the act," the constable said. "It looks like maybe he got his wish."

"But the rota idea got short shrift?"

"So Mr Hilton - he's the one who found the body - says. But apparently it was common knowledge in the village that Clough was skulking around here after dark. The locals even had a nickname for him: the Lone Ranger."

"But we don't think Clough's the victim?"

"Mr Hilton says not, sir. He thinks it must be the thief. Got more than he bargained for."

Baines had arrived at the same time as the CSIs, and had suited up to ensure he didn't contaminate the scene. The pathologist, Barbara Carlisle, was on her way. He watched the

CSIs measuring, combing the ground for clues, and taking photographs, finally feeling like a third wheel and seeking out one of the uniforms guarding the blue and white tape that cordoned off the scene. Now the three of them stood looking down at the body.

The shaven headed man lay on his side on a patch of grass between two plots. There was a lot of dried blood on his white tee-shirt, and a lot more in the wounds on his battered head. Nearby lay a set of bolt cutters and a spade, blood encrusted on the blade.

Baines hunkered down for a closer look.

"Not much sign of blood on the ground," he remarked. "Looks like he might not have been killed here."

"The Crime Scene Manager tends to agree, sir," the uniform told him. "He says it could have soaked into the soil, but he'd still expect to see some traces, the amount of damage the victim suffered. They're looking out for a primary scene, in case he was moved."

"Moved?" Baines frowned. "Why move him?" He shook his head. "Never mind."

The constable held up a finger. "One thing, sir. Mr Hilton says those bolt cutters would have been used to cut through padlocks on sheds. That's the usual technique."

"They padlock the sheds? What do they have worth stealing?"

"Beats me, sir. I dare say Mr Hilton will be able to tell you."

"Is he still here?"

"Yes, I asked him to stick around until you arrived."

"I'll have a chat with him in a moment. Is Phil Gordon the Crime Scene Manager?" The uniform nodded. "Then I'll find him and see what he makes of it so far."

"Looks pretty straightforward, though, doesn't it?" the uniform opined. "He comes back once too often and gets taken by surprise by an angry vigilante. Could be that Clough only meant to frighten him, but then he got scared himself. He lashes out, the guy goes down, then he keeps hitting him to make sure he doesn't get up again."

"Looks that way," Baines agreed. He could be back on the Leigh Fletcher case by tea time. "I still wonder why he might have been moved."

"Maybe Clough took it into his head to drag the body down to the gate, put it in his car, and dump it. But it was too much like hard work. Or maybe he changed his mind and decided he'd rather just leg it."

Something didn't add up. Baines thought he might put his finger on it in a moment.

"By the way," he said, "there was a yellow van down by the gate - an Astra, I think. Whose is that?"

"I'll run a check."

"Tell our friend Hilton I won't be long, would you?"

They headed off, and Baines stood scanning the white-suited CSIs for Phil Gordon's lanky frame. He spotted the crime scene manager near a shed and strode over to join him.

"Morning, Dan. I heard you'd pulled this one. It's looking pretty open and shut, though."

"You think?"

"This is Len Clough's shed. That's his padlock lying on the ground. The shackle has been cut through."

"Shackle?"

"The U-shaped piece that secures the lock. It's the quickest, most common way to get through a padlock. Just as well they're not that challenging, really, or a determined thief's just as likely to kick the door in. Much more expensive to fix."

"Sweet."

"Easy pickings, Dan. Even an old spade might fetch a couple of quid, and some fools still leave power tools, like strimmers, on their plots. And then there's the big, heavy post drivers."

"For bashing wooden posts into the ground, right? People actually steal them?"

"The metal, see? They can get a good price, even though the government is trying to crack down on metal theft. Not too many high value items, mind. Most people prefer to keep them at home, even though carting them to and fro is a pain."

"I was going to ask our witness what sort of thing gets pinched. Sounds like I needn't bother."

They walked back to the body.

"My brother's got an allotment," Gordon supplied. "They've had a couple of break-ins. It's as much the inconvenience as anything else. That and the idea that some scumbag thinks he can just take other people's stuff."

"Your brother ever talk about whacking a thief with a spade?"

"Nah, he's very philosophical about it. Like I said, you just don't leave anything on the plot that would be pricey to replace."

"Do we have a name for the victim?"

"Hilton didn't recognise him, but there was a wallet in his pocket." Gordon held up an evidence bag. "Credit cards, driving licence. One Gavin Lane, of Aylesbury."

"We'll need to check if he's got form. I'll bet that yellow van by the gate was his. Ready to load up with booty and drive away." He looked at Gordon. "So your take on all this is that Len Clough got his man?"

"That's how it looks and sounds. We'll check for prints on the murder weapon -"

"The spade?"

"Yeah, the spade. I'll bet they're Clough's prints. We'll dust his padlock too. Chances are we'll find prints we're able to match to the victim right here at the scene."

The spade. That was what had been bothering Baines.

"You've clocked that there's not much blood here?"

"Yes. We're looking out for copious amounts of blood elsewhere on this site," Gordon said. "This might not be the primary crime scene, although I suppose it's possible that he died right here and most of the blood has soaked into the ground..."

Baines squatted down and pressed his fingers on the surface. Even through the latex gloves he wore, he could tell what the soil was like. "It's bone dry and pretty compacted. Could the blood have evaporated?"

"We'll have to take some samples and get them analysed," Gordon said. "I dare say there's an answer to the riddle."

"But if you find nothing, would that suggest he didn't die here?" Baines persisted.

"It could, but let's not be hasty about that. This is a big site and we need to follow the evidence for the time being."

"All right. But if we do decide this really wasn't where Lane died, what's the murder weapon doing here?" he wondered. "Odd enough that Clough, or whoever did this, would leave it lying around in the first place. Odder that he'd move the body and then bring the weapon here too."

"You're right," Gordon admitted. "I was speculating that the victim might have crawled here from the primary scene, but it beggars belief that he'd have dragged the bloody spade with him."

Baines nodded. "I'll await your report. Meanwhile, I'd better get someone to bring Mr Clough in for questioning, always assuming he hasn't done a runner. Then I'll wait for Dr Carlisle. She'll be able to tell us more about the nature of the attack. "

"Will I, Dan?" the pathologist said sweetly, appearing like the Devil at the mention of her name. "Your faith never fails to touch me."

He watched as she crouched beside the body and started her initial investigations. He had questions, but knew better than to interrupt her.

"Time of death is never easy to determine," she said finally, "and this warm weather hardly helps. But I'd say he 's been dead several hours... at least eight, probably longer."

"So maybe late last night?"

"It's possible," she confirmed, with her trademark lack of absolute commitment. He often wondered if she'd made a mistake in the distant past by jumping to a hasty conclusion, but there was no way he would ever ask her.

"And not much doubt about cause of death? Blunt force trauma to the head?"

"He's certainly incurred some of that. But let's not be too hasty."

She carried on with her checks, at one point asking Phil Gordon to help her move the body.

"Well," she said at last, "there are no other obvious wounds, and no sign of strangulation or any other form of asphyxiation. You know me well enough to know I won't give you any firm conclusions on time or cause of death until I've done the post mortem, but blunt force trauma yesterday evening is certainly a very plausible theory. I suppose you've already worked out that he didn't die here. By the time he got to this spot, his heart had stopped pumping, so there's next to no blood."

"Yes, that's bothering both of us," Baines said, unease ticking at the back of his mind. "Well, I'll leave you scientists to do your scientific stuff. I'll talk to my witness and then we'll pull in our Lone Ranger -"

"Our what?" Carlisle looked mystified.

"Lone Ranger," he repeated. "Local nickname for our one man vigilante band, Mr Clough. Unless he has an alibi, he's looking like our prime suspect. If it's really our lucky day, he might even confess on the spot."

9

Archer had returned from her meeting with Gillingham to find that Baines had already left for his new crime scene. She was still annoyed, but her priority was breaking the news to the Fletcher family that Leigh's death was now being treated as murder.

The responses of the three remaining family members had all been different. Uncontrollable tears from the mother, and repeated questions about who would want to do such a thing. Such stoicism from the father that she wondered how he would be when it really sank in. Simmering rage from the sister.

Archer sensed again that Hayley Fletcher had a considerable temper. What was she capable of when it was truly unleashed? If there was real resentment against Leigh, the family golden girl, was she capable of violence?

Hayley's grief seemed genuine enough, but then Archer had seen people before who had killed partners, parents, children and siblings. In many cases, there had been a moment's red mist, a lashing out, the results as unintentional as they had been irreversible. The grief had been genuine, albeit mingled with remorse. Was that the case with Hayley?

The girl and her father had accepted a lift to the station, and her boyfriend, Kyle Adams, and Leigh's friend, Gemma Lucas, were each coming in with their own parent. Archer made arrangements for Kyle and Gemma to be made comfortable in separate rooms when they arrived and then she and Ross got the interview with Hayley underway.

Time was when police interview rooms were painted battleship grey, with grey furniture. These days, those at Aylesbury nick were duck egg blue with a blue fabric panel running round from roughly waist to shoulder high. No one seemed to know its purpose. The furniture was warm red-brown wood, but bolted down to ensure that angry suspects didn't throw it around.

The interview room she and Ross sat in with Hayley and Gareth Fletcher was probably the least threatening in the station, but it didn't exactly speak of home. There were no windows and, to Archer's mind, it always seemed to reek of sweat and fear. She could see the apprehension in father and daughter's eyes. Archer had stressed that it was all routine, but she guessed there must be some nervousness about being questioned by the police.

When everyone had said their name for the recording, Archer set out some ground rules for Gareth Fletcher's benefit.

"Before we start, Mr Fletcher, I want to make it clear that you're sitting in on this interview as a courtesy. Hayley is eighteen, and as such does not need a parent or guardian present, but I'm happy for you to be here supporting her. But I'd appreciate it if you tried not to interrupt this interview, nor attempt to influence Hayley's answers. Are we clear on this?"

Gareth nodded.

"Hayley is just helping us with our inquiries. She's free to go at any time, but we hope she'll want us to do all we can to find out what happened to Leigh. Is that all right?"

"It's fine," the girl said. She glanced around the room and seemed to shiver. "Let's get on with this."

Archer smiled. "Hayley, can you tell me how you and your sister got on as siblings?"

"Pretty well. We were more like friends than sisters."

"And has it always been like that?"

"Yes." She paused. "Well, I suppose we had a few fights as kids." Her expression softened. "She was always taking my dolls. Even when we both had the same one."

"Why do you think that was? Jealousy?" Archer didn't yet know where this was going, but it was interesting.

"I don't know. I've never really thought. Maybe. I don't know."

"Okay. Now you mentioned, when we spoke to you at your home yesterday, that Leigh had been a bit moody a year or so back, but that she'd come out of it. Can you describe those moods?"

Hayley thought for a moment. "I suppose I'd say..." She shrugged. "She went around with a face like a slapped arse and sometimes hardly spoke for days. I've seen teenage angst, even done it myself, but she had it bad."

"And do you think that's all it was? Teenage angst? Or do you think it was more than that? Maybe caused by something?"

The girl looked at her father, but he might as well not have been there. He had evidently segued into some private hell. Archer found herself wondering how long it would be before he became entirely unglued.

Hayley sighed. "I wouldn't know. You'd say things like, 'What's wrong with you?', and she'd be like, 'Nothing.'"

"How did it make you feel?"

"Honestly? It pissed me off. It felt like attention-seeking."

"Pissed you off how much?"

Hayley stared at her angrily. "Not enough to want to kill her, if that's what you're getting at."

Ross picked up the questioning. "But your dad said that all changed when she started going to chapel?"

"I don't know if it was going to chapel that changed it, not for sure. But yeah. It was around the same time."

"What made her start going? I think one of you said you're not a religious family."

She frowned. "Good question. Well, I'd say it sort of started just after Andrew got elected to Parliament. There was a big thank you party in the village hall. All the helpers were invited, and me and her got dragged along, even though we hadn't helped much. Leigh so did not want to go."

"Hang on," Archer stepped in. "I thought Mr Marling said she had helped? You say no?"

"I think the whole family spent a couple of hours one weekend stuffing leaflets into envelopes. We weren't exactly on the campaign trail, not me and Leigh, anyway. Dad did some canvassing. Andrew came to the house a couple of times. He's okay - not the usual suit you see in politics."

Archer cast her mind back. "May 2010. She'd have been - what? Thirteen?"

"Yeah. Didn't care about politics then, doesn't now. I mean..." Tears welled in her eyes.

"We know what you mean," Ross said, handing her a tissue. "Go on."

"Anyway, Andrew had also invited the local affluentials, and Pastor Marc was there. He was working the room. Fishing for souls, he said, but he was having a laugh at himself really. We asked him about the chapel, or maybe he cornered us and insisted on telling us." She frowned again. "It's funny. He only talked to us for maybe five minutes. A couple of weeks later, Leigh said she was thinking of going, and did I want to go too?"

"And did you?"

Hayley made a face. "Duh. Eight o'clock on a Sunday morning? Don't think so."

Archer laughed, but was intrigued. "But did she say why she wanted to go?"

"Not really, no. She mumbled something about wanting to see what it was all about, but that was about all we could get out of her. But you want to know what I think?"

"Please."

She glanced at her father. "Marc Ambrose is a well fit guy, and he's got this really cool voice. Seriously sexy. Leigh never got into the boy bands like I did, but I reckon she'd finally found someone she could drool over."

"She fancied him?"

"Well, yeah. Well, anyone would fancy him. Just not enough to get up early on a Sunday in my case."

"But Leigh started going?"

"No, not then. Not for about another year. I made her go, to be honest. She was so bloody miserable all the time, and I reminded her how keen she'd been. I thought something needed to change in her life and maybe a bit of happy clappy was worth a try. And it did seem to cheer her up a bit."

"I went once," Gareth suddenly spoke up. "Just to make sure everything there was above board."

"And was it?" Archer wondered.

"Seemed that way to me. A bit dull and old-fashioned really. Old-time religion, they'd call it in the States, no doubt. A lot of emphasis on it taking more than living a good life to get into Heaven. I thought it was harmless and that Leigh could be doing far worse in her spare time."

"Her other big love was swimming?"

If Gareth was aware that the questioning had switched to him, he showed no sign of it. "Since she was a little kid and had her first swimming lesson. She couldn't believe it when Graham offered to coach her."

"You like him?"

"He's got a good way with young people, and he makes training fun. So Leigh said, anyway."

Archer filed it away. Baines should be interviewing Graham Endean now, not doing Ashby's job for him. "Moving on, Hayley, tell me what you were doing on Friday night, please."

"I've already told the police all this. A sergeant."

"Now tell me."

The girl sighed. "I was out with Kyle. We went to the cinema in Aylesbury, left about half ten after the film, drove around a bit, then he dropped me home."

Archer could imagine what 'driving around a bit' translated into, but didn't pursue it. "And you got home about 11.30?"

Hayley nodded.

"What film did you see?"

"'World War Z'. Brad Pitt."

"And you went in his car?"

The girl stared at the table, breaking eye contact.

"Yeah - he drives an old Ford Fiesta, if you want to know. He sometimes uses his dad's van, but not Friday."

Archer wondered why she was bothering to introduce this information. It might just be nerve-induced waffling, she supposed, but she filed it away for now.

"And you can't think of anyone who'd want to hurt her? She hasn't been talking to anyone dubious online?"

"Like she'd tell me. But I doubt it."

They wound up the interview soon after that. Before sending Ross to collect Kyle Adams, Archer gave the DS a quizzical look. "Well?"

"She was lying when you asked her about Kyle's car, wasn't she?"

"The way she fidgeted? I'd say she was uncomfortable, at the least. What do you make of it?"

Ross pursed her lips. "Honestly? There was something about her evening with Kyle that she wanted to avoid talking about. Maybe they were just shagging in the back of the car and she didn't want to talk about it in front of dad."

"Maybe. Maybe we should get the CSIs to check out Kyle Adams' Fiesta. And any other vehicle he has access to."

"I agree. Now we know Leigh was dead before she arrived at the quarry, it follows that someone took her there - and I doubt it was in a wheelbarrow."

"It sounds like we definitely ought to chat to this Pastor Marc."

Ross grinned. "Suits me. Any excuse to drool over a well fit guy with a sexy voice."

"Down, girl. Let's take a moment and then get Kyle in."

* * *

Before they started again with Hayley's boyfriend, Archer went to the ladies' to splash some water on her face. As she looked at herself in the mirror, she played back in her mind the interview just concluded. Her thoughts lingered on Gareth Fletcher. She had almost fancied she had felt the waves of pain coming off the man. She was surprised that, having come along, he had shown little interest in proceedings, as if he had only been half there.

But then she had no idea what it must be like to lose a child. Losing her parents had been bad enough.

She wrenched her thoughts back to Hayley. Maybe the girl might have been pushed harder to see how deep some of her negative attitudes towards her sister really ran. But then she wasn't likely to suddenly leap up like some bad TV courtroom drama, saying, *"Yes, I killed her! And I'm glad! I hated her!"*

That didn't happen in real life. It would be interesting to see how Kyle Adams' story compared.

She thought about what Hayley had said about her sister's conversion to religion. Was it really the pastor's looks that had reeled her in, or what he had said? She was suddenly anxious to know more about his faith and what separated it from good old C of E. For all she knew - although she seriously doubted it - they sacrificed chickens and handled live snakes. But Gareth Fletcher would probably have mentioned that.

She made a mental note to see if the chapel had a website.

* * *

Kyle Adams was a wiry young man with unkempt hair, whiskers that couldn't decide whether they were stubble or a beard, and tattoos on both arms. He wore an earring and had a stud in his nose.

Kyle's father brought up the rear, a hunched-over six-footer with at least three beer bellies. Most guys in their forties were unfortunate if they had one. He also wore an earring. Maybe it was a genetic thing, Archer thought, and Kyle had sprung ear-ringed from the womb.

Ross started off by asking him to give a rundown on his movements on Friday evening.

To look at Kyle Adams, Archer would have expected him to be less than cultured. She had come across guys in London who looked very much like him, and who were barely capable of stringing a coherent sentence together. Some had been so inarticulate as to require subtitles. But, had she made that assumption, she would have been entirely wrong.

"I took my girlfriend out to the cinema. I'm sure she's already told you that." His accent was not cut glass, but would have got him a job as a BBC newsreader.

"Okay," Ross said. "Now, what time did you leave the cinema on Friday night?"

"I'm not too sure. After ten, I think. Before eleven."

"And you took Hayley straight home?"

"No. It was a nice evening, so we went for a drive."

"Where did you go?"

"Just around. We parked up on Ivinghoe Beacon for a while."

The Beacon was a well-known landmark in the Chilterns, overlooking several villages, including Ivinghoe in Buckinghamshire, as well as the 5,000 acre Ashridge Estate. Walkers knew the hill, as the starting point of the Icknield Way to the east, and the Ridgeway long-distance path to the west.

"Why there?" Archer prompted.

"Why not? We're a young couple who wanted to spend a bit of time alone together, if you get my drift."

She got his drift. She watched him drink some of the water that had been provided and then top his glass up from the jug.

"So when did you drop her off?"

"Around half eleven. Her mum and dad were on the step, looking out for Leigh. I drove around for a bit, looking for her."

Archer and Ross exchanged glances.

"Hayley never mentioned that," Ross remarked.

"She wouldn't have known. I dropped her off, asked her to ring me in the morning. I thought Leigh was off somewhere, up to something, to be honest. We've all had nights when we've come home later than expected, Sergeant."

"But I gather she wasn't answering her phone, either."

"I know. But you can't always get a signal in these parts." That was true. Just 40-odd miles from central London, but the Chilterns were full of flat spots. Technologically, Archer sometimes thought it was like living in the back of beyond.

"And," he continued, "it wouldn't be the first time a sixteen-year old forgot to turn on their phone, or let the battery die, would it? So anyway, after I dropped Hayley, I decided to cruise a bit and see if I could spot Leigh."

"For how long?"

"Maybe an hour."

Archer swapped another glance with Ross. That would take him up to 12.30 am, well within Barbara Carlisle's window for time of death.

"And did you find her?" Ross probed.

Kyle glanced at his father, then looked back at her.

"No, Sergeant. I didn't find her. Obviously."

"And you and Hayley didn't come across her after you left the cinema?"

"No, we didn't see her." His gaze slid towards his father. "I don't understand. What do you think I did?"

"We don't know, Kyle," said Ross. "Maybe you and Hayley saw her walking home from somewhere, late, soon after you left the cinema. Maybe you offered her a lift."

Archer knew that, for that to work, Carlisle's timing would have to be a little off. Possible, but unlikely, knowing the pathologist. She took up the speculation herself.

"Or maybe you picked her up and bundled her into the boot of your car, for a laugh. Or was it your dad's van you were using?" A quick check with DVLA had already confirmed that Adams senior had a white van for his business as an electrician.

He scratched himself and looked at the DS as if she had just invited him to give a dissertation on every one of Einstein's theories. He cast his puzzled gaze upon his father.

"It's a simple enough question, surely, Kyle?" Archer pressed.

"I understand the question, inspector," he replied finally. "I just don't get why you're asking it. Why are you wasting time with me, when you should be catching whoever killed Leigh? I didn't bundle her into anything. But, for the record, I was using my Fiesta. Why would I use a smelly old van when I can use a nice clean car?"

"A bit roomier, if you have romance on your mind," Ross suggested.

"You haven't seen the inside of Dad's van," Kyle said without missing a beat. "Romance isn't the word it calls to mind." He smiled at Ross. He had a charming smile when he turned it on, Archer decided.

She picked up the questioning again. "Can anyone verify that you used your car, apart from Hayley?"

"Me," his father, Joe, chipped in. "I was using the van on Friday."

"Have you no car, then, Mr Adams?"

"Of course. I might be a tradesman, but I don't have to take the white van when I take the wife to Le Manoir."

Archer thought she must be in the wrong job, if a sparks could speak casually of dining at Le Manoir aux Quat'Saisons, Raymond Blanc's Two Michelin Star restaurant in Oxfordshire.

"We use the Merc for anything like that," he said. "But it's a bit of a fag getting it out the garage just to get a bit of shopping in." He gave her a speculative look. "Why are you so interested in the van ?"

"You think Leigh was abducted and murdered, right?" Kyle said. "And you think a van was involved?"

"Not necessarily, but it might be easier to get an abductee into than the boot of a small car."

"I told you," Joe Adams said angrily, "I was using the van, not Kyle."

"Well, you would say that, wouldn't you, sir?"

"Look," he said, "I think we need a lawyer."

"That's your prerogative, of course, sir, but at the moment this is all informal. Kyle is helping us with our inquiries. We're just trying some scenarios out, to see what he thinks. That's okay, isn't it, Kyle?"

"I suppose."

She knew she was sailing close to the wind. If she got to the point where she was sure he was a serious suspect, she would have to read him his rights and advise him to bring in a solicitor. They weren't there yet.

"I take it you've got the cinema tickets still, or maybe a receipt?"

He visibly relaxed a little, letting out a breath. "I'm sure I've still got the receipt. I paid by credit card, and I like to check my statement."

"Okay," Archer said, as if that was the end of the matter. Kyle smiled, leaning back in his chair.

"Now suppose," she said. "Just suppose. You didn't like the film. Did you like the film, Kyle?"

"It was all right."

"All right. Nothing to write home about, in other words. Suppose you and Hayley left the cinema early and happened across Leigh on the way home. For some sort of laugh, you dump Leigh in the boot."

"We wouldn't."

"We all do things out of character sometimes, Kyle. Leigh got herself killed on Friday night. Out of character. Do you see?"

Kyle looked disgusted. "That's sick."

"What's sick is what we think was done to her. You want to help, yes? So humour me."

"All right." He leaned forward now, his body language aggressive. Not all charm, after all. "Tell me how this fantasy ends."

"You drive her around for a while, planning to let her out when you get to her parents' house, but when you see them out on the step, the joke's not funny any more. You drop Hayley, but you don't let Leigh out. You drive away and, when you do let her out, something happens. Maybe she finds the whole abduction thing exciting and makes a pass at you. Maybe you make a pass at her."

"Or maybe you saw her later," Ross chimed in. "After you dropped Hayley, you saw Leigh. You picked her up, intending to drop her home, but for some reason, it all went wrong."

"Did you fancy Leigh?" Archer pressed. "Did she fancy you?"

Kyle's father was out of his chair. "That's it. We're leaving. Unless you're charging Kyle with something. Helping with inquiries, my arse."

"Chill, Dad," Kyle said. "It's cool." He eyeballed Archer. "There was nothing between me and Leigh, Inspector. She was a nice kid. But a kid. And she was my girlfriend's sister. What do you take me for?"

Archer decided to change tack for a while. "How would you describe Hayley's relationship with her sister?"

"Better than me and my brother. I think they had a few rows, but what family doesn't?"

"Hayley seems to think Leigh was a bit over-indulged when she was young and moody, and that more recently she was getting too much praise from her parents."

"Does she? She's never said."

"Not to her boyfriend? How long have you been seeing Hayley, by the way?

He smiled disarmingly. "Ten months, three weeks and four days. It will be our anniversary next month."

"Congratulations." She would never have marked him for the romantic type, and chided herself for stereotyping him. "And she's never shown any resentment of Leigh?"

"She's said she can be a bit too good to be true sometimes. Usually when she's been pissed at her. I don't know that it was resentment though." He gave a little laugh. "I think she thought Leigh was Daddy's favourite, too, and that upset her sometimes."

Archer looked at Ross. "Help me out here, DS Ross. Didn't I ask Kyle whether Hayley thought her sister was over-indulged and over-praised by her parents? Whether she resented her for it?"

"You did, guv. And Kyle said she'd never said as much."

"Yet she called her," she made a show of consulting her notes, "'Too Good to be True' and 'Daddy's Girl'. That sounds like resentment to me, and also jealousy of her sister for being her parents' favourite."

He shook his head emphatically. "You know, that's why a lot of people think the police are just there to stitch you up. You give honest answers, and they twist your words."

"Tell me what you meant then, Kyle."

"Does he need a lawyer?" Joe Adams butted it. "All this stuff about the van, and now you're putting words into his mouth."

Kyle simply fixed Archer with his gaze, and she noticed for the first time what soft brown eyes he had. "Yes, Hayley thinks Leigh was a moody cow when she was younger. And yeah, she thinks her parents, especially her dad, think more of Leigh than they do of her. And naturally, her dying young will probably make it worse."

"So -" Archer began, but the young man held up a palm.

"Let me finish, please. My point is, these were things that upset Hayley, but mostly they were her parents' fault, not

Leigh's. Hayley didn't resent Leigh. She loved her. They were mates, as well as sisters. And, for what it's worth, I didn't share Hayley's opinion. I thought Leigh was genuinely nice. She never badmouthed anyone, that I know of. I can't say that about too many people I know."

It was quite a speech for someone Archer had expected to be taciturn at first sight.

Archer made a show of checking her notes. "Thanks, Kyle. You've been very helpful. I think we've got all we need for now, but I'll be sending some people to take a look at all your vehicles. Don't clean them, or it will look most suspicious. And Kyle - no foreign holidays, for a while, okay?"

10

Baines drew up outside the semi in Elm Farm, one of Aylesbury's newer housing estates. He had collected PC Megan Kirby, a family liaison officer, from the station en route. Uniforms had been despatched to locate Len Clough and ask him to come to the station and help with some inquiries. If they found him before Baines got back, he'd just have to cool his heels for a while.

"I fucking hate this part of the job," Baines said as he cut the engine and released his seat belt.

"It never gets any easier," Kirby said.

They got out. As Baines led the way to the front door, he noticed how neat the front garden was, how immaculate the paintwork on the fence and gate was. Checks had already been run on the man who had lived here, and he'd had some serious form. Breaking and entry, assault... Some nasty stuff, which had landed him a few spells inside. Years ago, he'd spent time in the army. Maybe that had fucked him up.

Baines wondered why someone like that would bother themselves with pinching a few bits and pieces from allotment sheds.

He paused in front of the door, varnished to a lustrous shine. Whatever else the man had been, either he knew how to do jobs around the house really well, or he wasn't afraid to splash out on quality tradesmen.

A deep breath, and Baines pressed the bell. A few moments, and then the sound of footsteps approaching. The door opened. A petite woman, her hair dyed blonde, her features pretty in a hard sort of way. She looked at Baines in puzzlement, and then her eyes slid locked on the uniformed constable beside him.

And she knew.

Her lips quivered. She swayed on her feet.

"No," she whispered, shaking her head. Then a shriek: *"Nooo-"* She made to shut the door in their faces, stood there with it half-open. Kirby shouldered her way past Baines, and Gavin Lane's widow fell into her arms, wailing her dead husband's name over and over.

* * *

Archer wasn't entirely sure what she had expected Leigh's friend to look like, but Gemma Lucas was a bit of a surprise. Like Archer herself, Leigh had been quite tall for a female - just under six feet - and had been slim, with a good figure. Gemma was about five feet five inches tall, and not quite as wide. Leigh had been pretty. Gemma was fairly plain looking, with quite bad acne. Her eyes were red, as if she had been crying for days. In the circumstances, it was entirely possible she had.

Her father, a pencil-slim contrast to her, with owlish glasses, sat beside her, holding her hand. The girl was visibly trembling. This was probably her first visit to a police station, and it could be intimidating. Of course, it was always possible she had something to be scared about.

Archer and Ross had been questioning people for almost two hours. Exhaustion was setting in already, and there was still a long day ahead.

"Gemma, just relax," she said soothingly. "DS Ross and I are just trying to get to the bottom of what happened to Leigh on Friday night, and you might well be the last person to have seen her alive. Can you tell me about Friday evening?"

Gemma hesitated. She seemed to stare at the left side of Archer's face for a long moment. When she did start to talk, her voice was a tremulous whisper.

"Could you speak up, Gemma, for the recording?" Archer said kindly.

"Speak up, sweetheart," urged her father.

The girl raised her voice. "Leigh came round about eight. We sat in my room, listening to music and talking. She left about 10.15."

She blinked at Archer, as if wondering what other questions there could possibly be.

"You're absolutely certain about the time?"

"Yes."

"How can you be sure?"

"I remember looking at my watch."

"And did you see her off at the door?"

"Yes."

Gemma Lucas was not the chattiest witness Archer had interviewed.

"When you were seeing Leigh off, Gemma, did you happen to see anyone else? Maybe someone hanging around?"

The girl considered the question.

"I don't think so. No, no one. I don't think."

"What about vehicles? Did you see anyone driving past?"

Gemma screwed her face in concentration. "I can't remember." She started to cry. "I'm sorry. I'm no use."

"You're doing fine," Archer said.

"It's all right, sweetheart," Gemma's father said, putting his arm around her shoulders. "You heard the inspector. You're doing fine, love."

Ross pushed a box of tissues the girl's way. She took one and blew her nose noisily. Archer waited patiently until she was more composed.

"What about parked cars, Gemma? Did you see any vehicles parked in your road that you didn't recognise?"

"Close your eyes, Gemma," Ross interjected. Gemma blinked and then obeyed, her eyes squeezed shut. "See the scene. You're seeing Leigh off. Do you open the front door, or does she?"

Long pause. Then, "She does. I'm behind her, she gets there first."

"Good. Just remember it all in your head and describe it to me as it happens."

Eyes still locked down, Gemma Lucas spoke falteringly at first, then gradually more confidently.

"Leigh turns round... on the step. She says, 'See you tomorrow, darling,' and I say, 'See ya.' She walks down the path, opens the gate. Walks through and closes it behind her."

"Very good. Does she turn left or right?

"Right."

"Is that usual?"

"Yes." Gemma frowned. "Why-?"

"Keep seeing the scene. Does she walk straight off, or does she hesitate?"

"Straight off."

"What else do you see?"

"Dad's car, in the drive. Next door's mini in their drive." She frowned. "Um, old Mrs Cooper's just coming back from walking her dog."

"Does she pass Leigh?"

"No, she comes from the other way."

Archer scribbled herself a note to ensure that Mrs Cooper had been spoken to in Bell's door-to-door.

"Good," Ross said. "Do you see anything else? Anything at all?"

"No. Nothing." She opened her eyes.

"Close your eyes again. See the scene. Is there anyone... anything... unusual? Out of place?"

"No." The girl shrugged. "I'm sorry." Then, "Wait. A van. Across the road, under the street lamp. White, I think, but the light..."

Ross's gaze flickered to Archer, then back to Gemma. "You're not sure about the colour? All right. Do you see the number plate?"

"No." There was a thin sheen of sweat on the girl's forehead from the exertion of concentration.

"Is there anyone inside?"

"Two men. I think they're men. Just shapes, really. They might have hats on. I don't know." A tear slid down her cheek.

"That's great, Gemma," Ross said finally. "Well done, thank you." She nodded to Archer, inviting her to resume the lead.

Archer had thought the DS was doing well with her cognitive interviewing technique until Gemma's eyes had suddenly flown open. From that point, she hadn't been sure she believed a word the girl said. She was tempted to press her, but decided to change tack.

"Well done, Gemma," she said, reinforcing the praise. "Now, can you help us out a bit more? It's all to help us find out what happened to Leigh."

"Anything. I'll do anything."

"Good, thanks. So, can you tell me about any boyfriends Leigh might have had?"

The girl looked suddenly flustered, her eyes darting her father's way, then looking at Ross. Then back at Archer, who kept her face as neutral as she could. She wasn't about to volunteer what she knew about Leigh's virginity, nor her parents' confidence that there had never been a boy or man in her life.

"Boyfriends?" Gemma repeated finally.

"Just routine," Archer assured her. "You know - who she went out with, when... that sort of thing."

"Er..." The girl was blushing. Her gaze slid away. "No one."

"Are you sure? This is important, Gemma. It might not have been recent, but we're pretty sure there was someone."

Gemma licked her lips again. "I... I don't want to get Leigh in trouble."

"Gems?" Mr Lucas said softly, taking her hand and stroking it. "Leigh's past trouble now. If you know anything, you've got to tell, sweetheart."

She looked torn for a moment, then sniffled and nodded.

"Well, she did see someone for a while, but I don't know who it was."

Archer and Ross swapped glances.

"Leigh was your best mate, Gemma," Ross said. "She must have given you a clue?"

The girl fidgeted, but not in the way that the dead girl's sister had earlier when talking about Kyle's father's van. There was more of a shy awkwardness about her.

"Didn't she say anything, love?" her father pressed. "I know you can't like talking about it in front of me and the officers, but you must. For Leigh."

Archer wished all young people's parents were like him.

"I don't know," she insisted. "Honest. She wouldn't say who it was, but she said it was serious. I had an idea it was someone she shouldn't be seeing, but I can't say for sure. There was one time she said, if anyone asked, she'd been shopping with me all afternoon."

"Can you remember the date? Archer urged."

"No. I think it was around the Easter holidays. Soon after, it seemed to have ended. I think he dumped her. She was so miserable for a while. But she got better."

"You say it was someone she shouldn't have been seeing. Like an older man?"

Gemma nodded.

"Married, maybe?"

"Maybe. I just don't know. It was all a big secret. But I think he was the only one. Nobody before. No one since."

"And when exactly was this going on?"

"I'm not sure. I think maybe it started about three years ago."

"How long did it last?"

"About six months? She was so unhappy - that must have started around April, May, the year before last. She was miserable for the best part of a year. Then she started to come out of it."

"Was that around the time she started going to chapel?"

"I think so, yes. I think it made a difference to her."

"Ever go with her?"

The girl shook her head. "I wasn't interested. She asked me, but I said no. At least she didn't start preaching to me."

Ross slipped in again. "Did she talk much about Pastor Marc?"

Gemma coloured again. "Yeah. She was always on about what a cool guy he was, not like the usual preachers. To be honest, I got fed up of hearing about him."

"You think she had a crush on him?"

"Maybe."

Archer picked up the ball. "Is there any chance she knew him before she started going to chapel?"

Gemma studied her face. "You think he was the one...?"

"I'm asking you."

The girl frowned. "I don't think so. I mean, I don't know, don't know who it was. I remember her mentioning him after she met him at some party. I think she was quite interested in his chapel, more than in him. Even then she didn't start going straight away." She shook her head. "I mean, she wasn't going to chapel when she was seeing this bloke. If it was the pastor, why wouldn't she? And why start going after he dumped her?"

"Maybe to be near him? Try and win him back?"

"Maybe." She sounded doubtful.

"Could that have been why she cheered up when she started going?"

"I suppose. I thought she'd just found something. God, you know?"

Gemma's father jumped in. "You're seriously suggesting that the pastor might have had an affair with Leigh, inspector? When she was..." - he must have been calculating - "... well under age? Thirteen, maybe?"

Too late, Archer wondered if her line of questioning ought to have been a little more circumspect.

"Absolutely not, Mr Lucas. We thought Leigh was seeing someone, and Gemma has confirmed that for us. But we have no idea who that someone was. All we're doing right now is ruling out possibilities. And we all know what young girl's crushes are. I gather the pastor is quite good looking, and maybe Leigh just got a crush on him on the rebound. But we really know no more than you. It's very important that neither you nor Gemma repeat any of this."

"Fair enough. But I'd hate to think he was fiddling with young girls who go to his chapel."

"Dad -" Gemma protested.

"We've really no reason to suppose anything of the kind at this stage," Archer assured him. "Honestly. We've no such suspicions."

This was true. But something was making her want to see Pastor Ambrose for herself, very badly.

"All right then. We don't want to make any trouble." Lucas gave Archer a hard look. "But if I find that something's happened that we could have stopped..."

"Thank you," Archer said. "And we don't want that either. If we think there's anything to investigate, we won't hesitate."

"Good enough for me. Is there anything else?"

"A couple more questions. You're doing brilliantly, Gemma. Now, how well do you know Leigh's sister and her boyfriend?"

The girl shrugged. "I know Hayley, from when I've been round there. She's all right. I've met Kyle a couple of times. I don't like him."

"No?"

"No. I think he fancies himself. He was always trying to chat us up when Hayley was out of the room. I don't think he was interested - at least not in me - but it was like he expected us to be falling at his feet."

"You said 'at least' he wasn't interested in you, Gemma," Ross played back to her. "You're saying he might have been interested in Leigh?"

"Probably not. He just flirted more with her than me." She smiled ruefully. "But I'm used to that."

"Did Leigh flirt back?"

"No way. We never talked about it, but I could tell it got on her nerves."

"One other question," Archer said. "Gemma, how did Leigh seem on Friday night?"

"Seem?"

"Well, was there anything different about her? How was her mood?"

"She was fine." But Gemma wasn't making eye contact.

"You're sure? She didn't seem upset, or preoccupied?"

"No. She was just Leigh."

Archer debated with herself whether to press it, and then tried a different tack. "I've no more questions for now. Is there anything else you'd like to tell me, Gemma?"

"Like what?" A slightly sulky tone?

"I don't know, Gemma. Anything at all."

The girl was crying again, her father's arm around her shoulders, his eyes pleading with Archer to leave his daughter alone.

"It's been such a shock for her," he told her. "Leigh was a real friend to her. Protected her from bullies, always on the phone to her or texting. She's just upset, that's all."

Archer stifled a sigh. "Here's my card, Gemma. If you think of anything at all that you wish you'd mentioned to me just now, give me a ring. Any time, day or night."

She watched them leave. Much of what Gemma had told them was useful, but she wasn't entirely happy. It wasn't clear whether the girl found some of the subject matter embarrassing, or whether she had been holding something back. She probably hadn't told an out and out lie, but maybe she hadn't told the detectives everything.

Archer only hoped they hadn't missed anything vital.

* * *

Gareth and Hayley Fletcher had returned home to be fallen upon by Gail, who fussed and asked questions about the interview, and offered food and drink. Hayley wanted neither, but her mother followed each refusal with the suggestion of some alternative refreshment. In the end, both to appease her and to put an end to her badgering, Hayley had accepted a cup of coffee and a biscuit and had taken them to her room, where they sat untouched on her bedside table.

She lay on her bed, staring at the ceiling, willing the thoughts and questions in her head to go away and give her some peace.

There was a light tap on her door. After a moment, it was eased open and her father's face appeared in the crack.

"I've just been listening to local radio," he said, "in case there was anything about Leigh."

She sat up. "And was there?"

"Nothing new. But they've found a body over at Westyate, on the allotments of all places. The police are treating it as suspicious. We know what that means, don't we?"

She just stared at him.

"I don't know," he went on. "This part of the world. I've always thought it was as safe a place to live as any. Now look. First Leigh, now this. Two murders in less than a week. Makes you think, eh?"

"Think what, Dad?"

"I just don't know what's going on any more."

"No," she said absently.

He stood there for a few moments, perhaps expecting a fuller response, maybe a full-on discussion about the state of the world in Aylesbury Vale. When she said nothing more, he shook his head in a despairing sort of way, exited and closed the door behind him.

Hayley stared at the closed door for a few minutes, then covered her face with her hands.

"Oh, Kyle," she whispered. "What have you done now?"

11

Baines returned to the station feeling low, and trying in vain to banish from his mind Marie Lane's grief at her husband's death.

It seemed that, when her husband wasn't helping himself to other people's possessions, he had a casual line of work helping a friend with various building jobs - fitting kitchens and bathrooms, the odd bit of light bricklaying. Yesterday he'd been on a kitchen job, and he'd phoned her twice in the evening - once to say the job was going on longer than expected, and once - about 9.30 pm - to say he and his mate were going for a drink, and not to wait up.

By that time, the kids had already been put to bed. She had turned in herself at around 11 pm, read a little, then gone to sleep.

When she had awoken to find that his side of the bed hadn't been slept in, she still wasn't especially worried. It wouldn't have been the first time he'd had one too many to drive and crashed out at his friend's, one John Butler. Just after 8 am she'd called his mobile, but it had gone straight to voicemail. So she'd phoned Butler.

Gavin wasn't with him. There had been no drink and, Butler had told her, Lane had been a bit off that day. Butler had in fact suggested the pub when they finished working just after 9 pm, but Lane had refused, saying he had to get home.

"So he told you he was going for a drink with Mr Butler, and he told Mr Butler he was going home to you?" Baines played back to her.

Marie Lane sniffled into yet another tissue. "I suppose I guessed then that he was up to no good. I kept begging him to give up robbing, but he hasn't exactly got a steady income and he takes his responsibilities as a provider seriously." Her head came up with something like pride.

Baines resisted the urge to say that stealing from people who had worked hard for what they had wasn't the most honourable way of meeting breadwinning responsibilities.

"But even if he'd been doing something shady, you would have expected him home by morning?" He watched her nod. "So what did you think?"

She shook her head. "Honestly? I thought he'd been caught. That the next I heard from him would be from a cell at the nick. It never entered my head that..." She broke off and wiped her eyes. "You say he was stealing from allotment sheds?" A frown creased her brow. "That doesn't sound his style at all. What could he expect to get? Lawn mowers? He wouldn't know what to do with them. TVs, microwaves, that sort of thing... that was his speciality. He knew how to shift them."

Her eyes blazed with sudden ferocity. "Fucking army. Men put their lives on the line for their country, but when they leave they've got no backup. They have to adjust to being civvies again, and it's hard. You've seen the stories. Homelessness, drugs, drink, crime..."

Baines let his gaze sweep the nicely decorated and well-furnished lounge. "He hasn't done as badly as all that, though."

She hiccupped a laugh. "We bought this place with what he came out of the army with, and a bit of money I inherited from my favourite aunt. There was enough left over for a few nice things to put in it. This is the best room. Some of the others are full of second-hand stuff that doesn't match. Day to day living?" She shrugged. "I do a shift as a dinner lady, and Gavin does his ducking and diving..."

"Did he never try for a nine to five job?"

"He had a couple of them, but - I don't know - maybe it was some sort of backlash from the military discipline. He couldn't get on with taking orders from people, not from civvies. He'd end up getting bolshie and he'd either leave or be asked to leave. What he was doing... it was a bit hand to mouth, but it seemed to suit him."

Collins leaned forward. "You say this John Butler said Gavin had been - how did you put it? A bit off? Was that normal?"

"Yeah, he could be a moody bugger."

"Had you noticed anything?"

Marie Lane shrugged. "I suppose he had been a bit quiet, the last couple of days. Maybe he was worried about money. Maybe that was why he went robbing sheds."

"Did you ask him if anything was wrong?"

"No, I don't do that. Only get my head bitten off. Best to let it go. He always came around, and he was a lovely man most of the time."

The tears flowed again, and Baines and Megan Kirby waited patiently for them to subside.

"I don't know what we'll do now," Marie said finally. "My money's not enough to keep us. I suppose I'll have to look into benefit, or sell the house. Do you know who killed him?"

"We're pursuing various lines of inquiry," Baines said carefully.

"Well, you catch him and you put him away. My Gav was a bit of a villain, but he never hurt anyone."

Baines bit his tongue again. Gavin Lane had been convicted of assault more than once. Baines would check out the details back at the station, but he thought the newly widowed spouse's image of a lovely man who wouldn't hurt a fly was decidedly rose-tinted.

He thought of Len Clough, waiting at the station to be questioned. Like as not, they already had their man.

"We'll catch him, Mrs Lane," he assured her. "It's what we do."

* * *

After the interviews concluded, Archer returned to the briefing room and stood studying the collection of crime scene photographs and handwritten notes on the board. Pictures of the three teenagers she and Ross had spoken to today would soon be added. She was thinking how fuzzy the picture still was when her phone rang. She glanced at the display. Ian Baker.

"I wondered if we were still on for tomorrow?" he said.

She blinked. "I don't remember agreeing that we were on."

"Ah, but you know you want to," he cajoled.

"Well..." She felt her resolve and her sense of practicality weakening, as they so often had before with this man. Tomorrow suited him better than her, she knew that, but what the hell? "I suppose if you could book us into that place in Huntingdon, although I don't know what time I'll get away."

"I've already made a provisional booking." She could hear the smile in his voice.

"You presumptuous, cocky sod." But she was smiling too. Typical Ian.

"What can I say? You know me too well."

"It's one of your more attractive traits. Not."

"So how's the case?" he asked.

"Frustrating, and not helped by the fact that Baines is working with Steve Ashby."

"That arsehole?" Baker sounded incredulous. "You mean they've actually got Ashby working a real case? Actually getting his hands dirty?"

"That'll be the day, Ian. More like he's up to his old tricks, I suspect. Get others to do all the work, but claim all the glory."

"More fool Dan for falling for it."

"Yes, well. Orders from Gillingham. And maybe he felt it was a better offer than my case. I might not have mentioned, but it's right on Dan's doorstep, and I've asked him to keep a bit of a low profile."

"Really? Your call, of course..."

Her hackles rose. "You think I was wrong?"

"Depends if there's a genuine conflict of interest. If there isn't, he's the ideal investigator, surely. Local man, local knowledge..."

"It's a tiny village, Ian. He's lived there well over a decade, and everyone knows he's a copper."

"We actually do have villages here, Lizzie, and local cops get involved in local cases all the time. I think maybe you're falling into the trap of stereotyping us bumpkins as extras from 'The Archers'. It really isn't like that, you know."

She did know. The year or so she had spent here had disabused her of that sort of thinking. Or so she had thought.

"You may have a point," she said. "He seemed to accept it with good enough grace, but..."

"Don't worry about it," Ian said. "There's no right or wrong answer, and you have to back your judgement. If your gut told you to keep him arm's length, maybe that was the right thing to do."

"Yeah, well. It looks like I've lost him to this death amongst the cabbages now."

He exploded with laughter. "Death among the cabbages?"

"I don't know the details yet. A body found on some allotments."

"A falling out over who had the funniest-shaped carrots, perhaps?"

"I'd never be surprised at what constitutes grounds for murder in this neck of the woods."

Baker was still chuckling. "Worzel Gummidge, in the vegetable patch, with the giant marrow? There you go - case solved."

"I'll tell Baines," she giggled.

"Look," he said more soberly, "I really have to go. Call me tomorrow when you're on your way, okay?"

They hung up and she found her mood was a little lighter. Solving real-life murder might be a little harder than a game of Cluedo, but at least she had a distraction from the demands of the job to look forward to tomorrow. A delicious shiver of anticipation ran through her. She remembered her earlier resolve. Talk first, fuck later.

Well, it was her rule. If she decided to break it, that was her prerogative.

* * *

The first thing Baines did on arrival at the station was to check that they had Len Clough safely stowed. He was assured that the suspect was waiting in an interview room, had had three cups of tea and some biscuits, and was becoming irascible about having to wait, especially as he wasn't actually under arrest.

"Has DI Ashby spoken to him?" Baines asked.

No, DI Ashby hadn't spoken to him. Ashby had checked in, had a coffee, and gone out again. He'd been informed that Clough was waiting, but been content to leave it to Baines.

Baines sighed and wandered into the open plan office. He spotted Collins and walked up to her desk. She was poring over some photographs.

"Joan, I need a favour. I've got a suspect waiting to be interviewed, and I shouldn't do it alone. Any chance you can sit in?"

Collins hesitated. "I'd be happy to, Dan, but maybe we should check with the guv - Lizzie - first."

"It won't take too long," he pressed.

She looked awkward, and Baines knew he was being unfair.

"Maybe I should ask DCI Gillingham," he said. "Although he won't appreciate it. There's no on else, though."

"Ah," said Archer, entering the room. "The defector."

He checked her face to see if she was having a laugh. With its lopsidedness, it could be hard to tell, but she looked deadly serious.

"Look, Lizzie -" he began.

"I know," she said. "You got a better offer. With DI Ashby, no less. I predict the start of a beautiful friendship."

"It's not like that-" he began again, and then he saw the twinkle in her eye.

"Anyway, why are you distracting one of my team?"

"Well..." He felt like a supplicant. He didn't like it. "I was wondering if Joan could sit in on an interview with a suspect. I'm a bit short of support."

"Let's have a word." She headed for the door without waiting for his response. With a glance at Collins, who simply cocked an eyebrow, he followed her into the corridor.

"Are you sure you've made the right choice?" she asked him.

"This case? I wasn't given a choice. I was told it was all decided."

"So was I," she admitted.

"Still," he said, "I can't deny that running the case myself isn't appealing. And, although everything points to the guy I'm about to interview, I've got my doubts. The scene is looking a bit staged to me."

"Just be careful. You don't need me to tell you that, as soon as you make a collar, Steve Bloody Ashby will be the one making speeches and grabbing the limelight. What's he actually doing, by the way?"

"He's going round the contacts he's made at other allotments that have been robbed recently. You know there's been a spate?" She nodded. "Well, Ashby's been, so he says, investigating it. So he's going back over the other cases to see if he can tie them back to our victim."

"How's he going to do that?"

"Christ knows. Meanwhile, I've got a prime suspect - albeit an unlikely one - to talk to, and no one to sit in with me."

"So take one of his team."

"You know as well as I do he doesn't exactly have a team. I don't suppose you...?"

She rolled her eyes. "Don't push it, Dan." She sighed. "All right. You can use Joan, but one good turn deserves another."

He knew he wasn't going to like it. "Go on."

"I still need someone to talk to Leigh's swimming coach, Endean. I take it you never got it set up?"

"Never got a chance."

"Can you make time for it after you've either charged your suspect or let him go? By all means keep Joan and take her with you."

He thought about it. "I guess you're pretty pushed, and there's a limit to what I can do until I've heard back from Phil Gordon and Barbara Carlisle. And Ashby won't have a clue where I am or what I'm doing. I'll ask one of the civvies to set something up."

"Fair enough, then," she said, "but we can't keep doing this. Next time you need more resources, you ask Ashby, or

Gillingham. They have to learn that there are consequences to putting you on a case like this."

They walked back to the office, Baines thinking it was easy for her to talk, but seeing her point. But he could sort of see Ashby's too, if he was honest. If he could establish that Gavin Lane had been responsible for all or most of the recent allotment break-ins, he could clear up several cases at the same time. Baines knew he ought to be hoping Ashby would find the link he was looking for and that Len Clough was Lane's killer. It was just that his gut told him neither was going to happen, at least not today.

* * *

When Baines, accompanied by Collins, finally walked into the interview room where Len Clough had been waiting for over two hours, he welcomed them with a sneer.

"No," he said, shaking his head emphatically, "I do not want another cup of bloody tea. I want to get this over with and go home. God, you hear about this sort of thing in Eastern Europe - the knock at the door in the night -"

"Hardly night time, sir," Baines protested mildly, "and no one's been holding you. You've been free to go at any point you chose."

"I know what 'helping with inquiries' means. One step short of arrest."

"Mr Clough, no one is arresting you. But we do need your help. Now, I'm very sorry you've been kept waiting for such a long time, but I've had to do an unpleasant job this morning - telling a lady that her husband is dead - and I do need to talk to you."

"So why bring me here when you're not ready? And if you weren't here, couldn't someone else have asked me your questions?"

"Not really, sir. It's my case. Anyway, we're here now."

Clough regarded him with muddy eyes set in a craggy face that was weathered to a leathery-looking texture, probably from hours spent on his allotment. Baines judged that he might be in his seventies, but there was a wiry vitality about him, in spite of his sour expression.

The man folded his arms. "Let's get on with it, then."

Baines introduced himself and Collins. They sat across the table from him, and then Baines asked him to account for his movements the evening before.

"Last night? I spent a bit of time up at my allotment. Went home just after ten, watched a bit of telly, then went to bed. I know it's not like car chases and the like, but that's the evening I had."

"Ten's a bit late to be working on your allotment," Baines suggested. "It must have been getting quite dark."

"Ah, but it was a bit cooler by then, and it's peaceful up there with my thoughts."

"Did you see anyone while you were there?"

He frowned. "Let me see. I arrived around 8.30, watered my plot, checked my crops to see what needed picking. A few other people were watering. The last one - Neil Goode - left about 9.30, then Doug Price came up around 9.45."

He paused, gave Baines a somewhat furtive look, and then sighed. "Oh, don't tell me that's what this is about? That bloody busybody has asked you to have a word with me, hasn't he?"

"Nobody has asked us to have a word, Mr Clough. But," he checked one of the notes that Collins had collected from his desk, "we did speak to Mr Price, and he confirmed that he saw you around the time you mentioned. He also said you were still there when he left, a quarter of an hour later. That was just after ten, around the time you said you went home."

"So what? I didn't take copious notes. I left soon after he did. What does it matter?"

"It matters, sir, because the body of a man was found on the allotments this morning," Baines told him. "We've spoken to as many allotment holders as we could get hold of and it sounds as if you were the last person known to be there."

Clough's eyes widened. "Man? What man?"

"We'll come to that in a moment," Baines said. "Perhaps you could tell me what you and Mr Price discussed?"

All the leathery skin on the older man's face seemed to tighten. "Oh, Lord. He's already told you, hasn't he? And now you think..." He gave his head a vehement shake. "No, no. I think I need my solicitor."

"That's your prerogative, sir, but no one's accusing you of anything."

Clough unfolded his arms and slapped his palms down on the table. "All right, then. Since you already know. We've had a number of break-ins. Padlocks cut through, stuff stolen from sheds. They keep coming back - the last time was just a couple of weeks ago - and you lot are obviously not interested. So yes, I've been going up there after dark in case they come back again."

He was staring at the table, as if the numerous coffee mug rings on the surface were making a fascinating pattern.

"Not something we'd recommend, sir," Baines said.

"Yes, well, you probably know what Doug thought. He said I was taking a risk. Either I'd get hurt, or I'd hurt someone else and get into trouble."

"And did you?" Baines wondered. "Did you hurt someone else?"

"No. As a matter of fact, after Doug left, I thought on what he'd said and concluded that I was being a bit of a silly old sod. Not worth getting my head bashed in for the few old tools in my shed - assuming anyone found them worth stealing."

"So you're saying you left soon after Mr Price and went straight home. Can anyone confirm that?"

"Not unless you can get my cat to talk, no. My wife passed away a couple of years ago, so now there's just me and Betty."

"Betty?"

"The cat."

Collins leaned forward. "Does the name Gavin Lane mean anything to you?"

"Never heard of him."

She showed him a photograph that Marie Lane had let Baines have. He studied it, then handed it back, shaking his head.

"Is this the dead man?"

Collins ignored the question. "Did you notice a yellow van parked by the allotment gate?"

"No. I would probably have noticed, too. It isn't the cleverest place to park, just before a bend."

A registration check, and also Gavin Lane's widow, had already confirmed that the vehicle was the dead man's.

Baines drummed his fingers on the table, thinking. He had a possible suspect here, with no alibi worth a damn, yet there was no real evidence against him. He let his gaze drift over the man opposite him. He might be well into his pension, but he looked strong enough to have hauled a body from wherever Lane was killed to where he was found.

The question remained, why had the body been moved? And why, at the point when Baines had left the crime scene, had the actual killing ground still not been identified? He hadn't been able to speak to Phil Gordon yet, and it was an important point. Something was out of kilter.

"You've been helpful, Mr Clough," Baines finally said. "You're free to go. We'd like a set of fingerprints, for elimination purposes, though."

"And that's it? After all this sitting around?"

"I'd also appreciate it if you didn't go far without letting us know."

"Oh, well, I'll cancel the round the world cruise, since you asked so nicely. And I take it you think this dead bloke was thieving from us when someone gave him more than he bargained for."

"I can't go into that."

"No. Just as you probably can't go into why the police are disinterested when decent people are being robbed, but are quick enough to give those same decent people the rack and thumbscrews when a thief gets what's coming to him."

He rose and Baines and Collins followed suit.

"Interesting to hear you say that, Mr Clough," Baines said. "Is that what you think about the deceased? He got what was coming to him?"

"Listen," Clough said slowly. "Whoever killed him, it wasn't me. But if he was the nasty bit of work who's been cutting our padlocks and stealing our stuff, then whoever stopped him deserves a medal."

* * *

Gemma Lucas sat at the kitchen table picking at the ham salad her mother had put in front of her by way of a lunch. Her dad had brought her home, grabbed a cup of coffee, then gone off to work.

At least Mum was leaving her alone, giving her space to grieve. No one could know how much she had lost in Leigh. The one true friend she'd ever had in the world. When Gemma had started senior school, she'd quickly become a target for bullies, because of her dumpy figure. Everyone else either joined in the bullying, laughed from the sidelines, or turned a blind eye, probably just grateful it was someone else on the receiving end.

Not Leigh, though. She'd stepped in, remonstrated with the bullies, done her best to shame them, even looked prepared to mix it with them if necessary. There had been belligerence, that was true, even a bit of pushy-shovey, but in the end her tormenters had gone in search of easier prey. From that moment, Leigh had become her friend and protector. They might have been an odd couple to look at, but they actually had a lot in common - their interests in music and TV shows, their sense of humour, even their ability to enjoy companionable silences as much as chatter.

And they had told each other almost everything. Gemma knew Leigh had secrets that had gone with her to her grave, but that still left masses of shared confidences, from silly little things to really big ones.

Now Leigh was gone, and she felt lost without her. Worse still, she felt she hadn't done all that she should have to help the police catch her friend's killers.

That van. She hadn't even remembered it until the Sergeant had taken her back through it. Was there more in her memory that hadn't been unlocked? Had there been something about the occupants that she had recognised after all?

That buried memory had unsettled her at the time, and now it triggered a scary new thought. If she had registered the van, even fleetingly, she must have looked at it, if only for a second. What if the people inside had seen her looking? What if they were scared now that she would say something that would give them away?

A cold little finger of fear ran down her spine. What if they came for her next?

Suddenly she didn't want to remember anything else.

She nibbled a leaf of limp lettuce. She wished Leigh was there to talk to. She would understand.

A tear slid down her face. Life was never going to be the same again.

12

Last night, Archer had done some digging online about the chapel at Little Aston. There wasn't a great deal, but it appeared that there had been something of a religious resurgence in the village during the 19th Century, leading to the formation of more than one non-conformist church there. In the latter half of the century, a local landowner had financed the building of the property now known as Little Aston Chapel.

As she and Ross got out of the car, Archer took in the condition of the building and judged that wealthy benefactors were a thing of the past. The slightly damp, musty smell inside added to the impression of decay barely held in check.

Baines had described Marc Ambrose for Archer, and she thought he definitely lived up to his billing. He reminded her of the actor, Rufus Sewell, who she'd always had a bit of a thing about, but was possibly an inch or two taller - she'd read somewhere that Sewell was about six foot, and she fancied that Ambrose was nearer to six two. As she and Ross entered the chapel, his eyes seemed to probe her soul when he looked at her, and she had to admonish herself sternly not to go all girlie.

Ross seemed equally impressed, but - thankfully - equally iron willed. So far.

The man with him, who was wielding a broom, looked about 50 - ten or so years older than Ambrose - and was in many ways his physical opposite. The pastor was tall and built like a ballet dancer. The other man was probably no more than five eight, but looked solid and muscular under his white shirt, like a former boxer who had kept himself in shape. He had close-cropped hair and a bullet-shaped head. His nose looked as if it had been broken on at least two occasions.

The two men were similarly attired, almost like a uniform: White shirt, dark, plain tie, black suit, polished black shoes.

The pastor's eyes twinkled as he walked towards her, a hand outstretched.

"You must be DI Archer and DS Ross," he said. "Although I don't know which is which."

Archer made the introductions.

"I'm Marc Ambrose. And this is Colin Crawford, one of our fellowship."

"Pleased to meet you." Crawford's voice was gravelly, with more than a hint of London's East End about his accent.

"Can we offer you anything?" The pastor's tone was light and almost without an accent of any kind. "Tea? Coffee? Juice?"

"Juice would be good," Archer said. "If it's no bother."

"Yes, juice, please," added Ross.

"Would you mind, Colin?"

"Course not."

Crawford disappeared into what Archer assumed was a kitchen. Ambrose gestured to the rows of seats that faced the simple altar at the end of the room.

"Not quite take a pew, I know," he said, "but please make yourselves comfortable." He waited whilst they sat down. "You said you wanted to talk to me about poor Leigh Fletcher?" He shook his head. "Terrible thing to have happened. Our whole congregation is reeling. And you think it was murder?"

"It looks that way, yes."

"Dreadful. Her poor family. I haven't known what to do." He frowned. "I know they didn't come here, nor go to the rivals up the road." Archer assumed he meant the local Anglican church. "When people aren't overly religious, you don't know whether attempts to offer comfort will make things better or worse."

Colin Crawford returned with two glasses of juice and handed them to the two women as if he was serving vintage champagne. Then he stood there, arms loosely by his sides, as if awaiting his next command.

"So how can I help?" Ambrose asked as they took their first sips.

Archer swallowed a mouthful of juice.

"You can start by telling us all about Leigh's relationship with the chapel."

Ambrose nodded. He came and sat down beside Archer. Colin Crawford continued to stand by like the world's ugliest dumb waiter.

"We met at Andrew Marling's victory celebration in 2010, after he got elected to Parliament. I don't normally mix with politics, but he hadn't been a bad councillor, and he was inviting community leaders as well as supporters, so I thought - why not?"

"How did you get talking to her?"

"I was just circulating - being an ambassador for the chapel, I suppose, and - if I'm honest - trying to drum up business. She was sitting in a corner with her sister. They both looked like they'd rather be in a cage full of tigers. There was something lost about Leigh, so I sat down beside her. Probably made some sort of a bad joke. I seemed to make some sort of connection. She showed a bit of interest in what we do here, and I hoped she might come along, maybe even bring her sister."

"But she didn't"

"Not then, no. But then, quite a while later - a little over a year ago, I suppose - she appeared at one of our services. Maybe the Holy Spirit had a hand in it."

Archer searched his face for some sign of conceit or insincerity. She didn't see it, but that didn't mean it wasn't there.

"Mr Ambrose -"

"Marc, please."

"All right, Marc then. You must know you're a pretty good looking man. She was an impressionable young girl. Do you really think the Holy Spirit would have been what drew her to you?"

He shrugged. "I've always thought that physical beauty is only skin deep, Lizzie - may I call you Lizzie?" His gaze lingered on her scar, and suddenly her left cheek felt as if it was burning. She had to fight the urge to touch it.

"Whatever stopped her from making her excuses and leaving as soon as I sat next to her at that party," he continued, "we can't escape the fact that she soon started asking me about the chapel, and why it's different to C of E."

"Which is?"

"That's a difficult question. Superficially, we don't go in for funny costumes, and we certainly don't do bells and smells." He frowned. "So we're more stripped down than what you'd call the mainstream churches. But, more importantly, I'd say maybe we place a bit more emphasis on forgiveness of sins and welcoming the Holy Spirit into our lives. And on placing our faith in what the Bible teaches us. Anyway, she came to us in the end. After that first service, I chatted to her over tea and biscuits and it was clear we had made an impression on her."

"The service, or you?"

"I'm just a mouthpiece, so arguably there's no difference."

"And Leigh kept coming back?"

"The second week, she arrived early, and helped put the hymn books out. The third week, she helped with the teas, and I was starting to see a very different girl to the lost soul who caught my eye at Andrew's party."

"And her relationship with you, as her preacher?" Archer wanted to know. "Did you become close?"

"I'm close to all my congregation."

Crawford abruptly took a pace forward. His arms were still at his sides, but his hands had balled into fists.

"Careful, Marc," he said in a low rumble. "Can't you see what they're trying to do?"

Ambrose gave him a slightly amused-looking glance.

"And what would that be, Colin?"

"They're trying to imply there was something improper between you and Leigh."

"Really?" He turned his piercing gaze on Archer, causing the whole of her face to burn now. "Is that what you're trying to do, Lizzie?"

She took a moment to compose herself. It took a greater effort than she would have expected.

"I'm just trying to piece together the truth."

"Well, that is the truth, whatever rumours you may have heard -"

"We've heard no rumours."

"No?" His eyes twinkled again. "Well, whatever. I love all of my congregation, just as I try to love those who haven't found their way yet. I do God's work, and it's God who draws people to this place, not me." He smiled. "You two should come one Sunday. It may be what's missing in your lives."

It was as if he had seen into her soul. She felt naked before him, and she blushed at what might have been revealed to him. Embarrassment turned to anger.

"You think there's something missing in my life, do you?"

"Every life has something missing, if they haven't known God."

"Well, I'm just fine," she told him.

"I'm pleased to hear it."

She realised that Crawford and Ross were looking at her. How had this man managed to turn the conversation and make it about her? Shaken, she reached for a question that would get the interview back on track.

"Did you ever see Leigh outside chapel?"

He looked amused again. "Do you mean see her as in see her out and about? Or see her as in private, the two of us getting together?"

"Just the two of you, one on one. Maybe some private Bible study?"

"The answer's no, Lizzie. She never asked for anything like that, and I wouldn't offer. I know how people talk in this village, and I know how vulnerable someone in my position can easily make themselves. The newspaper headlines are littered with priests who have been accused of improper behaviour."

Ross dived in. "In fairness, *Marc*, they're also littered with priests who actually have abused their positions of trust and influence."

"And you think that's what I did with Leigh?"

"You tell us."

"That's enough," Crawford said. "Please leave."

"We can easily do this at the station," Ross said, a tad more aggressively than Archer thought necessary.

"That won't be necessary," Ambrose said. "I've nothing to hide. I didn't see Leigh other than at services, and our relationship was nothing it shouldn't have been."

"Is there a Mrs Ambrose?" Ross said, mercurially changing the subject.

"No."

Archer had recovered her poise sufficiently to take up the questioning again. "Did you always speak to Leigh after the service?"

"Absolutely. She was finding God, and it was my job to help and encourage her on her journey. As it is with all my little flock."

"And how had she been recently? Had you noticed a change in her mood?"

He frowned. "Possibly."

"In what way?"

"Hard to say. I felt she was a bit preoccupied. I had the feeling she was struggling with something. To be honest, I'd all but made up my mind to ask if I could help in any way, but I left it too late." He studied her face again. "You don't think that had anything to do with her death?"

"We just don't know. And you have no idea what it was about?"

"I wish I did."

Archer nodded and then changed tack. "Did she ever talk about boyfriends?"

"No. As far as I knew, there wasn't anyone. Surprising these days, especially for such a pretty girl. I can't imagine there was any shortage of suitors."

"What about before? Did she ever hint at a relationship when she was a bit younger? Something that had ended?"

He smiled ruefully. "Not much help, am I?"

Archer thought she had probably got as much out of this interview as she was going to. She started to rise, and then sat down again.

"What about you, Mr Crawford?" She addressed the shorter man, who looked startled. "Anything to add?"

"Me? No."

"And where were you both between 11 pm and 2 am on Friday night?"

"Me?" the pastor came back immediately. "I was watching music documentaries on BBC4. They have some great stuff on a Friday night."

"I'll take your word for it. Mr Crawford?"

"I was fast asleep."

"Can anyone verify that?"

"You mean am I married? No, inspector. I'm a widower."

"Oh. I'm sorry."

"My wife was knocked down on a zebra crossing five years ago. It was soon after that happened that I found God, and He helped me get through it."

It was the longest speech Crawford had made since they arrived, but it left Archer feeling awkward.

"So, no," he continued. "No one can verify that I was tucked up in bed between the hours you mentioned. Not that I can imagine why I might want to kill Leigh."

"All right. Thank you both."

She gave them each a card with a request that they get in touch if anything else occurred to them. Back in the car, she asked Ross for her impressions.

"I don't know, guv. The pastor's too bloody pleased with himself by half. If he was ice cream, he would have been licking himself. He tries to do all this 'beauty's only skin deep' bollocks, but it's blindingly obvious he thinks he's God's gift."

"But do you think he was involved with Leigh?"

"Honestly? I don't know. If everyone who was the target for young girl's crushes - if Leigh even had a crush - went on to sleep with them, then half the population might be in trouble. I just thought he was too glib."

"What about Crawford? What did you think of him?"

"Creepy. I could imagine him doing anything for his beloved pastor. Probably without question."

Archer looked at her. "Really?"

"I think the local ladies aren't the only ones who have crushed on Marc Ambrose. I'm not saying Colin Crawford is gay, although there may be a latent subtext there. I'll bet that God getting him through his wife's death translates into Marc Ambrose getting him through it, and I'll bet he feels a massive debt of gratitude."

Archer thought about what the DS was saying.

"You think he might murder someone to get Pastor Marc out of a difficult situation?"

"I'm not going that far, guv. I do think we ought to keep it in our minds as a possibility."

"Okay. Let's do a bit of quiet digging on Mr Crawford. See if there's anything of interest."

* * *

Graham Endean's Princes Risborough home was an older style detached in a quiet cul de sac. His wife, Rachel, was an attractive brunette who made coffee for Collins and tea for Baines and brought it into the living room with water for her husband and a plate of home made muffins.

"I'd imagine you're always eating on the run," she said, "especially during a murder case. Help yourselves."

Baines needed no second invitation and reached for a muffin and a paper napkin. "Did you know Leigh, Mrs Endean?"

"No, not really. I mean, I meet all of Graham's protégés - the odd fundraising event, that sort of thing. A bit of small talk. But the training he does is his thing, like any job. I don't get much involved, so I don't really get to know the swimmers."

He nodded, taking in the room. Cool, clean and neutral. Creamy leather sofas. Maybe a reflection of the lady of the house. He imagined that Rachel Endean was the decision maker when it came to decor.

"Still, you must have gained an impression."

"Quiet, nice. Very focused on her sport. Maybe not the happiest of girls sometimes."

He swallowed a piece of muffin. "What makes you say that?"

"No more than a feeling, really.

Collins chipped in. "You don't get a feeling out of thin air, Mrs Endean. You must have seen something."

Rachel closed her eyes, evidently pondering this. She opened them again. "You're right, of course. All I can say is she seemed a bit withdrawn, preoccupied, on some of the occasions when we met. Maybe unhappy isn't the right word." She was still standing by the coffee table. "Anyway, it isn't me you've come to see. I'll leave you to it."

"For the record," Baines said, "where were you on Friday night?"

"Out with friends," she said immediately. "Dinner, a few drinks."

"Late?"

"We were home by eleven, I think. Our next door neighbour was putting rubbish in his bin, and can vouch for us."

Baines glanced at Collins and back at Rachel Endean. "You didn't have to think about that."

She smiled. "When we knew you were coming, Sergeant, it was obvious you'd ask us that."

She left. Her husband gave them an apologetic smile.

"I love her dearly," he said, "but she can be a bit fanciful. She's a serial attender of weekend courses. Psychology, studying people's auras... She thinks she can read people."

"Well," Baines said, "we don't so much do the auras thing. But, as detectives, we like to think we can read people too."

"Good to know."

Collins offered him the plate of muffins, but he waved it away. "Don't tempt me. I demand that the people I coach stay trim, and I need to watch my own waistline."

"Practicing what you preach?"

He gave her a thin smile. "So how can I help? I couldn't believe it when I heard that Leigh's death was being treated as suspicious. You think she was murdered?"

"It looks that way, yes," said Baines.

"Christ. Still, it makes more sense, in a way, than her getting herself drowned by accident. She was one of my best, you know. She would have gone to Rio." His voice caught. Baines asked himself if the emotion was genuine or affected. Couldn't be sure either way.

"How long had you been coaching her?"

"Since she was 12, so about four years. I knew some people at her club, they got in touch, and I took a look. She was a natural, the best I'd seen at that age since Christine Lindsay." He saw their blank looks. "You don't follow swimming?"

"I googled you," Collins said. "Bronze medal at Atlanta. Silver in the Commonwealth Games at Kuala Lumpur. Impressive."

"It could have been better, but we didn't have the funding. The sport got a big investment for the London Olympics in 2012, but it's been slashed again now. Anyway, Leigh wasn't quite ready for London, but she was on course for Rio."

"It must be a blow to you, professionally," Baines said.

"As a coach, I thought I'd been lucky having Christine. To have had two great talents in my career... Yes, it was a professional loss, but a personal one, too. Leigh was a lovely girl. Sure, she had some times when I thought she had a few problems, but what teenager doesn't?"

"She never confided in you?"

He picked up his water and toyed with the glass, making no move to actually drink from it. "No. I guess I was an old fart to her. Our relationship was purely professional. I worked her hard, and she always followed my guidance."

"So you wouldn't say you were close?"

"A close working relationship, sure, but we weren't what I'd call friends, if that's what you mean. At least, I hope you're not implying anything closer, if you get my drift."

Baines let that one go. "When did you last see her?"

"Tuesday evening. We had a session in the pool."

"Anything different about her?"

"Not that I noticed. But then Rachel's the aura reader." Another thin smile.

"Any contact since then?"

"Yes. She called me - it must have been Friday morning - to confirm our session for today. I would have been seeing her tonight." The corners of his mouth turned down and his eyes welled. "I'm sorry."

Baines took a few sips of his coffee, allowing the man time to compose himself, still trying to decide how genuine the emotion was. It seemed real enough.

"Mr Endean," he said when he had but his cup down, "we've heard that Leigh went through a particularly unhappy time a couple of years ago. Did you notice that?"

"You couldn't not. As I said, she was a teenager, so I didn't set any store by it. I didn't try to find out what was going on in her life. So long as she applied herself to her swimming - and she did - that was where my responsibility began and ended."

Baines wondered if he might be making a little too much of the coach/athlete relationship not being personal, but short of asking him outright if he'd had a sexual relationship with the girl, he saw little mileage in pursuing it further at this stage.

Of course, he could ask the question outright, but he wasn't convinced that he would be able to tell a lie from a truth with this man. Despite a few hints of emotion, Graham Endean seemed a bit too much of a cool - cold, even - customer to betray himself. Maybe he would crack under real pressure, but they were not at a stage where that was appropriate.

"Where do you stand on performance enhancing drugs?" he asked abruptly.

Endean blinked. "I hate them. It's against every sporting ethos I've ever stood for. If I thought one of my people was using them, I'd kick them off my books in a heartbeat. I've never had anything to do with them and never will."

The interview ended with Baines and Collins handing Endean their cards and urging him to contact them if he thought of anything.

In the car on the way back to the station, Baines asked Collins what she made of the coach. Her impressions were similar to his own.

"Worth checking up on that Christine Lindsay he mentioned," she said. "The name rings a faint bell, but I don't know why. She might give us an insight into how he works."

"Good idea. Do you think he's a suspect?"

"Do you?"

He pursed his lips. "I know I'm a bit on the fringe of this investigation, but this is a strange one. I still don't think we know nearly enough about our victim, let alone who might have harmed her. Maybe Lizzie's afternoon has unearthed something."

"Or Jason's school visit."

"I'd have liked to see that. I bet he delegated all the interviews with female students to the uniforms. All those young hormones presented with a nice-looking young chap like him... He'd have looked like a beetroot the whole time."

"Will you come to Lizzie's evening briefing?"

"Might as well, if only to report back on Endean. It depends on when Dr Carlisle is ready to do the post mortem on the Lane case."

The Lane case. Not as open and shut as had been imagined, but no leads and the trail already cooling. The reality of effectively leading the investigation seemed less appealing at the moment. At least in Lizzie Archer's team there were people you could bounce thoughts off, others out there digging up bits of jigsaw.

Maybe he was doing Ashby an injustice. Maybe he really did have contacts connected to other allotment break ins, connections that could shed some light on the darkness. Or maybe the DI was simply skiving.

He'd thought it would be a quick arrest, an easy cleanup that would be to his credit. Now it was already looking like a potential unsolved, something some future cold case investigator would pore over and conclude that the hapless DS who had been given the reins had been hopelessly out of his depth.

That wasn't going to happen, he resolved. He had - perhaps stupidly - promised Mrs Lane that he would catch her husband's murderer, and he was determined that he would.

He needed to press Phil Gordon, as soon as he got a chance, for anything forensic that could help make a dent in the case.

13

In the event, Baines's phone had rung just as he and Collins arrived back at the station. Barbara Carlisle would be starting the Gavin Lane post mortem within the hour, and would he like to attend? So Baines had dropped Collins off and set off for Stoke Mandeville.

"I can cover what Graham Endean said, no problem, guv," Collins assured Archer.

"I'm sure," Archer said. "Right, I was only waiting for you, and Dan if he could have made it. We need a catch up, I think. Can you ask all the team to assemble in the briefing room in about ten minutes? Best put your head round the DCI's door, too. I think he might want to sit in."

Archer thought she just about had time to make a coffee before the meeting. She returned to find Stephen Ashby standing by her desk.

"I don't suppose you know where the fuck Dan Baines is?" he demanded.

"Why, Steve..." She gave him the sweetest smile she could muster. "I'm not the one to ask. Isn't he part of your empire at the moment?"

He jammed his hands into his trouser pockets. "You tell me. I heard he'd gone off on an errand for you."

She smiled again. "Oh, that? That was just a little quid pro quo."

"In English?"

"I let Joan accompany him when he was interviewing a suspect in your case. He returned the favour. Before he was diverted onto your case, I'd asked him to talk to Leigh Fletcher's swimming coach, and I had no one else to send. It's done now, so he's all yours. That was all right, wasn't it?"

"You should have asked me."

She made her eyes wide. "Oops. But really, Steve, I had no idea where you were."

"Try my mobile next time."

"I heard you never have it on."

"Shit phone, shit battery, that's all," he blustered. "If you see him, tell him I want him. And don't sidetrack him again."

"I won't. I'd hate you to have to tell tales to Paul."

He looked torn between sarcasm and outright abuse, but finally walked away without another word. Archer grinned and sipped her coffee. Ashby may be a shit, but he was easy to wind up. It could be fun sometimes.

She drank about half her coffee and carried the rest into the briefing room with her. Gillingham was seated at the back, looking more than a little grumpy.

"So, Lizzie," he said as DC Bell, the last to arrive, planted his backside on a chair. "Tell me you've got some sort of breakthrough. Please?" he added hopefully.

"I think we're making progress, sir, but it's too early for it to all come together, I'm afraid."

"So what *have* we got?"

"Okay," she said. "As you know, DS Ross and I spent a fair chunk of yesterday talking to Leigh's family, and especially her sister and her sister's boyfriend. We also interviewed her friend, who may have been the last person to see her before she met her killer. I'll take you through it, but I'd be grateful if Jenny can fill in any gaps I manage to leave. DS Baines has managed to speak to Leigh's swimming coach but, as you know, sir, he's been called away to a new case. So DC Collins will brief us on that interview."

She ran the meeting through the main points of the interviews with Hayley Fletcher, Kyle Adams and Gemma Lucas. Leigh's mysterious boyfriend, who may or may not have been an older, married man. Hayley Fletcher's possible resentment of her parents' perceived favouritism towards Leigh. The feeling that each of the three had been telling less than the whole truth.

When she invited questions, Jason Bell's hand went up.

"Not a question, guv, but a bit more information," he said. "You mentioned Gemma's neighbour, Mrs Cooper."

"Oh, yes. I wanted to make sure she was spoken to during the door to door. Any joy, Jason?"

"Yes and no, guv," admitted the Scot. "She vaguely remembered seeing a van parked across the road when she came back from walking her dog. The uniform who talked to her got the impression she's a bit nosey, and wondered if someone was having work done."

"And were they?"

"No, guv. Besides, Mrs Cooper thought it was late at night for workmen to still be there, and she noticed there were two people in it. Didn't take much notice of them, though. Not even sure if they were men or women."

Archer turned to Ross. "About as observant as Gemma Lucas. But then, why would she, or Gemma for that matter, have taken that much notice?"

"My daughters are grown up," Gillingham commented. "They still go around with their eyes shut half the time. Do you think any of this is even relevant, Lizzie?"

"It at least merits a follow up." Her gaze slid back to Bell. "Colour? Registration?"

"Not much help there. It might have been white, or grey, maybe cream, but the light was poor. She didn't look at the number plate."

"Marvellous," growled Gillingham.

"CSIs are looking at Kyle Adams' family vehicles," Archer said. "There's a van he uses sometimes. If he and Hayley acted together and Dr Carlisle got her time of death slightly out, that's a possibility."

"For that matter," Ross added, "the timing works better if Kyle met Leigh after he dropped her sister off home, although that raises a gap of around 90 minutes where we don't know where Leigh was, or what she was doing."

"That was the other thing I wanted to mention," Bell said. "Not too much to go on at the school. Some of the kids are still very upset, some are morbidly excited to be associated with a murder. None of them came across as suspects, although there were a couple of lads who admitted to asking Leigh out and getting the brush off. She did it very politely, by all accounts." He blushed. "Ah, there was one Jack the Lad who speculated that... well, that Leigh and Gemma might have, you know..."

"Spit it out, for Christ's sake," Gillingham rumbled.

"Sorry, sir. He thought they might be, well, lesbians. But I got the impression he'd think that of any girl foolish enough to turn him down."

Archer twisted the cap of the pen she was holding. "Was he angry?"

"As in murderously, guv? I didn't think so, and I got no hint that he was covering anything up."

"Could there be a grain of truth in his lesbian fantasy?"

"Not unless Gemma and Leigh hid it really well. Which I don't think so. Here's a thing, though. There are two other girls they're friendly with. Hang out with them in the breaks sometimes. Names of Cathryn Rooke and Shannon Derry. Cathryn said Leigh came in upset a month or so ago after a family wedding. It seems Kyle asked her to dance a slow one, was dancing far too close for comfort, and Hayley made a scene."

Archer looked thoughtfully at the board, drew a line between photos of Leigh and Kyle and wrote 'Row at wedding?' next to it.

"Interesting," Ross said. "He got quite stroppy when we asked him if he had the hots for Leigh."

"Stroppy or defensive?" Archer questioned. "Of course, it could have been a storm in a teacup that Kyle and Hayley have forgotten."

"I sort of doubt that."

"Either way they didn't mention it."

"Relevance?" Gillingham demanded.

"It opens up some possibilities, sir, surely," Archer said. "What if Kyle had followed up on his advances at the wedding? Something happens behind Hayley's back, Leigh threatens to tell."

"Or," Ross put in, "maybe Hayley's still jealous. Kyle puts the blame on Leigh for leading him on, and Hayley eggs him on to punish her sister for it."

"All a bit dramatic for a teenage love triangle, don't you think?"

Archer fiddled with her pen again. "I don't know about you, sir, but when I was that age, anything to do with romance and sex had an intense, end-of-the-world quality about it. We've seen plenty of kids - especially girls - in this job who've got themselves into horrendous situations by imagining themselves in love." She shrugged. "I'm not saying Kyle and/or Hayley are necessarily prime suspects, but we neglect the power of teenage love at our peril."

"The idea of teaching her some sort of lesson," Collins ventured. "It plays well with her drowning in a bath. I mean, this Kyle works with his dad as an electrician, right?" Archer nodded. "So maybe he's rewiring a house while the owners are away, has a key. He lures Leigh there, or takes her against her will, maybe wants to scare her. He holds her under water in the bath - maybe Hayley's an accomplice, maybe he has a mate."

"But it all goes wrong?" Ross speculated.

"Exactly. Now he's got a body on his hands at a client's home. He thinks of the quarry, dumps her there in her underwear so it will look exactly what we first thought it was."

"A late night swim gone horribly wrong," Gillingham said. He nodded slowly. "Someone had better check what properties young Mr Adams has access to."

"One for you, Joan," Archer said. "Your idea, you follow it up."

"Me and my mouth," the DC grinned, eliciting laughter.

"There's also the question of the pastor from the local chapel," Archer said. "Marc Ambrose." She recounted hers and Ross's interview with the preacher and his friend or colleague - she wasn't sure what to call him - Colin Crawford.

"We need to do some more digging there," she concluded.

"Anything else?" demanded Gillingham.

"Not at the moment, sir."

"All right, I suppose. But, really, it sounds like there's nothing I can say or do for the moment to get the new Minister off our masters' backs, or our masters off ours."

"We need a break. Some useful forensics from a house or flat Kyle has access to, or from one of the Adams' vehicles. Something on Pastor Ambrose or someone else at the chapel, or the coach, Graham Endean. Beyond that, there's still the stranger scenario - that she was taken at random." She squared her shoulders. "We'll keep plugging away, sir."

Gillingham scowled. "All right." He heaved his frame out of his seat. "I'll go and explain to the Super yet again how we can't manufacture evidence out of thin air. You'd best get us that break, DI Archer."

"I'll do my best, sir."

* * *

The car was parked in a layby in a quiet country lane, its driver fiddling with a Smartphone. A second vehicle pulled in behind it and the driver got out and walked to the passenger side of the first car, climbed in. The phone disappeared into a pocket.

"Close the windows," the new arrival said.

"It's hot."

"Close them anyway."

There was a faint hum as the windows rolled up.

"Why all the cloak and dagger?" asked the person in the driver's seat. "Why drag me out here to talk?"

"To make a point. Because this is a conversation I really don't want anyone to overhear by some fluke or be able to lip read on any CCTV later."

A shrug. "So what's it all about?"

"There's a chance the police are going to ask some awkward questions soon, and you don't want to be giving them the wrong answers."

"What sort of questions?" Then, more quietly, "What sort of answers?"

"I think you've got an idea already. Now shut up and listen."

So the driver shut up and listened. Long before the other had finished speaking, the blood had drained from the listener's face.

"Why did you need to tell me that?"

"That's rich. You haven't said you mind what's happened, just that you'd rather not know about it."

"Exactly. If I don't know, I can't say the wrong thing."

"Yes, I thought about that. But you're so stupid, you're likely to put your foot in your mouth without realising what you're doing. No, it's better this way. If you know the score, you know what not to say and no one can trip you up. At least, they'd better not. Because I won't be the only one going to jail."

"But I didn't know you were going to -"

"Really? You knew I was going to do something, you just preferred not to know what. Well, now you do know. There were problems, I cleared up the mess, just like I always do. Only it's a bit less tidy than I'd have liked."

"I still can't believe it."

"Oh, do me a favour. When you heard what had happened, you must have put two and two together. You can't always expect bad things to go away without any shit sticking to you. Besides," the speaker went on, "I'm not sure I've finished yet. There may be one more loose end I need to take care of. Then you can relax and try not to mess up again."

"What other thing?" Wide eyes.

The occupant of the passenger seat smirked. "Now, that really would be telling."

* * *

"This is interesting," Barbara Carlisle murmured.

"What's interesting?" Baines asked.

Gavin Lane's corpse had been turned on its front. The pathologist was examining the back of the head. "These injuries. There's a lot of damage from a sharp object that might well be the edge of a spade blade - so, strictly, we're not talking 'blunt' force trauma."

Baines shrugged. "But you're confirming that it was the spade that killed him."

"That's what's interesting. I can't say for sure that the blows from the spade actually were severe enough to have caused his death. These, on the other hand, would almost certainly have proved fatal."

Baines was not one of those police officers who felt relaxed in the mortuary, but he'd attended enough post mortems to be able to put any natural squeamishness aside. He leaned in close, looking at the place at the back of the head to which the pathologist was pointing.

"Do you see?" she said. "All these gashes that the spade may have inflicted are relatively superficial. But these," she traced the area she was focusing on, "these are two massive blows with a very blunt instrument. You can almost make out its shape."

"So what do you think it was?"

"Oh, God, you're asking me to speculate again. Well, I'll indulge you on this occasion, only because I've seen something like it before. My suspicion is that it was a baseball bat."

Baines looked more closely at the indentations in the back of Gavin Lane's skull. He could see quite clearly the how the width tapered from top to bottom. Yes, it was probably the right width.

"So he was battered with a spade, then the bat was used to finish him off?"

"That's the other interesting thing. Looking at the wound pattern, I'd say it's more likely he was struck fatally with the baseball bat, then battered - in all probability post mortem - with the spade."

"But why do that?"

"I deal with the dead, Dan. You catch the killers. It's called division of labour."

He ran his eye down the back of the corpse. "These abrasions on the back and buttocks... Could they have been caused by dragging?"

"Almost certainty. Probably post mortem again."

"So the body was moved. This is all feeling weird." He took his phone from his pocket. "Can you excuse me for a moment?"

He stepped out into the corridor and keyed in Phil Gordon's number. The crime scene manager answered on the third ring.

"Phil, there's something I'm seeing in the post mortem that doesn't make a lot of sense," Baines said. "Have you had a chance to match those prints on the spade to Clough yet?"

"It's a match all right. But there's some blood on the handle, and the pattern's a bit odd."

"In what way odd?"

"I'd say whoever was hitting Mr Lane over the head with it was wearing gloves."

"So Clough's prints..?"

"It's probably his own spade. It's an old one. A number of the allotments had spades just left stuck in the ground."

Baines rubbed his forehead. "I don't suppose you found a baseball bat?"

"A what? Why?"

"Dr Carlisle thinks there was one used in the attack. That it might in fact be the real murder weapon."

"Well, we didn't find one, and we searched all the sheds."

"Did you find the actual killing ground?"

"No. And that worries me."

Suspicions were starting to form in Baines's mind.

"What's happened to that yellow van of Lane's?"

"It's in the pound. It's evidence of sorts, although -"

"Can you check it over, please?"

"What are we looking for?"

"Any possibility that Lane wasn't the last person to drive it. And especially any possibility that he might have been in the back. Check for blood. Any other traces you can find."

"Seriously?"

"Seriously, but don't spread it around. Lane's body was dragged to where it was discovered, and you've found no trace of where he actually died. Suppose he was killed somewhere else entirely? His head bashed in with a baseball bat, then driven to the allotments in his own car, dumped there, and a clumsy attempt to make it look as if an allotment holder killed him with a spade."

"They'd have had to have planned it well enough to have thought of bringing along a set of bolt cutters."

"Any prints on those?"

"No," Gordon admitted. "They look brand new and have been wiped clean."

"I doubt that Lane, in his death throes, would have had the presence of mind to wipe them."

The crime scene manager nodded. "I'm liking your theory. I'll check it out. But that would mean the killer was aware of the break-ins."

"Yes, well. I think Len Clough's antics were all over the village, and you know this part of the county. People like a good gossip and a good story. No doubt half of Thames Valley knows about it, so we can't assume it's just a local thing."

"You think they used Clough's spade to frame him?"

"Not necessarily out of malice towards Clough. More to assume we don't look elsewhere."

"Then it's someone who knows which is his plot," Gordon pointed out.

Baines let this sink in. "You're right. I'll need to find out who would have known." He pondered. If Lane hadn't been caught in the act of pilfering the plots, what had got him killed? "Let me know when you've got something on that van."

"Will do."

They hung up and he returned to the post mortem.

"I don't know what else I can tell you, Dan" Carlisle said. "Healthy man, reasonable physical condition. One minute, contemplating his evening. The next, a one way ticket to my mortuary slab."

As a police officer, Baines had always been more aware than most of the narrow tightrope everyone walks between life and death. Stepping off the pavement without looking, a lapse of concentration whilst driving, some other bugger's mistake behind the wheel, one more fatty burger to block the last tiny opening in an already clogged artery, an obstacle left on the stairs...

In his time, there were not many ways of changing one's status from living to deceased that he hadn't come across. With so many options available for leaving this life behind, it seemed almost unsporting for murderers to intervene with their own variations on life's uncertain theme.

"So what's your next move?" Carlisle asked him.

"I think I need another chat with the widow," he told her. "This guy wasn't what you'd call whiter than white, and he must have mixed in some dubious circles. I need to know more about who his associates were. Maybe he's been involved in a job in the recent past and it's led to this. Thanks, Barbara. This is really helpful."

"No extra charge," she said with a grin.

14

Baines called it a day at around 8.30 pm, feeling punch drunk and isolated. Running a one man murder inquiry without a senior officer to back him up was a situation he would have relished back when he was acting up for his last boss, before DI Britton died and Archer was brought in. But this felt all wrong. He just knew he was likely to be hung out to dry if the investigation turned to worms.

He'd returned to the station and almost bumped into Ashby as he walked into the building. The DI had torn him off a strip for doing the Endean interview without clearing it first, and then demanded to know what was happening with the Lane case. Why hadn't Len Clough been charged?

Baines had half expected him to explode when he heard that, far from being charged, Len Clough hadn't even been arrested, but for once he was surprised. Ashby listened while he outlined his theory that Lane had been murdered elsewhere and then dumped at the allotments.

"Christ," he muttered. "Paul wanted this cleared up quickly. Run me through your evidence again."

So Baines repeated himself. The lack of blood at the allotments, the fact that the murder weapon was almost certainly not the bloody spade, but something like a baseball bat. The illogicality, in the circumstances, of the spade and the brand new, clean wire cutters being found by the body.

"Fair enough," he said finally. "It's not so inconsistent with my own inquiries."

Normally, the idea of DI Stephen Ashby making actual inquiries would have had Baines stifling a guffaw, but he was intrigued and asked what he'd found out.

"As you know," Ashby told him, "I've visited most of the allotments where there have been break ins over the past four months. Waste of bloody time, but it kids them that we've got time to give a monkey's about the precious tools they choose to keep in a shed with a cheap padlock for protection." Baines winced. "Anyhow, it's obvious this is the work of some small-time pilferer who's got a market - probably down the pub, or some car boot sale - for this stuff. From what you tell me, Lane doesn't fit the profile."

"Lane's wife - widow - found it hard to credit," Baines said. "Didn't think it was his style at all."

"I have to admit, when I visited Little Aston allotments, I met Clough. He talked a good fight about what he'd like to do with these people, but I thought he'd most likely run a mile if confronted with an actual thief. I suppose anyone's capable of lashing out in fear, and he might have taken a baseball bat on patrol with him."

"But if Lane was killed elsewhere, that blows that idea out of the water."

"What's your next move?" Ashby made a show of looking at his watch.

"I'm hoping something shows up in Lane's van. If the killer's bodged this attempt to pin the murder on Clough, then maybe he's made other mistakes."

"Sounds like you've got it under control." The DI patted Baines's arm. "Got to go. We must have another of these catchups tomorrow."

Baines had watched in disbelief as the man sauntered away, got in his car, and drove off. For a moment there, he'd almost felt they were acting like a team, discussing the case. Now he wondered how much attention Ashby had even been paying. Still, at least he hadn't resisted Baines's instinct to shift the focus away from the allotments, and Len Clough.

But as he sat in his living room, gloomily contemplating beans on toast in front of the TV, Ashby's question came back to him. What, indeed, was his next move?

If he got lucky, Phil Gordon might find some evidence on the van. At least confirmation that it had been used to transport

Lane's corpse from the actual murder scene to the allotments. Maybe, if they got really lucky, some prints or DNA that matched something on the national databases. One thing he was sure of: it seemed unlikely that anyone from the allotments would have been responsible for the man's death.

So someone else had wanted Gavin Lane, dead. But why? Had he been in some sort of trouble: gambling debts? Talking business to the wrong sort of people? Stealing from the wrong people, maybe?

His wife had been the first to admit that he had been a bad boy, and even that she didn't always know what he got up to. But she had been at a loss to know why anyone would want to kill him.

The killers had tried to disguise what had actually happened as a vigilante killing, to pin it on Len Clough. Was putting Clough in the frame significant, or was he just a convenient patsy, thanks to his reputation for late night patrols? Was it all about deflecting any investigation from the real killer, or could some malice towards Clough be involved?

Baines had reached a point where he really needed to talk over where he had got to with the investigation. If he'd been part of a normal team on this one, and not a one man band, there would be a briefing tomorrow to look forward to. As it stood, all he had was Ashby, and he knew damn well that, even if he could get the chain-smoking DI to afford him a little more of his valuable time, he was unlikely to get any incisive insights.

He also knew that if he didn't get results, Ashby would make damn sure he shouldered all the blame. He had spoken to Gillingham about getting some augmentees from elsewhere to give him some support. There had been some vague talk of maybe finding a DC from somewhere, but he wasn't holding his breath

Easy talk from a man who seemed to cut his old pal more than his fair share of slack.

He took out his phone and scrolled through his numbers. Lizzie Archer was about halfway down the list, just after Karen. He stared at her name for a long moment before pressing the 'call' key.

It took so long for her to answer that he was about to hang up, convinced the number was about to go to voicemail. Then she picked up, stating her name.

"Lizzie, it's Dan."

"Oh, yes?" He could hear the caution in her tone.

"I wondered..." He hesitated. What had possessed him to call her? It wasn't as if they had the easiest of working relationships. Her being less awful to work with than a shit like Steve Ashby wasn't exactly a glowing recommendation. It didn't make her the ideal person to call in times of trouble, but he could think of no one better.

"Any chance I could find out *what* you might be wondering, Dan?" she demanded. "Or is this the latest guessing game craze? Do you have to guess what I wonder next? I'll give you a clue. It has to do with why on earth you rang me at home, apparently to say nothing."

"I'll just go then, shall I?" he snapped.

"Up to you, mate." She sounded amused. "You rang me, remember? Look, I'm fucking tired. I dare say you are, too. But if you need something, I'm here to help."

He was half-tempted to simply hang up, but he knew that would be unfairly taking out his frustration on her. It could damage their improving work relationship. Besides, he knew she had pretty good instincts, especially compared with some of the alternatives for brain-picking.

"Sorry," he said, "difficult day. Probably at least as bad for you, I know. But being on a case with Ashby is - well, I don't have to draw you a picture."

"Like working with the invisible man?" The words were barely out when she sucked her breath in sharply. The words hadn't even had a chance to sting him before she was babbling apologies.

"Lizzie," he said, then louder, "*Lizzie!* It's fine. Really. All this dancing on eggs is hopeless anyway. We can't go on doing it. I mean, I know you didn't mean the Invisible Man as in wife-murdering, child abducting psycho. Even Ashby's not that bad."

She gave a weak laugh. "So what did you want?"

"I, um, wondered if you could spare me an hour or so this evening? I could bring over a bottle, and maybe a takeaway if you haven't eaten. I'd really like your thoughts on the case and what I ought to do next."

"Oh. I was planning a shower and an early night."

"Never mind -" he began.

"Yeah, but what the hell? Make it Chinese and you're on. A nice white wine, please, and plenty of prawn crackers."

"You're sure?"

"Yeah. You might as well witness how little progress I've made here since moving day, and I can update you on the Leigh Fletcher case. How long will you be?"

"I'll order the food now. They'll say it'll be twenty minutes, which is about as long as it'll take me to get there and pick it up. I'll be with you in less than half an hour."

"Perfect. I'll be able to squeeze that shower in after all."

* * *

When she answered the door, her hair was still damp, and she had a towel in her hand. She wore a pale blue towelling robe and, by the look of it, not much more.

Baines stood there holding his brown paper bags, feeling a little uncomfortable about the situation, and also a little sad. Once you got used to seeing the ruin of one side of her face, you realised what an attractive woman she had been before the incident that had disfigured her.

"Barely had time for that shower after all," she was saying, holding the door open. "Well? Are you coming in or not?"

He walked in, noting the unopened boxes in her hall without comment, and waited for her to close the door. She pointed to the kitchen.

"Take the food in there. I'll put the oven on and you can stick the containers in to keep warm."

They went through and he put his bags on the work surface.

"Make yourself busy," she said as she fiddled with the oven knobs. "You'll find some plates in that cupboard." She waved a vague hand. "There's some beers in the fridge, or glasses in with the plates if you want to open that wine you brought. You can start sorting it all out while I put some clothes on." She was still fiddling with the cooker controls. "Damn. Why are these things so bloody complicated these days?"

He saw that it was a fairly new Neff oven, similar to the one Karen had splashed out on last year when her old one had died. He'd used it a few times, whereas he sensed that Archer had yet to make use of hers at all. In fact, the whole house still had a temporary, almost camping out, feel to it.

"I know how these work," he said. "Let me."

The dials on the oven were flush with the housing, but slid out when pressed, ready to turn and twiddle. The large one in the centre selected the type of cooking you wanted to do, and another, smaller one controlled the temperature. As he reached for the former, his hand brushed hers. He hastily withdrew it.

"Sorry."

"What about?" She frowned. "Are you turning this oven on or what?"

"There you go," he said when the fan whooshed into life.

"You'll have to talk me through that later. Back in a tick."

She disappeared, and Baines busied himself transferring the food containers from the bags to the oven and wondering why he'd been so momentarily flustered by that brief physical contact. It came to him that, apart from a handshake on her first day at the Vale, he couldn't remember them ever touching. Here, in her home, with her barely dressed, it had seemed a strangely intimate gesture, even though it had been accidental.

He found the plates and put those in the oven too, to warm. Left to his own devices, he made a brief tour of the ground floor of Archer's new home. The furniture from her London flat didn't seem to fit in, and was all exactly where he and Archer had virtually dumped it on Saturday morning. Nothing had been rearranged, just as it seemed that only a small handful of boxes had been unpacked.

He knew only too well how utterly a murder investigation could consume a detective. There were never enough hours in the day, eating was haphazard and often on the run, and you arrived home exhausted.

Still, the unlived-in feel of the house seemed sad, even though he instinctively knew that, if there was one thing Lizzie Archer would never forgive him for, it was feeling sorry for her.

What a pair of misfits we are, he thought. *Lizzie carries her scars right there where everyone can see them, and mine are so deeply buried most of the time that no one who didn't know me would know they were even there.*

The thought brought back last night's dream. There had been dreams before, of course, but there had always been some connection to the waking visions - particularly the QPR shirt. But in this dream, Jack had worn that suit. And he had spoken.

"I... can't. He'll... I just... can't."

What was he to make of it? His son had looked terrified of someone, but who? Or what?

Were the dreams and the waking visions all part of the same thing, or were the dreams just dreams?

Suddenly, he wished he hadn't come here. Tomorrow would have been soon enough for a chat with Archer. He could have hooked up with Karen, the one person he could tell all this stuff and not feel like an idiot. Instead, he was spending an evening with a Detective Inspector he still didn't feel he knew especially well, certainly not well enough to open up to about his private life.

"Where are those beers?"

She came in, wearing a pink shirt top with short sleeves and a white collar, and a pair of shorts.

"Sorry," he mumbled, moving to the fridge. "Miles away."

"Let's eat," she said. "I'm bloody ravenous. Talk afterwards, yeah?"

She dumped a couple of mats on the kitchen table and they spread the takeaway containers out. They settled on beer from the bottles, rather than wine.

For a few minutes, they concentrated on helping themselves and eating. Baines realised that, as well as no touching, they had never really done small talk either. He decided to steer clear of talking about their actual respective cases, but to settle on the relatively solid ground of a common dislike.

"Needless to say, I haven't seen Ashby hardly at all today," he remarked. "Have you?"

She shook her head whilst chewing, then swallowed a mouthful of beef with black bean sauce. "Not much, apart from complaints about you doing that Endean interview. But you know our Steve. God's gift to networking."

"All these contacts - half of who seem to be on the wrong side of the law - seem to be able to tolerate him more than we can."

"Well, I don't care, so long as he keeps out of my way."

"So, how's the house? Feeling at home yet?"

"To be honest, Dan, it's just a place to lay my head right now. With any luck, I'll start straightening things out at the weekend. Always assuming I can get any weekend, of course, with this case."

"Have you met your neighbours?"

"No, basically. They've already marked me down as an antisocial cow, I dare say. Not villager material. I doubt I'll be invited to the next barn dance, or witches' coven or whatever it is they do for fun around here." She cocked an eyebrow at him. "How long did it take you to get accepted, Dan?"

He laughed, nearly choking in the process. "Me? Accepted? Oh, everyone knows I'm a copper. They know what happened to my family back when..." He shrugged. "It was Lou who got involved, right from day one. I had no idea how many friends she'd made until she was gone. I've never had time for any village activities, nor the inclination, come to that. It's not obligatory."

"No, but I suppose there's something to be said for feeling part of a community. If you like that sort of thing," she added.

" Maybe when I've retired and I'm an old fart in a flat cap. I'll get an allotment myself and start frequenting the flower and produce show, entering my prize marrows and getting all grumpy if I don't get first place."

She closed her eyes for a long moment, then opened them again, shaking her head.

"Nah. Can't picture it somehow. Anyhow," she said abruptly, "you're my first guest here, and we haven't touched these beers yet. So, cheers."

She raised her bottle and he clinked his against it.

"Cheers. To your new home."

"Maybe I'll get a cat. What do you think?"

"I'm allergic to cats."

"I'll definitely get one."

He wasn't certain if she was joking or not. He swigged his beer and set the bottle down on the table. He was about to take another forkful of food when his phone rang. The display told him it was Karen.

"Do you mind?" he asked Archer, and got a shrug in answer.

He walked away from the table and into the hall.

"Are you home yet?" she asked after he picked up. "I wondered if I could come round."

He badly wanted to see her. "Well," he began, "I'm at Lizzie's right now, but..."

"Lizzie? What, your boss lady?" There was a momentary pause. "Twice in four days. Sweet."

There was something about her tone. "What do you mean, sweet?"

"She gets a house and suddenly you're always round there. Cooking you dinner, is she?"

"No. We're having a takeaway. And I'm hardly always here." He didn't understand. "Sorry, what's the problem?"

"What problem could there possibly be?"

"I honestly don't know. Look, it's hardly dinner. Just something to eat and then we're going to talk about a couple of cases. What if I swing by on my way home? Maybe we could have a chat then."

"No, you're all right. Have a nice night in with your girlfriend. Sorry I interrupted."

Baines was stung by the hostile note in her voice.

"Look," he said, "if you need me to -"

"Don't worry about it."

"Karen -"

"Don't *worry* about it!"

"Look," he said again, "I need to talk to you, too. I'll make some excuse and come now."

But the line had gone dead. He looked at the phone screen. 'Call ended', it said before returning to the main screen. He fleetingly wondered if she had lost signal, but he knew she had hung up. He was stunned. It almost sounded as if Karen was jealous. Of Archer?

He contemplated calling her back, but he knew the sort of sulky mood she would be in. It would be more grief than it was worth. Maybe he'd call around after he left Archer's place, depending on how late it was by then.

Upset and distracted, he went back into the kitchen. Archer was helping herself to more rice.

"Everything okay?" she asked.

"Yeah, that was just a friend. I might go round and see her after we finish here."

Archer looked as if she was seeing him in a new light. "Girlfriend?"

"Not exactly. It's complicated. She..." He tailed off, really not wanting to discuss his relationship with his sister-in-law with her. "She's just a friend."

"Must be a good friend if you're planning on popping round so late at night. I mean, it's half past nine now."

"So tell me about the Fletcher case," he said, shifting subjects abruptly.

She looked about to press him some more about his phone call, then shrugged and started digging into the sweet and sour pork.

"We're no further forward," she admitted. "We can't narrow down why, or in what circumstances, Leigh met with her death. We've almost got too many theories, and I can't begin to narrow down the possible suspects. It's four days since her death, and we've basically got nothing."

He chugged down some beer. "Okay. Theories first."

"Theories first. Well, there's this mysterious white van that her friend, Gemma said was parked opposite her house when Leigh set out for home. Uniforms have asked around, and no one had a visitor with a white van that night. Only one neighbour even saw it, and she's such a crap witness, she can't even recall the colour. But frankly, it's just as likely the van wasn't even involved.

"Then there's the fact that she's not a virgin, may well have had sex when she was under age. Was an older man responsible, or someone her own age? All we know for sure is that she became moody and then cheered up when she joined chapel. Gemma thought she was seeing someone inappropriate and the moods started after it ended, but that was her guess. She could be way off beam. I think it's possible that she was moody about something else."

"Maybe she got cheerier when she started going to chapel because the good looking pastor was giving her one for a while," Baines remarked. "Then it stopped for some reason, and he killed her - or had her killed - because she started threatening to tell on him. What does your gut say?"

"He fancies himself, that's for sure. Would he kill to protect his reputation? I don't know. But he's got this creepy mate, Colin Crawford. I can't quite fathom their relationship, but I reckon Crawford would do quite a lot for him. There might be a gay thing going on, or it could be just some sort of blind loyalty."

"Could it be something a bit less sinister? Something to do with other kids? Maybe from school?"

"She was generally popular, but probably not universally," Archer told him, her mouth half-full. "One of the lads had a theory that Leigh and Gemma were more than just good friends. That could give rise to a number of motives. They had a tiff and Gemma killed her. She'd have had to slip out of the house to do it, but she's quite a big girl. She might just be strong enough to force Leigh under, although I couldn't say for sure."

Baines took another swig of beer. "That all sounds a big stretch, though."

"It does. An alternative is one of the boys at school asked her out, got the bum's rush, and decided to teach her some sort of lesson."

"Maybe..." But he was doubtful.

"I swung by the swimming hole on my way home. They're holding some sort of vigil. I've got names of a number of regulars there, but I don't know..." She pushed her plate away.

"The kids who found her?"

"Yes, I know." Often the person who reported finding a body turned out to be responsible for the death. "But their alibis checked out. Friends and family can vouch for them, right through the doc's time of death window." She paused for thought. "Mind you, I understand they sneaked out of their respective homes on Saturday morning without their families realising they'd gone. I guess they could have sneaked out earlier, but why call it in? And where would they find a convenient bath or sink to drown Leigh in? What's the motive?"

He frowned. It sounded too thin to credit. "No chance the father did it? Maybe he was abusing her and she was going to tell mum."

"His wife would have to be alibiing him, which I frankly can't see at all. Then there's the sister's boyfriend. Something happened at a family wedding, it seems, that suggests Kyle Adams may have fancied Leigh. Maybe Kyle didn't like being rebuffed. Or maybe Hayley was jealous."

"Didn't we wonder if they both might be involved?"

"Another piece of unsubstantiated speculation, yes. That maybe they'd picked her up in his car or van and driven... I don't know, somewhere. Maybe they had access to a house or flat. Something happened and she drowned in a bath. Then they chucked her in the quarry. But Phil Gordon's team have found no evidence on the vehicles Kyle has access to."

"Doesn't mean it didn't happen."

"We'd wondered if Kyle and his father were rewiring a house. Maybe it was empty, they had the keys. But the dad says definitely not." She frowned. "There's one other piece of possible evidence. Phil says there were oil stains on Leigh's clothing. It's just possible that they came from the boot or back of a car or van when her body was being transported, but he says actually matching them to anything would be a nightmare. Besides, the interiors of the Adams family's vehicles are apparently spotless. The old man's got a thing about looking after his cars and vans."

"Wait a minute, though," he said. "How certain are you that they're from a vehicle she was in that night? I'm not saying they're not, but it seems to me you need to narrow the lines of inquiry down. If the oil does point to a vehicle, that at least probably eliminates her 16-year-old classmates. Not old enough to drive."

"Good point. Unless they were joyriding of course."

"Yes, that's possible. My point is, are we sure they're related to a vehicle at all? Because if the oil's incidental - say she could have slipped over in the street and picked up some oil from the road - then it's a red herring and their absence from her sister's boyfriend's car or van doesn't rule them out."

"Hmm. The sister wasn't quite as devoted to Leigh as we were first led to believe, and now we've got that wedding incident. I also wondered if Kyle could have met her by accident after dropping Hayley off."

"So there's one, maybe two, potentially serious suspects to focus on. Now, what about this pastor and his mate? You didn't really say whether you liked him for it or not."

"I'd quite like it to be him, to be honest. It would wipe the self-satisfied look off his face to be led away in handcuffs, and I can see why he might have done it. And his alibi's shaky. So is Crawford's."

"You need to find out more about them and their backgrounds."

"I've already got Jason digging. We should have some feedback at tomorrow morning's briefings."

"Ah," he sighed theatrically. "A briefing. Luxury! Trouble is, I think Gillingham's main focus is obviously the tragic teenage girl known personally to the new Home Office Minister. If he can clear that up and some poor sod of a jobbing builder with form is left as a statistic... well, I reckon he can live with that if he has to."

"Will it come to that though? You said you'd like to talk it through."

He briefly outlined his progress, or lack of it.

"So," she said, when he'd run out of words, "you're convinced this Clough character had nothing to do with it?"

"What would have happened if Doug Price hadn't happened upon him and made him rethink the wisdom of his stakeout is anyone's guess, but no. I believe him when he said he went home. Using his own spade and then leaving it at the scene, trying to move the body for no obvious reasons, the lack of any evidence that Lane was actually killed there... it all points to a bodged attempt to make it look like a vigilante thing."

"So the question is, if Clough didn't kill him, who did?"

"And frankly, Lizzie, I've got nothing at the moment. No idea where or how he met with his killer. No idea what the motive was for his murder. All I know is, I'm convinced it wasn't random."

"You've got Phil Gordon checking out the van. Maybe that will yield something. One thing's for sure - your killer is an amateur. He's made mistakes that we know of, and he may have made more."

"I hope so," he said gloomily.

"Have you talked to Lane's associates?"

"First I need to find out who they are." He shook his head. "This is fucking ridiculous. A DS trying to go it alone with a full-blown murder inquiry."

She took a gulp of her beer. "Look," she said, "make some use of Jason Bell for a day or two."

He looked at her, surprised. "Are you sure?"

"I'll try and manage without him. You need to speak to Lane's wife again. Really find out all about him. Who's who in his life, past and present. Draw up a list of people who need to be spoken to and start working your way through it with Jason. Somewhere in there you might find either your killer, or your motive, or even both. But then you knew all that."

It was true. There was a lot of work to be done, and there were no shortcuts. So why had he been sleepwalking through this case like a man wading through treacle?

The answer came back to him instantly. Too much else on his mind: feeling like a slightly spare wheel on the Fletcher case, for sure, and what he now saw as his self-pity at being unsupported by Ashby and Gillingham on the Lane murder. But also the disturbing new dream about Jack. Just to make matters worse, now it seemed Karen was going weird on him.

"And you're sure you can spare Jason?" he checked.

"No, but I'll let you know if I need him back. Jenny, Joan and I will have to take up the slack, that's all."

* * *

Jenny Ross pointed the remote control at her TV set and shut it off. The news had been as depressing as ever, and she intended to spend half an hour reading in bed with a cup of hot chocolate.

Her cat, Norbert, followed her into the kitchen, always on the lookout for a treat. Whilst Ross made her drink, she thought about the last couple of days, deciding she was enjoying working with DI Archer, who came across as a good boss and a good detective. Ross was wishing she could stay on the team. One thing was for sure. She was determined to give this case her all and show what she was capable of.

Mind you, she wouldn't mind working more closely with Dan Baines, who had been switched to another case. She'd always liked him. Okay, she'd always fancied him. The job had always got in the way of relationships for her, and there was something to be said for a partner who understood.

"Who am I kidding, Norbert?" she murmured, stroking the cat, who had now sprung up on the work surface. The word around the station was that Baines still mourned his wife, more than a decade on. After what had happened to his family, she thought it a miracle he functioned as well as he did. He'd gone on to gain promotion to DS and even done a stint as acting DI.

Baines and Archer - both had suffered in their way. She judged by the way Lizzie Archer's hand often strayed to her scar that she was very self-conscious about it.

She sometimes wondered what the office gossip was about her. She knew she had made a fool of herself that time with her ill-judged snog with Ashby - a creep she ordinarily wouldn't give the time of day. But she'd had a little too much to drink, he was flirting, and playing along had seemed like a good idea at the time. It had gone too far, and she was sure that lowering herself in that way had undermined her in her colleagues' eyes.

In the job, bad reputations were more easily won than good ones, and there was rarely any going back. She'd French-kissed Ashby far too enthusiastically in front of colleagues, and one of them had been Baines, who had avoided eye contact with her for days afterwards. At least Archer didn't seem to judge her.

As she carried her hot chocolate off to bed, she wondered, not for the first time, whether she should try online dating. There was even a site for people 'in uniform' to meet people who liked that sort of thing. She instinctively thought that was a bit creepy, smacking of naughty nurses and hunky firemen - and besides, she was plain clothes these days.

The thing was, even if she gave it a go, the chances were that the job would get in the way of half her first dates, let alone any sort of relationship.

She set her cup down on the bedside table, slid between the sheets, and picked up her book. Norbert stretched out at the foot of her bed and purred.

"Yeah, okay, Norbs," she murmured. "Fair point. You're the only man in my life, and that's how you like it."

15

After Baines's departure the previous evening, Archer had unpacked a couple more boxes whilst she thought about their conversation. It had been good to kick their respective cases around, and it had made her determined to try to whittle the potential suspects down to a few serious contenders, and see if they could be discounted before looking at the less likely ones. What they had been doing thus far was, she supposed, a bit too like throwing every conceivable name and possible motive in the air and seeing how many landed written side up.

And the strongest contenders did appear to be Marc Ambrose and Kyle Adams.

Before the meeting, she had got onto Phil Gordon again and asked if scenes of crimes could see if they could at least determine whether the oil traces found on Leigh's clothing came from the inside of a vehicle or from, for example, a road, a driveway, even the edge of the quarry she had been found in. He hadn't held out much hope. Oil trace was not like DNA. Getting an analysis was one thing; but, even if they had the vehicle in front of them, with similar oil stains, the chances of getting a definitive match that would stand up in court were slim.

He was, however, able to say that the Adams family's vehicles were all clean. At first, her interest was piqued.

"You mean they've cleaned them? Even though I told them not to?"

"No, no," he said quickly. "I don't think it's anything like that. All I mean is, all the vehicles are well looked after - even the van. There are barely any older stains inside, let alone new ones. I'd say that, if Leigh Fletcher has been transported in any of their vehicles - dead or alive - then that isn't where the oil stains on her clothing came from. They could have come from anywhere, Lizzie."

It didn't definitely rule the Adamses out, but she was no nearer to making a case against any of them either.

She'd collared Jason Bell first thing and asked him to give some support to Baines, but she had also asked him and Joan Collins to do some background digging into Marc Ambrose and Colin Crawford. The pair found her in the briefing room with Ross, mid-morning.

"Sorry to interrupt, guv," Bell said, "but we thought you'd like an update on that research you asked us to do."

"Ambrose and Crawford?" He nodded. "Please make my day. Tell me you've got something."

"Some interesting stuff, actually. I've been focusing on Crawford. He's done time."

That got her attention. "Really? What for?"

"It seems his wife was killed on a zebra crossing in 2008."

"Yes, he told me."

"Then you'll know."

Archer lifted an eyebrow. "Know what?"

"Oh." Bell reddened. "You don't know then."

She folded her arms. "Is this going to take all day, Jason?"

"Sorry, guv. It seems the driver who knocked her down just wasn't paying attention. He pleaded guilty to causing death by careless driving. The court accepted it was a one-off, momentary lapse and handed down a community order."

"And Crawford thought that a tad lenient?" Archer had an inkling of what was coming.

"I'd say so. Two weeks after the trial, he tracked down the driver, lay in wait outside his home, and beat the holy shit out of him in his front garden. Might have killed him if neighbours hadn't intervened."

"Custodial sentence?"

"Six years. He served three."

Archer absorbed the information. "So he presumably kept his nose clean inside. A capacity for quite a bit of violence, by the sounds of it, but who knows what state of mind he was in when he did it?" She fingered her scar, conscious that of how easily life can turn on a single instant in time, whether a driver's inattention, or a moment of red mist.

"No other form. And it seems he wrote an apology to his victim from prison. Even sent him money by way of some reparation."

"How do we know this?"

"Because the guy wrote to the authorities asking them to let Crawford out as early as they were able. It seems he was really cut up about that one horrendous mistake he made."

"And now Crawford's evidently got religion."

"Here's the thing. Towards the end of his sentence, Crawford met Marc Ambrose."

She stared at him. "Ambrose was inside, too?"

"No, guv. He was an official prison visitor. From what I've been able to piece together, Ambrose made quite an impression on him. If you believe it, Crawford appears to have found religion and turned over a new leaf. After he came out, he moved to Little Aston and became a regular and hard working member of Pastor Marc's chapel."

"And no new additions to his criminal record?"

"No, guv."

"So how's he making his living? I assume the chapel isn't paying him?"

"No, but he's been working quietly enough in a hardware store in Tring."

"Convenient for him." Tring was about four miles from Little Aston, just over the county border into neighbouring Hertfordshire. "Good work, Jason. Anything else on Crawford?" The DC, blushing as ever, shook his head. "Now, anything on Ambrose? Any criminal past there?"

"I've been checking on that," Collins said. "Nothing on record - except that, before becoming a preacher, he was a teacher, but he left the profession after some problems relating to one of his female pupils having a crush on him."

"How do you know this?"

"The police were called in at one stage, but they decided there was probably nothing in it. The story is that the pupil developed an infatuation and became convinced that her feelings were reciprocated. She started stalking him, weaving a fantasy relationship with him and telling friends about it."

"Fantasy?" Archer echoed. " I wonder. Did Leigh Fletcher have a 'fantasy' relationship with him too, one that stretched beyond her imagination?"

Collins glanced at her notes. "On the face of it, Marc Ambrose was entirely innocent. There was not a shred of evidence that he had ever done anything improper with that pupil or any other, but it's pretty clear that the school had a no smoke without fire approach. One way or another, his position became untenable, and he quit."

"Interesting."

"So we were thinking," Bell said. "Suppose our pastor was lucky to get away with it when he was teaching? Suppose there was fire as well as smoke? Now fast forward to more recently. Leigh Fletcher gets the teenage hormonal hots for the pastor, and he can't resist. Then things change - either he dumps her, or maybe she comes to realise it's wrong and threatens to tell. What would Crawford do for the man he looks up to?"

"Let's not get ahead of ourselves," Archer said. "I think we certainly need to know more about the pastor's subsequent history, and also his relationship with Crawford. But it's a good line of inquiry."

She turned to Ross. "Jenny, I want you to chat up Crawford. Find out all about his time since prison. And Joan," she looked over at Collins, "take away the paperwork Jason's gathered so far and find out more about the fascinating Marc Ambrose. How did he make the transition from teacher to cleric? Did he have any more teaching jobs, and what happened there? Who else did he visit in prison? It might or might not be relevant but, either way, I'd like to know for completeness."

She dropped by Gillingham's office soon afterwards to bring him up to date. He listened, face long.

"So what are you saying?" he asked finally. "That Kyle Adams is out of the running, but the local chapel minister is the prime suspect? Because I'm not seeing a great deal to suggest either."

"No," she said, "I'm not saying that. Honestly, boss? We're at that point you sometimes get to in an investigation where we're just spinning wheels. We desperately need a break. If there's something you think we're not doing that we should, I'd be the first to want to know."

"No, you're probably right. More's the bloody pity. One thing we might try, though. What about a press conference, with the family? There's nothing jogs people's minds like an appeal for witnesses by bereaved relatives."

"A good point, sir," she agreed. "I'll talk to the press office. Someone may just have seen something. Would you be part of that?"

He waved a dismissive hand. "No. You're the lead officer. You can front up the press conference. You should know, though," he added, "I had the lovely Claire King from the *Echo* on the phone this morning. The case is on the front page this week, and they're already thinking about next week's edition, so we may as well show that we're taking it seriously, leaving no stone unturned."

So that was it. Gillingham was always quick to worry about the PR dimension. With the local paper nosing around, and the possibility that the nationals might pick up on it, the last thing he'd want would be accusations of slackness.

"I've got two questions then," she said.

"Quickly, then. I need to see the Super in ten minutes."

"First, shall we come right out at the press conference and say we think Leigh was either deliberately or accidentally drowned elsewhere, before she wound up in the quarry?"

He sighed. "It's time we did. We don't seem to be getting very far by not shaking the tree a bit. Second question?"

She fingered her scar self-consciously. "The press conference itself. I think it's a good idea, but am I really the right person to lead it?"

"Why wouldn't you be?"

She wanted to tell him how reluctant she was for her horror mask of a face to be on national news. How it might be a distraction from the messages they wanted to get over to the public. Yet she had a feeling he already knew this. So what was he saying? That her scar shouldn't stop her doing her job like any other officer?

Or was he punishing her in some way? For what, though?

"It's your case, Lizzie, pure and simple," he said. "You know more about it than I do."

That hadn't stopped him before. And then it occurred to her that, in a case where a newly appointed government minister was taking a keen interest, Gillingham might actually fall over himself to let someone else field the questions.

She was prepared to bet that, if the case was resolved in a good way, it would be Paul Gillingham standing in front of the cameras talking up his division's success. If it all went to pot... well, Lizzie Archer would be the unforgettable scarred face of the investigation.

Suddenly, the thought of setting up that press conference felt like organising her own firing squad.

* * *

The weather showed no sign of cooling down and the small meeting room was stuffy and uncomfortable. Baines felt sticky and irritable. Phil Gordon, by contrast, looked cool in an open-necked pale blue shirt and a pair of oatmeal trousers.

"First of all," the crime scene manager said, placing a large clear plastic evidence bag on the table, "the bloody spade we found at the scene. I'm told the blood is definitely Gavin Lane's and we know the spade has Len Clough's prints on it."

"But we also know the obvious scenario just doesn't add up," Baines said, guessing that more was to come.

Gordon placed a smaller bag on the table. "The bolt cutters. No prints on them at all, and as we suspected, they look fresh out of the packaging. If Lane was really up there to rob the sheds, why brand new cutters? That seems odd to me. And besides, surely he'd have planned on taking the cutters away with him, so why bother wiping them?"

"He might have worn gloves for the job."

"He probably did, but would he have tried to get the cutters out of their packaging with gloves on? A bit fiddly, and why would he do it? I could even understand if he'd unwrapped them at the scene, but there's no packaging to be found."

"Maybe they don't come in packaging."

"I thought that, so I checked. They're a very popular brand, can be found in most hardware stores and garden centres and, yes, they come vacuum wrapped. So we have a guy who buys new cutters for the job, unpacks them at home, and then wipes off any prints in case he drops them while he's out blagging.

"Then there's the spade. There are plenty of Clough's prints on it. If he was the killer, why not wipe the spade? Come to that, why even leave the spade behind? No sign of Dr Carlisle's baseball bat. And look here." He indicated some smears and clear spots in the blood on the handle. "My guess? The spade was wielded by someone wearing gloves."

Baines nodded. "Hard to see why Clough would wear gloves to do the killing, then leave a spade with his prints on."

"Especially since, as I said on the phone, a pound to a penny, if you get him in he'll identify it as his. It's a bit of a museum piece. He probably leaves it stuck in the ground and doesn't lock it away - one less reason for anyone to cut off his padlock."

"Maybe the killer knew it was Clough's. Given his mouthing off about sorting out the thief, he'd be the perfect fall guy." He shrugged. "All right. I think we're agreed that Clough wasn't the killer, but we'd pretty much surmised that already. We don't seem any closer to any other suspect.

"Ah," Gordon said, a smile curving his lips. "But there's another mystery."

"I'm all ears."

"Your hunch that we'd find Lane's blood in the back of his own van was right on the money."

"So you reckon he really was killed elsewhere and then driven to the allotments?"

"Seems likely, but that's not the half of the puzzle."

"Tell me."

"We also found traces of blood on the driver's seat and the steering wheel. Not much, and definitely no prints - gloves again, I'd say. But the blood's Lane's, all right."

"So either he drove himself there after his head had been stove in with a baseball bat and then took a spade to his own head..."

"... or, more likely, the killer got some blood splashes on himself during the original attack," Gordon completed. "I'd say we've got a fairly incompetent killer who might have been better off not getting creative."

Baines nodded reflectively. "Maybe. It doesn't tell us why he was killed, nor by who, though. Still, pretty good work, Phil. I owe you a pint."

"It might be two. I was saving what may be the best till last. There were some hairs and fibres in the back of the van that don't tie in with Lane. I'm having them analysed. Don't get your hopes up yet, but cross your fingers."

Baines grinned at him. "If you can get me a suspect, I'll buy you the whole pub."

"You are on, my friend."

He walked back to the main office in slightly better spirits. Last night he'd gone to bed with the case weighting heavily on his mind and, when he tried to push the thoughts away, Karen's obvious upset that he was spending the evening with his boss had caused him more anguish. When he'd finally got to sleep, Jack had haunted his dreams again.

It had not been the same dream as Monday night's. He had been searching for something at Westyate allotments and kept catching glimpses of the familiar teenage version of his missing son, back in his Queen's Park Rangers shirt. Jack would appear from behind one shed only to swiftly disappear behind another. Baines called his name and hurried after him, but it was like chasing smoke. Every time he got to where he had seen the boy, he had vanished from sight, only to reappear somewhere else.

His expression had been unfathomable - sad or frightened, Baines could never tell. He badly wanted to tell Karen, but he wondered if she was even talking to him at the moment.

For some reason, the fact that the case he was working on wasn't going to be as simple as it had first appeared had given him a boost. A case that should have been Steve Ashby's had been dumped on him and, as long as it had looked like a quick clear up, he'd been left to get on with it. He had little doubt that the DI simply saw it as an escape from some tedious paperwork. Now it turned out to be something far more interesting, he just hoped that Ashby wouldn't be falling over himself to take it back, and that Gillingham would not be pressing him to do so.

The spade had been signed over to him, and he spoke to Jason Bell and asked the DC to get hold of Len Clough and confirm that it indeed belonged to him. His next step was to bring Gillingham and Ashby - if he was around - up to date with progress. But his thoughts returned to Karen. He wanted to try to make things right between them, so he headed out to the car park and dialled her number.

She answered immediately and asked him how his day was, with no overt hint that their last conversation had ended badly, but he was convinced that he detected a cool note behind the chatter. He decided to take the bull by the horns.

"Why were you so strange last night, when I told you I was at Lizzie's?"

"It doesn't matter."

"It almost sounded like you were jealous."

She snorted. "Yeah? You wish."

He sighed. "So what did you phone me about?"

"There was something I wanted to talk to you about. It doesn't matter now."

In Baines's experience, when a woman said something didn't matter, the chances were it was something of massive importance to her.

"It was just work," he said.

"What was?"

"Lizzie."

"Why do I care what you were doing with Detective Inspector Archer? It's not as if you and I have a relationship, is it? We're just good friends. Aren't we, Dan?"

He was utterly bewildered. "What are you saying? There was a time, about a year ago, when we might have had something more, but the timing was never right."

"My recollection of that is that I came to your house to say I wanted more than just a friendship. But you had to run because there was a dead body somewhere. Like it was going anywhere for ten minutes. And we lost an opportunity. Again."

He pushed a hand through his hair, sorry now that the conversation was going so badly. "Is that what you wanted to talk about?"

"No, Dan," she said. "Not at all. Quite the opposite. Well," she added, "sort of the same thing."

A Vauxhall Astra squad car pulled into a parking space and the driver gave him a cheery wave. "You've lost me," he said, waving back.

"Then I'll come to the point," she almost snapped. "There's a guy at work I get on well with. Mike, his name is. He asked me out."

He blinked. "And did you go?"

"I put him off. I wanted to talk to you first."

"But..." This was doing his head in. He had no idea what she wanted from him. His permission? For him to beg her not to? "It's not my business who you go out with."

He heard her suck in a breath. "You fucking blockhead. Ever since that will-we, won't-we business last year, I've been waiting for you to raise the subject again. I was prepared to give it - us, I mean - a try, but you've put it off, then put it off again."

His stomach was turning over. "You could have -"

"Could have what?" Bitterness seemed to crackle over the connection. "The ball was in your court. I thought you'd ask me when - if - you were ready. But nothing. Nothing," she whispered. "And then Mike asks me out."

"You could have said all that when you rang."

"I was going to. I actually imagined that, if I asked you first, you'd say, don't go with him. You'd say, choose me instead. But you were too busy snuggling up to the boss lady."

Her words were barely making sense to him. "We were not snuggling up. Look, can't we talk about it now?"

"Too late, Dan."

"What do you mean?"

"I've said yes." He felt as if someone had kicked him in the stomach, but she carried right on. "I deserve more out of my life than I've been getting. I think you deserve more too, but I'm not sitting around my whole life waiting for you to make a move."

He felt sick, yet had no real idea why. He had no claim on her. He had no right to any sort of a say in who she did and didn't see. So why did he mind this so very much?

Because he was in love with her, obviously. He'd never fully admitted it to himself before, but now it was so self-evident that he felt a fool for being so blind.

He took a deep breath. If he tried to think through a response, he knew he'd fumble it again, so he dived in, just letting the words flow. "You know how complicated it is. For us both. But you mean more to me than anyone in the world. I think I mean a lot to you, too. I think we could easily have something good together. Why not put this guy off, and we can talk about it?"

He heard her sigh. "No, Dan. It's too late. Shit timing to the end, I guess. I'm going out with Mike, and I'm going to see whether I like it. End of, my friend."

He didn't know what to do. What to say. It was as if he was watching a train wreck happening in slow motion before his eyes, the train wreck of his life. He felt he was losing her. Losing the best part of himself. He'd wanted to talk to her about Jack. No one else would even begin to understand. He wanted to beg, on his knees if need be. To tell her he loved her, needed her. Would do anything to be with her.

Yet he was struggling for the words and, in the meantime, he'd said nothing in response, and now she filled the gap. "Nothing's really changed, Dan. You were my best friend before this, and you still are, as far as I'm concerned. I'm just moving on with my life. Seeing people. It's not as if neither of us has had what you'd call a relationship since..."

It was true enough. For a while after Louise's death and Karen's subsequent split from her husband, neither of them had dated. Then both had tried seeing other people. All had been disasters, certainly Baines's dates had been, and he had blamed himself. He hadn't been ready emotionally, and now he thought that he had been measuring them all against what he had lost in Louise.

What he could still perhaps have with Karen.

"Yeah," he heard himself saying. "Yeah, fair enough. You go and have a good time. If it works out, I'll have to meet him some time."

"Maybe you could bring Lizzie," she said. And then she giggled.

"Ha fucking ha," he said. "Look, seriously. I'm a fuckup to the end. I hope he's good for you. You deserve something." Intellectually he meant what he said but emotionally he felt as if he was dying inside.

"He seems really nice," she said. "He makes me laugh, and he's really polite, like an old-fashioned gentleman. If he turns out to be gay or boring, or a serial killer, maybe we'll have that conversation after all." Her voice was tinged with sadness.

"Maybe we will. Although, if he's a serial killer, I don't want to know. Deal?"

"Deal. I suppose."

"So when's the big night out?" he wondered.

"Tonight."

"You just be careful."

"Yes, Dad."

He realised that his eyes were prickling with tears close to being shed, and he was about to ring off when she spoke again.

"There was something else. How are you fixed on Friday evening? It's important."

He somehow swallowed his pain and heaved some humour into his voice. "What? Are you going to bring this Mike round for me to vet?"

"Be serious for a moment. Are you still being haunted by Jack?"

"Dreams," he said cautiously. "No more sightings."

"We need to try and lay this to rest one way or another, Dan. It's not healthy."

Like he needed her to tell him that. Like he was happy that things were happening to his mind that hinted at him being not quite sane. "What do you recommend?"

"There's a medium appearing at the Waterside."

He watched a police motorcyclist, in his yellow high-visibility jacket, start up his machine. "I don't follow?"

An audible sigh. "Medium as in psychic. Waterside as in theatre. Name of Philip Weaver. A 'Mediumship Night', it's called."

His hackles rose. "And... you want me to go?"

"I've got two tickets."

"Then I suggest you take Mike."

"Don't be an arse. We - you - need to find out what's going on. You have these dreams, you keep seeing this teenager you're convinced is Jack, even though you haven't actually seen him since he was a toddler. You got angry the one time I suggested you see some sort of shrink -"

"Because I don't need one."

"Well, you sure as hell need something. Because either this stuff means something spiritual, or there's something wrong with you that isn't going to go away."

"And you think some charlatan, who plays on people's hopes and emotions... their pathetic hope that their loved ones are trying to communicate with them... you think that's the answer?"

"Listen to yourself. Tell me you don't, in your heart of hearts, hope - no, believe, actually - that Jack is trying to communicate with you already."

"I don't even know if he's dead."

"But maybe - just maybe - this guy can help. I don't know if he's the real deal, or even if I believe in all this psychic stuff myself. All I'm saying is, why not give it a go? What harm can it do?"

"Apart from wasting an evening?"

"So what if it's a waste? We can laugh about it afterwards. What are you afraid of?"

"Who's afraid?"

"I think you are, Dan. I think you're terrified that you'll hear something you really don't want to hear - and that you'll believe it."

"That's bollocks."

"Is it? Twelve years, Dan. Twelve years, and Jack's body's never been found. We don't know why the Invisible Man stopped after he took him, and we don't know what became of Jack. What we do know is this: for over a year, you've been having these dreams and visions, and it's high time you at least tried to understand them better."

"By seeing a phony medium?"

"He probably is phony, yes. But I've got the tickets now. Come? I can tell you how my date went."

"Unless it was rubbish, I won't want to know. Besides, I'm in the middle of a murder case."

"All right," she said. "If something breaks on the case and you absolutely have to work late on Friday, it can't be helped. Otherwise, come with me. Fair enough?"

"I'll think about it. Look, I've got to go."

"Hot date with Lizzie?"

"Oh, for Christ's sake," he snarled, exasperated.

"Joke. Bad joke. Friday, yeah?"

"We'll see," he said, and hung up. For a moment, on the edge of his vision, he thought he glimpsed a familiar figure in a blue and white shirt. He turned towards it, but there was no one there.

If it had been Jack, then he, like Karen, was not sticking around.

16

The day was passing too quickly for Lizzie Archer's liking. No, she corrected herself, the whole week was passing too damn fast. It had nothing to do with the TV cop show cliché about the first 24 hours after a serious offence being the 'golden period'. She knew this was something of a myth, or at least an oversimplification - the annals were awash with crimes that had been solved by days, weeks, months of hard slog. But the fact remained that Leigh Fletcher had now been dead for nigh on five days, with no real progress having been made.

She had spoken to the family about a press conference and they had been only too keen to be doing something. The irony that Hayley's boyfriend and, by association, Hayley herself, had not been ruled out was not lost on her. It would not be the first time a relative had made a passionate appeal for witnesses to come forward and then emerged as the prime suspect.

On a positive note, she had to admit that Gillingham seemed to be finally getting a grip. Local press coverage was probably playing its part, in addition to the inevitable Marling quotes, and it was only a matter of time before the story hit the national news. The murder of a photogenic young woman might have been enough normally, especially in the summer silly season, but it seemed to have got lost in the noise of Andy Murray's Wimbledon triumph over the weekend.

She called a quick team meeting for 1 pm and persuaded a uniform to nip out for sandwiches, pastries and decent coffees. It was a small gesture, but she hoped it would help the team feel appreciated.

When everyone had gathered in the briefing room and helped themselves to refreshments, she started by asking Joan

Collins what more she had found out about Marc Ambrose's past.

Collins took a quick sip of cappuccino, daintily wiped froth from her upper lip with a paper napkin, then took out her note book. There were a series of small paper tabs protruding from the edges of pages, part of the meticulous young DC's system for finding the notes she wanted quickly. She selected one, opened the relevant page and took a quick glance.

"Right," she said, "I started with the school where he had the original trouble, to see if they were aware of him having subsequent teaching jobs. I reckon it's fairly safe to say he didn't. They were a bit coy about it, but I suspect that, when they were approached for a reference, they found a discreet way of warning other schools off. They would never openly raise the possibility of him being inappropriately involved with a pupil - that could run the risk of defamation proceedings. But nor would they want to be blamed for keeping silent if something went wrong elsewhere."

"You don't know where he applied?" Archer checked.

"No, guv. They weren't that forthcoming. Said they couldn't remember and couldn't find the paperwork. Not sure I believed that. Still, there was one teacher he had kept in touch with, and he'd shared snippets of Ambrose's progress with other staff."

"And?"

"And it sounds like he realised fairly soon that his hopes of continuing his teaching career were zero. He did some bar work here in Aylesbury for a spell."

"That must have meant quite a drop in his income."

"Yes, but apparently he was always going on about what interesting people he met, and the pub in question was often frequented by groups of women."

Jenny Ross couldn't help but smile. "I bet that was a hardship for him."

Collins grinned back. "Put it this way. Reading between the lines, it's likely that more than one of those customers succumbed to Ambrose's charms. The teacher he kept in touch with felt he saw it as a perk of the job."

"Any suggestions that any of them were under age?"

"If they were, nothing came of it. In all fairness, unless they're in school uniform and clutching a cuddly toy, it can be hard to tell sometimes."

Archer tapped her pen on the table. It was a little thin still, but a picture was developing of a ladies' man who just might not have baulked at extending his appetites to quite young women, and who had clearly been in a position of some influence over Leigh. He wouldn't be the first sexual predator to seek out employment that gave him the opportunities he craved.

Which could explain why, when teaching had become closed to him, he had gravitated to preaching.

"So, what about him getting religion?" she wanted to know. "Did his old school know the story?"

"Oh, yeah," Collins said. "A real road to Damascus experience, that was. Seems like one evening the old pastor from Little Aston chapel just happened to walk into the bar by himself. He ordered a fruit juice and got chatting to Ambrose.

"It turned out that this pastor was a recovering alcoholic, who claimed he'd found the strength to renounce drink through God and attendance at the chapel. His faith had led him to train as a preacher, but he still went into bars once a fortnight to test and reassert his resolve. He believed that avoiding temptation was not enough."

"He had to confront it, head on?"

"Confront it, wrestle with it. And still have the will to resist."

"And that impressed Ambrose?"

Collins shrugged. "Put it this way. He turned up at the chapel the following Sunday morning, where - if you believe what he told this other teacher - he had some sort of epiphany. He found God and never looked back. He looked on the half-inebriated women who tried to flirt with him with pity, and followed his mentor's example by renouncing alcohol himself."

"Yet he was happy to sell the stuff?"

"Not for long. After about six months, he left bar work, saying that he could no longer be involved in the sale of booze."

Archer raised an eyebrow. "It all sounds a bit po-faced and holier than thou. Too good to be true?"

"The head teacher said he bumped into him around that time. He said that somehow, in Ambrose, the sincerity shone through."

Ross made a gagging sound, and everybody laughed.

"I'm only repeating what I was told," Collins said. "So, anyway, the next thing you know, Ambrose finds work in a Christian bookshop and the pastor sponsors him in beginning his own religious training."

"We must find out what that entails," Archer said.

"Ahead of you there. Well," Collins backtracked, flicking pages of her notebook, "I did some Internet searches, anyway. Most of the training and development is under the auspices of a local body. It acts, among other things, as a study and fellowship group."

"So does that mean the preacher, once he qualifies, can only operate in the patch where he was trained?"

"No, an accredited preacher has national standing, although the actual appointments are in the gift of senior people."

"Did you find out what the actual training is?"

"Yes, they do a course supported by local tutors. Examination is by continuous assessment. The course itself is organised on a national basis, but the actual training and examination is local."

"How long does it take?" Ross wondered.

"Typically, two to five years. Ambrose took just the two, and soon afterwards the old pastor at Little Aston stood down and Ambrose stepped up."

"And in all that process," Archer said, "is there any CRB check?"

Although the Criminal Records Bureau had been superseded by the Disclosure and Barring Service, old terminology died hard. The aim of the service was to prevent unsuitable people from working with vulnerable groups, including children.

"I didn't get that far," Collins admitted. "But surely they must do? Not that it means any red flags would have appeared against Marc Ambrose. There was never a formal investigation, so no impropriety was established."

"Still," Archer said, "get onto the barring service and see if he was checked. Just for completeness."

"On it."

"I don't like it. Did he really find God, or did he find a role that gives him access to adoring women, especially young ones?"

"Or maybe it's his equivalent of going to a bar in order to prove to yourself you can resist the booze?" suggested Ross.

"Maybe. But what if his resistance was lower than he thought? He briefly embarks on a foolish and illegal relationship with Leigh. What happens when it's over?"

"Say he sees the risk he's taking," said Ross. "It could be jail... certainly the sex offenders' list. Further damage to his work prospects. Maybe she threatens to tell."

"Okay," Archer said. "He's a person of interest then. The question is, if he did kill Leigh, was he working alone, or did he have help? Jenny, what else did you find out about Colin Crawford?"

Ross grimaced. "Nothing, so far. Nothing on line, nor on file, that we don't already know. He's not at home - or, at least, he doesn't open his door, and there's no sign of his car. He doesn't answer his landline or mobile either. Same with Ambrose. I've left voicemails, so maybe one of them will call back."

Archer pondered. "Just out of interest, what does Crawford drive?"

"A white Citroen estate."

She felt a moment's disappointment, then thought again. "Interesting. Easy enough, maybe, to take it for a white van at a quick glance?"

"Maybe."

"Keep trying." She checked her notes. "Joan?"

"Guv?"

"You were going to see if you could find any more about Marc Ambrose's prison visiting. Did you get anywhere?"

"Not really, guv. He was a visitor at Woodhill."

"That's Milton Keynes, yes?"

"That's right," Collins confirmed. "I'm not convinced it's going to be easy to find out who he did and didn't see, though. The guy I spoke to sounded pretty dubious. He said he'd make inquiries, but I wouldn't hold my breath."

"Damn." She thought for a moment. "We know Crawford was there, though, and that Ambrose saw him?"

Collins smacked the heel of her hand against her forehead. "Sorry. I should have checked that. I didn't, and I don't want to assume. I'll get on it."

"Thanks. Although I'm not sure where it will get us, unless it's to get some idea of who Crawford might still keep in touch with. Someone who would maybe help him solve a little problem. Still, worth seeing if you can find out anything."

"There's something else, guv," Collins added. "I tracked down Christine Lindsay. Graham Endean's old protégé."

"Anything?"

"Maybe." The DC passed her some copies of newspaper clippings. Archer skim-read them and then took a deep breath.

"Jenny," she said, "I've got a job for you."

* * *

Baines knew he needed to get a grip on his day but, try as he may, he was unable to keep his focus. In the aftermath of Louise's death and Jack's abduction, more than twelve years ago, he had always seemed able to compartmentalise his life. Colleagues had been concerned that he had returned to work far too early, yet he was somehow able to put all the private horror and misery in a box, seal the lid, and get on with his job. He had not shared concerns, more than once expressed by well-meaning workmates, that this wasn't healthy.

For a long time, things had run on a sort of autopilot until the end of each day, when he walked through the door of his home once more: the home where Louise had died, the home the Invisible Man had violated and stolen his precious son from. Home alone, he had been unable to hold down the lid of the box any longer, and the demons had emerged, capering and giggling.

He could have lost his sanity. He could have retreated into drink or pills.

He had chosen control.

And, eventually, he had been able to keep the lid permanently closed. The box had gathered dust, all but forgotten until just over a year ago, when the dreams had unaccountably started.

If he was asked to name one reason why he had come through it all as well as he had, that reason would have been Karen, and it had nothing to do with her resemblance to Louise - not just her looks, but her voice, her mannerisms, her way of putting things. No, it wasn't that she was a carbon copy of Lou. She understood how he felt, because she was going through the same hell herself. Somehow they had kept each other grounded, and he owed her a debt he could never repay.

He'd always been sure the right moment would come for their relationship to finally move beyond the close friendship it had become, yet that moment had never quite arrived. It was years since their failed attempts at dating other people, and maybe that had made him somehow complacent about her.

Now, suddenly, she was going out with someone else. This Mike. And he was more jealous than he would have believed possible.

Yet, at the very time that it seemed she might be moving away from Baines, she was still looking for ways to help him. This 'mediumship night', if 'mediumship' was even a word. Part of him was angry that she would even imagine he needed that sort of bogus comfort. He had always scoffed at these charlatans who found ways of making bereaved people believe that generalities and educated guesses applied to them and to their lost loved ones. Yet Karen apparently thought it might help him.

And, God knew, he needed help.

He didn't know why he'd been so vehemently hostile when she had told him she had tickets for the show. Sure, it had been presumptuous of her to get them without asking him first, but he'd known her intentions were good, and he'd also known he would wind up going, however much he protested.

Because, didn't a small part of him want to believe that some psychics were genuine? Were indeed able to communicate with the departed? He ached to know that Louise was at peace and to glean any news of Jack that he could get; to know once and for all whether the dreams and visions were entirely in his head, or a manifestation of something real.

Meanwhile, Karen had a date, and he hated the idea. He already had a mental picture of this Mike: dark, good-looking, suave, perhaps a bit too smooth, a bit too flash. Someone asking for a slap, in fact.

Whenever he thought of this imagined man and Karen together, he found that mental images of them kissing, and worse, soon followed, and he burned with jealousy. He wanted to call her, to try and persuade her to change her mind. To give their own relationship the chance they'd never quite given it before.

She was the woman he loved. Why in God's name had he never told her that?

Yet part of him resisted the notion of intervening, of trying to stop her slipping away from him. How would he feel if she turned him down? Utterly rejected, he suspected. And where would they go from there? An awkward friendship, bumping along the bottom until it petered out? It would be more than he could bear.

Mercifully, Jason Bell interrupted his tortured thoughts.

"Sorry to disturb, Dan, but I thought you'd want to know. Phil Gordon was right. Len Clough made no attempt to deny that the bloody spade was his when I showed it to him. He always leaves it on the plot, stuck in the soil, where anyone can get hold of it. Says its an old thing, not worth the bother of putting away."

Baines nodded. "So anyone attempting to disguise wounds inflicted with a baseball bat and deflect attention onto the allotment holders would have found just what they needed there."

"He says it's not the only spade left out, but the plan would work even if you didn't know which was Clough's. We'd just think the killer was another allotment holder, or perhaps that Clough had used someone else's spade, simply because it was closer to hand when he decided to jump Gavin Lane."

"Both are possible," Baines nodded. "But the real killer made too many mistakes. It's a very amateurish set-up."

"I'm inclined to agree," said Bell.

"I'm going to have to speak to the boss. He won't be happy with us for messing up his simple case."

As Baines considered how he might break the news, and what his next steps might be, he spotted Phil Gordon himself heading his way.

"Hi Phil," he greeted the crime scene manager. "Jason's just been bringing me up to date on the spade. It seems you were right. Clough doesn't deny that it was his own spade."

"Never mind that now," Gordon said. "You and Lizzie Archer will both want to hear this."

"She's not here just now. She went off somewhere with Jenny Ross a while ago. But what have you got that would interest both of us?"

Gordon's grin was crooked. "I'm glad you're sitting down. This is going to rock your socks off."

* * *

It was a relatively quiet day in the offices of the *Aylesbury Echo*. This week's issue was out today and, for Claire King and the paper's two other full-time reporters, there were a few days of gathering and writing stories before the mad rush to get the next edition ready to print.

Of course, the digital age dictated that things were no longer quite that simple. These days, local papers had an online presence that enabled them to publish up-to-the-minute stories almost as they happened.

King often thought her job title of 'Chief Reporter' was, at best, a little pretentious. At worst, it was downright hilarious. All she could say was that it enabled her some choice of which stories she covered. It meant that she could foist some of the ghastlier village events, and interviews with dull people whose story appealed to her editor, off on the more junior reporters (one of whose ages was almost twice her own 30 years).

If she was honest with herself, she had reached a point where the *Echo* was too small for her. She yearned to move up into the world of the big dailies, but needed something on her CV that would make them sit up and take notice.

Meanwhile, the long hours here meant she had little social life, and couldn't remember the last time she'd had anything worthy of the name 'love life'. At times when little was going on locally she was reduced to writing banality or soft-target knocking copy about one of the Vale's public services.

But mostly she enjoyed what she did

Today, she had definitely enjoyed herself. She ran her eye over the follow-up piece she had written about the death of young Leigh Fletcher. It had happened right under her nose in Little Aston, and she had been on the spot to get local people's reaction to the tragedy.

At the time, it had all sounded like one of those senseless accidents that occasionally happen, a pointless waste of a young life. Now it was clear there was much more to it.

Her editor, Ted Barton, had instilled in her - from the day he sent her on her first assignment as a junior reporter - his mantra for successful local journalism: "Always keep your ears and eyes opened and your pencil sharpened." Well, keeping her eyes and ears open had certainly come in handy on this story.

She always made a point of dropping into the Little Aston Village store on her way to work. They sold decent enough pre-packaged sandwiches that hadn't made her ill so far, and they saved faffing about getting one in town during the day. All of this week, the shop gossip always seemed centred on Leigh: initially on how the family were coping, how awful it was, how ironic it was that a county standard swimmer would die by drowning, and how out of character it was for her to be late night swimming in the quarry alone in the first place.

That had got what Ted called her 'news nose' twitching, even before the police had admitted there was more to the death than met the eye. There was a story behind the tragedy, she had known there was. So the revelation that the girl had been murdered had come as no surprise to her.

The question was, she thought, whether anyone could assume they were safe until somebody had been apprehended. The Vale had fallen prey to two serial killers within relatively recent memory. Was Leigh's death a one-off, or the start of a fresh reign of terror?

She had tried to contact the Fletchers for a sound bite, but had received a polite brush-off from a relative, saying they were asking the media to respect the family's grief.

She checked the headline to her story one more time:

Mystery Surrounds Girl, 16, Quarry Drowning

It would do nicely, she thought. Enough there to capture the imagination and catch the eye. She would run it past Ted, then post it on the website as the first of a series of reports as she conducted her own investigations. She already had tomorrow's instalment in her sights.

Open eyes and ears had gleaned the name of the best friend with whom Leigh had spent her last evening alive.

She waved at Sharon Skipper, the paper's IT wizard and general factotum. Skip ambled over, all nose rings and spiky hair.

"Can't be arsed to walk over to my desk?" she accused.

"Sorry," King placated. "Multi-tasking. I want to get this story posted and move straight onto the next one. Can you interrogate your technology and find me some contact details for a Gemma Lucas? She'd be about 16 and lives in Little Aston."

Skip made salaaming motions. "Your wish is my command."

"Thanks. I owe you one."

"You owe me hundreds."

King smiled. If the Fletcher family were reluctant to talk to her, maybe Gemma would be more forthcoming. Apparently the poor kid was really cut up about her loss. Talking about it might be good for her.

Good for the *Echo*, too. And maybe especially good for Claire King.

17

Christine Lindsay lived with her parents in a terraced house in the village of Stonehouse. The A418 Oxford Road ran straight through the village and, on the odd occasions when Archer had passed through it, she had thought of it as little more than a sign on the road. No pub, no shop, not many houses - hardly anything to mark it out as a place at all.

Yet, as Ross followed the satnav instructions to turn left off the main road and then second right, Archer realised - not for the first time since she'd moved to this area - that the signs announcing their entry into a village had misled her. Stonehouse's 'high street' ran parallel with the A418. Pub, church, store, village hall - all the main boxes ticked. No school that she could see, but by no means every village in the Vale had its own school.

A man in shabby jeans and a wrinkled tee-shirt was weeding an already immaculate-looking flower bed, kneeling on an equally immaculate front lawn, when they pulled up outside the house. Grey-haired, maybe a little overweight, but oozing vitality, Archer judged that he was in his early sixties - easily old enough to still be working, but he'd told Ross on the phone that he had taken early retirement and would be home. He rose as they got out of the car.

"Detectives Archer and Ross?" He held out a none-too-clean hand, drew it back, wiped it on his jeans, then offered it again for them to shake.

"Duncan Lindsay?" Archer said.

The man nodded. "Chrissie is waiting in the garden."

They followed him into the house, noting the ramp up to the front door. He led them through a small hallway into a lounge/diner that had seen better days. The carpet looked as if it had been in need of replacement for some years. To the rear of the room, a pair of French doors stood open and they followed Duncan Lindsay outside, down another ramp.

Christine Lindsay sat by a rotting garden table with the sun on her face. She didn't turn her head as the three emerged. Her father walked round in front of her.

"Chrissie, the two detectives are here," he said. He glanced at Archer and Ross, gesturing to two chairs, in similar condition to the table, that were placed facing his daughter. "Have a seat. My wife's out doing some shopping. To be honest, I'm not sure she wanted to be here when you came. Let me get you something to drink. Tea? Coffee? Squash?"

"I'm fine," Archer said. Ross said she was fine too.

"I'll leave you to it then. All right, darling?"

"Fine, Dad," the young woman said. "Nice to see someone new."

"She means it makes a change from my ugly mug," Duncan said with a grin, and then he disappeared into the house.

"So sit down, please," Christine said. "I can't look up at you."

As Archer seated herself, she tried to compare the figure in the padded wheelchair to the photographs she had seen of the young swimming hopeful. This version was thinner in every way - her body, her arms, even her face. Her dark hair was lifeless, her eyes hollow. Archer knew the accident had paralysed her from the neck down. If it was an accident.

"You want to talk about Graham?" Christine said. "Is he in trouble?"

"It might depend on what you tell us."

She shrugged with her eyes. "Ask your questions then."

"All right. What kind of man was Graham Endean when you knew him? What kind of coach?"

"He was a good guy. If he took you under his wing, he treated you like family. He knew when to push, when to back off." She paused, moistened her lips. "There's a glass of squash on the table. Can one of you put the straw in my mouth please?"

Ross moved to oblige. Christine drew on the straw for a few moments, then ejected it from her mouth.

"Thanks. Where was I? Yes, Graham was a good coach. He'd been there, done it, and knew what it took. I was fifteen, and we were going to the Athens Olympics together."

"That was when the accident happened?" Archer checked. "2002?" That would make her 26 now.

"26 September 2002. The day my whole life turned to rat shit."

"Would you mind telling us what happened?"

"I wish I could remember."

Archer frowned. "It was in the newspapers. I just want to hear it in your own words."

The young woman rolled her eyes. "Yes, well, the papers seemed to know a damn sight more about it than I did. I'm telling you, I don't remember. They told me it's not uncommon with trauma. The mind eliminates things that are too painful to remember. There's a huge slice of that evening that I just can't access."

Somewhere nearby, a wood pigeon had started its monotonous cooing. The sun slid behind a cloud, having the effect of momentarily darkening Christine Lindsay's face.

"It was just me and Graham," she said. "We had the pool to ourselves. I'd always had a hankering to try some high diving, and he'd always forbidden it. Said it wasn't my sport and I should focus on what I was training for."

"He was controlling?" Ross wanted to know. "Manipulative?"

"Graham?" Christine's eyed danced. "Not really. More focused and driven, I'd say. He told me once he thought he'd underachieved as a swimmer, and he didn't want what he referred to as his protégés to feel that way. So that night, apparently-"

"Apparently?" Archer checked.

"So Graham says. Something had got into me. I went up to the top board, despite him nigh on begging me to come down, and tried to execute a fancy dive. I'd never gone off any board before, had had no training. I utterly fucked it up. Sorry," she added, without any sense that she was, "but there's no other word for it. I broke my neck and knocked myself out. Would have drowned if not for Graham. He managed to pull me out. Saved my life, but probably aggravated whatever damage I'd already done to myself in the process. Damned if he did, damned if he didn't. I sometimes wish he'd left me to die." She said this with no sense of self-pity. It was very much as if she was simply stating a fact.

"But there were no other witnesses?" The sun had come out again and was beating on the back of Archer's head. "No one to confirm Graham's story?"

"No, but how else could it have happened?"

"And he had no reason to want to harm you?"

Christine's eyes blazed, the most emotion she had shown so far. "What? No way! Why would he?"

"You tell me. Your relationship - was it purely professional?"

She rolled her eyes again. "Oh, for Christ's sake. I see what you're doing. Leigh Fletcher drowns in mysterious circumstances and poor Christine can't remember her accident. The common denominator is Graham Endean, so naturally he was shagging us both. That's what you're getting at, isn't it?"

"Well? Was he?"

"No, detective. He wasn't. He was like a second dad to me. He'd never have thought of me in that way."

"All right." Archer paused, waiting for the anger to subside. "I don't mean to upset you. Now, you said, I think, he was focused and driven. How far might he have gone to make sure you won?"

"Drugs, you mean? Never. He'd have dropped me like a shot if I'd even suggested it. He hated the cheats in sport." She fixed Archer with a steady gaze. "Sorry if it doesn't help, but what happened to me was an accident, plain and simple."

"But only Graham Endean can say that for sure."

"Why would he lie? Why should it be any other way?"

"I don't know. Maybe he asked you to take something to give you a little extra. You got angry, threatened to expose him. He lashed out, you fell and broke your neck on the pool edge.

"He pulled me out, for pity's sake."

"So he says. Or, if he didn't proposition you with drugs, maybe his mobile rang and you overheard something you shouldn't. You asked difficult questions. Same outcome. He lashes out..."

"No." She blinked furiously. "Not Graham. He's not got a violent bone in his body." She frowned. "There's one thing I sort of remember, or think I do. They gave me plenty of drugs after the accident - not the performance enhancing kind. I was so far off my face, I could have hallucinated the whole thing."

A blackbird had alighted into a flower bed and was pecking enthusiastically for worms, showering soil over the show-standard borders and onto the manicured lawn.

"What was it, Christine?" Ross's tone was gentle but firm. "What do you remember?"

The woman in the wheelchair hesitated for several beats. "All right," she said finally, as if making up her mind. "I seem to think that my last clear memory, before I came round and found myself in hospital, is of Graham arguing with someone."

"On the phone?"

"No. A man. He came to the poolside. I'd just finished some lengths. I was still in the water and having a breather. I think I heard voices raised. At least, I don't recall this guy arriving. I didn't make out much of what they said. Graham told the man he could whistle for his money-"

"That's an old-fashioned phrase," Archer commented.

"Graham could be an old-fashioned guy. There was a bit more arguing. I'm fairly sure Graham pushed the man. Not violent, not really. More like, go away. And he did go. He told Graham - and, if it really happened at all, I remember this distinctly - he told him he'd be sorry."

Wheels spun in Archer's head. Sorry for what? What money did they argue over? Money for drugs? A loan shark, maybe? Good old blackmail?

"You're sure he left? He couldn't have come back and had something to do with what happened to you?"

"No," Christine insisted. "The accident happened just as Graham said."

"What did this man look like?"

"It was eleven years ago."

"Yet you remember the incident," Ross said calmly. "Your last memory before the amnesia sets in. Close your eyes and focus. See if you can see the memory."

"It's a waste of time."

"Humour me."

Christine sighed and then closed her eyes.

"You're in the pool," Ross prompted. "Which end?"

"Shallow end. Furthest from the boards."

"And Graham's to your left or right?"

The woman's forehead screwed up. "Right. The doors to the changing rooms are behind him."

"And you hear what sounds like an argument. Can you hear the words?"

"They were - are - echoing. Kind of muffled."

"You look round. To where the argument's going on?"

"Yes."

"Never mind what they're saying for now, Christine. The other man - what does he look like?"

"He's got his back to me. I can't see his face. I get the impression he's about Graham's age. Tall, over six foot."

"Hair colour?"

"Dark, maybe. The guy slouches. Keeps jabbing a finger at Graham. The echoes, the lapping of the water... the noise from the filters... I can't hear them."

"Just stick with what you see, not what you hear. Is there anything else you notice about him?"

"No... wait. Yes, actually. He wears an earring."

Archer felt her pulse quicken. The description, limited as it was, had struck a chord.

"When Graham pushes him, he staggers. Nearly topples backwards into the pool. It looks like there's going to be a fight, but he just shuffles off. Sort of shoulder-barges past Graham. Then he turns, just for a moment. Says, 'You'll be sorry for this'. Then he goes."

"He turned around?" Ross sounded as if she was barely containing her excitement. "You saw his face?"

"An impression." Christine's eyes fluttered open. "I remembered more than I thought."

"You did well," Ross assured her.

"We'll ask Mr Endean about it" said Archer.

Christine Lindsay pursed her lips. "Honestly, I doubt it has anything to do with Leigh."

Archer ignored the comment. "So, do you still see Graham?"

"No. He came regularly first of all, but the gaps between visits became longer. I haven't seen him at all since just before Beijing 2008. I think seeing me like this is too painful for him, but Dad thinks different."

"What does your dad think?"

"He thinks Graham was somehow to blame for what happened to me. That he should have done more to stop me. And that, once I couldn't swim any more, I was no more use to him. He found new people to work with and moved on."

"And your dad resented that?"

"I think so. But then he wasn't going to blame me, not the way I am now, and he sure as hell wanted someone to scapegoat. One of Graham's girls won a bronze at Beijing, and Dad hated it. Said he supposed Graham was happy now." She made a sour face. "Stupid. He was always going to move on. What else was he going to do?"

Archer placed a card on the table. "You've been a big help, Christine. If you think of anything else..."

"I'll call you. Well, not literally, obviously, but I'll get Mum or Dad to dial you up on speaker phone."

They found Duncan Lindsay still working in his front garden.

"All done?" he asked.

"With Christine, yes," Archer said. "We've just got a couple of questions for you."

"For me?" He looked surprised.

"Well, just one, really. Christine said you were resentful when Graham Endean started taking on new swimmers. Didn't like it when one of his protégés won a bronze in Beijing."

His eyes gave off sparks you could light matchwood with. "Good luck to the swimmers. I did blame him for what happened to Chrissie, yes. She was a fifteen-year-old and he was responsible for her. He let her take a header off the top board. I wanted to sue, but my lawyers said I hadn't a hope in hell. I've just given up a job I loved to make more contribution to my daughter's care, when she could be married with children and a future." He was spitting out words, his face puce. "What has she got now? You bet I'm resentful."

"Enough to seek a form of revenge?" Archer asked lightly. "Punish someone else to get at him?"

He barked a laugh. "Leigh Fletcher, you mean? You must really need a breakthrough in your investigation if that's the best you can do. I'm hardly going to kill someone else's daughter to punish Endean for helping to cripple mine."

"For the record, what were your movements on Friday night?"

"I was home with Chrissie. My wife had a book club meeting. One of her few bits of pleasure."

The two women thanked him and walked back to the car. Archer checked her phone, which had been on silent throughout the interview. There were three voicemails, but a check on her list of incoming calls told her they were probably Baines. He would have to wait, she decided.

"What do you think?" Ross asked as she started the engine.

"I think someone needs another chat with Graham Endean," Archer told her.

"You've got that press conference. Shall I do it?"

"Thanks. Tell you what, though. Did you think Christine's description of the guy Endean argued with rang a bell?"

Ross had slipped the car into gear. She turned to Archer with a half-smile.

"I was going to say the same thing. It sounded like a description of Joe Adams, Kyle's dad."

18

After Phil Gordon dropped his bombshell, Baines had phoned Archer three times, but every call went to voicemail. He tried to concentrate on some report writing while he waited to hear from her, but thoughts of Karen and her impending first date with the hated Mike kept distracting him.

He had gone so far as to check out the firm's website; there was only one Mike, and he looked a smug, oily bastard. He was sure that there was no prejudice in this assessment. It wasn't his fault that 'Mike Daniels' had a face he wanted to slap. Punch, actually.

Every time his mind returned to the subject was torture. He wanted to bombard her with phone calls, beg her to call off the evening so they could finally give their own relationship a real chance to blossom. Yet a part of him feared it would do more to damage the friendship they had than to deepen it into something else. His failure to make that extra commitment when he'd had a chance had hurt her, he could see that now. Yet instead of galvanising him into action to try and woo her back, he found himself in a funk of total indecision.

He was so preoccupied that he almost missed Archer's return, but spotted her heading for the little kitchenette with her kettle. Shaking himself, he locked his computer and went after her. She had just filled the kettle when he arrived in the doorway.

"Hi, Lizzie. Didn't you get my message?"

"I did," she confirmed. "It'll have to wait, Dan."

He could see she was tired. "Fair enough. Once you've made your coffee, maybe you'd swing by my desk?"

The kettle began to bubble. She shook her head.

"I won't be swinging anywhere, mate. I've got my own case to deal with, and I'm drowning in stuff to do as it is."

She left him standing there and got on with spooning coffee granules into her mug.

"You'll want to hear this," he persisted.

"About Gavin Lane?"

"Yes, but -"

Gavin Lane's your case, not mine."

"Actually," he said, "yes and no."

She gave him a hard look. "What's that supposed to mean?"

"Look, make your bloody coffee. I'll give you five minutes, then I'll come to you. Okay?"

She sighed. "All right. But it had better be good."

He sloped away as the bubble of the kettle became noisier. He guessed the Leigh Fletcher case must be frustrating enough as it was, and right now she might suspect him of looking for a way to draw her and her team into an investigation in which he had been left isolated. But maybe she knew him better than that. And she already knew that Gavin Lane's death on Westyate allotments was not the simple case of vigilantism it had first been taken for. Like the Fletcher case, someone seemed to have made clumsy attempts to make it look like something it wasn't.

He watched Archer walk back to her desk, mug of coffee in one hand, kettle in the other. As he started to rise, his phone rang. As he talked to his caller, she returned the kettle to her drawer and locked it away, then glanced over at him, beckoning. He carried on talking as he rose and headed her way.

"But you're as sure as you can be, without the tests?" he was saying as he arrived at her desk. She pointed to the threadbare chair next to her and he lowered his tall frame into it. "Okay," he said. "Okay, Phil, thanks. Yeah, I know, I know. Big drinks. Yeah, see you." He looked at Archer. "That was Phil Gordon."

She raised an eyebrow. "I'm glad you told me that. I'm such a rubbish detective, I imagined you were talking to your sister."

He blinked. "No, it was -"

She rolled her eyes. “Get on with it. And please try to keep it brief.”

He half-smiled as the penny dropped, then became serious.

“Okay. I think I mentioned that Lane did some kitchen jobs and the like when he wasn’t doing anything illegal? He used a yellow van, and it was left parked by the allotment gates. I asked Phil to check it for blood, thinking it might have been used by the real killer to transport Lane’s body from the original murder scene to the allotment before making a half-arsed attempt to stage the aftermath of a vigilante attack.”

“So that was Phil on the phone, confirming that Lane’s blood had been found in the back?”

“What?” He shook his head. “Oh, no, he’d already done that. This is more interesting. He’d noticed some hairs and fibres in the van and they reminded him of samples found on Lane’s clothes.”

“But he didn’t need them really, did he, with the blood?”

He smiled. “Well, not to confirm that Lane’s body had been moved in the van, no. But Phil thought they also looked familiar in relation to another case. He’s had them tested and found a match for the hair and for fibres found elsewhere.”

“And...?”

“And the same sort of fibres were found on Leigh Fletcher’s clothing. More to the point, the hairs are hers.”

“You mean...” She sipped more coffee, her eyes wide. “So, Phil thinks Leigh might also have been transported in the back of Lane’s van at some point?”

“He’s sure of it, Lizzie.” Baines was no longer attempting to contain his excitement. “It’s pretty obvious that the same van was used to take Leigh’s body to the quarry.”

“My God.” She set down her cup. “The van’s definitely Gavin Lane’s?”

“He’s the registered owner, yes.”

“And your theory is - what, exactly?”

“It’s still pretty half-baked, but try this. Lane is involved in Leigh’s murder in some way. His van is used in her abduction - ”

"We were looking for a white one," she murmured. "Gemma thought it might have been cream."

"One was spotted near her friend's house," he said. "I remember. But the street lamps in Little Aston give a slightly sickly yellow glow. Easy enough to assume that all vans are white and make a mistake. Lane's is quite a pale yellow."

"Okay, so Lane's lying in wait for Leigh..."

"He must have had an accomplice. Probably the boss in whatever they were up to - which, of course, we're no closer to figuring out."

Archer nodded. "Gemma said she thought there were two figures in the van she saw. So they abduct her and take her somewhere, where she gets drowned, probably in a bath - either by accident or design. As you say, our theory's still a bit flaky about motive, or what exactly happened, but let's say Lane did have a part in her death. Then what?"

"Well, he was a bit of a bad boy, but murder's way out of his usual comfort zone. Maybe it wasn't what he thought he'd signed up for. He got worried, nervous, maybe even felt guilty. Whatever. Whoever he was working with - or for - gets nervous and decides he's a threat or a liability. He lures him somewhere - maybe with the promise of money - and then lamps him with a baseball bat."

"The killer would probably have already planned to leave him on the allotments and stage the scene."

"Which means he would have known about the previous break ins, and Clough's one man guard force - but to be honest, that seems to have been pretty common knowledge in the village, and - knowing how gossip travels - the legend may well have spread across the Vale."

"All right," she said. "I'm buying this. But here's the thing. Was the whole allotment setup just a clumsy effort to wrong-foot us? Or a deliberate attempt to implicate Clough? Was there even a connection between Len Clough and Leigh's death?"

Baines pursed his lips. "I see what you mean. Or it could be that whoever was behind Leigh's murder had it in for Clough and saw a way of disposing of whatever threat Lane was posing, and getting Clough into trouble at the same time."

"Or none of the above."

They sat in silence for a few moments, each deep in thought.

"Well, thanks a lot, Dan," Archer finally said, a hint of irony drizzling into her tone. "This case just got a whole lot more complicated. I suppose we ought to tell Gillingham we think we've both been working the same case. Still," she added, "it looks like you're back on the team."

"Maybe he'll put Ashby in charge," Baines suggested with a grin. "The Lane case is nominally his, after all."

"Like he'd want it. Besides, I'm not leaving it to him to catch Leigh's killer. The kid deserves better than that." She drank some more coffee. Checked her watch. "Let's speak to Gillingham."

She was in the act of rising from her desk when Baines spotted Jason Bell heading their way, notebook in hand, an excited look on his face.

"Sorry to interrupt," the DC said, practically skidding to a halt in front of Archer's desk. "You'll both want to hear this."

"Christ," Archer groaned. "I should put a sign up: 'Open House'."

"If you're busy -" Bell stammered.

"It's fine, Jason. Let's hear it."

"Guv, you asked me to give Dan a bit of support, and one of the things he asked me to do was talk to the guy Gavin Lane often worked with - a John Butler. See what he had to offer about what Lane might have been up to lately, what his mood was, and also get a list of other associates."

"And?" Baines prompted, fearing that Bell might be preparing for a long tale.

"Not much about Lane that his wife hadn't already told you. He seemed a bit preoccupied and short tempered, but that wasn't exactly a one-off. Nothing especially remarkable. But the list of associates has one interesting name on it."

"Jason..." Archer's impatience was palpable. She glanced at her watch again.

"Sorry. Well, as you'd expect, he did quite a few jobs with different tradespersons involved. One of them is a Joe Adams. I'm thinking that's Kyle Adams's father. Quite a coincidence, don't you think?"

The whole mood changed, as if the Scot had flicked a switch. Archer looked at Baines, her eyes bright with excitement, then back at Bell.

"More of a coincidence than you'd think, since we've just connected Lane's murder with that of Leigh Fletcher."

Bell gaped. "No way! How -"

"Dan will fill you in. Look, I'm going to speak to Gillingham. Dan, find Jenny Ross. She was going to talk to Leigh's coach about someone he might have argued with a few years back. She'll bring you up to speed, but from the description we have, it could just be Adams. Of course, it could be plenty of other people, too."

"And if he confirms it was...?"

"Then I want you to hook up with her, find Joe Adams - Jason, you can help them with that - and go and talk to him. I'll want to see how his story of the argument compares with Graham Endean's - that's the coach. I want to know if he still harbours ill will towards Endean, I want to know what he was doing the night Gavin Lane was killed, and I want his alibi for Leigh's death to be rock solid."

"Should we arrest him, if we're not happy?"

"Use your judgement. You know our custody sergeant. If you think you've got a case for holding Adams, and that the sergeant will buy it, then do it. If you don't think so, but you still think some serious questioning is in order, see if he'll come in voluntarily."

"This changes everything, doesn't it?" Baines said. "Are you going ahead with the press conference?"

"The boss's call, but I would. We're a long way from cracking the case, but these new dimensions make it all the more interesting. Let's hope we get a good public response. Two murders within a few miles of each other is bad enough. A connection is ten times worse. Who knows if it's over yet?"

* * *

As Claire King walked up the short tarmac driveway to Gemma Lucas's front door, she found herself wishing she'd chosen something different to wear today. She had a liking for alarmingly short skirts and had found, on the whole, that they did her no harm when trying to get men to open up to her. Women were a different matter, but then she usually knew sufficiently in advance that she had an interview to conduct, and could tone down her dress as necessary.

But the idea of having a chat with Leigh Fletcher's best mate had been a bit spontaneous, and so she'd had to go with what she had on. The look might actually be something the girl could identify with, but it might set the parents' teeth on edge if they were feeling protective of her. If they were anxious to keep the press at bay, then looking a bit young and fluttery might not be the ideal image.

She'd scrubbed off her makeup and tied her long blonde hair back in what she hoped was a preppy, serious look, and she'd done up all but the top button of her blouse and popped on her glasses. The spectacles had plain lenses and were purely for effect on the rare occasions when she was trying for gravitas. It would have to do. She rang the bell.

She needn't have worried. Gemma's mother confided that her daughter had been terribly withdrawn since Leigh's death. If King could get her to talk about how she felt, it might be usefully cathartic. So she had left it to Gemma to decide whether to speak to the journalist.

King hadn't known what she would find when she finally met Leigh's friend. She'd half-feared that the girl would be a sobbing wreck, her eyes raw with crying. The reality was slightly different. Gemma was pale beneath her acne and looked desperately unhappy. Her eyes looked as though there was little going on behind them. She shrugged and said, "Whatever," when her mother asked if she was willing to talk to a journalist.

"Perhaps we could do this in your room, Gemma?" King suggested. "You might feel more comfortable in your own space."

Another shrug, but the girl headed towards the stairs. The mother nodded and the two women followed. As she watched Gemma's short, rotund frame lumbering upstairs, King found herself wondering about the nature of her friendship with the dead girl. Leigh would not have been the first attractive person to choose a plain friend to make their self stand out all the more. Perhaps she hadn't been quite the good girl she was made out to be. The thought was interesting but, King thought, may just have been an over-cynical one.

Gemma sat down on the bed, picked up a pink teddy bear, and hugged it to her.

"Nice bear," King commented. "He looks quite new. Present?" Maybe the girl's parents had brought it for her as some sort of comfort in her grief.

Gemma nodded. "Leigh gave it to me for my birthday."

"When was that?"

"20th of June."

"Just a couple of weeks ago." King gave her a bright smile. "Happy birthday for the 20th."

The girl shrugged once again. In other circumstances, it would be starting to annoy her by now, but Gemma Lucas's pain was almost palpable. King hated asking grieving people how they felt. She would delegate such jobs when she could. But she was certain there was a real story here, tantalisingly within reach.

She asked Gemma how close she and Leigh had been, what the dead girl had been like, and what sort of a friend she had been.

Really close. Always together. A great person, a great friend. All communicated with as few words and syllables as possible.

And all possibly inhibited by the mother's presence. She glanced at Mrs Lucas, who stood in the doorway wringing her hands.

"You know, I'm parched. I've been running around all day and not had a drink for hours. Could I be a pain and beg a cup of tea? Milk, no sugar?"

The woman frowned and looked at her daughter. "Will you be okay for a moment, sweetheart?"

Gemma nodded.

"Milk, no sugar?"

"Please."

"Coming up," Dawn Lucas said with forced brightness.

King waited for her to depart, then quietly pulled the door to. "Just us girls now," she said. "Is that better?"

Shrug.

"I bet your family are walking on eggshells around you, being all morbid and gloomy, because they think that's respecting your grief."

Nod.

"It doesn't help, does it?"

Shake. And then, "They mean well. Every time I mention Leigh, they steer me away from talking about her. Like that's going to make her less dead."

King smiled. "Don't be too hard on them. They didn't expect you to be in this situation, and they're out of their depth. They don't know how to help you, so they create a sombre atmosphere, when what you really need to do is talk about your friend." She put her pad and pen back in her bag and sat down next to the girl.

"So talk about her."

After a few moments, Gemma did.

19

DCI Gillingham had managed to get hold of Steve Ashby, and the DI sat in the briefing room with Archer, Phil Gordon, and Gillingham himself.

Gordon had told the DCI about the CSIs' discoveries and the evidential connections between the Lane case and that of Leigh Fletcher. Archer had explained how Joe Adams might have a tentative connection to both victims. Gillingham in particular, but Ashby too, had asked a few questions, but they had mostly listened attentively.

"Of course," Gillingham said when Archer had finished, "I trust Phil to know his stuff." He turned to the crime scene manager. "How sure are we that these hairs and fibre mean that both Leigh and Lane have been transported in the back of Lane's van at some point?"

"As confident as I can be - or at the very least, it links the two victims. It's always possible, I suppose, that evidence was transferred from one to the other in some way, but it still connects them. Either way, I reckon we're dealing with a single case here."

"A single killer?" Ashby checked.

"My reading is that Lane was involved in Leigh's death," Archer said. "Maybe he killed her, maybe he was an accessory. But he was working with or for someone who, for whatever reason, decided to take him out too."

Gillingham nodded. "That's good enough for me. We need to pool the two investigations, decide who'll be the lead DI."

Archer felt a sick feeling in her stomach as the boss turned to Ashby. "How about it, Steve? This could be a big, high profile case. I need someone experienced to lead the team."

Ashby hesitated. Archer would have bet that he was weighing the kudos that could be gained from a result against the glare of public failure - to say nothing of the amount of work that could be involved.

"I dunno, Paul," Ashby said finally. "I've got a lot on, right now..."

Ask him like what, a part of her wanted to say. But a bigger part of her wanted him to be let off, because she wanted this case badly. Leigh Fletcher deserved justice, and Archer wanted to get it for her.

"Maybe I should just have oversight?" Ashby suggested. "Fairly hands-off, but Lizzie can keep me posted and we can chat through any problems she encounters."

Aghast at this worst of all worlds scenario, Archer stared at Gillingham, who seemed to be weighing the suggestion.

"No," the DCI said finally. "That won't work at all, Steve. I need one DI focused on the case and reporting to me. Fragmenting the lines of communication will just foster confusion. No, you're right. Best you focus on the other balls you have in the air. Lizzie's pretty steeped in the Fletcher case, and Dan Baines is up to speed on Lane, so I guess all the bases are covered."

Ashby nodded slowly, his face mingling both disappointment and relief.

"Press conference in just over an hour, boss," Archer said. "Do you still want me to lead it, now it's looking like there are two connected murders?"

"Yes, you lead," Gillingham said. "You know the Fletcher case better than anyone. I don't think we'll be too specific about our suspicions of a link to Lane's death just yet. Make the conference about Leigh Fletcher alone. We want people who may have seen a white, or possibly yellow van - that's how we bring the Lane connection in - in the area last Friday night, or saw anything at all suspicious, to come forward."

"Also, anyone who knew Leigh, knew about anything that might have been worrying her," Archer added. "We've questioned everyone we can think of, but you never know." She frowned, her thoughts coming into focus. "There was a reason she was abducted. Someone wanted some hired muscle to help, and they used Lane. But was killing her the plan all along? Or just scaring her?"

"To prevent her from saying something?" Gordon speculated.

"Or maybe she had something incriminating they wanted to get hold of," she said. "The burglary, the mugging... it's got to all be connected. I'll get Joan to look over the files one more time."

"Good thinking," said Gillingham. "And find out what Lane was doing the night Leigh died - and who might have hired him for some dirty work. Maybe this Joe Adams. You were looking at his son, but maybe the dad's a better fit."

"As I said, Dan and Jenny are on that. It may come to nothing, of course. He won't be the only tall guy with an earring in these parts, and besides, we don't even know what the row with Endean was about yet. But we'll certainly screw down Lane's movements the night Leigh died. If no one can account for him, we've got a strong scenario to work on."

"But still no motive or suspect," Ashby observed, his first contribution since his offer of oversight had been spurned. "Why don't I speak to one or two of my dodgier contacts? See if anyone was putting out feelers for a hired thug around the time Leigh died."

"Good idea, Steve," Gillingham said with a smile. "That would be great."

Ashby the team player. Archer glanced at Gordon, who briefly made an astonished face at her. She shrugged back. Ashby saw the gesture and gave her a hard look. Archer smiled insincerely at him.

"Thanks, DI Ashby," she said with exaggerated warmth. "Like the boss says, that would be great."

"Great," Gordon added, his eyes dancing.

Ashby looked at them in turn, frowning. They smiled back. "Well," he said, "that's great, then."

* * *

After the meeting broke up, Archer followed Gillingham back to his office.

"Was there something else?" he asked her as he settled in his comfy chair.

"Not really. Just... thanks. I know you were pretty sceptical at first about Leigh's death being anything but an accident."

He opened his mouth as if to speak, closed it again, looked thoughtful, then told her to close the door.

"This bloody case," he said. "As soon as it became clear that Golden Boy Marling was a friend of the family and taking a close personal interest, the whole thing became political. Oh, I know he's a good guy, and a hard working constituency MP. He's given the police a lot of support over the years. But that kind of keenness in a politician who has the ear of the Chief Constable isn't what I'd call comfortable for likes of me."

"The Chief's still keeping up the pressure?"

"The word's come down that she's made it clear that she wants a quick clear-up. She'll not be happy when these new developments hit the fan."

"So..."

"So nothing. We have evidence that two murders have been committed. I like to keep the brass happy, but we all know whose career will be over if we get it wrong and it comes back to haunt us. And these things have a nasty habit of doing so," he added.

There was something about his tone. "You sound as if you speak from experience?"

"What?" Suddenly, he looked flustered. He stared at his desk and fiddled with his pen. "No, no, not really." He looked up at her again. "Let's just say we all make mistakes. You'll make one, one of these days, Lizzie. Take my advice. In the long run, you're better off getting it out in the open there and then. Keeping quite just makes it worse."

"But we're not keeping these murders quiet," she pointed out, confused. "We've got a press conference coming up."

"So we have." He looked like man who'd just walked away from a patch of quicksand. "Look, I meant what I said about you taking the lead, but if you'd like me on the platform with you? I could kick things off, then hand over to you? Add a bit of weight to the team?"

"That would be good," she said, stroking her scar and feeling strangely touched by this little extra support. "I'd like that, Paul."

"Done, then. Make sure you pick me up when you need me. I'll be right here."

Walking back to her desk, she replayed the conversation in her mind. She couldn't shake the feeling that Gillingham had almost let something slip, some skeleton in his past that was still in the closet, scratching at the door with bony fingers that demanded to be let out.

* * *

Paul Gillingham sat with his elbows on his desk, twiddling the Montblanc fountain pen his wife had given him for his birthday a couple of years ago, wondering if he'd said too much to Lizzie Archer about the error of judgement that haunted him for so long. He didn't know what had made him say it, other than he always tried to be firm but fair with his team and to give them the benefit of his experience when it seemed right to do so.

He wondered if she would go away puzzling over what his own indiscretion had been. Maybe not. Even if she did, she would probably imagine it was something relatively minor - some procedural blunder that he'd not owned up to when he should.

She would have no idea of the truth, which was just as well. But, he thought, just letting it slip that there was something there to be found had probably been a little foolish.

He would need to guard his tongue more closely in future.

* * *

Baines was waiting outside Graham Endean's house when Ross emerged. He waited until the swimming coach had closed his front door and then got out, raising a hand to attract his fellow DS's attention.

"You got my text?" he checked as she came across to join him.

"Yes, thanks. He was pretty open about the argument though. It was Joe Adams, all right. Endean claims he did some electrical work for him - a light fitting and a couple of plug sockets. A few days later, fuses started blowing. Adams showed no urgency about coming back to sort it, claiming a heavy workload, so Endean didn't pay his invoice."

She took out a packet of cigarettes, offered one to Baines. He shook his head, so she lit one for herself and took a drag. "The night of Christine Lindsay's accident, Adams showed up at the pool, demanding his money. Endean told him he'd got someone else in to do the job properly and Adams could whistle for it. Adams got aggressive and got in his face, so he shoved him away. Nigh on pushed him into the water. Adams made some bravado threat and buggered off."

"And Endean didn't see fit to mention either Christine's accident - if that's what it was - nor the handbag fight with Adams - to me?"

"To be fair, Dan, he was hardly evasive about it. Said he'd assumed we'd know about the accident - it was in the local press at the time, and you can find the story online. And he didn't think anything of Adams' threat. He insists that Christine's accident was just as she told Lizzie and me, but then it's the version he told her in the first place, so who knows? I get the impression of a man who blames himself for what happened to her."

"But is that because he should have stopped her taking a header off the board, or because something else happened?"

She shrugged. "Only one person knows the answer to that. I don't see how Adams could be involved though, not if Endean says he saw the whole thing. Why would he lie?"

"Let's find Adams and get his take on it. See if the stories match. My car - we can pick yours up afterwards." He gestured at the fag. "Chuck that thing away, though. And a word to the wise. Don't smoke around Lizzie."

She gave him an off look. "We're outside. It's not like I'm smoking in the office, like a certain DI I could mention."

"She doesn't like it. Her father died of lung cancer, and she's as anti-smoking as they come."

She ground the butt under her foot. "Do you always stick up for her like that?"

He barked a laugh. "Stick up for her? Is that what you think? When she first arrived, I thought it might come to blows. And that she might just win."

"Really? That dolt Ashby thinks you'd like to get into her knickers. He says he can't decide if it's lust or career ambition. I know he's an utter twat, but..."

"Yes, he is." Baines's hackles rose. "A twat who's always making snide remarks about her scar, which she got trying to stop someone getting hurt in a pub fight. She wasn't even on duty. The guy had a broken bottle. She still made the arrest." He opened the driver's door of the Mondeo. "I'd take her over twenty Steve Ashbys, any day of the year."

He got in, and she climbed in beside him.

"For the record," she said, "I would too." She stared straight ahead. "Look, I know I made an idiot of myself with him at that party, and I can imagine what some people think of me over it. I can't believe, even after one drink too many, that I'd have gone anywhere near him, let alone..." She coloured.

He was surprised, and felt a little awkward, that she was opening up in this way. Yet he couldn't help feeling sorrier for her than he would have expected. Anyone whose claim to fame at work was locking lips with a slimeball deserved a bit of sympathy.

"Not my business," he said. "Besides, people will always gossip in our job. It makes a break from dwelling on some of the shit we see every day. You said yourself that Ashby's saying things about Lizzie and me - which for the record are bollocks."

"Yes, but I can't say that about what happened at the party. I wish I could."

He started the engine. "I'm not much for advice, Jenny, and we don't know each other especially well. But, for what it's worth, you just have to try not to care what people think or say. They're going to do it anyway. One day - maybe this week -

you'll do something that will give them something more positive to talk about."

"You think?"

Baines didn't answer. He was the man who had let the woman he loved slip through his fingers by doing too much thinking. He was the last one to be helping anyone else sort out their life.

* * *

Local TV were there for the press conference, and one of their makeup girls was preparing Archer for the cameras. It felt uncomfortable. She wasn't actually saying anything about Archer's scar, but it was pretty obvious that she was bothered about it and wondering how to broach the subject. Archer guessed she was itching to plaster a load of slap over it, but didn't want to do so without some sort of discussion.

The drunken hothead who had slashed her with the broken bottle had managed to damage some branches of her facial nerve, leaving her with a slightly lopsided mouth, despite the surgeon's best endeavours. And, although they had done what they could with the scar itself, it was still very conspicuous. For a year or so, it had gradually faded a little, but there was still a clear, slightly puckered, crescent-shaped white line.

Experiments with growing her hair long to hide it, and with various makeups and other cosmetic cover-up options, had done little to improve matters. In fact, she had felt they simply drew more attention to the freak show that was the left side of her face. In the end, she had decided to put up with it as best she could and get on with her life. That decision hadn't stopped the stares, nor did it help her feelings of vulnerability when meeting a new person or - as this evening - when she was on public display.

The girl was still hovering with her pot of flesh-coloured cream, and Archer took pity on her.

"You won't be able to do much with my scar," she said. "It is what it is."

"Oh, no, no." She reddened. "It hardly notices. It's just that, under the lights..."

"Anything you can do is great."

The girl frowned. "If you're sure?"

"Sure. Every little helps."

She sat watching her reflection in the mirror as the girl - she couldn't have been much more than 19 - worked on her with creams and powders. It was all very subtle, and - despite her doubts - she found herself impressed with the result. Only a magician could have done anything about the droop, but she thought the actual scar would be hard to spot unless you were looking for it. And the makeups that had been applied didn't look unnatural, nor had they been piled on with a trowel.

"Thanks, um..."

"Georgia," the kid supplied.

"Thanks, Georgia, that's really good. Maybe you could show me afterwards how you do that, if you'll still be around?"

"Well..." She hesitated. "I was heading off soon, but I could easily hang on. Give me a chance to get my phone out and catch up on my social networks."

"Great," said Archer, who never understood the attraction of Facebook, Twitter and the like. "I'll see you after the media circus then."

* * *

The room used for the conference was not packed out - Gillingham's underplaying of Leigh's death had so far avoided the national high profile such crimes sometimes attracted - but there was a good attendance from local TV and press, as well as a smattering of journalists from the national dailies. She also spotted Andrew Marling's agent, Chris Russell, at the back, presumably looking for an update to take back to his master.

The conference went much as planned. Archer explained that, since 16-year-old Leigh Russell's death by drowning in Little Aston Quarry, the police had been trying to ascertain the circumstances of the tragedy. There were now strong reasons to believe that she had been abducted on her way home from an evening with a friend, and that what had followed had led directly to her drowning. The police were especially keen to speak to anyone who may have seen a yellow or white van in the village or near the quarry around the time that Leigh died, as they may hold the key to the investigation. All calls would be treated in confidence.

She then repeated the van's registration number and the telephone number for witnesses before handing over to Gareth Fletcher, who made an impassioned and tearful appeal for anyone who may have seen something or know something to come forward.

It had been made abundantly clear that no questions would be taken following the statements, but that did not deter one reporter from rising in her seat and calling to Archer.

"Inspector, Leigh died on Friday, and you've known about this van since yesterday. Why has it taken so long to make this appeal?"

Claire King from the *Echo*. Her body language made it clear that she wasn't going to sit down until she had an answer.

Archer marshalled her thoughts, wondering where King had dug up this information. She could see the interest in the eyes of other media representatives. Ordinarily, a local reporter wouldn't be too much to worry about, but she had been put on the spot on a platform aimed at attracting national attention.

She licked her lips. "Ms King, that's a fair question. But the truth is that we've only just determined that this vehicle may have been involved. Until recently, the possibility of abduction has been just one of many lines of inquiry. I don't want to compromise the investigation by saying any more, but -"

"And yet Leigh's best friend, Gemma Lucas, told you yesterday that there was a strange van parked near her house when Leigh set off for home on Friday night."

Archer fought down her rising irritation, knowing it wouldn't help to let it show.

"You're quite right about that. But, as I've said, this has been one of a number of -"

"Sure," drawled King. "One of a number of lines of inquiry. But it's getting on for a week since Leigh's death. We all know about the golden 24 hours, and how your chances of solving a crime diminish after that. Why didn't you take Gemma seriously before?"

Archer wanted to say that there had been no real reason until the Monday to begin to suspect that Leigh's drowning had been anything other than an accident and that only now did they have compelling evidence linking her to this particular vehicle. But she was wary of going into too many details.

"Is this true?" Gareth Fletcher hissed from her right. "Hayley said you kept on about Kyle's dad's van."

Gillingham rose from his seat at the end of the table.

"Ladies and gentlemen, thank you for your attention. That concludes our statements for tonight. Rest assured that further statements will be issued as soon as we have more information."

He gathered his papers and looked pointedly at Archer. She stood and shepherded the Fletcher family from the table, following Gillingham out of the side door. She glanced back once at Claire King, who looked pleased with her evening's work. The reporter already had her mobile phone in her hand, keying something in.

Outside, Gareth Fletcher grabbed Archer by the arm. "I want an answer to my question."

Archer very gently removed his hand. "And you'll get one. Perhaps we could go to one of the interview rooms?"

"For what? More spin?"

"We can chat in my office," Gillingham suggested.

Gareth Fletcher rolled his eyes and then nodded. He, Gail and Hailey followed the two detectives. Archer felt control slipping through her fingers as they entered the DCI's lair. He settled the family into chairs at his meeting table and perched on his desk, facing them. Archer was left feeling like a spare part.

"I understand your concerns," Gillingham said, directing his words at Gareth, but glancing at Gail and Hayley too, so as not to exclude them. "But this is a fast-moving situation. Please don't mention this outside this office, but we've had a breakthrough only this afternoon. We've found that a van connected to a separate crime has some forensic evidence that strongly suggests it was used in Leigh's abduction."

"You've already found the van?" Gareth blinked. "So - what? You've caught the killer?"

"Not yet, unfortunately. I'm reluctant to say any more on that at the moment. What I can promise you, Mr Fletcher, is that this is real progress in finding out what happened to Leigh and catching those responsible."

"But... so what about what that reporter was saying? That you've known about the van from the beginning?"

"It's not that simple," Archer said, butting in. Gillingham glared at her, but she was determined not to stand there like a lemon while her boss did all the smoothing.

"It sounds simple to me," Hayley snapped. "You made me and Kyle feel like criminals, and you kept on about his dad's van."

"I'm sorry if it felt that way," she said, "but at the start of the case we were still trying to establish what had happened to Leigh. It looked like an accident, but it soon became clear that we were looking at something worse. We were interested in Kyle's father's van because - to be honest - it is quite common for vans to be used in abductions, and we weren't able to rule anything out at that stage. We were still covering as much ground as we could, testing everyone's stories and trying to build some sort of picture.

"We subsequently heard from Gemma and another source that there was a van parked near her house around the time Leigh left, but under the glow of the street lamps the colour must have been indistinct. People assumed it was white. It's actually a pale yellow. At that stage, we didn't have a registration number, didn't even know for sure that the van was even involved. Even if we'd appealed for anyone who saw an unspecified white van in Little Aston, I doubt it would have got us far, in all the circumstances."

Gareth scratched his forehead. "So what's changed?"

"I wish we could tell you more." Gillingham stepped in again. "But I'm afraid Leigh's death is now part of a wider investigation, and we don't want to compromise either case. Just releasing the details of the van will have tipped off the killer that we've connected Leigh's death with the other crime.

It's a bit of a balancing act, I'm afraid. That's why we're asking you to keep this to yourselves and not spread it around."

"I'm not at all sure you've told us anything you didn't just say to the press."

Gillingham spread his hands in a 'What can I do?' gesture.

Gareth shrugged. "All right. Whatever it takes to catch our girl's killer. But one person I will be talking to is our MP. He'll make sure there's no slacking."

Great. Marling's agent had doubtless already reported back to his boss, and now there would be complaints to him from the dead girl's parents. It would mean more pressure on Gillingham.

Soon afterwards, the family were being given a lift home and Archer had finally been instructed to sit.

"Well, you fucked that up, Lizzie," Gillingham declared from his power chair. "You should have just ignored Claire Bloody King's question."

"Maybe, but the damage had already been done with the Fletchers, as soon as she opened her mouth. And Hayley would have put two and two together with hers and Kyle's original interviews anyway."

"Yes, but you gave the press more fodder. By answering her, you allowed Claire's question to become an issue." He shook his head. "And what will the family do when they hear Joe Adams is now a person of interest?"

There was a tap on the door and Joan Collins looked in.

"Sorry to disturb, boss, but the PR guys wanted you to see this. Just up on the *Echo*'s website."

She handed him a printout, which Archer could see was from a webpage. He scanned it, thanked Collins, waited for her to depart, then handed it to Archer.

Mystery Surrounds Girl, 16, Drowning

Police Concealed Vital Van Clue?

"Fuck," she growled, reading on.

"You've done media training, haven't you, Lizzie?"

Gillingham's tone was pointed. She ignored it, reading on. One sentence made her pause and re-read it.

"In all honesty, Paul," she said finally, "this is mostly predictable stuff. Making something and nothing out of a few scant facts."

Gillingham rose from his comfy chair and leaned forward with his knuckles on his desk. He reminded her strangely of the statue of Guy the gorilla at London Zoo. That included his facial expression.

"It may be predictable," he said, "but it's powerful. It makes us look shifty and inept. And the reporters from the dailies who were here will pick up on this piece. If we're not careful, the whole point of the appeal will get lost in all the finger pointing."

"Claire would have written this piece anyway. And, in fact, she'd have written about the van anyway."

"Really?" he snorted. "How so?"

She counted to five before she replied. "You only scanned the article, sir. If you'd read it through, you would have noticed that she spoke to Gemma Lucas earlier today. Gemma told her about the van she'd mentioned to us."

Gillingham's arms were folded now. "And how did she know to speak to her? Has there been a leak?"

The very suggestion made her want to hit him. She had seen leaky teams in the Met, suspected backhanders were being received from journalists in return for titbits. It had nearly always coincided with dubious leadership. If she suspected one of her team of those sorts of tricks, she would report it in a heartbeat.

Slowly and deliberately, she folded her own arms. "You've worked in Thames Valley for years, haven't you?"

"What's that got to do with it?"

"Seen a few communities in that time?"

"Of course, but -"

"Claire King lives in Little Aston herself. I bet she keeps her ears open. She'd know who the last person to see Leigh alive was, and now we have a bit more to worry about than her stirring up a non-story about some titbit we held back on."

"Oh, really? Enlighten me?"

"It says here," Archer stabbed the page with her finger, "that Gemma is a key witness to what happened to Leigh that night. That she saw the van that she was almost certainly abducted in. Paul, these people already killed Gavin Lane, probably to silence him. Gemma Lucas could be in danger."

He shook his head. "But... she saw nothing."

"That's not what Ms King says here. It's common knowledge that Leigh had been at Gemma's the night she died and it's clear that, when Claire decided to spin a mystery out of Leigh's death, she went to see her. This dangerous crap is the result. We may know she can't identify anyone, but the killers don't. Will they want to take the chance that she can?"

"I don't know," he said doubtfully. "We haven't got the resources to start protecting everyone the press says is a potential witness to a crime."

"I'm not saying that. But we should at least do a risk assessment. Have the local PCSOs keep a casual eye and ear out and, if necessary, warn the Lucas family to be on their guard."

"I'll think about it," he replied. "We don't want to scare them unnecessarily, nor have them setting new hares running in the community. Leave it with me. And don't think it gets you off the hook for that shambles just now. I should have followed my instincts and put Steve Ashby in charge of this investigation."

"That would have been funny," she scoffed. "The man who wasn't there." She looked him in the eye. "I don't get it, boss. Why do you cut Ashby so much slack?"

For a moment, his gaze slid to his desk, and then he eyeballed her right back. "What you're saying is close to insubordination." Archer recognised bluster when she heard it. "Now go, before one of us says something we'll both regret. But you'd better get your bloody act together, Lizzie. Right now, I'm more than half-wishing I'd left you at the Met last year, instead of giving you a chance."

Cold fury bubbled up inside her. She thought Gillingham was being unjust on so many levels, and the last remark had been, in her opinion, entirely unfair. She'd done a good job at

Aylesbury Vale and hadn't got anything wrong in this inquiry so far.

Her scar itched underneath the makeup and she fought down the urge to rub it, as well as the powerful impulse to throw some barbed words back at the DCI.

"I'll wish you goodnight then. Sir." she finally said through gritted teeth.

As she turned to go, Joan Collins appeared in the doorway.

"A Mr Russell is keen to speak to you, sir," she said.

As Archer stifled a groan, Gillingham told Collins she had better show Russell in. He did not so much ask, as order, Archer to stay.

Despite the pressure he was exerting at the moment, Archer still had a lot of time for Andrew Marling. She didn't see why she should extend this indulgence to minor party officials, especially an election agent, whose role when there was no election on was a mystery to her.

Moments later, Chris Russell was entering the office, wreathed in smiles.

"It's good of you to spare me a moment," he said.

Gillingham told him to have a seat. Archer was still standing, so he lowered himself into the one nearest the DCI's desk.

"I'll come to the point," he said. "You know how concerned Andrew is about Leigh Fletcher's murder, and now there's this second person killed in his constituency. Only a criminal going about his unlawful business, I know..."

"And a human being whose death we will investigate every bit as thoroughly as Leigh's," Gillingham said with a vehemence that surprised Archer.

Russell smiled again. "Of course. Although I understood there was a prime suspect in that case. I'm surprised there's been no arrest yet."

Gillingham folded his arms, slowly and deliberately. "You know I can't discuss the particulars of a case with you, sir, although I'm willing to brief the Minister."

"Really? The Minister has asked me to keep an eye on developments for him. I think you'll find he'll take it ill if you don't cooperate. Nobody wants to make it all official, through the Chief Constable."

Archer held her tongue, knowing that if she opened her mouth she would seriously regret what came out. Gillingham looked about to explode. He sat there with his arms folded, whilst a gathering storm seemed to envelop the room. Then he sighed and unfolded them.

"Well," he said. "I don't suppose it can do much harm. We're not convinced that Gavin Lane's death is as simple as it looks, and we have evidence that links Leigh Fletcher to his van. We think both murders are in some way connected, and we're following a number of leads. With luck, the appeal tonight will jog some memories and someone will have spotted the van in Little Aston on Friday night - perhaps even got a look at the occupants."

Russell frowned. "What about this friend of Leigh's? Gemma? That reporter said she had seen it."

"She claims not to have noticed anything about the people inside, although I suppose it's possible her memory will be jogged if we have an actual suspect in custody."

"Let's hope so. Anything else I can feed back to Andrew?"

"Not for now, no."

"Okay." Russell rose. "Thanks for your time." He handed cards to both Gillingham and Archer. "I'll tell you what I'll do. You keep this channel of communication open and I'll strongly advise Andrew to back off for now. Give you guys some space to do your jobs. I dare say you have enough on your plates, without politicians flexing their muscles."

Gillingham looked surprised, then pleased. "That would be a big help, yes. We'll keep you posted on anything that doesn't compromise our investigations. How does that sound?"

"Sounds good." There were handshakes all round before the agent took his leave.

"That's a relief," Gillingham said. "If he sticks to it, that is."

"I don't know," Archer told him. "Why do I feel like we've just done a deal with the devil?"

He shook his head. "That's something you're going to have to learn, Lizzie. Sometimes this job is all about deals with the devil." He spread his palms. "Look, let's forget earlier. We were both a bit wound up, and we all say things...."

She found it amazing that he could impugn her ability and her professionalism, several times over and then ask her to forget it, but she was suddenly too tired to argue.

"Okay," she said.

He waited for her to say more, then shrugged.

"Go home and get some sleep."

She stalked back to her office and immersed herself in work. Only later did she remember the makeup girl, Georgia. When she looked for her, she had gone.

20

Joe Adams sprawled in a recliner in the room he had described as his den. Apart from the recliner, there was a small desk, a sofa, and a slim unit with bottles of booze on top. The builders' beige walls were adorned with pictures of the Adams family (every time those two words were linked in Baines's mind, the theme from the TV show played in his head), some more photos of Adams with his mates, one of him with some Chelsea footballers, and a widescreen TV.

Adams wore a crisp white tee-shirt and a pair of dazzling multi-coloured shorts. He had offered Baines and Ross a beer and, when they had declined, shrugged and got himself one. He took a long swig from the bottle now, smacked his lips, and wiped this mouth with the back of his hand.

"Ah," he sighed. "That's good. So what's all this about? Tell me you're not still persecuting Kyle."

"Hardly persecuting, sir," Ross said. "We chatted to a few people in connection with Leigh's death, including Kyle. Now we'd like a word or two with you."

"Really? I suppose I'm a suspect, is that it?" He was leaning forward in the chair now, with a pugnacious jut to his chin. "You think I'd kill Leigh? Why? What possible motive would I have?"

"Let's not worry about all that now," Baines said. "We're carrying out our inquiries, that's all."

"Yes, well. I was here the night Leigh died. My wife will vouch for that. Or maybe you'd suspect her of lying to protect me?"

Baines thought he was becoming increasingly aggressive and defensive for someone with nothing to hide. He thought that was interesting, but put the feeling aside for now.

"Let's leave Friday night for a moment," he suggested. "There are a couple of other things you might be able to help us with."

"I can't think what." He chugged some more beer down. "You people have been out of your depth from the word go on this. I never used to believe the local cops were a bunch of dozy flatfoots. Now I'm wondering." He took another swig, examined the bottle, finished it off. He stood up. "Let me get another one of these."

"I'd rather you sat down and answered our questions."

"Yeah, well," smirked Adams, "life's full of disappointments, right?"

He hunched his way out of the room, his height somehow putting Baines in mind of the Addams Family's butler, Lurch. The tune jingled in his head once more. He shot Ross a weary glance.

"This is going to be a long evening."

Adams returned, beer in hand, and flopped back down on his recliner.

"Come on, then," he growled. "We might as well get on with it."

"Thanks," Ross said. Baines detected no sarcasm and mentally congratulated her. "Now, the first thing I want you to do is cast your mind back to September 2002. The 26th, to be precise."

The electrician blinked. "Oh, right. I'll just put a call in to my secretary." He scowled. "How the fuck can I cast my mind back to then? It doesn't mean a thing to me."

"Then let me refresh your memory. You saw Graham Endean, the swimming coach. Confronted him, in fact, or so he says."

He closed his eyes as if he was trying to remember, although Baines couldn't decide if that was genuine or a big show.

"Right," he said after a few moments, "I'm with you now. Yeah, I went to see him at his poncey pool. He owed me money and he was avoiding me."

"His side of the story, sir, is that you bodged a job and he was refusing to pay until you put it right."

"Yeah, right. There was nothing wrong with my work. It was a piece of piss little job. I tried to tell him that, if he was having fuses blow, it was his wiring, but he wasn't having it. Dick. He thought I was going to rewire half his bloody house on the back of a stupid little job like that. He must have thought I was born yesterday."

"It got heated, according to Mr Endean," Ross said, making a show of consulting her notes. "A bit aggressive. Maybe a bit violent."

"Nah. Well, yeah, all right, he got a bit shovey. Yeah, I remember now. I was lucky not to end up in the pool. Arse."

"But you threatened him."

"Nah," he repeated. "Who's telling you those porkies? Endean, I suppose."

"And another witness. Christine Lindsay."

He frowned. "Oh. Oh, yeah, she was there. Bloody shame what happened to her. Same night, I seem to remember. But what's any of this got to do with Leigh?"

Baines slid into the conversation. "All in good time. DS Ross asked if you threatened Mr Endean."

"Told him..." Ross made a little show of consulting her notes. "Ah, yes. 'You'll be sorry for this'."

Adams took another swig, maybe buying time. "Did I say that?" Shrug. "It sounds like me. But it wasn't a threat. Probably something to say. I might have meant I'd take him to the small claims court."

"And did you?"

"Nah. Not enough money in the job to piss about over."

"So did you get even that very night? Where were you when Christine Lindsay had her accident?"

"Christ, I dunno. Home, I expect. It was ten years ago. More, maybe. What? Endean's trying to blame me?"

"Should he?"

"Look..." He reached out and put the beer bottle down on the edge of the desk. "Why would I hurt the girl? If I wanted to get at Endean, I'd have a pop at him. I know people who..." His eyes widened. "Christ! You think that's what happened with Leigh? Is that what fucking Endean's saying?"

He slumped back in his seat. "Fuck. I can't believe it. Look, if he says I had something to do with that accident, maybe you should look at him for the blame. And why would I suddenly take it into my head to hurt Leigh, after all this time, just to get at him? It makes no sense. No sense at all. I wrote the money off and moved on. And now that bastard's trying to pin everything on me?"

"No one's pinning anything on you, Mr Adams," Baines assured him. "Certainly not Mr Endean."

"Then where's this crap coming from? First you all but accuse Kyle, now me. I wanna lawyer."

"That's your prerogative, sir. We're just talking. No one's accusing you of anything. You say you were home on Friday night, with your wife?"

"Yeah." His whole attitude had become surly.

"Can anyone apart from Mrs Adams confirm that?"

"Nah. Kyle was out, and our daughter's on holiday with her mates." He frowned again, then became animated. "Hang on, though. Me and my wife sat outside until quite late. It was a nice night, so we had salad and stuff outside and polished off a bottle of wine. Maybe the neighbours heard us talking, or saw us from an upstairs window."

"We'll check," Baines said.

Adams grinned like a man who has just heard the most ironic joke in history.

"Yeah. You do that. Why the fuck would I hurt Leigh? She was practically Kyle's sister-in-law."

"That's right," Ross beamed back at him. "I heard he got very friendly with her at a wedding not so long ago."

He stood up. "That's it. You arresting me?"

"Not at the moment."

"Arresting Kyle?"

"Not at the moment."

"Then fuck off out of my house."

"Sit down, Mr Adams," Baines said, keeping his seat. "Don't give us a reason to make this in any way formal."

"I'd like to see you try."

"Gavin Lane," Baines threw into the mix. "Know him?"

"What? You're trying to pin that on me, too?"

"So you know he's been murdered too?"

Adams rolled his eyes. "I see the news. I might be a tradesman, but I do have a brain."

"I understand you knew him."

"We did the odd job together. Big jobs, major refurbs, you know? Where they bring a few different trades in. Can't say I really knew him, though. Who says otherwise? What's it to do with Leigh?"

"Maybe nothing," Baines said, essentially lying. "Your name came up as one of his associates."

"I wouldn't go that far. I worked with him a few times."

"A beer or two at the end of the day?"

"No. I didn't like him. You never knew what mood he was going to be in. He could go off to use the toilet, nice as pie, and come back angry. I can't be doing with that at work. I certainly wasn't going to do it on my own time. And no, I didn't dislike him enough to kill him. Didn't I hear you had someone for that?"

"No," Baines said, wondering how far the assumption that Len Clough was guilty had already spread.

Adams sighed, throwing himself down upon the recliner. He grabbed his beer and took a savage swig. "What do you want from me?"

"For the moment, we just want to know your movements for the nights Leigh Fletcher and Gavin Lane died. You knew them both, after all."

He stared at Baines, then Ross, then back at Baines. "You're thinking it's the same killer? The word is that Gav was robbing from allotments and got whacked by one of the growers."

Baines ignored this. "So the night Gavin Lane died, you were..."

"That was - what? Monday night? I worked, I came home. Went to bed about eleven. And, since there were only the two of us in the bed, only my wife can confirm that."

Baines nodded, irritated that Mrs Adams wasn't at home. Apparently, Wednesday night was always ladies' night out for her. Adams was vague about what was on tonight's agenda. He thought it might be book group. Usual suspects, different activities each week of the month.

"Get her to call me in the morning," Ross said, handing him a card.

"Are we done?" Baines detected a petulance in his voice.

"For now," he said.

Outside, they loitered by the cars.

"We'll get someone to check that alibi with the neighbours in the morning," Baines said.

"Sure, but are we really any further forward?"

He leaned against the Mondeo. "Not really, no. I mean, the guy knew both Leigh Fletcher and Gavin Lane, but the idea that it's all to do with a minor altercation over some piddling unpaid bill seems... well, it can't be the whole of the story. And it's hard to see how he could have been responsible for what happened to Christine Lindsay. Endean was there, after all, and has said what he reckons happened."

Ross took out her cigarettes. "What if Endean was lying?"

"In what way?"

"Christine has a nasty accident, but can't remember anything. Suppose it didn't happen the way Endean said? Maybe he tried something on with her, maybe he simply egged her on to make that dive. Suppose Joe Adams came back, saw it all, and has been blackmailing Endean ever since?"

"So how would that lead to the two deaths we're investigating?"

She lit up, took a drag and inhaled. "All right. So Leigh finds out what really happens. Either Endean lets something slip or maybe Leigh speaks to Christine and has her suspicions aroused. We should check whether the two girls have any communication."

Baines thought he saw where this was going. "So Adams is blackmailing Endean, who tells him the truth is about to come out anyway and the golden goose will be cooked. Adams knows Gavin Lane's a bit of a villain and he pays him to help him abduct Leigh and stage her death. Then he silences Lane for good measure." He frowned. "Endean must have been paying a hell of a lot for that to be worthwhile. I don't think swimming coaches are rich."

"He was a top swimmer before he was a coach, Dan. Who knows how much he made out of sponsorship and TV appearances? I seem to recall he was on a couple of pundit panels during the London games."

He nodded. "It's a theory, and as good as any we've got. That's the trouble, though, Too many bloody theories and not enough to pull it all together and make a concrete case. I still think the reason Leigh died is the key, so yes - it's worth finding out if Christine has been in contact with her."

"I'll ring her in the morning," Ross said, consulting her watch and yawning.

"I'll update Lizzie and then head for home." Where doubtless he would torture himself imagining Karen with smarmy Mike. "There's a stone we haven't turned, Jenny, I'm convinced of it. Maybe it has to do with the Fletchers being burgled, maybe with Leigh being mugged. I think Joan's still got the files on those two crimes. I'll have a look at them with her tomorrow."

She took another draw on her fag. "Fancy a drink?"

He was tempted for a moment. She wasn't at all his type and, despite her obvious embarrassment about her encounter with Ashby, would be forever tainted by it in his eyes. Yet here was a woman asking him to join him for a drink. It might be just a drink - or, just maybe, the chance of a drink and something else.

Karen was moving on. Maybe this was what he needed. Some sort of catharsis.

"A drink?" she repeated. "You know? In a pub?"

He pressed the button on his key fob, unlocking the car.

"You know what?" he said. "I'm wiped out. Maybe some other time?"

21

The hotel in Huntingdon had become a tradition in Archer's long-distance relationship with Ian Baker. It wasn't really much more than a glorified pub and the decor, although generally fresh and clearly quite recently updated, still nodded a little too much towards the past for Archer's taste. But it was comfortable, offered decent food at a fair price, and had king sized beds.

She had arrived at around 10 pm, exhausted and ravenous, but the sight of Ian, seated in a corner of the bar with a pint, had lifted her spirits immediately. His dark-brown hair was immaculate as ever, and his ice-blue eyes shone as he spotted her approaching. He had the sort of chiselled features she always liked, and was a snappy dresser - tonight's ensemble consisted of a crisp blue Oxford shirt with white butcher-boy stripes, dove-grey trousers with creases you could cut yourself on, and black loafers that looked fresh from the box.

It was a look that contrasted with a Norfolk burr when he spoke that could fool people into thinking he was something of a yokel. Archer knew better. He had as sharp a mind as anyone she knew, and a gift for lateral thinking.

Ian had originally booked a table in the restaurant, but Archer was past formal dining, so they settled for bar meals - scampi and chips for her, a pie for him. The conversation over food was limited to general chit-chat about their respective journeys and the sort of day they had had. He was sympathetic about her ordeal by press conference, and Gillingham's treatment of her after Claire King had sprung her question.

"He was probably right," she admitted as one of the bar staff removed their plates. She was on her second glass of Pinot

Grigio and feeling more relaxed. "I probably should have ignored her."

"The question was still out there," he said. "Your answer was almost irrelevant. Local journalists, eh? I've encountered the whole range. Some don't know their arses from their elbows, others think they're going to win prizes for what they write for a little local rag. Then there are the half-decent ones who want to move on to bigger and better things."

"Claire's probably in the latter camp, although she's probably getting to the stage where, if it doesn't happen soon, it might not happen at all." She shrugged. "But I didn't come here to talk about her."

"Nor did I." He grinned at her. "What say we take these drinks up to our room?"

It hadn't quite been what Archer had meant and, if she had wanted to follow through on her resolve to have some real conversation with him before lovemaking diverted them both, that was the moment to insist on finishing their drinks in the bar.

Instead, it was quite some time later, lying in bed with her head on his shoulder, his arm encircling her, that she tried to make some conversation - although they were both sleepy and she knew it wouldn't go on for long.

"This is lovely," she ventured. "I really wish we could get a decent chunk of time together. There's so much we still don't know about each other."

"Really? I think I know you pretty well, Ms Archer. I know what you like for breakfast, I know what you look like when you're asleep..."

She propped herself up on one elbow. "You watch me sleep?"

"Sometimes. You sleep like you do most things - sort of intently."

"You think I'm intense?"

"Oh, yeah." His free hand began to slide down her body. "Let me give you an example."

She caught the hand and held it, arresting its progress, knowing where it would lead.

"Seriously, though - wouldn't you like to spend some real quality time together?

She watched his face, a part of her scared that she'd see he didn't like the idea at all. But he just smiled and stroked her face.

"It would be nice. Life gets too much in the way. Job in the week, kids at the weekend..."

"I'd really like to meet your kids, you know. I mean, they can't expect their parents to live like monks or nuns forever more."

"I know, I know." He closed his eyes the way he did when something was especially difficult. "I'd like nothing better. It's just a matter of timing. Maybe I need to pick my moment and introduce them to the idea that their old man is seeing someone, and then take it from there. But I need to do it carefully."

"I do understand." She wanted to ask him when he thought the right time might be, but the last thing she wanted to do was sound pushy or needy and scare off the first decent man she'd been involved with since her partner, Rob, had dumped her in the wake of her disfigurement.

"Let me see if I can engineer a weekend some time," he said. "You're right. These snatched nights here and there aren't like a proper relationship. We should have some time to do all the things that other couples do. Browsing round little shops. Walking in the rain together."

She snuggled closer. "It sounds perfect."

"Give me some time, Lizzie, and I'll try and make it happen. I just need to make the space."

"And then pray that a big fat case doesn't get in the way," she pointed out.

"I'll put the word out," he said seriously. "No murder and mayhem on our weekend away."

"That'll do the trick," she said, yawning. It sounded like progress. A weekend away - it sounded like one of Bridget Jones's mini-breaks. Hopefully without the slapstick.

Sleep was coming for her now. Her last thought before surrendering to it was that she wished it could always be like this.

* * *

Baines was awakened from a troubled sleep by the telephone chirping shrilly. As he picked up, he glanced at the illuminated face of his bedside clock. It was after 1 pm.

"Baines," he mumbled, an uneasy feeling settling in his stomach. A call in the small hours often meant that someone had met with a violent end.

"It's me," said a small voice.

"Karen? Are you okay?"

"I'm in Milton Keynes. Can you come and get me?"

His fuddled brain tried to grasp the concept. "MK? What are you doing there at this time of the morning?"

"Can I explain when you get here please? I'm all on my own and it's dark, and there's some groups of young blokes around, and I'm scared."

"Where exactly are you?"

"The railway station."

"Sit tight. I'll be 25 minutes, tops."

"Okay." But her voice still sounded shaky.

Still trying to wake up properly, he heaved himself out of bed and hastily threw on some clothes before grabbing his wallet, mobile phone and car keys. Outside, Little Aston was asleep and it was pitch black. Even the sliver of moon that he had noticed last night had disappeared from view. He unlocked the Mondeo, got behind the wheel and started up.

As he drove through various villages on the way to the fast A4146 Leighton Buzzard bypass, he tried to think why Karen would be in Milton Keynes city centre at a time like this, apparently with no means of getting home under her own steam. Then he remembered why he had struggled to get off to sleep.

She was supposed to have been on a date with Mike from work. Mike, who was so funny, like an old fashioned gentleman. Had he taken her to MK? If so, where was he now? Or had the date fallen through, and she'd gone there for some other reason? But if that was the case, surely she'd have her car. Maybe it had broken down, but Karen would simply have called her breakdown cover in that case. She was not normally some helpless damsel in distress when things went wrong, yet he'd detected some teariness in her voice

Soon he was on the A5. He exited at the junction for Central Milton Keynes and headed towards the railway station, noticing the array of lights burning on store signs, and in their windows. It had always been a mystery to him why, in an age when everyone was supposed to be so conscious of their carbon footprint, businesses were allowed to burn enough fuel overnight to power a small country.

He pulled up at the front of the station. Karen was nowhere to be seen, but he found her just inside the entrance, leaning against a wall and looking small and vulnerable. She spotted him and hurried over, taking his arm.

"What's happened?" he wanted to know.

"Please, can we just get in the car?"

He led her back to the Mondeo. As soon as they had got in and closed the doors, she threw her arms around him. She was shaking and sobbing. His own arms went around her, making a protective circle.

"Hey," he said. "Hey, shhh. What is it? What's wrong?"

She pulled away, her face a mess of smeared mascara and snot. "Have you got a hanky?"

He had pushed one into his pocket when dressing, an automatic thing his mother had drummed into him. Always make sure you have a clean handkerchief. He handed it to her and she blew her nose.

"Please, Dan," she said, like a child, "take me home."

He put the car in gear and drove. Sat next to him, she alternatively scrubbed at her eyes and sniffled into the handkerchief.

"So what's happened?" he asked again. "I thought you were out with lover boy tonight."

"Don't call him that," she replied with shocking venom. "Don't ever call him that."

There was something about her tone that alarmed him.

"What's happened?" he repeated, more demanding now.

She leaned back, her head resting on the cushioned restraint. "Please. Just drive. I'll tell you when we're indoors."

He had the wisdom to just shut up and drive then. It had been a very long time since he'd seen her so upset, and he had to wonder why, and because of whom, she was upset now. It had to be to do with her colleague, Mike the Gentleman. If he'd done anything to hurt her...

Baines realised he was gripping the steering wheel far more tightly than was necessary. He tried to relax, but the anger still raged inside him. Whatever had upset Karen, it must have been bad to have shaken her up so. Somebody was to blame, and Dan Baines might just have to make them regret it.

Halfway home, she suddenly stirred and said, "Shit. I haven't got my house keys."

He glanced her way. "Not like you to forget them."

"I didn't. They were in my handbag when..." She put a hand over her face.

"When what?"

"Can we go to your place? Can I stay with you tonight?"

"Of course," he said without hesitation. "But where...?"

"I'll explain. Promise."

Some 20 minutes later, he was turning back into his own driveway. He noticed that Karen was still shaking when she got out of the car, so he slipped an arm around her shoulders as they walked to his front door.

Once inside, he offered her coffee or tea. She asked for something stronger, so he poured liberal measures of single malt whisky into two tumblers.

They sat side by side on his living room sofa. He had stopped yawning at least. The return drive had woken him up. He waited patiently until she had taken two or three sips of the drink. She seemed a little calmer, although she was staring into the bottom of the glass, as if at something only she could see.

"So tell me," he prompted.

"Christ. I must look such a frightful mess."

"*Tell* me."

She nodded, sniffled again, took another sip of whisky.

"You know I was out with Mike tonight?" He nodded encouragement. "Well, he was really lovely at first. We went to the cinema. He held my hand through the film, and it was fine. Crap film, though. Anyway, there's this scene where these characters sneak into a public toilet and have sex. And he leans close to me and whispers, 'He's not very convincing, is he? I could do better.' And then he says, 'There's a toilet here, you know.'"

Baines gawped at her. "Tasteful," he remarked. "The perfect gentleman."

"Just for a moment, I thought I'd misunderstood. I couldn't imagine he was suggesting what he seemed to be suggesting. I tried to pass it off as a joke. Said something like, Thank you, but I went before we came out. But then he pulled my hand into his crotch - right there in the cinema - and said, 'Meet me in the gents in five minutes.' With that, he gets up and goes."

Baines was stunned. It was a picture he really didn't want in his head.

"What did you do?"

"Do? I told myself it was a joke in poor taste. That he wasn't as mature as I'd thought. That he'd needed to go to the loo and made this stupid joke. But when he came back ten minutes later, he seemed annoyed. He sat through the rest of the film sort of rigid, staring ahead, ignoring me."

"Great technique."

"Anyway, when the film was over, he acted like nothing had happened. Perfect gentleman again, helping me on with my jacket, holding my hand on the way out of the cinema. He'd already booked a restaurant in the centre for us to eat at after the film, and I decided to go with him, even though what had happened had made me a bit wary of him. I thought it was just a bad judgement on his part. That maybe even I'd given out the wrong signals."

"Christ," he said, hoping he was wrong about where this was going. "If I had a pound for every abused woman who thought it was her fault."

"Oh, no," she said. "He didn't really abuse me. At least, not physically. Anyhow, we had a nice meal, and he was funny and charming, and I relaxed a bit. He'd said when he picked me up that he was out of practice, and he hoped he didn't make too much of an arse of himself. So I was prepared to give him the benefit of the doubt.

"We'd come in his car, and he walked me back to the car park. I was feeling a lot more comfortable as we started driving. Then he asked if I'd like to go back to his place. I said that was daft, because he'd only have to drive me home after coffee. You know what he said?"

"Tell me."

"He said that wouldn't be necessary, as I'd be staying the night. That he had more than just coffee on his mind. Or, if I preferred, he knew a place where we could park up."

"Cheeky git. What did you say?"

"I was angry. Embarrassed. I said I must have given all the wrong signals if he thought I was going to put out on our first date, especially in a public place. I told him I wasn't the dogging kind

"He got angry. Said too right, I'd sent out the wrong signals. Said he'd assumed I must be gagging for it. Then he said we could take it slower if I wanted. He could spend the night at mine instead."

"Nothing if not persistent."

She put down her glass. "What, you think it's a joke?"

"I think he's bloody immature. These are not great chat up lines." He was speaking calmly, almost flippantly, to try and reassure her, but he felt his own indignation rising at anyone who could treat Karen like that.

"So I told him, quite coolly, that we weren't about to spend the night together anywhere. And that was when he stopped the car and told me to get out."

He had been about to sip his whisky. The glass halted halfway to his mouth. "*What?* Just like that?"

"Just like that. At first I thought he was joking. I asked him to please take me home. He said I was a little tease, and I could get out of his car right now. I could tell he was getting really worked up, and I was scared. I undid my seat belt and got out. I was so flustered, I forgot for a moment that my handbag was on the back seat. As soon as I was out, he roared away. My purse, my house keys - everything was in my bag except my phone. For some reason, I'd zipped that into the inside pocket of my jacket, otherwise I wouldn't even have been able to call for help."

He was lost for words, indignation turning to rising rage. "Unbelievable."

"I didn't believe it either, not at first. I thought he'd calm down and come back for me. At least bring my bag back. I waited half an hour before I realised that wasn't going to happen, and I was already getting frightened. I'm really sorry to have disturbed you so late."

"Don't be stupid." Then the dam burst. "What a fucker. Where does he live?"

"What? Oh, Berkhamsted." A small town in Hertfordshire a few miles over the border.

He had slammed his glass down on the coffee table and was reaching for his jacket. "What's the address?"

"What?" She looked at him. "What do you think you're doing?"

"I'm going round and getting your bag back."

"I don't know the address. A road off the High Street, I think."

"What's his surname? I'll check the directory."

She let out a great sob. "Can you just stop? Please? I've had more than enough macho bullshit for one night, Dan."

He stood there, his arm through one sleeve, horrified at her distress, mortified that he might have helped cause it.

"But you'll need your things."

"He'll probably give me my bag in the morning, making some lame excuse about his behaviour. If not, I'll ask him for it."

"What if he's difficult?"

She attempted a smile. "I'll call the police."

Privately, he wasn't going to let this go. For starters, he was going to find out who this Mike was, and have checks run on him at work. He realised in hindsight that he should have done that before Karen ever went out with the bastard. He might just be a pushy lout who expected women to fall at his feet, but he might equally have form for sexual assault. The pattern certainly fitted in with some rapists and molesters he had come across.

"I'll tell you what you can do, though," she said as he threw his jacket aside again.

"What's that?"

"Hold me."

He sat down beside her and she sank into his embrace, her head on his shoulder. He was conscious of the warmth of her and the smell of the delicate perfume she wore. For a moment, it was so like holding Louise that he almost wept. When he had mastered that emotion, a stirring in his groin told him there was something else he was going to have to control. The desire to kiss her was almost overwhelming. And he knew that would be a disastrous mistake, after what had happened tonight. He looked at his watch.

"It's well after two," he said, and his voice sounded husky to his ears. "We both ought to go to bed, or neither of us will be much use tomorrow. I'll make up a bed for myself on the sofa.

Her own replying voice was small. "I don't think I want to be alone, Dan."

She nuzzled his neck and he hastily held her away from him.

"I really think that would be a bad idea, Karen."

"But why? A bastard like Mike shows me how lucky I am to have you. I don't want other men. I want you, Dan. I -"

"Don't say it," he said, pressing a finger to her lips. "Please. We're both tired, and you've had a horrible experience. We made one mistake a long time ago. I don't want the next time to be another off the cuff misjudgement."

"Bad timing again," she murmured, not looking at him, the corners of her mouth turned down in misery. Then she dashed the tears from her eyes with the heels of her hands and looked at him, her eyes still glistening. "What if I don't want to wait any more?"

There was a hunger in her eyes that matched what he was feeling inside. "You're upset. You're vulnerable. I don't want to take advantage of you. I -"

The rest of his words were lost as her mouth closed over his and he found himself responding to the kiss, all thoughts of being sensible, taking things slowly, driven out in a heartbeat. All the years of longing crumbled away like a breaking dam. When the kiss finally broke, leaving them both gasping, it was Karen who stood up, extending her hand to him; Karen who led him upstairs to the bedroom.

Much, much later, he held her in his arms, so giddy with happiness that he thought his heart would burst. This felt so right, after so many wasted years, so many missed opportunities.

"Well," he said shakily, "I suppose this means I'd better come and see your psychic on Friday."

She shifted her position so that she could look at him. "You're coming?"

"Wouldn't miss it. I just hope he doesn't conjure up my scary Great Auntie Peggy."

She stifled a yawn. "There'll most probably be three dead bodies between now and then."

"Yeah," he said. "But as you recently reminded me, they won't actually be going anywhere."

"Nor am I, Dan. I don't want to be without you, ever again."

"And I don't want you to be," he said, kissing her.

"Maybe I could bring some things round at the weekend? A few clothes and toiletries? If you don't think that's a bit too forward?"

"You want to move in here?" He liked the idea, but he was surprised at how quickly things were moving.

"If you'll have me." Her eyes searched his face. "You don't want me to?"

He hugged her. "I want. A lot of ghosts in this house, though."

"Ghosts of people we love," she said, her eyes glistening again. "They won't hurt us. In fact, I rather think they would approve."

* * *

Not so far away from where Baines and Karen lay talking about the future, someone else was wide awake, staring through the darkness at the ceiling.

Everything was falling apart. The Leigh Fletcher murder had made the national news, with her family's emotional appeal prominent, but the local BBC news reporter had also noted that the police were linking a van seen in the area the night she'd died with another case, and had been quick to point out that there had been another recent killing only a few miles from Little Aston.

It was obvious that the reporter had joined up the dots, and absolutely certain that the police had established a connection between the two crimes.

How had it come to this? It had all escalated out of hand in the space of a few days. Every attempt to fix things had simply dug a deeper hole, and there seemed no alternative but to keep digging. It was obvious that there was at least one more loose end that had to be tied off in some way. It might even require another life to be sacrificed.

Well, at least there would be no need to try and wrong-foot the police next time. Trying to make Leigh's death look like an accident and Gavin Lane's murder appear like a spot of over-zealous vigilantism had proved futile - not entirely unexpected, but still a disappointment. Either ploy had only ever been going to work if the scenario had been taken at face value.

So if there did have to be another death, the chances were that the police would make the connection immediately. Even the most bungling of coppers could not be that stupid. The only thin ray of light was that it would be that bit easier next time. Leigh Fletcher's death had been a mess, but there had been no sense of remorse afterwards. Just a problem to be solved. That and the sense of power.

Taking out Gavin Lane had involved no great moral debate. It had been a job that needed doing, and there had even been some satisfaction in doing it. Murder was not - could probably never be - simple. But it wasn't the big deal people made it out to be, either.

The thought that, even with killing fellow human beings, practice made perfect, elicited a smile. Maybe it was something you could even get a taste for.

Now the stakes were so high that whatever it took to sort out the mess would have to be done. It could be seriously bad news for one person in particular.

22

The alarm had awoken Archer at 6 am. After the momentary disorientation of waking up in a strange room, she had smiled at the sight of Ian Baker curled up next to her in the bed. He seemed in no hurry to stir, so she got up and went to shower.

As the jets of hot water tingled on her skin, the messy end to the press conference and its aftermath had played themselves back in her head over and over, and each time it all seemed worse. She still seethed with the injustice of some of Gillingham's words, but the knew he was probably right on one count: she should not have risen to Claire King's questioning, and by doing so she had probably fuelled the journalist's sense of a story of police incompetence. Now there was the real risk that the media could undermine what was already a difficult investigation.

It would have been tempting to share a leisurely breakfast with Ian, but she knew she needed an early start. She made coffee in the room while she was dressing, resisted his suggestion of a quickie before she left, and set out to beat as much of the main rush hour as she could.

When she parked the car she was starving, so she made the snap decision that she could spare ten minutes and she cut through to the local Costa Coffee with Americano and something sugary on her mind. As she stood in the queue, dithering between a blueberry muffin and a chocolate twist, her gaze panned absently around the tables. So absently that it almost didn't register that she recognised the pair sitting in a corner by the window.

Stephen Ashby was deep in conversation with a leggy blonde whom Archer was beginning to see far more of than she cared for. She knew there was no accounting for taste, but somehow she doubted that Claire King was having coffee with the DI for his good looks and charm. And there was only one other thing she could think of that would interest a journalist in a copper. Ongoing revelations in the media about the scandal of phone hacking by certain national newspapers continued to uncover tales of illegal payments to police officers for information.

Now here was Ashby, who Archer would put nothing past, brazenly having coffee with the very journalist who had so effectively railroaded her press conference last night.

The temptation to leave the queue and confront them was almost overpowering, but she knew it would cause great harm and do little or no good. They would deny that their meeting was anything but innocent or, worse, cause a scene. King would have something else to write about, if she chose - although probably not, if she was slipping Ashby brown envelopes.

In the end, she decided to store the encounter away for the time being.

She walked out of Costa with her coffee. The decision on pastry she had solved by taking both the muffin and the chocolate twist. She had been skipping a lot of meals since the Leigh Fletcher inquiry had got under way, and she doubted that a couple of cakes would make her fat.

As she passed Costa's window on her way back to the station, she glanced in at Ashby and King. The journalist was scribbling something on a pad. Neither of them noticed Archer. But she noticed her own reflection, and the sight made her think about the makeup girl, Georgia, last night. She had made Archer's scar look less monstrous. Looking back, she remembered how it had unexpectedly lifted her confidence before her appearance in front of the cameras. But the hiatus after Claire King's interruption had meant they never had that chat about how she had achieved the effect.

In the office, she had barely sat down when Joan Collins came her way.

"Got a moment, guv?"

"Always got time for you, Joan." Carefully, she uncapped her coffee and took a sip. The caffeine began to kick in immediately.

"I've got some more details about Gavin Lane," she said.

Prior to last night's press conference, Collins had been tasked with digging deeper into Lane's past. Archer was impressed that she already had something to report.

"Let's hear it then."

Collins slid into the chair next to Archer's desk.

"As we know, after he left school he did a spell in the army. He was a sapper, and it seems he had an aptitude for the practical side of his work, but had had problems with discipline and had also had anger issues."

"Go on." Archer took her muffin out of its bag and broke it into four pieces.

"After he came out, it seems he drifted around building firms, doing some casual work here and there, supplementing his income with a little burglary. He's served two stretches for burglary, amounting to eighteen months, and another six months for assault."

"What do we know about the assault?"

"He did some sub-contract work for someone who was a bit bossy. Suffice it to say, those anger issues kicked in again. I also found out that - although nothing was ever been proved - he was suspected of administering beatings on more than one occasion on behalf of local gangsters."

"Was he now? So not just the good boy gone wrong his wife would have us believe."

"Let's just say it must be true what they say about love being blind."

The caffeine jolt and the sugar rush from her muffin were making Archer feel more human.

"Interesting," she said. "Makes him sound more and more like someone capable of holding a young girl under water."

"Maybe losing his temper and going too far?"

Archer nodded, imagining an accomplice vainly trying to get him to release Leigh's shoulders as she slowly drowned. In her mind's eye, his face was set, hard fury at being denied what he was after. She knew it was only one of many possibilities, but it was at least plausible. A thought occurred to her.

"You were digging into Marc Ambrose's prison visiting days. I wonder if he saw Lane? Come to that, I wonder if Lane and Colin Crawford were in the same jail at the same time?"

Collins smiled. "If we can establish that they knew each other, we'd be starting to build something plausible to work with, wouldn't we?"

"Work with Jason. Let's get to know Gavin Lane like the back of our hands. Who did he see, where did he drink, did he have any bits on the side? I want his whole life story, past and present, and I want it today. How are you on miracles?"

Collins' grin stretched wider. "Miracles? No problem. Just don't go asking the impossible."

Archer feigned disappointment. "Oh, all right then. Oh, and Joan?"

"Guv?"

"There was a girl called Georgia who did my makeup last night. Can you try and get her contact details for me?"

She almost regretted the impulse as soon as the words were out, half-expecting Collins to look at her strangely or, worse still, pityingly. But the DC neither batted an eyelid nor missed a beat.

"No probs."

* * *

Baines watched Collins walk away from Archer's desk, and then ambled across to talk to the DI himself. The imminence of last night's press conference, and the flurry of urgent tasks, had precluded a proper team briefing, and he was keen to catch up and share the results of last night's meetings with Graham Endean and Joe Adams. He'd sent Archer a couple of texts, but they were no substitute for a face to face.

One thing was certain. Nothing was going to puncture his mood today. He still couldn't believe how suddenly and easily his relationship with Karen had finally made its long overdue gear shift.

He had to admit to himself that he had awoken alone with a momentary panic. What if Karen had woken up feeling that last night had been mere comfort sex, and a huge mistake to boot? What if she had dressed and left without a word or a note?

But he had found her downstairs, making breakfast and complaining about how abysmally stocked his fridge and food cupboards were, a charge he could hardly deny.

He had dropped her at work on his way in, having elicited her promise to contact him if her bag was not returned. If he had needed any convincing of just how deeply he cared about her, his desire to take apart the man who had treated her so appallingly did the job. He still wasn't one hundred per cent sure he wouldn't find a way to pay him back.

Meanwhile, there was a job to do. He arrived at Archer's desk and made a pretence of knocking on an invisible door. She rolled her eyes, but mimed opening it.

"Are we having a team briefing this morning, or what?" he enquired. "I only ask because -"

"Oh," she said, looking momentarily flustered, but recovering fast. "Yes, sorry, Dan. It was all a bit of a whirlwind last night, and you've doubtless heard about the shambolic end to the press conference."

He was disarmed by her apology. "No?"

"Maybe Ashby hasn't heard yet. I'm sure when he can be arsed to show up, DCI Gillingham will be telling him all about it. Claire King of the *Echo* has stirred things up a bit, and apparently it's my fault."

"What happened?"

"She asked why we'd known about a possible connection to a van in Leigh's murder since Tuesday and only mentioned it last night. There's also a crappy online article, full of innuendo implying that we couldn't find our own backsides in the dark, and making a big deal about Leigh's best mate, Gemma Lucas, being a key witness."

He shook his head. "Oh, great. Let's hope whoever killed Gavin Lane doesn't decide to eliminate her, too."

"That's my worry, but Gillingham isn't inclined to do too much to protect her. Actually, one thing for your to do list would be to contact the family and at least put them on their guard. For Christ's sake don't scare them though. Get their confidence, Dan, and get them to report any concerns or suspicions to you."

"Sure. I suppose that'll mean more demands for action from our MP."

"I can't blame him for that." She shrugged. "I'd probably do the same in his shoes. But there might be good news there. His agent was at the conference and said he'd try and get his boss to back off."

"Gillingham will be pleased."

"Meanwhile, I've got Joan and Jason digging out as much as they can find on Gavin Lane, and I think Jenny and I will have another chat with Pastor Marc Ambrose. I'll call a snap team meeting around noon and we can have a proper catch up then."

"Okay." He made to leave, but she held up a finger.

"You might like to know I spotted DI Ashby and la King having a cosy coffee in Costa this morning. What do you make of that?"

The very idea astonished him. "I know what I don't think," he replied. "I don't think Claire's so hard up that she'd have romantic designs on Steve, not even as a trade off for a story."

"No, but I bet he'd be capable of believing otherwise. He probably imagines that reek of stale cigarette smoke he carries with him is enough to drive any woman wild."

"It would make them mad, you mean. Seriously, though. You think he's leaking her information?"

"Possibly. Although, unless he's getting briefings from Gillingham, I'm not sure how much of an inside track he can give her on the case we're working."

"You're probably right," he said. "Still, if she publishes something explicitly linking Leigh's death to Gavin Lane's murder, we'll know where it came from. You're saying nothing to Gillingham in the meantime?"

She shrugged. "What good will it do?"

He returned to his own desk via Joan Collins, who dug him out the Lucases' contact details. Gemma's father was at work, but her mother was at home, as was the girl, whose parents had decided to give her the rest of the week off school to try and come to terms with her grief.

Half an hour later he was in their kitchen, watching Dawn Lucas make coffee for him. He wasn't especially thirsty, but he often found that accepting a drink attached some sort of informality to a visit. It made a policeman seem more human, he supposed.

"You didn't say much on the phone," she said. "I suppose it's more questions for Gemma?" She pursed her lips. "I do understand you're trying to find out what happened to Leigh, but it's not helping Gemma move on. We had a reporter here yesterday, too."

"So I heard. It might be an idea not to speak to them again, if you can avoid it."

She looked at him sharply. "Really?" She stirred the coffee and pushed it towards him. "Have you read her latest piece in the online *Echo*?"

"No," he admitted, "but I've heard about it."

"Gemma told you about that van two days ago, and you hold off on issuing an appeal. The *Echo* rightly embarrasses you and you ask me not to talk to them again. Is that what this is all about? Asking us to help you limit the PR damage?"

He blew on his coffee. "Not quite, no. Claire King can write what she likes. But, if you read her article, you'll probably know we're investigating a possible connection to another murder."

"So?"

"So, if ...if," he repeated, "there's a link, and these people have killed not one, but two people already, then it mightn't be wise to broadcast the fact that Gemma may have seen something."

He let his words sink in, watched her eyes widen. "You think they'll want to... oh, Christ!"

Her hands flew to her head. He recognised the first stages of panic and set his mug down.

"It's nothing to get alarmed about," he placated.

"But she saw nothing. She barely noticed the van, let alone who was in it." There was a phone on the wall, and a directory on the work surface underneath it. She seized the book and started riffling through it. "I'll ring the *Echo*. Make it clear Gemma didn't see anything. Get them to say that."

"No," he said, firmly but gently. "That's not a very good idea. You're better off keeping your heads down than drawing more attention to yourselves. Bad people are unpredictable and don't always do what you expect."

"That bloody woman," she said abruptly. "Worming her way in. Doesn't care about us, just her story." She slammed the directory down. "What are we going to do? What are you going to do to help us? I mean, is there some witness protection scheme?"

"Please," he pressed, holding up his hands. "There's no need to panic. I didn't want to scare you. I really doubt you're in any danger. Just keep your eyes and ears open and, if you see or hear anything in the least suspicious..." He put his card where she could see it. "Give me a ring. Or, in fact..." He took out a pen and turned the card over. "I live in the village myself."

"I know, I've seen you around. You're the one whose family..." She tailed off. "I'm really sorry."

"Thanks, but it's you I'm concerned with now. I'm putting my address and my home number on the back here. My mobile's on the front. If you're worried - any time, day or night - just give me a call."

Her smile was faltering but genuine. "Thank you."

He picked up his cup just as a plump girl with acne trailed in, hugging a pink teddy bear to her. Despite the fact that it was mid-morning, she was in a dressing gown over pyjamas.

"Hello, sleepyhead," the mother said, a little too brightly. "Sleep any better?"

"Not really. Who's this?"

Baines introduced himself. "Nice bear. Does he have a name?"

She gave him a look that said 'duh'. "She's a girl, obviously. Her name's Harriet."

"It was a birthday present from Leigh," Dawn Lucas explained. "Now I can't separate them, can I sweetheart?"

The girl shrugged. The way she was squeezing the poor thing, Baines doubted if Harriet the bear would be in one piece for too long. Already he could see a loose seam near the neck.

"Can I have some juice?" she asked.

Her mother fussed about, getting a glass, while Baines wondered why a 16 year old girl couldn't get her own juice. He doubted that her friend's death would have rendered her hands useless. Perhaps her mother was pandering just a little too much. Or maybe Gemma was milking it.

Or maybe I'm getting old and cynical, he told himself sternly.

"So have you come to ask me more questions?" Gemma asked him as she tucked Harriet under one arm and took the drink from her mother with her free hand.

"Oh, no," her mother said quickly, shooting Baines a warning glance. "Mr Baines was just coming to see if we were all right."

"Someone drowned Leigh on purpose, didn't they?" Gemma fixed Baines with her gaze.

"We think so, yes."

"Are you going to catch them?"

"Yes," he said, feeling like he'd wandered into a TV cop show where detectives routinely make promises to kids with no prescience of whether they can deliver.

"Good," she said. "Pity we don't execute people in this country." She slurped her juice. "Is there any chocolate, mum?"

Shortly afterwards, as sure as he could be that he'd done all he could for the family, Baines left. He didn't notice the car parked across the road, nor the figure behind the wheel, observing his departure.

* * *

Dawn Lucas had finished loading the dishwasher and was just about to ask Gemma if she wanted to go with her to the supermarket when the doorbell rang. She glanced at her watch, wondered who it could be, and actually had her hand on the latch when she remembered her conversation with DS Baines. He'd said it was nothing to worry about, but she'd felt uneasy ever since he'd advised her not to broadcast the possibility that Gemma might have seen something.

She released her grasp on the latch and peered through the spy hole. The face was familiar, and she immediately relaxed.

Patting her hair into what she hoped was a semblance of order, she opened the door. Said hello.

"So sorry to trouble you," her visitor said, with a warm smile. "I just thought it would be the right thing to do to drop by and see how Gemma's holding up."

"We were just about to go to the shops," she said, feeling a little unwelcoming as the words left her lips.

"Oh, well then..."

He looked disappointed. Maybe he even thought she had a problem with him. It was true they didn't exactly move in the same circles, but the couple of times their paths had crossed, she had found him charming, to put it mildly.

She vaguely remembered that the police had asked Gemma some questions about him in their first interview, but nothing seemed to have come of it. It was surely routine.

"Oh, look," she said. "Ten minutes won't make much difference. I can at least ask you in for a quick cuppa. If you've got the time."

"Always got time for a cuppa," said Marc Ambrose.

* * *

There was no sign of the Pastor when Archer and Ross walked into Little Aston Chapel, but Colin Crawford was there, pushing a broom around. Archer wondered how dusty one building could get.

Their heels clicked on the wooden floor and the sound echoed in the room. Crawford stopped sweeping and turned round. For a fleeting moment a scowl passed across his face, to be replaced by a neutral expression, rather than a smile.

"Officers," he said.

"Mr Crawford." Archer greeted him in kind. "Busy, I see."

"Got to keep on top of it." As if to underline the point, he gave the broom a quick twitch, presumably attacking some speck of dirt that only he could see.

He was fully suited and booted, jacket and tie immaculate, his outfit either identical to or the same as the last time they had seen him. The weather outside was warm again, and the chapel windows were closed.

"Aren't you hot?" she wondered, also wondering why on earth he needed to look like he was attending a board meeting just to do a spot of light cleaning.

"Hot?" He frowned. Perspiration stood on his forehead, rendering her question unnecessary, yet he pondered on it. "Well, yes, it is warm in here. I might have a glass of juice. Ladies?"

"I'm afraid this isn't a social call, Colin. Where's Pastor Marc?"

"Pastoral work," he intoned.

"Any idea where?"

"Am I my brother's keeper?"

"Genesis 4:9," Ross said, surprising Archer. "Didn't Cain say that, after murdering his brother?"

His smile was thin. "I can assure you, the pastor is quite safe. Now, if you will forgive me -"

"Let's talk about you, Colin," Archer said. "Let's talk about your jail time."

"With the greatest respect," he said, "I've paid my debt to society. I don't like to talk about those times now."

Archer took a couple of paces towards him, not quite invading his space, but closer than she thought would be comfortable.

"Tell you what. Let's make it something you like to talk about, here and now, or you can put that broom down and come with us to the station."

He leaned on the broom handle and looked her up and down. Then he treated Ross to the same scrutiny.

"Very tough talk for two little ladies," he said. Abruptly there was something chilling in his eyes, something ugly about the set of his mouth. "You think you can make me go anywhere

I don't want to go? You'd need to come back with a bit more muscle, I think."

Archer itched to wipe that look off his face, to make him eat his words, but Jenny Ross forestalled any action she might have contemplated.

"We might surprise you, Mr Crawford. But why put us all to the trouble? We're interested in a man called Gavin Lane. You were in Woodhill at the same time." Collins had dug that much up quite quickly. "Did you know him in prison? Or since, come to that?"

He frowned and stared at the ceiling, as if seeking inspiration from the Almighty. But not before Archer saw the cold look in his eyes momentarily replaced by what might just have been fear or panic.

He looked straight at Ross, his unreadable mask back in place.

"Kevin Lane?"

"Gavin," Ross prompted.

"Gavin Lane." He chewed on the name. "No, it rings no bells. Do you suspect him of something?"

"At this precise moment, we suspect him of being dead," Archer told him. "Either that, or the man we have in the mortuary is descended from Lazarus."

"Really? So sad. But weren't you investigating poor Leigh Fletcher's death?"

"Oh," said Ross, "you know us little ladies. Great multi-taskers."

"I've had this thought, Colin," Archer said. "Maybe whoever killed her thought females were weak and inferior. Maybe he liked to talk a bit macho to them to cover up his own inadequacies."

"Who knows?" Ross added, her expression angel-sweet. "Maybe he'd been in prison and spent a lot of time being buggered six ways to Christmas? That would make him question his masculinity."

The ugly mouth and ice-cold gaze were back. "I don't know any Gavin Lane, and I don't know who killed Leigh."

"And Pastor Marc?" Ross prompted. "Does he know the answers to either of those questions?"

He sighed. "My advice is to stop wasting your time. You'll find nothing bad about Marc. He saves souls. He doesn't take lives."

"Well, alleluia."

While Ross was baiting Crawford, a new thought came to Archer. "Colin, why is it that, whenever we come here, we find you? I thought you were working in Tring?"

"You've been doing your homework, but not thoroughly enough. I'm only part time. I don't need much to keep body and soul together these days, and it means I can do more to help Marc."

"One last question," she said. "Where were you late on Monday night and in the early hours of Tuesday?"

He blinked. "Most probably in bed. Why?" His face darkened. "Hold on. Is that when this Kevin Lane of yours died? I told you, I've never heard of him. Why are you trying to pin it on me?" His voice was rising.

"Calm down, Colin," said a cool voice behind them.

They turned to face Pastor Marc Ambrose, who stood in the doorway. The sun streamed in, bathing him in light and making him look like some depiction of a saint. Archer felt his eyes upon her and felt herself flush. Whatever else Marc Ambrose might be, he was certainly always easy on the eye. She shook herself mentally.

"Lizzie," he said. "Jenny. How kind of you to call. I'm sorry I wasn't here, but I'm all yours now."

"Marc," Crawford said urgently, "they've been trying to -"

"They're just doing their jobs, I'm sure. We must do all we can to help. Now," he said, striding into the room, his eyes on Archer, "I think I heard you mentioning a Kevin Lane, Colin. Would that be Gavin Lane, in fact? So sad to hear of his passing." He stood close to Archer. He was wearing a subtle aftershave that she found herself liking very much.

"Lizzie, I'm sure Colin is speaking the truth when he said he'd never come across Gavin," the pastor said. "But as for me... yes, I knew him."

23

Baines had arrived back at the station to find that Archer had not yet returned - which meant he had at least a little time to spare before the team briefing. He wandered into the car park and phoned Karen.

"I was worried about you," he told her. "Did you get your bag back?"

"It was on my desk when I got in," she said. "No one said anything. I reckon he arrived early so he could leave it before anyone else arrived. No note or anything."

"Have you seen him?"

"Passed him in the corridor. Bastard smiled and said good morning. I cut him dead. Not literally, more's the pity."

So the creep wasn't in the least embarrassed by his behaviour. Baines felt fresh anger welling up. "Let me know if you want me to hurt him for you."

She giggled, and he was glad to hear it. "Sounds a bit career limiting. Best not. I'm sure I can handle it, so long as he stays away from me, apart from work stuff."

"And everything's there? In your bag?"

"Seems to be, not that I've done an inventory. He'd have to be a special kind of pervert to nick anything out of this handbag, I can tell you."

Baines had knowledge of what a creep like this Mike might think of doing with access to what women carried in their handbags - keys, diaries, credit cards. All the information in a phone, but thankfully Karen had kept that in her pocket.

"Get your locks changed," he advised. "Just in case."

"In case?" She paused. "You think he might have copied my keys? Surely not."

"Please," he urged. "Don't take the chance."

He felt the same fury rippling through him that he'd felt last night, when his instinct had been to find out where the scumbag lived - misusing police resources if necessary - and confront him, possibly with some mild (or not-so-mild) roughing up involved. He badly wanted to do that now, but he was well aware that he would simply make worse what must already be an awkward work situation for her.

"I'll buy you a late supper after the show tomorrow," she said. "My knight in shining armour."

"I'll hold you to that," he said, trying for a light tone. "Repayment for the tosh you're making me sit through."

"Promise me you'll approach it with an open mind. You're seeing things that didn't ought to be real, correct?"

"I suppose."

"No suppose about it. Which means, Sherlock, that only one of three things are possible. Either they are real after all..."

"Neither of us really believes that. Especially as I can see them and you can't."

"Very good, Sherlock. Or you're going round the twist..."

"Not a welcome prospect. Sounds like a lot's riding on option three."

"Option three is there really is something supernatural at work. If I knew what exactly, I'd be the one up on stage tomorrow night. But look. Let's say it really is supernatural. Who's to say someone like our medium can't make contact with it? All I'm saying is, give it a go. I'll be the first one to laugh if he's obviously a con man."

"All right, all right," he laughed, a little of his anger dissipating. "Open mind it is."

"Gotta go. I'll text you about meeting up. And Dan?"

"What?"

"Thanks. For being there."

She broke the connection. As he returned his phone to his pocket, he spotted Archer and Ross getting out of their car.

"We could almost have the briefing here," he suggested as they joined him. "Not as stuffy as inside."

"I need Joan and Jason," Archer said. "Besides, it may be sunny out here, but I don't fancy inhaling too many exhaust fumes."

They went inside and, within twenty minutes, were seated in the briefing room, Gillingham in his usual place at the back. Archer waited for the team to settle down and then walked over to the board, where photographs of everyone associated with the case stared out at them. She held a ruler in her hand and used it to tap three of the images.

"Marc Ambrose. Colin Crawford. Gavin Lane. I can tell you that, as of today, the three are definitely connected. Crawford and Lane in the same prison at the same time - overlapping by about three weeks, as far we can establish."

"And Ambrose?" Baines asked.

"Glad you asked that, Dan. He and the prison are the real common denominator. He freely admitted to Jenny and me that he visited both Lane and Crawford when they were serving time in Woodhill. Crawford is sticking to his story that he never met Lane, and that might just hold water."

"Doesn't mean Ambrose hasn't introduced them since," offered Ross.

"Very true. Gemma Lucas said she was vaguely aware of two men in that van the night Leigh was killed. If Ambrose wanted something incriminating that Leigh had, or just wanted her silenced -"

"Or both," Baines suggested.

"Or both, then a couple of old contacts with histories of violence might just be the dream team. Dan, you've established the contact with Lane's widow. I'd like you to go back to her and press her on whether she's come across either of the other two."

"Will do. I'll take Joan, if that's okay. And you say Ambrose volunteered the connection?"

"Maybe he knew we'd winkle it out in the end and he preferred us to hear it from him. It stops us catching him in a lie and makes him look honest and transparent. Right," she said, tapping two more images. "Graham Endean, Leigh's coach.

And Joe Adams, the father of Leigh's sister's boyfriend. Not only is there a link through the Fletchers, but - you tell it, Dan."

So Baines outlined last night's interviews and the fact that Adams and Lane had also known each other.

"It's all a bit thin, in my honest opinion," he said, "but we've only really got speculation to go on with the pastor, haven't we?"

"Any chance the pastor links in with Endean or Adams or both?" Gillingham piped up.

"Nothing obvious," Archer admitted. "How did you get on with the Lucases, Dan?"

He shrugged. "I think they got the message to be on their guard without me actually terrorising them. Gemma? I don't know. I mean, I'm sure she's devastated, but I'm not sure she doesn't see herself as some sort of tragic heroine in a drama."

"I sometimes wonder if kids today know the difference," Ross said.

"I tried to make her think about the van she saw," he said. "See if she could remember anything at all about the two men. They were parked under a street lamp, remember? But she insists she barely noticed the van, let alone its occupants."

"It was worth a try," Archer said.

"It might be worth going back with Joan and going over what Leigh might have confided in her about her love life."

"Good idea. Maybe tomorrow. Focus on the widow Lane this afternoon. Jenny, maybe go with Jason and see if Leigh's family can think of anything else. Be subtle, but we're looking for indications that Marc Ambrose was too friendly with Leigh."

Gillingham spoke up from the back. "Lizzie, this is your show, but you're sure you're not investing too much time in this pastor?"

Baines watched her face, saw a frown come and go. Then she nodded.

"Fair question, sir. The truth is, we're not exactly knee-deep in suspects, nor possible motives. If there's anything we're missing, I'm hoping it will come out as we keep going back to people. What we do have is the van that was almost certainly used to take Leigh's body to the quarry and subsequently to transport Gavin Lane's to Westyate allotments. We have connections between Ambrose and Leigh, Ambrose and Lane, and Leigh and Lane."

"You could substitute Colin Crawford for Marc Ambrose and get the same equation, guv," Jason Bell threw in, his cheeks reddening as all eyes turned upon him.

Archer nodded again. "That's a good point, Jason. Jenny, when you and Jason talk to the Fletchers, see what they have to say about our Mr Crawford. Did he show an unhealthy interest in Leigh? Did he seem... I don't know, jealous, when she spoke to Ambrose?"

"I'll ask," Ross agreed, "but it rather sounded as if Leigh's life at the chapel was a bit of a closed book to the family."

"I know, but they may still have seen something some time, or maybe Leigh made some passing remark." Archer turned back to Gillingham. "I know we're light years from an arrest, sir, but -"

"Don't worry," the DCI said benignly, startling Baines. "Some cases are like that. At least some of the heat may be off from above." He briefly reported Chris Russell's visit the night before.

"Okay, everyone," Archer said when he had finished, "work to do. Any last questions?"

Collins put her hand up. "For Dan, really. Jason and I have been looking at those files you asked to see - the robbery at the Fletchers' and Leigh's mugging. I don't know. I've had a feeling that something was staring me in the face, and I think Jason has hit upon it."

Archer turned to the Scot. "Tell us, Jason."

He nodded and opened the file, from which he extracted two photographs enclosed in transparent plastic document holder and held them up.

"This is typical of the pictures from the scene," he said. "It looks thoroughly ransacked, doesn't it?"

Baines vaguely knew the house, which was tucked away in a corner of a cul de sac. By all accounts, the thieves had broken in during the afternoon when the family were either at work or school. No one had seen anything.

"It's just..." Bell handed the pictures to the person nearest to him and they began to circulate. "I don't know. Something. So I looked at the list of missing items" He removed another document holder, this time containing a typed sheet. "Almost all electrical goods. A TV, iPod and speakers, all the cameras and computers."

The list, too, was passed round. As Baines scanned it, he sipped machine-produced coffee and grimaced at the taste.

"Not *almost all,*" Collins corrected Bell. "*Nothing but* electrical goods."

"So they knew exactly what they were looking for," he suggested.

By now, Gillingham had the pictures. "You think? So why are the tellies in the lounge and two of the bedrooms still there? And the microwave in the kitchen?"

"That's sort of my point, sir," Bell said, red-faced. "If it was just an opportunist robbery, why go to all that trouble and then leave half the goodies behind. And why trash the place like that? I mean, there's no jewellery on the list, nothing like that. If all they wanted was electrical goods, why rummage through drawers?"

"I might say it was just mindless vandalism," Collins said, "only it doesn't really look quite like that. I've seen scenes where thieves decided to trash people's homes for good measure. There's been graffiti on the walls, stuff smashed for the hell of it. I remember one place where one of them had taken a crap in the bath. Silly sod left his DNA in the process and might as well have signed his name on the wall. This isn't like that."

"The fact is, it isn't like anything," Bell said. "But I know what this does remind me of. I visited a house once that was supposed to have been burgled. When you walked in, it looked thoroughly done over, but somehow it looked more like a film set than a ransacked house. As if someone had tried to create a look. A couple of items were broken, but they were low value, high street stuff. There were some expensive-looking lamps and mirrors and, surprise, surprise, they were untouched."

"Don't tell me," Archer said. "Insurance fraud."

He nodded, grinning now. "We found the allegedly stolen items stashed in the garage."

"You think this is what this is?"

"That's one possibility. I don't suppose anyone bothered to verify that the family were really where they say they were. I suppose they could have got someone else to do the job. But I don't know... all that stolen stuff can't be worth more then five grand put together. I get the impression the Fletchers aren't short of a few bob, so why?"

"One of the kids, maybe needing cash for drugs?" Ross speculated.

Bell smiled. He seemed to be growing in confidence as people took his thinking seriously. "The TV that did go missing was Leigh's. Could she have flogged her own stuff and claimed it had been stolen? Perhaps Leigh wasn't such a nice girl as she was painted. Maybe she got into other shady stuff and it got her killed. Although, if she ripped off her own home, she must have had an accomplice with transport. Maybe she did have a boyfriend, but she's managed to keep him secret."

"But isn't that just speculation, Jason?" Trust Gillingham to pour cold water on something.

But Bell smiled again. "You're right of course, sir. Even if she was seeing someone at the time of the robbery, that doesn't mean she's still seeing him. Maybe she stopped having sex once she found religion."

"But kept up the drugs, and didn't mind a little burglary? If so, she's the biggest mass of contradictions I've come across in quite a while."

"What about the sister, though?" Baines chipped in. "She's old enough to drive."

"And she's got a boyfriend," Collins added. "Whose father has connections to Gavin Lane and Graham Endean."

"So what are you two saying?" Gillingham demanded.

"I don't know," Bell admitted. "I just think there's something not sitting right. This robbery, Leigh's mugging, were not coincidences. They're something to do with her death."

"I agree," Archer said. "Good work, Jason. You could be onto something, so keep thinking on this. Right, everyone - a lot to do."

* * *

Archer was thinking about making herself a coffee when Collins hurried across and pressed a slip of paper into her hand.

"Almost forgot. Those details you wanted, Lizzie."

She stopped, looking at Collins blankly. "Details?"

Collins dropped her voice so she was barely audible. "The makeup girl. I hope it helps."

She felt a flare of annoyance. "Helps?" she said, trying to sound casual, but feeling anything but. "Why, what did she say?"

Collins raised her palms defensively. "Whoa, nothing. I didn't even speak to her. I just spoke to the company, told them what I wanted and they gave me her email and mobile."

Archer looked about her. They were alone in the corridor.

"So why the crack about it helping?"

As soon as the words were out, Collins looked mortified, and Archer realised it was her own sensitivities that were the problem.

"I'm really sorry," Collins was saying. "I didn't mean to be presumptuous."

"No," Archer said. "It's me who should be sorry, snapping like that. Don't worry about it, Joan - and thanks."

It was Collins' turn to check that they weren't overheard.

"Lizzie, if you don't mind me saying - everyone here has pretty much got used to your - you know." She touched her own cheek. "We don't care about it. But on telly last night, it was barely noticeable, and it didn't look as if you'd been made up with a trowel, either."

Archer examined the other woman's words to see if there was a compliment in there.

"Thanks," she said. "I think." She wanted to end this conversation.

"All I'm saying is, when you asked me to get those details, I guessed you wanted her to help you do your own makeup. And I thought, great. We can all do with a boost in confidence. Oh, fuck, I'm making a mess of this. Keep your mouth shut, Joanne."

Yes, you are, Archer thought. Yet she was also touched by Collins' kindness. Impulsively she squeezed her arm.

"It's fine, Joan. Thanks for the information - and for the support."

Collins' dark eyes searched her face. "You're sure we're okay?"

"I'm sure."

"Thank God for that." She glanced across at Baines's desk, where he stood looking restless. "I'd better go."

Collins hurried away. Archer stood with the slip of paper in her hands, her thoughts a jumble. Even if Collins kept her thoughts to herself, if she changed her makeup to try and disguise the scar, everyone here would still know what lay beneath the slap. It would be like a bald man suddenly sporting a wig. The thought made her shudder, and she abruptly screwed the paper into a ball and tossed it into her waste paper bin.

24

Baines and Collins arrived at Marie Lane's home. She must have been looking out for them, because she opened the door as they walked from the car.

"More questions?" she said as they walked into the lounge, which looked as if it had been hastily tidied.

"Sorry," Baines replied. "More questions."

She sighed. "Coffee? Tea?"

"Actually, no thanks, if that's okay. We don't want to take up any more of your time than we have to."

"Fine. Have a seat then."

They sat.

"Have you got anywhere?" she asked. "With finding out who killed Gavin, I mean?"

"We're following some leads," Baines told her, "but nothing I can really tell you about yet. We've spoken to the couple of contacts you've given us so far, but we've drawn a bit of a blank, so we thought we'd have another look at the people he knew."

Marie Lane shook her head. "Gav was hardly Mr Social and, as I've told you, half the time I never had a clue where he was, who he was with, or what he was up to."

"Does the name Marc Ambrose ring a bell?"

She looked blank.

"Pastor Marc Ambrose?"

"Pasta Marc? What, does he do an Italian cooking programme on the telly?"

"Not that kind of pasta. A pastor as in a preacher."

She guffawed. "A preacher? Gav had nothing but contempt for religion after what he saw in Iraq."

"He was in Iraq?"

"Yeah. He saw what people did in the name of religion, and he said some of the things our people did weren't much better. Not that he had a problem with that."

Baines looked at Collins, who shrugged.

"What do you mean?"

"He said some people on our side didn't always go by the Geneva convention. When they wanted to get information out of people, for instance. He didn't much care - as far as he was concerned, he was in a war, and you did what you had to - but it was our politicians' holier than thou attitude he couldn't stomach."

"So he didn't know Marc Ambrose? Maybe as a prison visitor, when he was in Woodhill?"

"It's not a name I know, but I doubt it. Why are you interested in him?"

"How about Colin Crawford? He was in Woodhill at the same time as Gavin."

She creased her brow. "Doesn't ring a bell. He didn't talk a lot about life inside, though. For all I know, he met both those people. Still, a preacher... that sounds unlikely."

Collins spoke up. "What about his time in the army? Did he speak much about that? You said he talked about getting information out of people?"

"Yes. He never named names, but one time what he saw was torture, pure and simple."

"What did they do?"

"They put the man in a bath, full of water, and they kept holding him under. They got him to right the point where he thought he was going to drown, and then they let him up. They were going to keep doing it until he talked."

"And did he talk?"

"Gav said no. In the end he really did drown."

* * *

With the rest of the team out and about, Archer was left alone with her thoughts. She played back this morning's conversation with Marc Ambrose and found herself dwelling more on its personal side than the professional. He had spoken to her as if she were the only person in the room, and she remembered feeling flattered at the time, whilst reminding herself that he couldn't fancy someone who looked like her. She'd had those feelings, even though she thought he might well have had slept with Leigh Fletcher when she was underage, and could well be involved in her death.

Not that she fancied Ambrose - far from it. He was much too obviously convinced of his own charms for her liking. And the man in her life, Ian Baker, might be maddeningly difficult to actually get to spend time with - as much her job constraints as his own commitments - but he also had never seemed to give a damn about her scar.

She had thought she had reached the point where she had to accept the damage that split-second encounter with a shard of glass had inflicted on her. Accept that her looks were what they were, stop kidding herself that she could do anything meaningful about them, and move on.

Except she had never really moved on. Every time she met someone for the first time, every time she was on show, like the press conference, her thoughts about how her looks were being judged overshadowed everything else. The girl, Georgia, had changed that for an evening, boosted her confidence. Okay, so Claire King, and then Gillingham, had conspired to deflate her, but that had been a professional matter. It had nothing to do with her looks.

It occurred to her that she had yet to make her coffee, and she removed her illegal kettle and her jar of coffee from her drawer and made her way to the kitchenette to make herself a drink.

Last night with Ian, she felt their relationship had taken a small, but significant, step forward. He had talked about introducing her to his kids, and she knew what a big deal that had to be for him. She imagined a future where she joined him on the weekends when he had the children. She hoped she would get on well with them. It could be like a proper family, albeit on a part time basis.

Assuming her horror mask of a face didn't give them nightmares.

The kettle had boiled. Coffee made, she returned to her desk, juggling mug, kettle and jar and hoping Health and Safety never spotted her. Once the kettle and coffee jar were safely locked away, she retrieved the paper Collins had given her from her bin, smoothed it out, and stared at it. Maybe she would give Georgia a call after all. Not now, but soon.

Maybe.

She was raising her coffee to her lips when her phone rang, startling her and almost causing her to spill it. She set it down on her desk while fumbling for the phone.

Two minutes later, she was hurrying to her car.

* * *

En route to the Lucases' home, Archer had made some calls. One was to Dan Baines, but the call went to voicemail. She was irritated. He was supposed to be Dawn Lucas's first port of call. Apparently the woman had called him first and similarly got no reply. But in all fairness, she reminded herself, there were still flat spots in the Chilterns where mobile signals died.

And he was probably talking to Marie Lane. Archer was the only member of the team not engaging with suspects or witnesses, so it made sense for her to go.

She beat the two uniforms in the squad car to the house by about five minutes. By the time Gemma's mother had shown her what had happened, Phil Gordon and a team of CSIs had arrived.

Gemma and her mum had been out shopping. They had returned to find the place ransacked. Mr Lucas had been at work and was hurrying home as quickly as he could.

As soon as Gordon turned up, Archer steered him into the kitchen.

"I'd be interested in your first impressions, Phil. Not forensically, but as a crime scene. I want to know if I'm reading it right."

Gordon gave her a speculative look. "Any clues?"

"First impressions please, Phil. I'm not going to colour those with my own thoughts."

"Fair enough."

While the CSIs went about their business, Archer got the uniforms - who were there for little more than backup - making teas and coffees. Gemma and her mother sat miserably on the sofa.

"What's the world coming to?" Dawn Lucas demanded. "A lovely girl like Leigh murdered, and now this. And the Fletchers had been burgled too."

"How quickly did you know you'd had a break-in?"

"The moment we walked in." She made a sweeping gesture with her arm. "Can't miss it, can you?"

The lounge looked like a mini-hurricane had hit it. Things had been tossed around and sideboard drawers stood open.

"But you had no sense of anything wrong until you got in?"

"What, like a sense of foreboding? Or a feeling someone had been here? No, not until we opened the door." She gave Archer a scared look. "You don't think this is to do with Gemma, do you? I mean, your Inspector Baines told us to be careful. You don't think it was, you know...?"

The killers, she wanted to say. You don't think it was the killers? But she clearly didn't want to scare or upset Gemma any more than she was already scared and upset.

"I don't know," Archer admitted, "but this is a robbery. You were out. It could just be an opportunist thing."

But she no more believed that than she thought the other woman did. Especially after hearing Bell's ideas about the Fletcher raid.

"Have you spotted anyone unfamiliar hanging around?" she asked. "Maybe even a stranger at the door? Or even someone familiar who maybe you don't usually see much of?"

"No. Well, the pastor from the chapel came asking after Gemma. We're not chapel goers, so he's not a regular visitor."

The hairs on Archer's neck tingled. "Pastor Ambrose? Did he stay long?"

"We had a very quick cuppa, then Gemma and I had to go shopping."

"And you told him that?"

"I think so." Dawn Lucas looked at her. "That was all right, wasn't it?"

"I'm sure."

"When were you actually out?"

"Oh, I don't know. From just after ten to maybe half eleven. We came back and found this."

She recalled Ambrose's appearance at the chapel, thought about how long she and Ross had been there with him. The time frames in which he could have broken into, and ransacked this house would have been tight, but not impossible.

"Look, will you be okay for a moment? I'd like to have a look around and speak to my colleague."

She moved carefully from room to room, the paper suit she had donned before entering the house rustling softly. Each room had been trashed, but to her eye it looked more like the perpetrators wanted it to look ransacked than the work of dedicated thieves. Her thoughts went back to the photographs taken at the Fletcher house after their own break-in. This had the same stagey feel, but at the same time somewhat different.

Only in Gemma's room did she think a little more purpose had been displayed. Drawers had not simply been emptied. Things had not just been tipped on the floor and left. Items were more spread around, as if someone had gone through them. The duvet had been pulled back and pillows removed from cases. A large pink bear lay on its back in a corner, its glass eyes staring at the ceiling as if it was suffering an outrage in silence. She picked it up and sat it on the bed, then went and found Phil Gordon.

"Phil, how does this compare to other burglaries you've attended?"

He nodded. "I wondered if you'd spot it. The short answer is, it doesn't. It looks like someone's made a cursory attempt to make the place look turned over, but really things have just been tossed about."

"Have you been in Gemma's room?"

"It looks as if there's been a proper search in there, doesn't it?"

"It does, Phil. I wonder if they found what they were looking for. Whatever that might have been."

He shrugged. "One thing's for certain. Whoever broke in here had no finesse. Just rammed something in between the back door and its frame and forced it open with brute force and ignorance. Not too much of a risk, as it's not really overlooked."

"Interesting. Did you attend after the Fletchers were burgled, by any chance?"

He nodded. "As a matter of fact, I did. I remembered it almost as soon as Leigh was identified. But that was nothing like this. Much more finesse, as if the thief really knew what he was about."

She told him about Jason Bell's theory that those thieves had been looking for something specific and had turned the place over to make it look like a more general burglary.

"But now I'm thinking Gavin Lane did the Fletcher break in," she said, "only now he's dead. What if someone was looking for something at the Fletchers', never found it, and has now tried their luck here? But with Lane gone, whoever was giving him his orders decided to do this one themselves."

"Looking for what, exactly?"

She shook her head, frustrated, feeling the key to the past week's events were almost in reach.

Yet somehow this crime scene turned her thoughts in a new direction.

"I'll go and have another word with Gemma."

The Lucases didn't look as if they had moved. Archer pointed to an armchair.

"May I?"

"Sure," Dawn Lucas said listlessly.

"Gemma, can I ask you something?"

Shrug.

"I don't suppose Leigh gave you anything for safekeeping?"

"No. I'd have said, obvs. Like what?" She looked tired, and Archer thought that explained her sullen attitude. She was also very likely scared to think someone had invaded her home so easily.

"I don't know," she confessed. And, as soon as the words were out of her mouth, she thought perhaps she did know, after all.

Bell had speculated on something to do with drugs, maybe even insurance fraud. But the fact was, Leigh had been targeted twice by a thief, almost certainly Gavin Lane, almost certainly because whoever was paying Lane feared she had something damaging to them.

So what was it? Her phone had been stolen, and so had cameras, iPods and computers. All storage devices.

And suddenly it made sense.

Suppose the thieves had really been after was files, whether documents, photographs, or both? Suppose, when they hadn't got them, they'd either tried to scare Leigh into giving it up, by holding her under water, or had simply killed her to silence her for good.

But then Claire King's emphasis on the friendship between Leigh and Gemma had made them think that maybe Leigh hadn't been holding what they were looking for, but had asked the person she was most likely to confide in to look after it for her.

Something incriminating.

"Maybe something like a CD or a USB stick?" she suggested.

The girl shrugged again. "No."

Inspiration struck Archer. "Did she maybe lend or give you a music CD that you've never played?" Perhaps an incriminating CD was concealed inside an innocent cover, although that would have risked Gemma opening it.

But Gemma was already rolling her eyes. "A music CD? What would I do with that? Even Mum downloads all her tracks these days. I've never owned a CD player. What, do I look like a pensioner?"

Archer smiled tightly. "I'll take that as a no."

"I'm sorry," Dawn Lucas said. "She isn't usually so rude."

"She's not rude. I just need to remember what century this is." She turned to the girl again. "All right. Has she ever passed you a file, in whatever form?"

Anger sparked in Gemma's eyes. "Oh, I see. You think maybe she said, if anything happened to her, I was to take it to the police? And what? I would have forgotten it? Decided not to?"

"No one would blame you for being scared."

"She was my best friend! How many more times? She hasn't given me anything."

"Okay." Maybe this whole idea of an incriminating file was just the product of her overactive imagination.

What was more, Marc Ambrose had dropped round, today of all days. Had been told they were going to be out. Coincidence?

Before leaving the Lucases, Archer had asked one of the uniforms to remain there until she was relieved and insisted that Gemma should not go out on her own. She could see she was scaring the family, but that was preferable to some of the alternatives.

She drove back to the station, an uneasy feeling at the back of her mind that something was still being overlooked. Right from the start, she and the team had homed in on the revelation that Leigh had not been a virgin and may have had underage sex. From there, they had developed theories focusing on who the sex might have been with, and what they may have had to lose if it came out - and that had placed Pastor Marc Ambrose firmly under the microscope.

She chided herself, not for the first time, about being too fixated on the good pastor. What if it wasn't about him? What if it wasn't even about the sex? What else could it be? Drugs at school? But that made no sense. The idea of a school kid engaging Gavin Lane's services and subsequently murdering him seemed ludicrous.

But then, what if drugs were being supplied from outside the school? Or by a teacher?

Possibilities swirled around in her brain. Whatever else, she sensed that she may have made the cardinal error of too quickly liking one suspect and one motive. There was plenty about Marc Ambrose that she disliked. It didn't necessarily make him a killer.

Not that she thought the focus on Ambrose had allowed other leads to go cold. They had asked a lot of questions in a lot of places and come up with nothing. Whatever both she and the killers were searching for was the key. She was sure of it.

But what was it? And who would get to it first?

* * *

The killer was philosophical about the latest setback. Smashing into the Lucases home while they were out had been a risk, but it had been something of a buzz, too, even if it had all been for nothing.

How had everything got so out of hand? Had the stakes really been so high as to justify two deaths? Maybe, maybe not. But, from the moment Leigh had drawn her last breath, there really had been no going back.

There was just the possibility that the very thing that had caused all the trouble in the first place had either never really existed, or had been destroyed. But if Gemma Lucas had it, that would explain why it hadn't turned up at the Fletchers.

It might also explain why Leigh had been prepared to die, rather than put her friend in danger. Well, Gemma Lucas was in danger now, all right. If she was dead, she couldn't say anything, couldn't suddenly produce the item her best friend had entrusted her with. It was always possible that she knew nothing, had nothing. But the risk of leaving her alive was too great.

Another unfortunate fatality was necessary, and soon. At least this time there wasn't much point in trying to wrong-foot the police. The previous two attempts at doing so had failed, and no one would believe for a moment that this death was a coincidence, or an accident.

Although... what about suicide? The fat girl, distraught about her best friend's death, decides life isn't worth living any more?

The killer smiled. Maybe one last piece of stage management was worth trying after all.

25

The team reassembled, pooling the results of their latest investigations. Ross and Bell had been unable to make any useful headway with the Fletchers; if Colin Crawford had in any significant way figured in Leigh's life, it was news to them. The pair had checked out the whereabouts of the family members, as well as that of Joe and Kyle Adams at the time of the robbery at the Lucas home. All had cast-iron alibis, with witnesses to support them.

The news that Gavin Lane had witnessed, maybe even been a party to, a water torture in his army days had struck everyone as significant. Maybe he had talked about it, and this had brought him to someone's attention as the very person to get information out of Leigh. Or maybe he had first been engaged as a thief, and had then suggested another way of getting at whatever his paymasters were so afraid of.

The information went some way to assuaging Archer's irritation that Baines had forgotten to charge his phone and missed Dawn Lucas's call.

For the first time in this case, Archer was feeling that surge of adrenalin she got when the elements of a case begin to come together. For too long, there had been too many possible suspects, too many theories, and too many fragments of facts. Now, at last, some pieces of the puzzle could be set aside, and she thought they were within a whisker or two of seeing the real picture.

Everyone, Gillingham included, agreed with Archer's analysis that the killer or killers were still looking for something - almost certainly media files - central to the whole investigation, yet no one could see how that took matters further. It would be interesting to hear what had been taken from the Lucases' home. Gemma's iPad went everywhere with her, so the thieves had been thwarted there but, in any case, the girl had been insistent that no file of any description had been entrusted to her.

"As far as she knows," Bell pointed out.

Archer looked at him with interest.

"Well," he continued, "what if Leigh hid something in Gemma's room and didn't tell her? She just didn't want it with her or in her home where it was vulnerable."

"But that means the thieves may have already found it," Collins groaned.

"If they have, then we're screwed," said Gillingham gloomily. "I know I was sceptical about the Fletcher break-in being related to Leigh's murder, but I agree now - this burglary at the Lucases, at this particular time, is more than just coincidence. There's something out there that points us to the killer. To think it might have slipped through our fingers..."

Ross held up her hand. Archer smiled, thinking she looked a bit like the cleverest girl in class.

"Jenny?"

"I'm just thinking - you know, Leigh did give Gemma something recently. For her birthday. A big, pink teddy bear. Did you notice if that was still there, guv?"

Archer's heart jumped as she saw where the DS was going. "Yes, it was. I picked it up off the floor."

"Well, what if Leigh hid something inside it and didn't tell Gemma? She wanted it somewhere safe, but didn't want to risk Gemma knowing about it."

Baines snapped his fingers. "I saw it too. I even remember noticing that some of the stitching around the neck didn't look too clever."

"So what if Leigh had unpicked it?" speculated Ross. "Unpicked it, slid something small inside the stuffing, and sewed it up as best she could? Then presented it to Gemma?"

"It's worth a try," said Archer. "Joan, can you get onto those uniforms I asked to keep an eye on the Lucases? Get one of them to get that bear off of Gemma and bring it here?"

"Better still, go yourself, Joan," Gillingham said. "She might not want to part with it. Show her your tender side."

"Have I got one?" Collins said. "And I thought I was hard as nails."

Archer grinned. "Yeah, right. Well, DC Hard as Nails, don't wait for this meeting to end, unless you've anything new for us. The sooner we get our hands on that bear, the better."

* * *

The waiting was unbearable. Archer had a good feeling about Ross's idea. If it came to nothing, they were back at square one - maybe even worse than that, given that the Fletchers and the Adamses at least had been ruled out of personal involvement in the break in at the Lucases. Of course, it was possible that, if any of them was involved in all this, they had found another Gavin Lane to do their dirty work.

She doubted it though. The amateurishness of the whole crime scene suggested that the burglar had little or no prior experience, and she also strongly suspected that whoever was behind it would not wish to bring in another outsider, not after Lane had proved more liability than asset. No, this raid had the hallmarks of someone doing the job themselves. Someone who had thought they were cleverer than they were.

Leigh Fletcher's death had been made to look like an accidental drowning; Lane's to appear like a vigilante attack. Both had been clumsy attempts to throw the police off the scent, but both had been undone by some fairly routine forensic work. Even the robberies, with specific targets, but made to look like more random raids, had finally been spotted for what they were.

It suggested either stupidity or a big ego. And the thought of a big ego made her think of Marc Ambrose all over again, the man who had impressed Leigh at a party and who'd had just enough time to turn over the Lucas home today before swaggering into the chapel and admitting he knew Gavin Lane. What better way of looking innocent than to come clean?

In less than an hour, a triumphant Collins had returned with the pink bear Gemma had christened Harriet. There was some good natured teasing about how it suited her, and one wag took a surreptitious photo that would later appear on the station notice board with the caption ‘Joan and her latest squeeze’. But the whole team wanted to see if the bear did indeed contain a significant clue to the case, so Archer took it into the briefing room, where everyone could gather round. Even DI Stephen Ashby deigned to grace them with his presence.

“This is the weirdest bloody post mortem I’ve ever attended,” he commented. It was the first time in her life that something he said actually made Archer laugh.

“If you’d be so kind, Nurse Baines,” she said, playing along, “scalpel.”

Baines passed her the slim pen knife he kept in his drawer. She selected a blade and picked at the already loose stitches. When she had opened the seam a reasonable amount, she peered into the opening.

“The stuffing doesn’t look right,” she commented. “I wouldn’t be surprised if something has been pushed in here.” She started to push her fingers in experimentally, then stopped. “Joan, your hands are smaller than mine. Don’t want to ruin the bear more than we need to.”

“It’s only a bloody teddy bear,” commented Ashby.

Archer rolled her eyes. “It’s a dead girl’s last gift to her best friend, Steve.”

Collins’s started working her fingers into the stuffing.

“There’s something here,” she said, after a few moments. “It feels like... guv, I think Jenny was right.”

Seconds later, she had withdrawn a USB stick and Bell was firing up the laptop that sat on the end of the table.

“What do we reckon, then?” speculated Gillingham. “Emails? Photographs?”

“I should have opened a book,” sniggered Ashby, making Archer think that his earlier joke about an autopsy had only been funny in the way that sooner or later a roomful of monkeys might accidentally type the soliloquy from Hamlet.

The computer took an age to warm up, but Bell was finally able to link it to the projector and insert the USB. He soon had a menu on the screen. There were six files - five emails and two photographs.

"Photos first," she instructed Bell, although she was dreading what she might be about to see.

The young DC double clicked on the first photo icon and an image filled the screen.

If the couple in the first shot had been of similar ages, the selfie, taken in a park, might have been quite sweet. Just two people, snuggling in the sunshine with a bandstand in the background.

Archer studied Leigh's face. The girl's smile was enigmatic: shy, yet at the same time there was a boldness about it. A child tracing her first faltering steps towards womanhood, in love for the first time.

Had the person beside her been around her own age, there would have been a touching innocence, but this was a man old enough and, Archer knew, intelligent enough to know better.

Perhaps he did. There was something fake about his smile, as if he already knew this picture was a mistake.

"I want to know where that park is," she said.

The second showed the man with his top off, his hand raised in a warding gesture, clearly taken by surprise. Reflected in a mirror behind him, Leigh, also topless, smiling wickedly as she took the picture with her camera. The room instantly recognisable as the girl's.

They all stared at the two images, which Bell had now placed side by side on the screen.

"They're date-stamped," Baines said quietly. "Look at the date."

"She must have been... what?" said Gillingham, the anger in his voice palpable. "Thirteen?"

The second picture had been taken one day later than the first. Archer remembered Gemma Lucas saying that Leigh had once asked her to cover for her absence, around the Easter holidays. The dates seemed to fit in with that.

"Emails," Archer commanded Bell.

He opened them one at a time. Email streams, the girl declaring her love and hinting at activities that she ought not to have been indulging in at her age, especially with this man. The man almost as romantic. The last stream, the man backing out of the relationship, evidently reassessing the wisdom of what he had been doing with Leigh Fletcher. Her desperate attempts to make him change his mind. In the end, urgings from him to destroy the very files that had found their way onto this USB stick, and her promises to do so.

Somehow, he had discovered the existence of the stick and taken desperate measures to get it back. A young life wasted to protect a reputation. An accomplice snuffed out to ensure his silence. The bastard at the bottom of it getting on with his life.

It made Archer feel sick to her stomach.

No one had spoken for a long while. It was Gillingham who broke the silence.

"Right. Let's arrest the fucker."

26

The four-car convoy rolled into Little Aston: two squad cars, Baines's Mondeo, and Jenny Ross in the pool Focus. Ross peeled off, heading for Gemma Lucas's home, her feelings mixed. She'd been given an important job to do, but she would rather have been in on the arrest.

Archer had suggested this. The files on the USB stick had been pretty damning, but were only proof of an improper, under-age sexual relationship with Leigh Fletcher. By themselves, they weren't conclusive evidence of murder. Archer and Gillingham were fairly confident that, once they had the suspect in custody and started pressing him, a strong case would begin to build. But if they could place him inside Gavin Lane's van the night Leigh died, that case would become almost irresistible.

Archer had asked Ross to bring photographs of Gavin Lane, the suspect, and Lane's van with her and, using these as prompts, make another attempt at getting Gemma to remember what she had seen last Friday when she said goodnight to her friend for the last time.

An anxious-looking Dawn Lucas opened the door, the chain on until she had identified Ross.

"What now?" she demanded. She was scared. The knowledge that her home had been invaded, almost certainly by Leigh's killer, must have the whole family on edge. Dawn's husband stood in the hall behind her. No surprise that he'd come home from work after the burglary.

"We're making an arrest," Ross said. "I can't say more than that at the moment, but if charges result you should be able to relax."

"Who is it?"

"I can't say. What I'd really like is a quick chat with Gemma."

Ross waited in the lounge with Gemma's father whilst Dawn called the girl down. When Gemma appeared, she looked somehow diminished. In less than a week, her best friend had died, her home had been broken into, and she had been warned that she might be a target for a killer.

She looked at Ross, glanced around the room.

"Haven't you brought Harriet back?"

"Sorry, no. We need to keep your bear a little longer, but we're taking good care of her."

Gemma nodded, but she looked miserable.

"Let's sit on the sofa," Ross suggested.

The girl sat down beside her, leaving acres of space between them. Ross had to ask her to come closer. Gemma budged up, closing maybe half the distance. Ross herself shuffled along until she was satisfied.

"Now," she said to the girl, "remember when we first met, Gemma? I asked you to remember back to when you saw Leigh off on Friday night, and to see the scene as you saw it then. Remember?"

"Yes, but -"

"I want you to do it again, but this time I'm going to show you some pictures. Okay?"

The teenager shrugged, her body language negative.

"You've got to help, sweetheart," her father said. "For Leigh."

So Ross went through her cognitive interviewing technique once more, the reason Archer had earmarked her for this task, helping Gemma to remember herself back into the scene to the point where Leigh was saying goodnight and Gemma was noticing the van. At that point, she slid her hand into the folder she had brought with her and withdrew three photographs.

"I want you to keep that scene in your mind, Gemma," she said, "but look at this photograph. Could this be the van?"

Gemma looked, her memory sharpened, her eyes widening.

"It could be. Yes. It looks like it. Could be," she said again.

"Stay in the scene. "You said you thought you glimpsed two figures inside that van. Describe them to me."

Gemma shook her head. "I told you. I hardly noticed."

"Maybe you've just forgotten. Do you recognise either of these men?"

Ross showed the girl two more pictures. One was Gavin Lane. The other was a group photograph, five people in total, the man now suspected of taking part in Leigh's murder and then killing Lane prominent.

Gemma looked. Looked again. Looked at Ross, then at each of her parents in turn. Closed her eyes, concentrating.

"Oh my God," she whispered. "I remember."

* * *

Baines's Mondeo and the squad cars pulled up outside the suspect's house. A couple passing by rubbernecked the vehicles. Gillingham, in the Mondeo with Baines and Archer, scowled at them, and they hurried on their way.

The whole squad would have liked to have been in on the arrest, but Gillingham decided to stick with the two other detectives, plus four uniformed officers. Even then, he admitted it was probably overkill, but he made no bones about wanting to humiliate the suspect.

"If I had my way," he had said, as Baines drove them to Little Aston, "I'd have the whole media hoopla. Nothing would please me more than to see this fucking hypocrite on the ten o'clock news, being bundled into a police car in handcuffs. But we'd probably get stick from above." He paused. "The mad world we live in now, I'll probably get stick anyway, for daring to nick someone like this without asking permission first. Well, sod that. We're making this collar, and we're doing it my way."

Baines had rarely seen the boss so fired up for making an arrest. Archer had told him that Gillingham had identified with Leigh Fletcher's family, related Leigh to his own teenage daughters. Ever since he had looked upon the photographs the girl had hidden - that she had apparently died, rather than give up - he had been in a bullish mood.

They were acutely aware that all they really had at the moment was suspicion of sexual activity with a minor, but that was enough to get the suspect into custody. It wouldn't be the first time a single piece of evidence had caused a suspect to crumble and confess all. Baines wondered if the man wasn't tougher than that, but it remained to be seen.

When the rubberneckers were well clear, Gillingham cracked his door.

"Right," he said. "Let's do this."

The DCI was first to the front door, ringing the bell, hammering on it for good measure, and flashing his warrant card.

"DCI Gillingham," Andrew Marling said, blinking. "How can I help?" He looked over Gillingham's shoulder, his smile looking fake now. "This is quite a deputation. Is it about Leigh Fletcher? Have you made an arrest? Come in, come in." He turned away and started down the hall with a spring in his step. Too springy for Baines's liking. "Chris and I are in the kitchen, about to have some coffee. Would you like some?"

Gillingham turned to the others, shrugged, and followed him.

Marling lived in a double-fronted detached house at the smart end of Little Aston. The hallway was not especially wide, so Archer fell into step behind her boss, Baines bringing up the rear. The uniforms waited outside, as arranged, in case the suspect bolted.

The kitchen was at the end of the hall. To reach it, the little procession had to pass an open door into what Baines glimpsed as a well-appointed lounge. Considering that Marling had split with his long-term girlfriend just after the election, citing 'different life goals' as the cause, the house didn't look in desperate need of a woman's touch. Marling had good taste and kept the place immaculate. Baines tried to imagine the minister doing housework, failed utterly, and presumed he employed a cleaner.

Marling's agent, Chris Russell, was in the spotless kitchen, drawing coffee from a fancy machine. Seductive aromas played around Baines's nostrils.

"Look, Chris," Marling said, "some colleagues from the local force, about poor Leigh. At least, I assume, so - unless you're behind with your parking tickets?" he added with a forced chuckle.

All the natural charisma, all the genuine, nice guy, man of the people façade was crumbling before the detectives' eyes. But if Chris Russell had noticed, he showed no sign.

"We're just having some coffee," the agent said. "What can I get you? Americano? Cappuccino?"

Gillingham smiled. "Actually, we won't be stopping. Andrew Marling, I'm arresting you -"

"What?" Marling squawked.

"- on suspicion of the murder of Leigh Fletcher. You do not have to say anything -"

"You're kidding me."

"This isn't funny, guys," Russell chipped in.

"- but it may harm your defence if you do not mention when questioned something which you later rely on in court. Anything you do say may be given in evidence."

Marling's eyes widened in what Baines thought was terror. Every drop of blood seemed to drain from his face, and he swayed. The man tried to speak, but nothing came out. He tried again.

"Chris?"

Russell looked from Marling to Gillingham, lips pursed, as though he was appraising the situation.

"Better just go with them," he said finally. "It's obviously some stupid mistake."

"We'll show you the evidence when we get to the station, Mr Marling," Gillingham told him. "Then you can explain how it's all such a big mistake."

"Evidence?" The Minister covered his face with his hands. "Oh, my God."

"Shut up," hissed Russell. "Shut up and say nothing until you're lawyered up."

"Good advice, Mr Marling," said Gillingham. "On the other hand, they do say confession is good for the soul. And we've got some interesting stuff at the station. But then, you already know what we've got, don't you? You've tried hard enough to get your hands on it. Killed a young girl for it."

"No -"

"Take him," the DCI said.

* * *

"I'd best be heading home," Leigh says.

Gemma looks at her watch. Just after 10.15. The evening seems to have flown.

"I don't see why you can't stay a bit later on a Friday. There's no school tomorrow, and we're not kids."

"Yeah, I might ask them about that. But," she stretches and stands up, "I'd better not be too late. Don't want them worrying."

"They don't seem to worry about Hayley."

Leigh smiles. "This is true. But then Hayley's with Kyle, the knight in shining armour."

Gemma, who secretly quite fancies Kyle, only manages a half-hearted smile back. She stands up herself, watching her friend pick up her phone from on top of the duvet and stuff it in her pocket.

Downstairs, Leigh looks in on Gemma's parents and says goodnight, then the girls walk to the door. Leigh opens it. Outside, the street is deserted.

"Still warm out." She moves out onto the doorstep, half turns. "See you tomorrow, darling."

Leigh has a training commitment in the morning, then the girls have plans to go shopping.

"See ya," Gemma says.

She watches as Leigh walks down the path, opens the gate. Walks through and closes it behind her. She turns right, as usual. Gemma watches her for a moment, turns to go inside.

Hears a vehicle start up.

She turns her head, a reflex response to the sound, just in time to see the headlamps of a van come on, across the road. She'd barely registered its presence before.

It moves off, heading in the same direction that Leigh has taken. As it passes right under the street lamp, she glimpses two faces. Two men, in what look like beanie hats, which seem pointless on a hot night. For an instant, the one in the passenger seat seems to look right at her. Then the van is on its way and Gemma goes inside and closes the door, the vehicle and its occupants already forgotten.

* * *

Baines removed the handcuffs from his pocket. "Hands behind your back, please, sir."

Marling was weeping now. "No, please..."

"Surely those things aren't necessary," said Russell. "Mr Marling will come quietly."

Marling's teary eyes darted his way. "You said it was all sorted."

Gillingham gazed at the agent with new interest. "Is that a fact?"

"Andrew," grated Russell, "for the last time. Shut the fuck up."

Marling was backing away from Baines. Archer's phone rang, but she ignored it.

"It wasn't me," Marling snivelled. "None of it. Okay, me and Leigh... yeah. But the killing? No. No." He jabbed a finger in his agent's direction. "It was him. All of it. All right, yeah, he said he'd sort it, but I never dreamed... He took it too far. None of this is my fault."

"Shut it, you fucking fool," Russell blustered. "Just shut it. They've got nothing."

"No?" Marling said, reaching in his pocket. "I've got this."

"Keep your hands where I can see them," snapped Gillingham.

"Just my phone. Please," the MP implored, drawing out a Smartphone. "You'll see... Just a second." He manipulated the touch-buttons on the screen. Voices emerged from the phone.

"Close the windows." It sounded like Russell.

"It's hot." Marling.

"Close them anyway."

The whirr of windows rolling up.

"Why all the cloak and dagger?" Marling again.

As the voices continued to flow from the phone, Russell stared at his boss. "You recorded it?"

"Quiet," Gillingham snapped.

Everyone listened to the rest of the conversation. Baines's phone rang. He checked it. Ross. He dismissed the call, reminding himself to return it as soon as possible.

Meanwhile, Russell looked as if he was weighing a difficult decision. When the recording ended, Marling turned off the recorder and put the phone down on the worktop.

"I guessed what our secret meeting might be about, Chris," the MP said. "I'm not as stupid as you think. I took precautions." He looked at Gillingham. "You see? I didn't kill anyone, had no part in those two murders. It was all his idea."

"Fair enough," Gillingham said. "I'm arresting you both."

"I don't think so." Russell yanked a long-bladed knife from a block by the sink, brandishing it.

"No, Chris," yelped Marling, "you're just making it worse."

"We all need to calm down," Archer spoke for the first time. "This isn't helping you or anyone else, Chris. Now, why not put the knife down?"

A warning leapt to Baines's throat but, before he could utter it, she had taken a tentative step towards Russell, who immediately grabbed her by the arm, pulling her to him and holding the knife to her neck. The agent's face creased into a smug smile.

"Right, Inspector" he said. "You and I are walking out of here. Don't get creative, or you'll have more than just a scar to worry about."

* * *

Ross drew up outside Andrew Marling's house, double parking and blocking in Baines's Mondeo, but not giving a damn about that. She had half-expected the Mondeo and the two squad cars to have already left, but they were still here. There was still time to make sure they got this arrest right, first time.

She'd tried phoning both Archer and Baines, but neither was picking up, so she'd jumped in the car and driven the short distance to Marling's property at speeds just short of reckless.

"What's going on?" she asked the nearest uniform.

"Search me. I thought they'd go in, caution him, cuff him, and bring him out. We've been told to hang on here."

She dithered, wondering if there was anything to worry about, whether something had gone wrong. But, apart from the small matter of the suspect being a government minister, this should be a straightforward enough collar. She didn't want to barge in and mess up whatever the others were doing, but she had important news.

The photographs had unlocked a memory that Gemma Lucas had been either unable or unwilling to access. She'd had only a glimpse of the two faces in the van when Leigh had set out for home - but the photographs had jogged her memory even better than Ross had dared hope. She had unhesitatingly identified Gavin Lane, but it was the girl's response to the second picture that had surprised her.

She supposed it should have been obvious that a teenage girl living in the village - even one completely disinterested in politics - might have remembered seeing the local MP parked opposite her house the night her friend had died.

Only she hadn't seen Andrew Marling. No, faced with the second photograph, she had pointed to another face in the group. That of Marling's agent, Chris Russell.

The tumblers had spun in Ross's head. Maybe Marling was still in some way involved in the two murders. In all probability, he was behind them. But, at the very least, his trusty agent had done his dirty work for him with Leigh. In all probability, Russell was behind Lane's murder too.

Did her colleagues know that yet? Did it matter? It probably did, for all sorts of reasons.

"The rest of you wait here," she told the uniforms. "There's been a development that the others need to know."

She walked up the drive towards the front door. She was two thirds of the way there when it opened inwards, revealing a scene that made her blood freeze.

* * *

There had been a long period after her injury when Archer had wondered if she would ever be able to walk into a dangerous situation again. The bottle attack and its consequences had rocked her confidence in so many ways. When an occasion had finally arisen when she needed to dig deep for some courage, she had somehow managed to find it, but this was different.

A sharp edge close to her face, touching her throat. Held by a man who had killed twice and clearly now felt he had nothing much to lose. One slip could be disastrous. Asked how she would respond to such a situation, the words fear and panic may have come into her mind.

Yet, now it came to it, she felt only calm.

"Chris, you're being stupid," she said evenly. "Where do you think you're going to go?"

"Let me worry about that," Russell said. "I'll think of something. I always do." He manoeuvred her round so his back was to a bank of cupboards, close to the kitchen doorway.

"Are you the driver?" he asked Archer.

"No."

"You are now." He looked from Gillingham to Baines. "Whoever's got some car keys, give them to her. Now."

"Do it," Gillingham said. Baines retrieved the keys from his pocket and pressed them into her hand.

"Now," Russell said, his gaze darting from face to face, "we're walking out of here, and no one's going to try and be a hero. Anyone even comes out of this kitchen before we're out of the house, and my hand might slip."

"If anything happens to her..." Baines began.

"Yeah, yeah. Save the macho bullshit."

"There are uniformed officers outside," Gillingham said.

"So? I've got a knife at your Inspector's throat."

Archer read the helplessness in Baines's eyes, imagined how she would feel if it was she who was watching something unfold that she was utterly powerless to influence. But what was uppermost in her mind right now was Russell's readiness to take a hostage, without a second thought. He had already shown amply that he was not much troubled by conscience. Whatever the precise circumstances of Leigh Fletcher's death, she was fairly confident that the man had lost not a moment's sleep over it, and he hadn't hesitated to kill Gavin Lane when he felt the man had become a liability.

Archer had little doubt about the fate that awaited her, once her usefulness as a hostage had been exhausted.

Keeping Archer close to him, Russell slid sideways into the narrow hall, keeping his back to the wall. He had to shuffle them both along so they could move towards the front door whilst he watched the officers in the kitchen. By now Marling had slid to the floor, knees drawn up to his face and hands over his head, but no one was taking much notice of him any more.

Russell and Archer reached the door.

"Open it," he ordered her.

She smiled sweetly. "You open it."

"You're in no position to argue."

"No? I thought you needed a hostage? I'm not much use to you dead."

"I could just take your eye out."

"You could. But I thought you wanted me to drive."

He stood there for a moment, then sighed. "Awkward cow."

She had hoped he would try to open the door whilst still threatening her with the knife, that he might relax his grip enough for her to try something. But he pushed her so she was up against the wall, face first, the knife held against her neck with his right hand whilst he pulled the door inwards with his left. In the close confines of the hallway, she thought her chances of disarming him and coming off unscathed were less than even. Better to bide her time than to wind up a dead heroine.

"Move," he said, pulling her away from the wall so she was in front of him again, and then he walked her out the door.

Ross stood a few yards away, her expression frozen in horror.

"It's all right, Jenny," Archer said lightly, determined to keep the situation calm. "Chris and I are going for a drive in Dan's car."

Ross frowned. When she spoke, her tone matched Archer's for lightness, all bar a slight tremor. "You'll have a job, guv. I've blocked him in."

Archer glanced beyond her and saw it was so. Russell had evidently done so too, because he swore.

"It's just not your day, Chris," she observed. "Why not give it up?"

"Not a chance," he sneered. Then, to Ross, he said, "Give her your keys." He was becoming agitated, Archer could tell. The situation was like dry kindling, needing the slightest of sparks to blaze out of control. Her chances of keeping things cool were sliding away.

"Give them to me, Jenny," she said. Ross nodded. Her eyes met her DI's and an understanding passed between the two women.

Ross stepped towards her, holding the Focus keys out. Archer extended her hand for them but, as the DS released them, she withdrew her hand by the barest fraction so that they brushed her fingers and dropped to the tarmac below.

Russell snarled with frustration, and that was when Archer judged that his attention was most likely to have been distracted.

Praying that she was right, and that her self-defence skills weren't too rusty, she whipped up her left hand, grabbing Russell's knife hand and rolling his arm downwards and outwards, away from her throat. At the same time, she stamped down on his instep, drawing a satisfying bellow of pain from him.

To complete her manoeuvre, she needed to spin to her left, but Ross had dived in, grabbing the killer's other arm, impeding her. For an instant it was a mess, and she thought he was going to get away from her as, screaming curses, he tried to pull away towards Ross, his superior strength already telling. She felt her feet scrabbling for purchase on the tarmac drive.

Then the uniforms were there, pulling Russell away. Baines was there too, twisting his knife arm until the weapon fell from his grasp. Jenny Ross was sprawled on the grass next to the drive. Seconds later, Russell was secured, and Gillingham was leaning into his face, panting.

"Please resist," he growled. "Please give me an excuse to punch your fucking lights out."

But the fight had gone out of the killer.

"Cuff the bastard," Gillingham said, "then go and get the other one."

As they put the cuffs on Russell, Archer held out a hand to Ross, who was still on the ground.

"Well done, Jenny. Up you get."

"Not sure I can, guv."

Only then did she see how pale the other woman was, and the red stain spreading over her torso. Her gaze slid to the knife, still lying where Russell had dropped it. There was blood on the blade.

"Boss!" she bellowed at Gillingham, who, along with Baines, was watching two uniforms manhandling their prisoner into their car.

The urgency in her voice got both their attention, and they turned to see what was amiss. Baines moved fastest, already ripping off his jacket. Gillingham had his phone out, punching numbers.

Archer stripped off her own jacket and pressed it against Ross's wound. The injured DS groaned. Baines rolled his jacket up and laid it under her head.

"I picked the wrong day to try and be Wonder Woman." The words were slurred, just about audible. "All I did was get in the way."

"No," Archer denied. "You were brilliant."

Gillingham was bawling into his phone that an officer was down, an ambulance was needed yesterday.

"I don't feel brilliant," Ross whispered. "I think it happened when the three of us were doing the okey cokey."

"Does it hurt?" Baines asked.

"Not so bad." Barely even a whisper now. "Everything's fuzzy, though. I could do with a drink."

"I'll get some water," said Archer.

Gillingham, who had just got off the phone, came over and squatted down, taking Ross's hand. "Ambulance shouldn't be long."

The uniforms were marching the handcuffed Andrew Marling out of the house. Archer had to wait for them to pass, then started down the hall towards the kitchen. She found a glass and began to fill it.

Then Gillingham's voice, hoarse with emotion, came from outside. "Don't worry about the water, Lizzie. We won't be needing it after all."

27

The atmosphere around the office was sombre, with none of the usual banter. Even black humour was beyond the squad today. A dark and gloomy pallor had settled over the whole station. The case might have been solved, all bar the formalities, but there was none of the usual sense of triumph. Everyone was stunned by Jenny Ross's sudden and violent death.

By the time they had been in a position to interview Marling and Russell, both had refused to say anything without a lawyer present. After consulting with his solicitor, Russell had promised a statement, but only after he had been allowed to sleep.

Gillingham had been incandescent. Archer thought he would have cheerfully beaten a confession out of the suspect, but in the end she had persuaded him that letting Russell stew overnight might be no bad thing. They decided to make Marling sweat too.

Meanwhile, they had listened several times over to the conversation the MP had recorded on his phone. It pretty well told the whole sorry story, but they wanted to hear it first-hand from Russell. One thing was certain: whatever pathetic attempt he might have made to wriggle off the hook had been blown out of the water by Ross's death.

At precisely 9 am, Gillingham and Archer sat across a table from suspect and solicitor in the most claustrophobic interview room the station had to offer. Baines and Collins were in another room, questioning Marling.

Archer was beyond tiredness. She'd spent some time with Ross's distraught parents, then gone home, heated some soup, found she couldn't face it, and fallen into bed. But she was sure she hadn't slept at all. Every time she closed her eyes, she saw Jenny Ross, blood spreading from a knife wound.

"I'd like to start by challenging the so-called incriminating recording of my client," Russell's solicitor said. Adina Walker was a handsome black woman, in her late thirties, with an accent you could cut glass with.

Gillingham's grin was wolfish. "Go ahead and knock yourself out, Miss Walker. The fact is, we didn't make that recording. Andrew Marling did. I think, if he was going to fake a recording to put your client in the frame, he'd leave out all the stuff that's going to send him to prison and destroy his career.

"Besides," he warmed to his subject, "we have techie guys who can do stuff I don't begin to comprehend, but which will prove the tape is genuine and that your client's voice is on it."

"We'll see," she sniffed.

He shook his head in a world-weary way. "We will indeed. Even if you were able to lay a glove on that recording, we still have the matter of your scum of a client stabbing a police officer to death in front of other officers."

"I must object to that sort of language."

"Oh, shut up," he snarled, waving her objections away. "What I'd like to hear now is your client telling his story in his own way. My strong advice is that he does himself a favour. I want the truth, and I want it now." He directed his gaze upon Russell. "Things might go slightly easier for you if you make a clean breast of it. Not that I'm able to offer you any deals, of course."

Walker had a brief, whispered conversation with Russell, then cleared her throat and said, "My client wishes to make a statement."

Gillingham's smile was almost tiger-like. "Wise decision."

Russell sighed heavily. "All right, then. I want you to know that none of this would have happened if Andrew's old girlfriend hadn't been such a selfish bitch. Seven years, they'd been together, and when he got elected he asked her to marry him. What does she do? She decides that being married to an MP with ministerial ambitions isn't for her. Some feminist crap about not wishing to live in his shadow."

"Right," Gillingham said.

"With that, she upped and dumped him. He was devastated. Oh, he hid it well enough in public, but inside he was hurting, and it must have triggered some sort of mid-life crisis. Meanwhile, it seems that silly little cow Leigh Fletcher had had the hots for him ever since his victory party after the election. They don't call him Britain's coolest MP for nothing, you know. He's got this way of talking to you in a room full of people and making you feel it's just the two of you. Maybe that was how it started.

"Anyhow, he must have made a big impression on her, because she hooked up with him on social media and started sending him direct messages. I guess she caught him at a vulnerable time, and maybe part of him was flattered. I don't know. I knew nothing of it at the time."

"You're sure about that?" Archer pressed.

"I had no idea, or I would have nipped it in the bud before it got as bad as it did. He didn't confide in me until it was a mess. It took about six months, but it seems one thing led to another, and he slept with her a few times before coming to his senses and breaking it off."

Archer was sickened by the matter-of-fact way in which Russell described what amounted to the grooming and, essentially, rape of a young, impressionable girl - not much more than a child. He all but portrayed Marling as the victim.

Yet she remembered now how genuinely upset Marling had been at the Fletcher house when she had visited soon after Leigh's death. She had half-wondered if this was an Oscar-worthy performance by a consummate politician. Now she guessed it had been authentic grief. Maybe that was a small thing in his favour.

"So he confided in you in the end?" she prompted. "When was this?"

"It was only when he was being tipped for future promotion into the government that he realised what a career limiting move he'd made, and he started thinking the whole thing was a ticking bomb. What worried him most was some indiscreet emails and at least one even more indiscreet photo she'd taken. He assured me there was nothing sordid about it; she'd been a young girl in love, and for a little while he'd been silly enough to fancy he felt the same."

"Silly?" she echoed. "Now, there's a word."

"Please continue, Mr Russell," Gillingham said, shooting her a warning glance. Archer berated herself. She shouldn't let her feelings get away from her.

Russell took a sip of water. "When he ended the relationship, he all but begged her to delete everything, and she promised that she would. Then she got mugged for her phone and he got worried that she hadn't actually done it."

"Hold on," Gillingham said. "You're saying the mugging was nothing to do with you?"

The other man smiled. "Is that what you'd decided? No. I promise you, it was just a random thing."

"Really?" Archer eyed him sceptically, but could see no artifice there.

"Nothing to do with me. As I say, I knew nothing about the affair at that stage. Anyway, he got in touch with her and she promised that everything had been deleted from the phone and her computers. But then," he rolled his eyes, "she admitted that she'd transferred them to a USB stick. Some tosh about keeping them to remember him by. She said they were quite safe, but he was scared."

"I bet he was," Gillingham remarked.

"He urged her to either destroy the stick or hand it over to him. It seems she got angry. Said he should have thought of all that before he used her and threw her away. Probably just temper, but he was terrified now that she'd decide one day to hand it over to the press or to you guys."

"But," Archer said, "even without the files, she still might have raised a complaint."

"She might, and it would have been damaging. But even more damaging with the evidence. Without the files, it was her word against Andrew's.

"Well," he continued, "I told him what a bloody fool he'd been, but I thought I could make it go away. I'd invested a lot of time in Andrew's political career, after all - helped him organise his election to the parish council, been his agent when he got on the district and county councils, and made damn sure he got into Parliament at the first attempt.

"We were going places together. I was convinced he'd be in Downing Street within ten years. As his influence in the party rose, so he'd become ideally placed to get me on the ladder. I had my eyes on a nice Euro MP seat in a few years' time. I wasn't going to let this one lapse flush all that down the loo.

"I figured that, if I could get the evidence away from her, then the most she could do was talk, and we could spin it as the romantic delusions of an impressionable kid."

"So you had her home burgled?" Gillingham surmised.

Russell shrugged. "I'd had my bathroom re-tiled about three months before by a guy called Gavin Lane. Funnily enough, it was Andrew who recommended him to me. Real bleeding heart, is Andrew. Likes to know of any ex-cons moving onto his patch, not so much because of any threat they might pose, but in case he can help them get a second chance. No," he added, seeing the look in Gillingham's eye. "Seriously. Andrew Marling's the real deal. If he hadn't made this slip-up, he'd have made a great Prime Minister one day."

"Such a shame about the slip-up." Archer was beginning to wish she could have this creep to herself for half an hour.

"It was," he agreed, missing the irony in her voice. "Well, I got chatting to Lane. Told him I was aware of his history and it didn't matter so long as he did a good job, and he started opening up over the odd cup of tea. Told me quite a bit about himself - about the army and he talked about his brushes with the law since he came out. I gained the impression he could turn his hands to most things, if you know what I mean, and that he wasn't exactly flush for cash.

"He'd left me his card in case I wanted any more work, so I rang him, arranged a drink. I wasn't sure how he'd react, but I came right out and told him it wasn't his DIY skills I needed. I said if he could get hold of all Leigh's devices - her phone, any laptops, computers and so forth, but especially any USB sticks, I'd make it well worth his while."

Gillingham looked more puzzled than Archer suspected he really was. "Why did you suppose those files would ever come out? Did you not think she might keep their secret?"

Russell spread his hands. "Look. Andrew said she was pretty cut up about him breaking off their relationship and now, with all these celebrities being outed for various sex crimes after the Jimmy Savile scandal, there was always a chance that Leigh would take it into her head that she'd been a victim too, especially if he got into the government."

The former DJ and TV presenter Jimmy Savile, had been a popular charity fundraiser associated with the Vale's own Stoke Mandeville Hospital, and knighted for his good works. In 2012, just a year after his death, hundreds of allegations of child sex abuse and rape had come to light, leading to a string of similar complaints against other public figures. Savile turned out to have been one of the most prolific sex offenders in Britain's history.

"Yet Leigh had kept silent so far." goaded Archer.

"So far," Russell agreed. "But who knew what was on her mind? For all I knew, she'd had blackmail in her sights from day one. For all I knew, she was biding her time, waiting for him to rise to high office so she could milk him financially or expose him."

Despite her earlier determination not to let her feelings show, Archer found herself shaking her head in disgust.

* * *

Andrew Marling's solicitor was from an expensive London firm and suited and booted in what Baines suspected cost more than his entire wardrobe.

The MP wept a great deal, but his version of how it had all started would turn out to match that of his erstwhile agent.

"I don't know now how the thing with Leigh ever went so far," he said. "I'm not a paedophile."

"You need to check the definition of that word," Baines retorted.

"Yes, all right. I just mean I'm not really into kids. I mean, I'm not into them at all. It was just a bad period in my life. The woman I loved had left me, I had the election triumph and a great future predicted, and no one to share it with. I suppose Leigh was in the wrong place at the wrong time. She practically stalked me, you know."

"You should have resisted," Baines said.

"I was flattered that a young kid like that had taken such a shine to me."

"You should have resisted."

"I suppose I was emotionally vulnerable."

Baines found his hands making fists. "You were vulnerable? What about her? Thirteen years old."

"She wasn't so innocent. She instigated most of what happened. I only slept with her twice, and then I came to my senses and realised it was wrong."

"It took you two times to figure that out?" Collins rolled her eyes. "I'm surprised you didn't go back for thirds, just to make sure."

"I was a bit of a victim here too."

Baines sighed. There was really no point in challenging the man's skewed view of the world. "Poor you," he said. "Go on."

Marling looked from Baines to Collins, then he straightened his shoulders and nodded. "I deserved that. You're right, of course. I can try and justify what happened to myself, but there's no excuse. I should have been stronger."

He wiped his eyes and blew his nose. "There's something else, though. I really did believe I was in love with her for a while. Maybe I was. I still have feelings of tenderness for her, even now. She was a sweet girl. She swore she'd tell no one, and I believed her. But later I started to worry that she'd see it differently one day.

"It was the Jimmy Savile thing that really shook me. Women coming out of the woodwork decades later. Well, I would have toughed it out if it came to it, but as you know now, I'd been a bit indiscreet in some of my emails to her and stupidly allowed her to take at least one really dangerous picture. She said she'd deleted them all, but later - after her phone was stolen - she admitted she'd kept a copy on a USB stick. I couldn't stop worrying about it. In the end I confided in Chris, and he said he'd make it go away."

* * *

"Anyway," Russell continued, "Lane was up for helping at a price. He broke into the house and took everything that she might have stored data on. But it wasn't there. So you know what the silly little bitch did then?"

"I'm sure you'll tell us," Gillingham said with a mildness Archer suspected was only skin-deep.

"She got in touch with Andrew and told him what had happened. Said he wasn't to worry. She'd done a thorough job in wiping all traces of him from the devices, and the USB stick was in a totally safe place. Some crap about them being her secret treasure, all she had to remember him by."

"So she was still loyal to him."

"Maybe."

"You don't think she guessed who was behind the thefts?"

"No. Maybe. Who knows? But I was still worried that if she started talking, evidence or no, it would be very damaging. With those files - well, they were dynamite by all accounts."

Archer felt a lump in her throat at the naïveté of an adolescent girl who fancied herself in love.

"She said Andrew wasn't to worry," Russell continued. "No one would ever know."

"But you didn't trust her?" Gillingham said.

"I think Andrew might have been inclined to. I thought it was touching but dangerous. It could have been a crafty hint that she had something against him that she might use one day. I wasn't having it."

"Go on."

"So I spoke to Lane again. How would he go about getting his hands on that stick? He said he'd been pretty thorough when he'd ransacked the house and would have taken a stick if he'd seen one."

"Did you tell him what was on the USB stick?"

Russell snorted. "You're joking. I'd paid him enough for him not to get nosey. Anyway, he guessed we hadn't got what we wanted, and that was when he said he knew a way to get her to tell us where it was. Something he'd learned in Iraq. Results guaranteed." He smiled. "I wasn't sure if he was just joking at first, but then I decided to ask him if he'd do it. I think he'd have done anything for enough money. On the surface, he was a chirpy tradesman, but I could see he had a streak in him that was hard as they come."

"So what happened next?"

"Lane tracked her movements and habits for a couple of weeks, and it was clear she spent every Friday evening at her friend's. We decided to pick her up after she left her friend's house."

Archer leaned forward. "We?"

"He said it was a two-man job. So we wore ski masks and picked her up in his van. Lane was very good at making it clear to her that she wasn't to scream. He scared the shit out of me, so God knows the effect he had on her."

"Where did you take her? We know she didn't drown in the quarry."

He smiled. It wasn't a pretty sight. "You're right. Well done, detectives. No, we had a bit of luck there. It turned out that our Mr Lane wasn't exactly true to Mrs Lane. A contact of his was away a lot and let Gavin have a key to his house to use whenever he wanted - no questions asked. We took her there blindfolded. She was pretty scared, but she still wouldn't give up the memory stick - wouldn't say anything about it - so Lane ran a bath. We made her strip to her underwear, and then we put her in."

"He held her under the water?"

"Oh, yes. He kept pushing her shoulders down, so her head went under. He didn't need much help from me - he was pretty strong. I just kept shining a torch in her face and asking her questions when he let her up. I disguised my voice, not that she'd heard it more than once or twice, and I kept asking her where the stick was. And you could tell how scared she was. But you know what?"

"Go on," growled Gillingham, looking sickened.

"Well, here's the irony. You know what I think? I think she thought we were the ones who wanted it to harm Andrew. She really was loyal to him, even after he dumped her, and she was determined not to betray him."

"You could have let her go, when you decided that, surely?" Archer said. "She probably wouldn't have said anything about what you'd done to her."

"No," Russell agreed. "We'd already told her we'd kill her family if she said anything. I reckon she believed us."

Archer shook her head. "In that case, she had two reasons for silence. She wanted to safeguard Marling, and she wanted to safeguard her family. If she talked about you torturing her, somewhere along the line she might have been under pressure to tell what you were after. She might have decided just to keep her mouth shut."

He frowned. "Maybe. I hadn't thought of that. Maybe she would, maybe she wouldn't."

"What was your plan if she agreed to give you the USB stick?" Gillingham asked. "I take it she didn't have it on her?"

"No, we searched her. The plan was for us to take her home, and for her to put it in a bag and drop it down to us from an upstairs window. We were going to threaten to burn the house down with her and her family inside if she didn't."

The DCI banged his fist on the desk. "That makes no fucking sense."

"I must protest -" Adina Walker began.

"Noted," snapped Gillingham. His gaze swivelled back to Russell. "You could have made those threats without abducting and torturing her at all."

"Yes, I suggested to Lane that he just put the frighteners on her. He said this way would prove to her that we meant business."

"The plan wouldn't have worked anyway," Archer said. "The stick wasn't in her house."

"No, I guessed that later."

"We'll come to that in a bit," Gillingham said. "How did she die?"

"She wasn't cooperating, and we were getting nowhere. Gavin started to get cold feet, wanted to give up, but we'd come too far. I think I said before, he'd do anything for money, but that's not right. I suppose he drew the line at killing. Well, I wasn't giving up. I said I'd have a go at her. So I held her under, the way he had. She must have been exhausted, because she didn't struggle much."

He frowned. "You know, it's funny. Looking at her face, under the water, her trying to hold her breath, was sort of fascinating. I knew I should let her up, but a part of me wanted to see how long she could hold it for. Lane started yelling at me, saying that was enough, tried to pull me away, but I kept holding her down.

"I distinctly remember turning my head round to tell him I'd had enough of pissing around. When I looked back, there were all these bubbles. And that was fascinating, too."

Archer felt chilled to the bone. She glanced sidelong at her boss, whose jaw was violently clenched.

"Then what?" Gillingham asked, and she had never heard such seething anger in his tone.

"When it was over, I felt more relieved than anything else. At the back of my mind, I think I knew it had always been going to end that way. We still didn't have the stick, but at least Leigh wasn't going to be talking to anyone.

"Gavin was panicking. He'd got a dead girl in the bath at his friend's flat. What were we going to do with her?

"And then I thought of the quarry. I thought if she turned up there, drowned, everyone would assume it had finally happened - a young life lost, an accident Andrew had long been warning about. Hell, we could even make political capital out of it. So we dried her off and dressed her. She'd clawed at both of us when she was putting up a fight, and I knew enough about forensics to know someone might spot skin under her nails, so we found some nail scissors and cotton wool buds and made as sure as we could that there was nothing to find."

"So you took her to the quarry?"

"Yes. We waited until about three in the morning, when we thought the chances of anyone spotting us were negligible. We put her in the back of Gavin's van, drove her over there, and threw her in. Her clothes, we folded and left there."

Archer leaned forward. "Did you tell Marling?"

"Not then. At that stage, I thought I'd done as much as I could to protect him, although I was still worried about that memory stick coming to light."

"Then Lane got greedy. Rang me up and said he'd not banked on risking a murder charge. He said the price had gone up. At first, I laughed it off, but he was saying things like, I was the one who'd killed her. Meanwhile, you guys were saying the death looked suspicious. You weren't buying the accidental drowning. He was asking for stupid money, and I just knew that, even if he got it, he'd be back for more."

"So what?" Archer interjected. "What was he going to do? Shop himself as well as you?"

"He said he could find ways of pointing the finger at me but keeping himself in the clear. I thought it was all bollocks, but I also thought the USB stick had suddenly become the least of my worries. He was becoming a liability. I couldn't trust him not to do something that would land me in the shit."

"So you decided to kill him too? Just like that? Even though you couldn't seriously believe he posed a threat?"

"You don't understand. It was all getting out of control. I'd tried to make sure Leigh had nothing on Andrew, and that had gone way too far. She was dead, and there was still a USB stick somewhere. Now here was Lane, trying to blackmail me. Yes, it was probably all piss and wind, but I felt I couldn't take any chances, not now. Gavin Lane was one problem I could deal with, and I thought I knew how to get rid of him without any possibility of suspicion falling on me.

"I knew there'd been a series of allotment thefts in the constituency. There was one the night Leigh died, over in Wendover. And I'd heard talk of some sort of vigilante action in Westyate. It had sounded hilarious to me at the time - the squash and carrot brigade making like Rambo. But all of a sudden I saw a way of getting rid of Lane and turning suspicion elsewhere. No one would ever guess he'd been involved in Leigh's death, and you'd think he'd been caught in the act by an angry allotmenteer."

"I think we know what happened next," Gillingham said. "But just for the record, if you would."

Russell took a long sip from the glass of water in front of him. "I told him he could have his cash, but I wanted to hand it over somewhere discreet, where he could count it. I made a big deal about it being a one-off payment and him counting it in front of me, so he couldn't say afterwards that I'd short-changed him. You know the car park at the bottom of Westyate Hill?"

"I know it," Gillingham confirmed. It was a popular spot for walkers to set off from, but also notorious for car theft and break-ins.

"I got him to meet me there after dark. When he got there, I told him to open his van so he could count his money on the sill at the back. Then I opened my boot and gave him a briefcase. There was no cash in there, of course - just a load of Andrew's old election flyers.

"I also had my baseball bat at the ready in the boot. As soon as he carried the case over to his van, I picked up the bat and followed him. He put the case down on the sill, and that was when I hit him, as hard as I could.

"I'd thought I might have to hit him several times over to finish him off, but he went down like a sack of spuds. I hit him once more, then I checked his pulse. He was gone. I hadn't thought it would be so easy." He gave an ironic little chuckle. "Clearly, I don't know my own strength."

Gillingham made an impatient twirling gesture with his hand. "Get on with it."

Russell picked up his thread. "I'd brought some polythene sheeting with me to avoid getting too much blood in the back of the van. Getting him in there wasn't easy, but I managed it, and then it's only about a quarter of a mile to the allotments. I waited until it was late enough that I'd be really unlucky if anyone spotted me, and then I drove there.

"It was a bastard dragging him up the slope in the dark. I knew several of them left spades sticking out of their plots, so I stopped by the first one I saw that had one. I wore gloves, of course. I arranged the body to look like he'd been attacked from behind by an angry plot-holder, then I got the spade and gave the back of his head a battering. I hoped I'd done enough to hide the original injury, and that no one would look that closely in any case."

"You didn't know who the spade belonged to?" wondered Archer.

"Didn't know, didn't care."

In spite of her disgust, she almost laughed at the trick coincidence had played. They'd thought Len Clough's spade had been singled out.

"I'd bought some bolt-cutters - cash - in a little hardware store north of Milton Keynes. Not too local. I went round cutting a few padlocks off, then put the cutters by the body, as if he'd dropped them when he was attacked. After that, all I had to do was shove the van keys in his pocket and walk back to my car."

"But you must have been in a bit of a state by the time you got home?" Archer pressed. "Blood and dirt? Your wife must have noticed." Mrs Russell had been outraged to be told of her husband's arrest. Had declared her intention to complain to Andrew Marling, and had been nonplussed to be informed that this would not be possible "for the foreseeable future".

"She didn't suspect a thing," Russell said. "I had a change of clothes in the car, and we have a sink and a water supply in the garage, where she fiddles with her plants. I was able to have a quick wash and change before I came in the house. I'd told her I'd be late home, and she was already in bed and asleep. I've since burned the clothes along with the plastic sheet and some garden rubbish."

As they had agreed beforehand, Gillingham didn't waste time explaining the forensic evidence that had linked Leigh and Gavin Lane to the back of Lane's van, nor how the ham-fisted attempt to make Lane's death look like a vigilante attack had not been nearly convincing enough. All that would come later.

"What about the robbery at Gemma Lucas's home?" Gillingham asked. "Did you arrange that?"

"No, I did it myself. I wasn't going to bring anyone else into the equation. I'd read in the paper how close the girls had been, and I started to worry that Leigh might have confided in her, or even given her the USB stick to look after. I was watching the house. I saw that bible-basher from the chapel drop in and then the girl and her mother went out, and I saw my chance. I suppose my break-in lacked finesse, but it was effective. I didn't find the stick though."

"We did," Gillingham said with a smile. "The funny thing is, we had a different suspect in our sights altogether until we saw those files. What a pity for you that you never found it."

Russell shrugged.

"Tell me," the DCI said. "When you said Marling would be lowering his profile on the case, but you asked me to keep you posted?"

"Very good." The killer nodded. "Yes, I told Andrew to back off. The less pressure he put on you, maybe the less effort you'd put into the case. Probably a forlorn hope, but..." He spread his palms. "And, of course, if you were giving me progress reports direct, I'd have an inside track on the investigation."

"Is that it, Chief Inspector?" Adina Walker asked. "My client will be tired."

"One last question, I think," Archer offered. "When I went to see the Fletchers, you and Mr Marling were there. Did he know then what you'd done?"

He gave a hollow laugh. "He didn't have a clue. He was just an MP doing his duty by constituents he thought had lost a child in a dreadful accident. He was pretty cut up about it, as a matter of fact. Yes, he confided to me that some of his worries might be over, but he had no idea what had really happened, not until it became obvious that the police were suspicious about the death. As a matter of fact, he was pretty broken up about it. I think he still had some sort of feelings for her.

"After I killed Gavin Lane, I decided to tell him what I'd done. He was horrified, but I reckon his main concern was that someone might find out. I had no idea he'd recorded the conversation, although thinking back, I remember him fiddling with the phone when I joined him. He must have been setting it to record." He sipped some more water. "Have I been helpful, Chief Inspector? Do you think I'll get a lighter sentence?"

"For this? I can't say," Gillingham said. "Maybe you'll get away with kidnap and manslaughter in the case of Leigh Fletcher. Maybe you can even get some sort of provocation taken into account for Gavin Lane, although it's obvious it was entirely premeditated. But you're still going to jail for the rest of your miserable life, if I have anything to do with it at all."

"But you'll say I co-operated?"

"Sure. You might get a day off your life sentence."

* * *

Marling was weeping again.

"Poor Leigh. What happened to her... it was the last thing I wanted. When she died, at first I wouldn't allow myself to believe it had anything to do with the files or with Chris, but there was always this little voice in my head telling me otherwise. He had this ruthless streak that had got me where I am today. He often says that, without him, I'd be a popular middle-ranking social worker by now. But I always thought he had a dangerous side."

"DI Archer said you seemed genuinely upset when she saw you at the Fletchers' home," Baines said.

"I was. At that stage, I desperately wanted to believe Leigh's death was a stupid, senseless accident." He swiped at his eyes. "But then Chris told me to meet him in that layby. At first I couldn't imagine why he'd want to meet in such a bizarre place, but I soon guessed at the truth. I saw no way out, so I decided to record what he said, to at least show I had nothing to do with it if the truth came out. A sort of insurance policy. Even though a part of me had feared he'd been involved in Leigh's death, I had no idea he'd killed again - that Gavin Lane - not until he told me. I felt sick."

"But you said nothing," said Baines, feeling somewhat nauseated himself. In part, he pitied Marling. He believed the MP when he said he hadn't made the running with Leigh and had allowed himself to be flattered and become infatuated - at a time when he himself was vulnerable - by the attentions of a girl way too young, but still pretty and vivacious. And it seemed he had genuinely cared for her.

But if the relationship had been wrong, the man's choices thereafter had had appalling consequences. "As a result of your inaction - your cowardice - three people are now dead, including a fine police officer. All so you could hang onto your precious career. Well, it's not just your career you've lost now, Andrew, and it won't just be sex with a minor you go to jail for, Andrew. You're looking at aiding and abetting murder, and we'll have a look at conspiracy to pervert the course of justice too."

If he'd wanted to be really hard on Marling, he would also have pointed out how little the inmates cared for nonces, but he stopped short of that level of cruelty.

He leaned towards the suspect. "There's something else, though. Leigh died rather than give up those files. Files that would get you into trouble. You really believed that was so she could blackmail you some time in the future? Or, more likely, because she was determined to keep your sordid little secrets safe from someone who might want to use them against you? What do you reckon? I know what my money's on."

Marling stared at him, taking in his words. Then his face crumpled and he started to sob. Baines glanced over at one of the uniforms standing by the door.

"Take him away."

* * *

Around the middle of the day, Archer ran into Baines in the corridor. He looked as grim as she felt.

"I don't know about you," she said, "but I still feel unclean after sitting in the same room as Chris Russell. How are you feeling?"

"Sad, more than anything," he replied. "Marling really was one of the good guys in most regards. He'd dedicated his life to the community, and might well have made an above average prime minister one day. Then he loses his girlfriend, a pretty child spots a gap and decides to fill it, and everything goes straight to hell."

She looked at him questioningly. "You sound sorry for him."

"No," he said. "At least, not exactly. If he'd left it at that and got caught, bang would have gone his career, probably prison, certainly humiliation. Left to his devices, maybe that's what would have happened. Or maybe no one would ever have found out. The irony is, neither he nor Russell would have known the USB stick even existed if it hadn't been for that random mugging."

"We thought it was all part of the killer's campaign to get hold of the files. But the jungle drums told Marling about it, he contacted Leigh, and she found she couldn't keep the stick a secret from him."

Baines nodded. "That was what really started the whole thing. Ultimately what got her killed."

But Archer shook her head. "No, Dan, what really started it all was Marling's weakness. The same weakness that wouldn't let him say no to Leigh wouldn't let him say no to Russell, either. And Russell really didn't give a shit about anyone but himself. He would have killed Gemma Lucas next, you know. He admitted that he'd toyed with waiting for her and her mother after he broke into their house. He'd weighed up whether the element of surprise would enable him to slit both their throats with a breadknife before they knew what hit them."

"But that's..."

"Insane? Not quite. I think he imagines he played a bigger part in Andrew Marling's success than is really the case. He fancies himself as a fixer who was on his way to fame and fortune. The reality is that he was helpful to a man competing for safe seats, and one with more than enough charisma to hold them without Russell's help."

"A fantasist then?"

"And one who doesn't think things through properly. I think he'd rather do something about a problem than do nothing, even if it doesn't solve it. So he killed Leigh and was prepared to kill Gemma, even though it would have taken him no nearer to getting hold of that stick. He was prepared to take me hostage, even though he was never going to get very far. And poor Jenny..."

She felt cold all over as Ross's death played itself over for her in flashback yet again. A sudden impulse came over her - she had no idea where it came from - and she found herself saying that she felt like getting good and drunk tonight, and did he fancy joining her?

He looked awkward. " I would, but..."

She felt embarrassed, guessing at what he must be thinking. "Sorry. Bad idea."

"No," he told her. "Good idea. But I have plans."

28

Normally after a case was brought to a successful conclusion, especially a high-profile one, everyone involved would go out for a celebration drink. But Jenny Ross's death had cast a pall over the whole station. The place was like a morgue.

They would hear later how the knife wound inflicted by Chris Russell had caused catastrophic damage to a number of internal organs. They would also learn that Chris Russell could become violent in times of stress. His wife had been on the receiving end on more than one occasion but, like many an abused spouse, had taken the blame upon herself.

It was a day that Dan Baines would never entirely get out of his mind. He felt shame about the slightly mean attitude to Ross that he had harboured when she had first joined the team. He felt guilt that she, not he, had been the first to help Archer to tackle Russell. He would never lose the sense that he hadn't moved swiftly enough, that there was something he should have done that would have prevented what happened.

But what had really unnerved him was teenage Jack's appearance in Marling's doorway at the precise moment Ross had died. He had looked at Baines with sadness and compassion. Baines had blinked and the apparition had disappeared.

He took it as a sign of sorts, and he wondered now why he had been so resistant to Karen's idea of seeing this medium tonight. At worst, it would be a waste of an evening. At best, it just might, against all his low expectations, give him some of the answers he sought.

The only person who seemed to take anything positive home at the end of the day was Steve Ashby. Midway through the afternoon, having hardly been seen all day, the DI arrived in the station with two uniforms in tow, and two young suspects. One went by the name of Craig Bragg. The other was Kyle Adams, Hayley Fletcher's boyfriend. Both proceeded to confess to a string of allotment break-ins.

The very last piece of the puzzle fell into place. From the outset, Archer had been sure that Kyle and Hayley were hiding something, and that feeling had persisted even after she had ceased to see him as a serious murder suspect. On the night Leigh Fletcher had died, Kyle and Craig had been breaking into the Wendover allotments. Later, Hayley would admit that she'd suspected her boyfriend was into something shady to do with allotments - had even feared that he'd been somehow involved in Gavin Lane's death - but had been adamant that she had neither known for sure, nor wanted to know.

When asked how he'd solved the crimes, all Ashby would do was tap the side of his nose, grin knowingly, and whisper. "Contacts, my boy." He was at a loss to understand why no one felt like celebrating his 'result'. Baines wanted to punch him in the teeth. Claire King's online scoop on the arrests made Archer wonder if the journalist was one of those contacts.

Now, with the office behind him for the weekend, but with the sorrow of the day still very much in his mind, Baines sat with Karen in Aylesbury's impressive Waterside Theatre, watching the medium Philip Weaver at work.

It was only Baines's third visit to the theatre. It had been officially opened in October 2010 by Cilla Black, and had divided the community over both the ballooning cost of the build and its modernistic design, which was not to everyone's taste. Baines himself rather liked it, and certainly had no complaints about the comfort of his seat. His feelings about Philip Weaver himself were far less positive.

Weaver wore tight black trousers and a crimson shirt, open at the throat. He wore a headset with a microphone that allowed him to pace around the stage. His lustrous black hair was tied in a ponytail, and his face looked as if it had been chiselled from granite. Baines judged that he was in his early 40s, and thought he had 'con-man' written all over him.

So far, it was very much what he expected. Weaver would claim to have a message from the spirit world, throw out a name, and watch the hands going up. He would link the message to one of those audience members by what Baines thought had to be a combination of fishing questions and vague statements. Invariably, some sad soul would become convinced it was a loved one speaking directly to them through Weaver. There would be an assurance that the deceased was happy and at peace, and announce something the gullible bereaved would imagine only they could know.

Baines had to admit that the man was good, but then that was his job. But surely it simply boiled down to a sophisticated repertoire of mind-tricks?

He felt half-relieved by his conviction that there really was nothing in it. Half-disappointed that there would be no answers for him tonight.

Weaver finished telling an elderly woman that her late husband had always known about her losing her wedding ring and secretly buying an identical one - and that he'd never been angry about it. She had wept with joy and relief at a weight finally off her mind, and Baines supposed that this charlatan did no actual harm and, just maybe, the odd little bit of good.

"Alas, I have time for only one more message," Weaver said. "But remember - you can check my website for my next appearances. Someone on the other side may have a message for you." He emphasised the last word by extending his arm and pointing his finger. He seemed to be pointing right at Baines, who supposed the whole audience probably had the same impression.

"Now," Weaver said, "I have a message from a lady. I'm getting a name beginning with 'L'. Lucy?" Pause. "No, maybe Louise?"

Karen nudged Baines in the ribs. He looked at her in mingled panic and bemusement.

"A message for Don?"

"Would that be Dan?" Karen called out.

"Dan. Dan, yes. My mistake."

"Oh, please," Baines whispered. "Why did you do that?"

"He's right here." Karen lifted her hand and pointed at her companion.

"Can we get a mike to Dan?" Weaver said.

A girl in a red tee-shirt with Weaver's name emblazoned on it in bold black type was already at the end of their row, passing a microphone along.

"Hello, Dan," said Weaver. "I have a message from Louise that might be for you. Yes, I'm getting the strongest sense that you're the person she wants to talk to."

"Okay," Baines said, embarrassed, looking at the floor.

"I think you loved Louise very much, and her passing was especially tragic and painful for you."

"Yes." Baines was 39. It wasn't hard to imagine that the lost loved one might be a spouse, and that losing them at a young age would be especially painful. But besides, any loss was painful and tragic in its way.

"She says you're not to worry about her. She is at peace, and she's happy where she is. And Dan?"

"I'm listening." He just wanted this charade over.

"She begs you not to go on holding hate in your heart."

"What?" He looked up. This hadn't been in any of the previous scripts.

"You've harboured a hatred, haven't you, for the person you hold responsible for Louise's death?"

Baines started to relax. It was a fair bet, he supposed, that losing someone - especially a relatively young loved one, as he thought Weaver was surmising - would make you want to blame someone. This wasn't about the Invisible Man. It was generic.

"I suppose so," he said.

"Louise says, don't. It will eat you alive."

That certainly sounded like Lou, but...

"Okay. Fine."

Weaver's expression changed abruptly. Even from his seat in the stalls, Baines swore he saw alarm flash across the medium's chiselled features. It was a look that might have been for effect, but seemed sufficiently genuine to unsettle Baines.

"There's more," the medium said. "It's about your son. Jack?"

Baines's mouth was suddenly dry. Karen clutched his arm so tight that it hurt. He half expected the teenage apparition that had been haunting him for well over a year to materialise on stage beside Weaver. The fact that he didn't was somehow even more unsettling.

"Dan? Do you have a son called Jack?"

Baines looked at Karen and she nodded encouragement.

"Is he with her?" he asked cautiously. "With Lou, I mean?"

"No." Confusion. "No he isn't with her. Has he... passed over?"

"Yes. No. I don't know."

He sounded mad, even to himself. Audience members were craning their necks to see him.

"You don't know?"

"It's complicated. What does..." He swallowed. "You know, what does Lou say?"

"She says... she says don't try to find Jack. Don't try to find out about him."

"What does that mean?" If he still doubted that Weaver was in the least bit genuine, that didn't seem to matter now. "Ask her what it means."

"All she says is, don't worry about her, and don't look for Jack. She says no good can come of it."

"No good? What does that mean?" He was on his feet, shouting now.

"I'm sorry, Dan. She's gone. These connections are so brief..." Dan had seen enough of human emotion to be able to tell when somebody was unnerved, and that was certainly the word for the man on the stage now. All his flashy poise and sharpness seemed to have evaporated.

"That's all we have time for tonight," Weaver said, but there was none of his previous panache. "You've been a wonderful audience. Goodnight - and may your departed loved ones watch over you."

After the house lights went up, Baines and Karen had recovered their jackets from the cloakroom. Neither of them spoke of what had just happened. But when Karen headed for the exit, Baines took her arm.

"We're not going anywhere."

"Aren't we?"

"I'm going to have a private word with this guy."

"Oh, Christ. You're not going to make a scene are you?"

He looked her in the eye. "It's been a fuck of a day, with Jenny. Now this. This was your idea. Get some answers, you said. Well, I'm getting some."

He found a steward. Flashed his warrant card. "We need to get backstage. Speak to Mr Weaver."

The young man looked uncertain. "My manager's not around right now. You'll have to wait..."

Baines showed him his warrant card again. Held it in front of the steward's face.

"I'm afraid it can't wait. It's urgent. I strongly suggest you take us to Mr Weaver now, unless you want to obstruct justice."

"Dan -" hissed Karen, tugging at his sleeve. He ignored her.

"Of course," the young steward said. "Right away, officer."

Moments later, they were in Philip Weaver's dressing room. Not palatial, but not a broom cupboard, either. Sweat hung in the air. A girl was removing the last vestiges of makeup from the medium's face. Baines showed his warrant card once more, and Weaver asked the girl to come back later.

With most of his makeup removed, Weaver looked older than Baines's first impression. Maybe as old as 50. He looked tired, but he nodded to Baines as soon as the three of them were alone.

"You're Dan. From the end of the show. You're a policeman?"

"That's right."

"But this isn't really police business, am I right?"

"So - you read minds as well?"

"No. But you've got questions. I would have, too." Weaver shrugged. "I'm not sure how much I can tell you. I gave you Louise's message, word for word."

Baines bit his lip, part of him hardly able to credit that he was even having this conversation. "But you said Jack wasn't with Louise. You even asked me if he'd passed over. Why didn't you know? Didn't Lou say?"

"She didn't, I'm afraid. Sometimes, the spirits only say what they want - or are permitted - to reveal. Sometimes they don't know things themselves. Yet, if your son had also passed over, I would have expected him and his mother to have found each other." He frowned. "She talked about you searching for him. Is he missing, is that it? You don't know if he's alive or not?"

Baines thought he saw it then. "Oh, come on. You know who I am. You knew who I was before I set foot in the place."

"I'm sorry?"

"That's what you do, isn't it? You check the names of everyone who's bought tickets, trawl through the Internet, and try to link them to a bereavement. The death notices - leaves behind a wife, Ivy etc, etc. And you find out just enough to make yourself plausible." He was shaking with rage, or some other emotion. "You know about the Invisible Man. You know he murdered my wife. Took my son."

Karen pawed his sleeve. "Dan, the tickets were in my name, remember?"

He stared at her wildly. "You, then. You must have been mentioned in the press at the time. The grieving twin sister." He turned his bale back on Weaver. "That's it, isn't it?"

"Dan," Karen said quietly, "just listen to yourself."

"Dan, I'm sorry," Weaver said. "Really I am. That's not how I work at all. I simply don't have time to do all that - what you said. For a start, the theatre would have to be in on it, for me to get the names, and someone would blab. Believe it, don't believe it, but I get my messages from the spirit world. The gift has been in my family for at least four generations, and I think my own son has it, too."

He laid a sympathetic hand on Baines's shoulder. "There's only one thing I can really add to what I've already told you, but it will offer you no comfort. Quite the reverse, in fact."

Baines's shoulders sagged. He was so tired. And, when he thought about it, his theory about how Weaver worked was almost as fantastic as the notion of speaking to the dead. "Tell me anyway," he said, really not sure he wanted to hear it.

"You're sure?"

"Dan, maybe -" Karen began.

"Just tell me. Please," he added.

"All right. Just before I lost the contact with Louise, she said what I told you. Not to look for Jack. No good could come of it. But I didn't tell you how she sounded."

In his head, Baines was still 100% sceptical of this man. Yet in his guts, he felt as cold as ice.

"And how did she sound?"

"She sounded afraid, Dan. She sounded frightened - for you. And for Jack."

29

Lizzie Archer drained the glass of sauvignon blanc she had ordered from room service, looked around the hotel room, and asked herself for what felt like the one thousandth time what she was doing here.

It seemed such a mad impulse now, this spontaneous drive down to King's Lynn. She had felt Jenny Ross's death like a kick to the stomach. She relived how she had somehow held it together through the interview but, when that had terminated, she had fled to the ladies' where only a fist jammed in her mouth had muffled the howls that she was unable to contain. The struggle that had led to Ross's fatal wounding played over and over, right in front of her eyes.

It wasn't that she'd grown especially close to Ross. This was the first case they had worked together, and the woman had only ever been an augmentee to her team. Yet Archer had found herself liking her, despite her occasional over-eagerness to please. And it was Ross who had been especially instrumental in solving the case. It was entirely possible that no one else would have thought of seeking the incriminating USB stick inside Gemma Lucas's teddy bear.

Gillingham had, for once, been surprisingly sensitive, ordering team members to head off for the weekend by five at the latest - an unprecedented move, by all accounts. But home in her new house, facing unpacked boxes, the loneliness had been overwhelming.

In the past three years, she had lost her looks, and with them the man she had hoped to marry; she'd had to get away from London and the Met, and all her familiar colleagues, to try and make a fresh start to life and her career; and then she had lost her mother. Her father was long dead. She had a brother who barely spoke to her, even on the rare occasions they were in the same room. And, worryingly, she suspected that Dan Baines - with whom she still occasionally came close to falling out - was the nearest thing she had to a friend these days.

She hoped to God she hadn't sabotaged the steps they'd recently taken in their working relationship by inviting him to get drunk with her. It had been stupid, and she wasn't sure how genuine his regret had been. Maybe he really did have a prior engagement. Or maybe it was the first excuse to hand.

She desperately needed someone to talk to. Someone to hold her, too. She realised that she needed Ian Baker like never before. It might be a difficult relationship for them to manage, but he would at least understand.

So she had searched the Internet for hotels in King's Lynn, made an off-the-cuff booking before she could change her mind, and driven the nigh-on 140 miles to get here. Since then she had called Ian's mobile a few times, only for it to repeatedly go to voicemail. She'd left messages to call her, but had given no indication of where she was, not in a voice message. She didn't want him to think something weird was going on.

Which, she thought, it just might be.

She knew that his family circumstances made weekends at least as difficult as the job, especially when he was on a big case. But, even if he could only manage to see her for five or ten minutes, she thought she would take it.

Five or ten minutes to stop feeling so lost and alone.

She glanced at her watch. 9.20 pm. She picked up her mobile and speed-dialled Baker again. After a few rings, it was answered.

"Ian Baker's phone?" A woman's voice. He must still be at work. She felt a twinge of sympathy for him.

"Hi," she said, "I wonder if I could speak to DI Baker."

"Who is this?"

"It's DI Lizzie Archer from Thames Valley Police. Ian and I met on a case we were both involved in last year."

"Oh, I see," the woman said, cheerfully. "Well, he's just putting our youngest to bed."

Archer froze as the implications hit home.

"He got away from work a little earlier than usual," the woman prattled. "We've been out to the cinema and then for a pizza. As a family - wonders will never cease! Well, I suppose you know exactly what it's like?"

The room started spinning, ever so slowly.

"So... is this Mrs Baker I'm speaking to?"

"That's right. He shouldn't be long. Shall I get him to call you?"

Her stomach roiled. "No. No, that's okay. It'll keep."

"Perhaps I can give him a message?"

"No, no message. I'll catch up with him on Monday."

"You're sure? Okay. Well, you have a great weekend."

"What? Oh, yeah, you too."

Archer broke the connection, rose from the bed on shaky legs, and lurched into the bathroom. She barely had time to lift the toilet seat before she began to vomit. She'd eaten little all day, so it was mostly dry-heaving.

She stayed on her knees for what felt like eternity, willing the cold sweat and dizziness that threatened to overwhelm her to go away. At length she felt able to get herself over to the bed and lie down. She was crying again: not this time for the death of a brave colleague, but for a cruel betrayal. Baker had told her his marriage was over. That his relationship with Archer was hurting no one. He'd even talked about introducing her to his children when the time was right.

All based on lies. She'd been nothing more to him than a bit on the side, a glorified fuck buddy. She even imagined him thinking what an easy lay she must be - a woman who few men would fancy, with her face in such a state; a woman who'd just be grateful to get a shag when he could spare the time. Perhaps he had confided in some of his mates at the station. How they must have laughed.

She found three miniatures in the mini-bar: scotch, gin and vodka. She drank them down neat, straight from the bottle, one after the other, felt like puking again. Managed to keep them down.

So she had no one. Here she was, in King's Fucking Lynn, miles from anyone she knew, apart from a lying, philandering bastard she never wanted to see again.

Her phone rang. She snatched it up. Baker. The temptation was to ignore the call, but she made herself answer.

"Lizzie? It's Ian. What's up?"

"What's up? What's fucking up? I ring you up and end up having a cosy chat with your lovely wife, that's all. While you put the kids to bed. After a lovely family night out."

"I'm sorry," he said softly. "I didn't want you to find out that way."

"Find out what?"

"That we've decided to get back together."

She snorted a laugh into the phone. "Don't lie any more, Ian. That wasn't a woman you've just got back together with. It was a woman you never left. You told me you were divorced."

There was silence at the other end.

"Well?"

"Yes, all right. I shouldn't have told you that. But we were going through a rocky time, and I thought it would come to splitting up. I didn't want you to feel that you had any part in that."

"Shut up," she sneered. "You're making this up as you go along. The truth is, Ian, that you're happy enough with your family life, but if you can get a bit on the side, that suits you fine and you don't mind lying to get it. I doubt I was the first."

"I care about you, Lizzie," he said. "I do. I heard about that policewoman who was stabbed in the Vale. Did you know her?"

Even then it would have been easy to pour her heart out, but she was under no illusions now that his would be the sort of sympathetic ear she needed. Her hurt and her pride would not let her cheapen herself any further.

"I hope your prick drops off," she spat, and she hung up.

For a long moment she sat there staring at the phone in her hand, wondering if Baker would call her back with more bullshit. But he did not. She thought of some things to say to him if he did call and then felt cheated of an opportunity to say them.

She considered calling down to room service again and asking them to send her up a bottle of vodka, but a voice in her head that sounded uncannily like her mother's urged her not to let a snake like Ian Baker drive her to drinking herself into a stupor.

So she made herself a cup of insipid-looking black coffee and, while it was cooling, rummaged in her handbag. She found the scrap of paper she was seeking, smoothed it out, and rang the mobile number on it.

It was answered on the fifth ring.

"Hello," she said, "is that Georgia? Georgia, sorry to call you so late. This is Lizzie Archer - you did my make up for the press conference in Aylesbury the other day. Yes, yes, that's right. I was the one with the scar."

ALSO BY DAVE SIVERS

Archer and Baines Novels
The Scars Beneath the Soul

The Lowmar Dashiel Mysteries (crime fantasy)
A Sorcerer Slain
Inquisitor Royal

Short Story Collection
Dark and Deep: Ten Coffee Break Crime Stories

DAVE SIVERS

Dave Sivers was born in West London and worked for years in the public sector, occasionally moonlighting as a nightclub bouncer, bookmaker's clerk and freelance writer.

The Scars Beneath the Soul (2013) was his first contemporary crime novel and introduced detectives Archer and Baines. His published work also includes two 'crime fantasy' novels, featuring the personal inquisitor Lowmar Dashiel, and the anthology *Dark and Deep: Ten Coffee Break Crime Stories*.

He lives in Buckinghamshire with his wife, Chris.

www.davesivers.co.uk

36394034R00197

Printed in Poland
by Amazon Fulfillment
Poland Sp. z o.o., Wrocław